A NEW YEAR'S RIDE

BOOK ONE OF THE RIDE TRILOGY

ELMIRA WYLDE

A New Year's Ride

© ELMIRA WYLDE 2025

This book is a work of fiction. Any references to persons, living or dead, or places, events, or locations are purely coincidental. The characters are all productions of the author's imagination.

Please note that the work is intended only for adults over the age of 18, and all characters represented are 18 and above.

Cover art by Ashley Howard

For my best friend, because you were by my side through all of it.
For my husband, because you believed in me before I did.

Contents

This book contains explicit sexual content and profanity.

Some topics may be sensitive to some readers, including but not limited to:

Death

Violence

Breeding Kink

Mild BDSM

Gun violence

Mention of drugs

Slurs

Emotional abuse

Panic attacks

A New Year's Ride

As we pull away from the parking garage, a wave of anxiety pushes and pulls its way around in my chest. Today was my last day at work, and while it's been a bittersweet day, it isn't the reason for my spiraling emotions. I've kept them at bay, but I can barely hold myself together anymore. I'm not sure what has made me so high-strung tonight. Maybe it's the thought of bringing in a new year with someone I don't feel connected to. Or maybe it's that gut feeling you have when something upsetting will happen, and you know you can't stop it, so you're preparing to watch the shit show, and you're on the edge of your seat until it's over.

I glance at my nails, seeing the tiny piece of skin coming off in the crease on my thumb. I've been trying to get it all day, but all I've done is make my thumb ache, chip my nail polish away on the edge, and create a raw spot on the side of my finger. "One more shot," I mumble to myself, and bite down with the edges of my teeth.

"Quit that! It's disgusting. Go get your nails done like a real woman," Sebastian yells as he swats my hand out of my mouth, then grabs the steering wheel to stop us from swerving off the road.

I cling to the edge of my seat as the car swerves back into the proper lane. My heart hammers in my chest as I sit with my head pressed into the headrest. It's always like this with him behind closed doors; I'm used to it, but I know he will be the ever-charming boyfriend once we are at Amber's party. To be honest, the emotional whiplash has taken its toll on me mentally. I'm tired.

I let out a breath, ready to escape the hell he has trapped me in. All of our friends and their friends will be at this party tonight; everyone my parents desperately want me to get to know. Sebastian will turn on that fake, golden boy personality that I quickly caught onto, and I will mingle with people I couldn't care less about. I met Sebastian at Amber's birthday two years ago, and everyone was up in arms about it, except for his parents. They were so thrilled he "finally found someone to calm him down." For nearly two years of my life, all I've done is uncover hidden drug use, anger issues, and the fact that most of the girls in our inner and outer circle have had their chance with him and regretted it immediately.

Everyone assumed his relationships were either one-night stands or quick flings, but once I got to know him, I realized how awful he truly is, and no one will open up about it. Maybe they fear what his family will have to say in retaliation, even my parents panicked when I told them I wanted to cut my ties with him. They wouldn't hear my reasons; they just told me I was being choosy and refusing to accept that everyone has their flaws. I roll my eyes as the past conversations flash through my mind, feeling his cold stare on the side of my face when I look out the windshield.

I often wonder if the images I post of us on social media get pity likes or if he's somehow blackmailed everyone into liking him. By posting us, am I helping sell his 'good-boy' image? An idea springs forward, and I smile as I pull out my phone. If he wants to keep that sweetheart reputation, he can do it himself from now on. One by one, I begin deleting our pictures from my social media accounts. What's the saying? New Year, new me?

Yeah. New year, new me.

No more illusions to help my parents' lives look perfect, so they can climb the social ladder. No more helping my so-called boyfriend look like he is Mr. Perfect. This year will be all about what I can do to be better for myself. Sebastian stomps on the brakes, stopping the car abruptly. His sudden action sends my phone onto the floor next to my feet. I look over at him in disbelief and clench my teeth as he lets out a loud laugh and slaps the steering wheel several times, hysterical at the idea of annoying me. I lean forward and grab my phone, clenching it so hard my hand hurts.

"Should have been paying more attention, Ava! Now look at you, fumbling around in the dark, you're so clumsy; it makes me sick. You need to get off of it anyway, we're here." His words are laced with venom, but I don't care anymore. After tonight, I'm done for good.

I toss my phone into my clutch, feeling satisfaction at deleting the bulk of him from my online life already. Over time, I've tried to convince myself that he's rude like this when we are alone, and it would get better, but it hasn't. Now his true colors come out, no matter where we are, and he blames me for it later. I've also noticed that he has been worse, even belittling me in public.

I don't want to look at his smug face anymore. I can't live like this. He has tried for too long to break me down, but I refuse to let him eat at me anymore. I don't need him, and my family doesn't need to tie itself to his. He will be the downfall of everyone, and I will make sure to sever every link between us. My parents have worked too hard to build themselves up from nothing to be torn down by this man-child who doesn't know how to treat people with basic courtesy.

We turn into Amber's long driveway, hope blooming in my chest. The large front yard looks like it goes on forever, but Sebastian catapults us forward, weaving around the parked cars like he is racing to get inside. A few people have parked in the center of the wide pavement, but he drives through the grass to get around them, heading towards the back of the house before coming to a complete stop in front of Amber's garage doors. I immediately get out and run towards the house as fast as I can in the rhinestone heels strapped to my feet.

I push through the wooden back door, into the grand kitchen, then take a deep breath, grateful to no longer be in the vehicle with my soon-to-be ex-boyfriend. My spirits are immediately lifted as a few people turn around and greet me. I smile and wave at them as I press further into the room. Some of these people I would consider friends, but most of them aren't. I don't waste my time stopping to talk to any of them. Amber told me she would have a bartender for the night, and she wasn't lying. A crowd stands around, talking in groups as a guy busies himself, pulling bottles from the setup behind the high countertop that cuts her kitchen in half. He mixes drinks quickly, sliding them across to serve them before moving on to the next person without breaking a sweat.

Amber is seated at the end of the island with her two sidekicks, both clinging to her like a lifeline. They weren't always like that, but over the years, the girls have attached themselves to her like leeches. Wherever she goes, they follow, and for some reason, they now live for her attention. I suspect it has something to do with her brief relationship with the head photographer for a well-known modeling agency, but I don't want to assume their true motives. Emily is the first to notice me, giving a small wave as she leans into their conversation to announce my arrival; I give a small wave back but don't care to speak to her. In fact, I'd rather she pretend I don't exist at all, but I can't be so lucky.

From what Amber had told me, Sebastian and Emily had a thing going on for a long time, until Sebastian announced me as his girlfriend. Emily never got over him and decided to seek revenge by spreading rumors about me being the cause of their separation, even though it is well known that he has gotten around even when they were together.

Regardless, she stirred up unnecessary drama, and when I refused to speak to her directly about the situation, it fueled more opinions and rumors. Honestly, I didn't care much then, and I don't care now either. I want to put it all behind me, but now and then, I hear someone question where we stand, especially when Amber invited us both to her parties like this one.

My parents never knew Emily's family personally until the whole shit show went down, and after they realized my parents are new money, they wouldn't stop inviting them places. My family, as smart as they are, couldn't understand that there was obviously a bigger picture they weren't seeing until one day, Emily's mother called asking for money.

People don't like their secrets to be yelled from the rooftops, especially when it comes to money. Unfortunately, Emily backed down and has been friendly with me ever since. I remind myself often to keep my walls up when she's around. I know she's only being nice because she's afraid of being blackmailed. It isn't something that I would ever consider, because I'm not like them. The idea of it alone makes my stomach roll. It's okay, though, because I really don't need a back burner friend who wants me around because of what I can afford to do for her. After that, the rumors died down significantly, and Emily seemed humbled, but I still don't trust her.

Emily is fake and attaches herself to anyone she thinks will benefit her, and I've said so from the moment I met her. However, Amber believes she is in the same position as I am: to get close to people and make the family important. It's been drilled into our heads for a long time now: gain connections, build relationships, and make sure always to save face. So, I play nice, smile, and speak to everyone, but it's all for show. I'm not one for making myself look like a fool, but that's what it feels like I'm doing when I mingle with the ones I don't consider friends.

I can say with certainty, though, that nothing makes me feel like a bigger fool than when I have to defend Sebastian, and it's probably how I ended up belittled by him every day. Thinking back on the situation, I should have just let Emily have him, but I was doing what a good daughter is supposed to do. I think that I've been mostly passive through all of this because deep down, I don't think Sebastian is anything to fight over, and I was hoping he would leave me. Sometimes I wonder why he hasn't, because there is no way this has been enjoyable for him. Unfortunately, that's not how this works, and it won't ever be that easy.

I take a deep breath, repeating my new mantra: New Year, New Me. Enough with the shitty memories, tonight is a new beginning, and I plan on having fun with my best friend, and the ones I keep at arm's length, too. I deserve some fun after what I have put up with. Eventually, I make my way through the small crowd of people milling through the kitchen to find my place beside Amber and release a sigh of relief.

"I'm finally here!" I yell out loudly, gaining a few whoops and cheers from people in the crowd who are happy to see me. I wave at them from across the room, hoping that tonight we all have a great time. I won't let two bad apples ruin this party for me; I've been looking forward to this for the last two weeks. We all screech in excited agreement, and Amber slides several shots in each direction for us to throw back, hugging me before grabbing her alcohol and downing it immediately.

On my fourth shot, I decide to start pacing myself or be married to the bathroom toilet for the rest of the night. I never really considered myself a lightweight, but according to everyone else, that's exactly what I am. If I want to make the most of my night, I need to slow down. My skin crawls when Sebastian comes up behind us, introduces leech number two's boyfriend; I watch as the girl melts when he smiles her way. In my buzzed state, I let a small laugh escape me as I imagine the two girls making kissy faces together in photos; 'leech' fits them perfectly.

The guy and Sebastian are loud as they scream about some people in the next room who are annoying them and threatening to fight, but I know Sebastian is all talk. I busy myself by getting away from them, not interested in them puffing out their chests to beat on it and talk shit to people that can't hear it. I wiggle past the guys, silently putting distance between us, as I glance over my shoulder, Emily is watching me like a hawk. Of course, she noticed my attempt to distance myself from the man she wants. My eyes roll to the sky; how desperate can one person be?

I turn my back on her to escape the sea of people that seems to be multiplying. The kitchen is crowded now, and as I look outside, the pool area is filling up quickly, too, despite the cold weather. I watch as a group of guys jump into the freezing pool, but their screams and shrieks are drowned out by the thumping music and buzzing conversation that has filled the house. A guy runs in front of the large kitchen windows completely naked, screaming at the top of his lungs. I lose my mind with laughter before heading to the pool house and turning the pool's heater on as high as it can go. It will take a while for the water to be warm enough to consider jumping in, but by then, they will all be gone or too drunk to care about swimming again.

As I go further into the pool shack for some towels, I hear thumping and moaning coming from the dressing room. I cover my mouth with a towel to muffle my cackling, so I won't kill their vibe. Turning my head, I hold a hand to the side of my face to block my vision, giving them some sense of privacy as I pass by the curtain. Someone should be getting lucky tonight, even though it won't be me. Jealousy washes through me as I go back to the pool; Sebastian wasn't exactly the best when it came to sex, but I do wish there was a chance of getting something from him before I call it quits. Not that it would matter much anyway, I always finished myself at the end of the night after he fell asleep.

With a deep sigh, I toss their towels on a folded lounge chair and head back to the main house to see why no one else is out here watching the shit show. Walking up the sidewalk, I hear Amber on the phone with someone as she paces in circles. She yells into the phone, telling the person on the other end that people need to leave. The guy Sebastian introduced earlier nearly rips the door off its hinges to stick his head outside.

"They've gone out front but aren't leaving, just stumbling around talking shit. I'm sorry about your couch. We can get you a new one this weekend. I'll help you get it delivered if you want," he says before being pulled back inside by another guy.

Screams erupt from inside but become muffled by someone turning the music up louder. Looking over at Amber, I can see the tears threatening to spill over as she holds the phone. She looks towards her house and starts yelling frantically for the person on the phone to hurry over to handle the situation. She turns and looks at me as I walk up, the tears finally falling from her eyes.

"Oh my God, Ava! Someone just pissed all over my white couch, and Roger had to toss the guy outside with his pants still down! None of us even knows who he is. My brother told me to call the cops, but I can't." She stops to take a breath, shaking as she sucks in air. "Can you imagine what my parents will say if they learn about this? There have never been this many people here before; I don't know who invited extras." She's full-on sobbing by the time she finishes, leaning in to lay her head on my shoulder. Her body shakes as she cries on me, and I can't help but notice the stench of alcohol coming from her. I knew she had been drinking before I got here, but holy shit, she smells flammable.

"What? How do you not know the guy? I thought we said no strangers this year," I ask.

She pulls back from me, ready to explain, but her eyes narrow as she glares at someone over my shoulder. I spin to see who the target of her wrath could be and freeze on the spot. A tall, menacing man who looks like he could be a bouncer has come around the corner with a beer in one hand, attempting to light a cigarette with his other. He stops when he sees us and flips the lighter closed before smiling widely.

"Hey, pretty lady-"a woman shrieks from inside, cutting off whatever he was about to say.

Amber and I take off running towards the open door, grateful for the opportunity to get away from the creep that has wandered up, and ready to investigate what could be happening now. To our surprise, everyone went back to the party, the piss couch forgotten; people circle the kitchen island where the bartender was once handing out drinks. Chanting and cheering spread through the crowd, but we can't see through the sea of people to see what's happening.

"Is there a fight?" I ask, nearly screaming.

"I don't know! What are they saying?" Amber screams back, panic flooding her face.

Another shriek sounds out before Emily pushes through the door. I notice her hair and clothes are disheveled, far from her usual, perfect, primed self.

Her eyes meet mine and drift back to the crowd, then she yells out, "Hey!" The noise dies down instantly, all eyes turning to look at her. "What the hell are all of you doing?" She yells. A petite blonde girl stands on the counter before hopping down and pushing her way towards Emily. She pulls her shirt down as she steps forward, looking a little ashamed of herself. Her eyes drift up to meet the pissed off gaze of Emily before both the girls smile at each other.

"Shots!" She screams, pulling Emily into the crowd to join her.

Amber and I are left off to the side of the show, staring after them. I think we are both surprised when Emily licks salt from someone's chest and takes a lemon from their mouth. My friend's kitchen is completely trashed, but no one seems to care; they just keep drinking. Sebastian steps up beside me, shoving a solo cup into my hand. As he tries to lift it to my face, I resist the urge to pour it on him instead. I don't want to accept anything from him, but the party is wearing on my nerves. Everyone here is starting to annoy me, and Amber is getting more pissed by the minute. It's only a matter of time before she lashes out.

I take a sip of the drink and immediately regret it. The liquid is strong, with a flavor reminiscent of gas, pine, and oranges, but I down it before tossing my cup at the crowd. I laugh as a guy turns to glare at me, wiping drops of my drink from his hair and shoulder. What do I care if he's upset about something being spilled on him? He probably isn't even meant to be here. I look over at Amber, ready to make a joke about the stuck-up attitude coming from the guy, but she shakes her head. She places her cup on the table behind us and weaves through everyone to leave the room.

Sebastian nudges me on the shoulder, his way of telling me to figure out how to fix her before she tells everyone off and shuts it all down. But before I get the chance, the naked pool guy comes barreling into the house, chasing after people who have stolen his clothes. I stare at them and call for Amber to check out the displayed goods as someone yanks the small towel from his hand when he runs by. Instead of Amber coming back, her brother rushes in and pushes the birthday suit guy out the door. A couple of girls let out sad groans once the guys are out of sight.

Roger goes over to the speakers, unplugging every cord he can get his hands on. The music stops, and people immediately yell out their frustrations. "Whoever lets them in can take them home. In five minutes, any face that's here that I don't recognize will be forcefully removed." He yells out, making eye contact with several people before walking down the hall, repeating his message.

Two

Kellan

Finding the party we heard about was pretty easy; a lot of these rich assholes have security gates to keep unwanted people out, but this house didn't. It also helped that cars lined the left side of the driveway, and some even parked on the street. Choosing to be a complete nuisance later on, I roll right up to the front door, revving my bike to announce our arrival. A couple of pretty boys stand on the front porch, eyeing us but never saying a word. Not even a whisper when Tracy walks right up and takes a beer from their hands to drink it herself. They stand there, staring at the three of us with panicked expressions, letting her take one can after another from their hands.

It's actually pretty funny. Watching this five-foot-tall woman walk up to any man and do something to them, daring the guy to react. I've told her a million times that she'll eventually be humbled when she picks a fight with the wrong person, but she never listens. We're not a club, but most people think we are up to no good, so they move out of our way or let us do what we want. I guess in Tracy's mind, she feels a little more invincible when John and I are with her; sure, she sometimes goes too far with her nonsense, but I'm not her keeper.

Tracy downs the last beer before tilting her head back to let out a loud howl. I shake my head, still getting used to the weird shit she does sometimes. She has been working at the shop for nearly a year now, mainly focusing on the street cars that come through the shop for us while we work on the bikes. It's been both a blessing and a curse having her around, but ever since she got that Rebel, she's been tagging along on our rides, too. I can't complain about her too much, though. She's quick to diagnose any problems the kids have with their cars and get them out of our hair, but John has been becoming more obsessed by the day. It was bad enough having her show up to work in shorts so short they barely covered her ass, but now I have to wipe the drool from his mouth myself to keep the peace between them.

John parks his bike and storms off, heading around the back of the house, still a little bitter from being turned down by her earlier. I imagine he's taking a walk to clear his head or get her out of sight; it's not his first time being turned down by a woman, but he's stuck on this broad. I let him go off, not really caring much about his temper tantrums these days.

A New Year's Ride

I half jog up the stairs, pushing my sweaty hair out of my eyes before walking into the front door that looks like it's seen better days, and gently press it closed, checking the latch to make sure it catches before going any further into the house. Just because I'm here to cause a little trouble doesn't mean I'm gonna trash someone's home. I'm here for entertainment purposes, not to rack up charges if someone were to think I was vandalizing their shit.

The smell of piss hits me immediately. Usually, these rich snobs have houses cleaner than a Hilton hotel, but I guess this one didn't get the memo. Covering my mouth and nose, I move past the group of girls who stop speaking to stare at me in disbelief. I spot the keg of beer in the corner, but I know there is more than this available to drink. The place is too fancy to have one cheap keg. As I walk, squeals and laughter draw my attention to an enormous kitchen. A bartender is mixing drinks, with several bottles lined up on the wall and counter. A group of women is arguing and covering up someone else with a towel; she's obviously naked underneath, and it has stirred up some drama between all of them.

Two short blondes are taking turns licking each other's necks in the corner, picking up shot glasses and knocking them back one after the other. Two guys stand a little too close to them for my comfort, but I know better than to cock block these weird bitches. The last time I did that, the two broads bit my head off, and I'm not one for hitting a woman, but they didn't hesitate to slap the shit out of me for getting in their way of a good time.

The bartender gives me a suspicious look, but I ignore it. "I'll take an Old Fashion," I tell him. If I'm going to be dealing with these snobs all night, I might as well get a good buzz while doing it. I grab the glass as soon as he puts it in front of me, noticing he poured a generous amount. He's either getting paid well or he doesn't want me coming back anytime soon. I chuckle and walk away, hearing someone yell about not knowing who the fuck everyone is.

Three

Ava

Emily and her blonde friend bounce over to us, eyes shining, until Emily notices Sebastian's hand creeping up the back of my skirt. He catches their gazes and quickly tucks his hands into his pockets. I feel relieved when his hands are no longer on me. My skin feels like it's trying to peel off to escape his touch, but I'm stuck between him and the crowded counter.

"Look, a few of us are heading to my parents' house across town. They won't be back for another two weeks, and, uh, it seems like Amber will be doing some cleaning up for a while." Emily is talking more to Sebastian than to me, but I know he will answer for both of us. He always does.

"Plus, her brother is killing the vibe," the blonde adds.

Emily looks back and forth between us, as if she doesn't know which of us will respond first. I shake my head in disbelief; she wants me to leave them alone so badly that she's willing to leave Amber behind with a mess on her hands just to have time alone with Sebastian. I get the hint. I decide to give her exactly what she wants and leave the three of them behind, pushing past all the drunks asking for more alcohol than they need. I swipe the rest of Amber's gin off the counter and head into the massive house to find her. The music has been turned back up, thumping loudly from the living room. Someone keeps increasing the volume to drown out the shouting as Roger wrangles people out of the house.

My steps start to falter from the alcohol, but I'm not nearly drunk enough to keep dealing with Emily and her friend. My face begins to heat, too, and walking down the hallway to find the stairs feels like it's taking longer than usual. I touch my face to feel the warmth and smile. It's been a long time since I've drank, and I have no regrets right now. Glancing back at the kitchen, I see Emily pressing closer to Sebastian to talk to him. I try to slow down to see his reaction to her, but I trip instead, landing on my ass with my arms propping me up. The whole house is so loud, I feel as if the sounds are deafening. I scoot across the floor, propping up against a wall, searching for something to hold onto.

Emily stands on her toes, making herself taller as her hand reaches to pull Sebastian's face closer to hers. Their lips touch as her friend grabs onto Emily's shirt sleeve and tugs a few times, pointing in my direction.

The three of them glance down the hallway at me, but regret is only written on the face of the girl I don't know. I hold her gaze the longest, wondering how she could be the only one with sense in the trio. Emily's expression is smug, as if she is the winner of a competition I didn't sign up for. Sebastian just stands there, expressionless.

I realize they both came back at the same time earlier. Emily's hair was a mess because of him. He used to mess up my hair when we made out in his car, before he made my life absolute hell, and the worst side of him took over. I scramble to my feet as quickly as I can and head toward the foyer. The blonde girl calls after me, but I don't turn around to face her. I knew something was going to happen tonight. I've mentally prepared, but witnessing it myself has cut me deeply. I don't want to put on a show; I don't want to cause a scene. I just want to leave.

Yes, my plan was to leave Sebastian once we were alone, but I didn't think he would stoop to such a low level. I didn't expect him to be willing to go back to Emily after everything they did to each other. But you know what? Who am I to get in the way of them? Honestly, they deserve each other.

Four

Kellan

I down my whiskey in a few gulps, letting the drink warm my insides, and take a deep breath before setting the glass down on a random table. Before I can take another step, a Richie Rich pretty boy steps into my path.

"You," he says with a growl. I'm a little impressed by his tone. Most of the time, these uppity guys don't look twice in my direction, but here he is wanting to stand toe to toe. "I don't know you," he declares.

I look him up and down, then gesture to myself. "Of course, you wouldn't know me," I smirk as I shoot back at him. All these guys are the same, thinking they're famous or some shit because of who their mommies and daddies are, but I couldn't care less. I'll knock him on his ass just like any other regular Joe. Besides free drinks and ruffling a few feathers, I don't want to get into trouble tonight, but if a fight breaks out, I'll gladly take the chance.

He grabs the front of my jacket, ready to make a move I've seen too many times. Several people around us turn to see the commotion, but I stand still, smiling. *Let this little fucker take a swing at me, please.* I silently pray, hoping he will give me a reason to release some stress on his pretty boy face. I've been wound up tight lately; I need the release. He notices the circle of people moving in on us, ready to announce when the fight will break out. The tension is running high, but I still stand there, grinning ear to ear. It's a trick I learned from my brother; you stand there smiling, and it pisses them off more. They fight sloppily when they are mad, and to make it even funnier, they can't fight their way out of a wet paper bag to start with.

The guy shoves my shoulder, trying to push me back, but I don't move. I plant my feet the moment he touches me. Yeah, I'm a little stronger than that, boy. My grin widens as he looks me over. I might not be the tallest or the biggest in the room, but I make my presence known. I handle motorcycles every day; he's going to need to put some real effort into taking me down.

"Outside," he says as he points at the rickety door behind him.

"Sir, yes, sir," I mock him, hoping to rile him up more, but he doesn't take the bait. I make my way to the door, disappointed that I could only have one drink before being thrown out with not even a punch tossed in my direction. Tracy is still sitting on the porch; the guys from earlier are still frothing at the mouth over her giving them attention. At least one of us is having a good time tonight. Buckling my helmet on, a sense of loneliness fills my chest. Sure, I've been alone most of my life, but bringing in the new year solo feels heavy. Fuck's sake, I'm starting to mope. I'm only 33 years old, but I feel at least a decade older, especially when I show up to a party and it's a bunch of college-aged kids trying to have a good time. I didn't think tonight would be the night I'd find Miss Perfect, but I was at least hoping for someone to spend some time with.

It's been a while since I've been with anyone, and I half expected to bring in the new year with someone tonight, but this crowd isn't who I thought would be here. Tracy starts to walk down the steps of the house, but I wave her off. If pretty boy puts his hands on her, she won't hesitate to throw him around. As bad as I'd love to watch that shit, I think I've outworn my welcome. Besides, she's got the guys on the porch entranced, and who am I to stand in her way? I should go anyway; there's a bar across town calling my name.

Five

Ava

Amber and her brother round the corner, herding people towards the door. I down the rest of the drink and toss the cup over my shoulder before I meld myself into the crowd of people escaping them. The group of people will give me enough coverage to slip out, then I'll Uber to my apartment.

A loud rumble startles me, causing me to jump and cover my ears. My eyes immediately fix on the motorcycle parked a few feet away from the bottom of the stairs, idling loudly. A slim, muscular man pulls straps together under his chin as he gets onto the seat. His legs move, tightening the jeans in a way that nearly makes my eyes pop out of my head. I openly gawk at his impressive build. Even as he sits on the bike, I can tell he's tall. He revs the engine again as he balances the bike beneath him, motioning for someone to stay where they are.

The crowd on the porch has started to part, unsure of which direction the man is about to take. I take a few steps forward, taking in the view; his face is completely hidden behind his full-face helmet, but I still feel a strong pull to him. He's wearing a black hoodie, dark denim jeans, and black leather boots. When he places his hands on the bars in front of him, I can see tattoos peeking out of the sleeves around his wrists. Oh my God. I don't know who he is, but his physique alone makes my knees weak.

My insides suddenly squeeze as I watch him, when a loud thud sounds behind me, followed by several people yelling my name at once. Turning, I see Sebastian, Amber, Emily, and her friend all rush towards me. I quickly retreat down the stairs; I've seen enough of them for the night, and the party will only be awkward if I stay here with them. It will also be embarrassing if they leave together, though, and I'm left behind. I'm the odd man out here.

I can explain all of this to Amber tomorrow, but I have to get out of here before they all make a bigger scene. The last thing any of us needs is for our parents to find out about Sebastian and me from this crowd. The act will send them all into orbit. Emily takes a step down, coming right for me. I look back at the guy on the motorcycle, feeling his eyes on me as I back away from Emily. Yeah, I've got to get out of here.

I quickly jog to the motorcycle, watching as he pushes up a visor on the helmet. Immediately, I stare into the bluest eyes I've ever seen. The rest of his face is hidden, but I can tell he is smiling. His cheeks are pushing up past the padding on the inside of his helmet, and I thank the stars he's welcoming as I throw my leg over the seat behind him. Everyone stops running towards me, staring in shock at what I've done. The stranger revs the bike loudly, warning them not to come any closer, before he grabs one of my bare knees and steers my foot to a pedal off to the side. I do the same with my other foot a second before he jerks us forward. Grass flies behind us as he steers us towards the driveway.

"Oh shit. John!" A woman screams at the top of their lungs, but the sound of the motorcycle cuts off her voice.

My heart is pounding in my chest. I've never done anything like this before, and I'm with a complete stranger. As we make it onto the smooth driveway, I look around nervously. Am I supposed to hold onto his jacket the whole time? I settle for his broad shoulders, but he grabs one of my wrists and places it a little too low in front of him; I yank my arm back in alarm. Panic floods me as I begin to wonder if we are going fast enough for me to be seriously injured if I were to jump off.

He holds his hand up as if surrendering, but when we reach the end of the quarter-mile driveway and bounce down onto the street, I'm thrown around on the small seat, nearly falling off completely. My heart beats faster; I'm terrified but excited. He pats one of my knees again, then one of his shoulders. I glance at my hands on his back and see my fists have grabbed onto his jacket so hard the fabric is riding up, revealing tattooed skin lower than I could imagine.

He reaches around his waist with one hand, and I take it. He places my hand on his stomach and gives a thumbs-up, followed by the O.K. signal over his shoulder. I lace my other arm around and lock my hands together. I don't want to have to touch him more than this, but his warmth is welcoming. As we race forward, my skirt blows up around my midsection, sending me squealing from the cold air attacking me. I let him go to tuck the bottom hem under each of my thighs, hoping he didn't see the show that I just put on for anyone who may be standing on the side of the street.

The cold January wind bites at my face and hands, but I have nowhere to escape the chill. I tuck my head behind his and stare down his spine, but now I can't see where we're headed, and I'm still uneasy about who this person might be. My legs start to shake as we slow down and pull into a neighborhood. I don't recognize any of the houses, but I'm relieved the wind is no longer biting at me.

We make another turn and pull up to an empty driveway, but he doesn't stop the engine. He throws his leg over, gesturing with both hands for me to stay, and walks into the garage of the house to our right. The street is empty and dimly lit, with only the motorcycle's idle sound filling the night. I sit perfectly still as it rumbles beneath me. The heat from the engine radiates close to my legs. I'm afraid it will burn me if I move even an inch, but the warmth is welcoming.

I sit in the dark for a few minutes before he returns, holding a helmet in one hand and what looks like a leather jacket in the other. His visor is still closed, completely hiding his face from me. I lean to look behind him, wondering if this is his house or if he just stole these things. I mentally slap myself for suspecting the worst about someone's generosity; he's obviously just trying to make sure I'm safe and as warm as I can be without pants. No one expects a crazy person to jump on their motorcycle in the middle of the night, and he must have known these things would be here.

He flips his visor up and holds the helmet out to me, but before I can grab it, he shoves it onto my head. It's a snug fit, but padded and comfortable. I look up to meet his gaze, but his determined look keeps me quiet. I sit patiently as he loops a strap from one side of my face, under my chin, to the other. I stare into those beautiful blue eyes and can't help but wonder if he has looked at mine this closely. Why did he let me come with him?

Once satisfied with the helmet, he steps away and hands the jacket to me. I push my arms through, but the sleeves are too long. He steps up beside me, folds the sleeves nearly in half so my hands are visible, then grabs the bottom and starts the zipper. He stops so I can finish it myself, but I silently wish he wouldn't. Something about those big hands taking care of me stirs feelings I've never known before. I could watch him all night; the way he moves is mesmerizing. His long fingers are thick and calloused, with faded, scarred tattoos on his knuckles. My skin tingles, but I'm not sure if it's from the cold or from thinking about all the ways he could use those hands on me.

Shaking out of my thoughts, I pull the leather strap to the center of my chest and wait for my next silent instructions. He's staring at my foot, which suddenly feels warm under his scrutiny. He inhales deeply through his nose and blows it out quickly, obviously frustrated. I look down at my frozen foot, the rhinestones on my shoes reflect the dim lights, shining like a beacon in the night. Oh. I suddenly feel naked. I have no suitable pants or shoes for this ride to carry on any longer.

These are the heels I bought last year for my birthday after Sebastian conveniently forgot to get me a gift. I've nicknamed them the 'fuck me' heels. And now that this man is staring at them with dark eyes, I don't regret wearing them at all anymore. I wiggle my polished toes to see how numb they are to the cold. I'm pleasantly surprised they can still move at all. He shakes his head and throws his leg over the seat in front of me.

As the motorcycle's weight is shifted, I wobble and sway, forgetting that I should be holding on to him, or at least shifting my weight to help balance myself. He doesn't seem to mind my lack of experience as he straightens the bike in the lane, then walks us to a stop sign.

"Have you ever ridden before?" He yells over his shoulder, his voice deep and gravely. I shake my head, then remember he can't see me that well.

"No," I yell over the motorcycle's loud idle.

"Alright, you need to bring your hands and arms closer up here," he pats the metal lump in front of him. "When we slow down, you can sit back a little. Follow my movements when we're in turns."

"What do you mean?" I ask him.

"When I lean, you lean too. You don't have to lean as much as I do, but you can't sit straight in the turns." He waits for me to respond. I nod and put my hands where he showed me, hoping I'm able to do this.

We leave the same way we came into the neighborhood, and once on the main road, he guns us forward. If anyone back there was asleep, they aren't now; I wouldn't be surprised if a few car alarms went off in the distance from the noise coming from the machine I sit on.

Six

Kellen

John is going to kill me when he finds out I took his leather jacket, but I couldn't let the girl freeze to death on the back of my bike. I could kick myself for not being more prepared and bringing an extra helmet, but by the grace of God, John's kid left this one behind when he moved out. It was pretty funny seeing the damned thing fit so perfectly on her head. I'm almost certain it's a youth size, but I'll take whatever works. I just wish there were some boots or something in that storage bin, too. The shoes this girl has on now look like they cost more than the helmet I'm wearing, which wasn't cheap by any means.

What the hell am I going to do with this chick? I can't take her to the shop, it's not exactly dirty, but I haven't cleaned all week. There's no way I'm taking her back to my mom's apartment either, and she'll freeze to death before we get to my place. I take that back; I've changed the sheets and shit at the shop because I left a human-sized oil stain on them two days ago. I hate sleeping in filth, but somehow I always find an oil stain on my sheets. I bet nothing would make this chick more hot and ready than rolling in motor oil.

I stifle a laugh at my sarcasm. The only thing she's hot and ready for is getting away from the people who were about to jump her ass. One of her hands squeezes into a ball on the front of my jacket as I pick up our speed. I know she's cold, but the way she's inching closer to my lap makes my dick twitch in my jeans. I tell myself not to get too worked up over the broad, but damn, her legs are as bare as they can get; it's hard not to think of a woman naked when she's pressed against me with hardly any clothes on in the first place.

I should be slapping the shit out of myself for thinking about her that way, but at least I'm not the guy she was running from. I slow us down as we come up to a traffic light, and I feel her grip soften.

Don't let go, baby. Not yet.

I sit up, planting my feet on the pavement and let my arms rest against her legs. We might only be here for a minute, but if I can give her any warmth, I will. If I can feel the cold on my legs, I can only imagine what she's feeling. I hold up my hand, signaling to ask if she's okay, but she doesn't move. Lights explode overhead, filling the sky with flashes and bangs as the firework show begins. I feel like we've sat here long enough without the light changing, probably not recognizing us as a vehicle. I look around, making sure no one is nearby, and run the light.

I need to get her out of the cold.

Seven

Ava

We pull into a diner on the outskirts of town and come to a stop near the front door. When he turns off the motorcycle, silence blankets us. My ears ring for a moment as the rumble dies down. As he kicks the stand from the bottom of the frame and leans us over, I feel like I will fall off. My leg goes out instinctively to keep myself upright. I swear I hear him laugh under his helmet.

He stands and stretches his arms above his head, letting his shirt and jacket ride just above his jeans for barely an inch before he sighs and begins working on the strap under his chin. When he pulls the helmet over his head and places it in front of me on the seat, I almost gasp at the sight of him.

He's gorgeous.

His hair is short, a dark shade of brown or black; his lips are full but flaunting an old scar on his bottom lip that extends down to his chin, covered in a light stubble. But his eyes are what keep drawing me in. I've never appreciated a shade of blue as much as the one shining from his eyes right now, and even though this man is a complete stranger, my mind starts racing as I think of all the things I'd let him do to me. I'd have a story to tell and a dreamy man as my highlight. The best part is, it would all be true. Everyone already saw us leave together.

A surge of confidence rushes through me; he was at the party, so someone must know him or have seen him. Amber has cameras, so they could figure out who he is if anything happens to me, but I doubt he's dangerous. He would have already hurt me if that were the case, right? I swing my leg over the seat and stand in front of him, sizing him up. He remains still in front of me, not moving a muscle. Instead of loosening the buckle on his helmet, he stares back into my eyes.

I reach up to touch the buckle of the helmet, knowing it's not as complicated as I think it is, but not wanting to look like a fool in front of him. The metal is cold under my fingertips as I trace what feels like a capital D, the strap scratchy on the skin of my neck as it's pulled tightly underneath. He reaches up and swats my hand away but doesn't immediately start working me out of the borrowed gear. Instead, he smiles and grabs the lower part of the helmet, slightly shaking it back and forth, which causes me to wiggle around unsteadily on my feet. I thought I'd sobered up enough during the getaway, but apparently not, since I'm still wobbly.

"Let's get something to eat and figure out our next move," he says, heading towards the sidewalk.

I start scratching at the strap, finally finding the end of it and pressing it through the metal piece, forcing it to loosen and eventually come completely apart under my chin. I pull it over my head and run my fingers through my hair as he opens the door. He takes the helmet as I walk by. The metal rings jingle behind me before suddenly stopping. I turn around to see him sliding into a booth and walk towards him, taking the seat across from the gorgeous stranger.

We sit silently at the booth, pretending we're not sizing each other up. The fluorescent lights reflect off his dark brown hair as he tilts his head down to pull his phone from his front pocket. He looks up at me and grins when I quickly look away. It's embarrassing to be caught ogling someone. But I'm fighting myself to resist climbing across the table and kissing those perfect lips until they fall from his face.

He notices my sudden shyness and ruffles his hair before running his hand through it to fix it. I'm unsure if he's reading me like an open book or just fidgeting. I notice the tattoo wrapping around his wrist again, but I still can't tell what it is. The idea of being with a bad boy has suddenly turned me on. I become more flustered the longer I look at him, losing the confidence I had just minutes ago. He exchanges smiles with the approaching waitress and orders coffee and water for both of us. A pang of jealousy hits my chest as he smiles at her, showing off his perfectly straight teeth and wide-set mouth.

Don't look at him. I want to scream in her face until she retreats and gouges her own eyes out. I am surprised at my near outburst of violence. I thought leaving Sebastian behind with everyone would feel freeing, but this anger I have lingering inside me is threatening to swallow me whole. Blue eyes stare at me from across the table, studying me as I fight a silent battle. Heat begins to pool low inside my abdomen as I stare at his mouth. I realize how desperate I am to know how it feels. His voice breaks my thoughts like a rubber band popping my skin. I painstakingly push the thoughts away and tune into the rest of his sentence.

"-But yeah, the coffee here isn't the best. What about you?" He waits patiently for my response.

"Yes, I drink coffee," is all I can manage. What was he babbling on about?

"So, they were yelling at you back there. What's all that about?" He asks as he takes a napkin and cleans the table off. The waitress comes back, setting two cups of coffee and a glass of water between us, giving me time to consider telling him about the night's events. After riding on the back of his motorcycle, wearing someone else's clothes, and sitting in a shady diner on the outskirts of town, my dating issues aren't what I'd like to focus on, but I guess I need to explain myself.

I watch as his long fingers grasp the handle of a mug. He pulls it toward him and stirs in a packet of sugar and a creamer. What else could those fingers do? As he lifts the cup to his lips, he uses it to hide a smile. My face flushes; of course, he saw me looking at him. I'm sure it's hard to miss. I pick up the laminated menu to hide behind it, afraid that if I look up at him again, my body will throw itself into his lap without a second thought.

"My boyfriend was kissing some other girl," I grumble. He snorts at my short explanation.

"And the girl stepping up to throw the first punch was that the one he was loving on?" His eyes stare at me over his mug, gauging my reaction to his question.

"It was, but she isn't the physical type. None of them are. She was probably going to scream at me to make the whole thing more embarrassing than it was." I stop explaining Emily to him, unsure of how much of the situation I should share. "Who do you know there?"

"Nobody, really. Some guys wanted their shit worked on, and they were talking about it when they were in the shop." His large shoulders rise and fall as he shrugs. "Figured I would go just to be a bother."

"Why?" I ask him, confused by what he means.

"I don't know. I didn't have anything else going on, and that side of town always gets annoyed when people like me show up. Just so happened I had two more people come with me, so they were three times as annoyed." he explains, but I still don't understand. This is a grown man wanting to bother strangers?

"What do you mean by 'people like you'? I press him. He doesn't answer, just stares at me with those icy blue eyes until I feel a shiver run down my spine.

"Why were you running from the girl if she wasn't going to lay hands on you?" He asks.

"I told you, I didn't want to be yelled at in front of a million people." Are we speaking different languages?

"So what? Get yelled at in front of some people and yell back," he says, as if it's that easy. I roll my eyes, the action making his jaw feather. Oh, that's hot. I should annoy him again. Wait, no, he's my ride home. "I hardly think that's the whole story. Most women I know would claw out anyone's eyes for even looking in their man's direction. You just let her have him, just like that?"

I bite my tongue to keep from screaming at him. "It's not like he was a prize to be won," I whisper. My eyes begin to burn as his words cut into me. I didn't think he would understand; he is just a stranger after all, but I also didn't think he would be the judgmental type. Maybe I made a mistake, and I should Uber home like I had intended.

Eight
Kellan

Poor little rich girl; caught her boyfriend sucking face with another rich girl. I try my best to cover up my laugh, but it's just so damn comical. Having everything in the world given to you on a silver platter, but crying over some douchebag that doesn't know what it means to get his hands dirty. I watch as she shifts, uncomfortable by me telling her how she should have handled the situation, but when she rolls those pretty brown eyes in annoyance, I resist the urge to spank the living daylights out of her.

She slams her menu down, rage filling her features. For a moment, all smart-ass comments leave my mind. I thought she was pretty when she fearlessly threw her leg over the back of my bike, but she's beautiful when she's angry. I blink, wondering if this is a dream for a second. Her lips twitch as she mutters under her breath, but I can't make out what she's saying. My blood pulses through my body, drowning out everything around us.

The fire in her starts to die down as she stares out the window. What could she be thinking of to calm herself down that quick? I watch as the anger on her face is slowly replaced by sadness until her shoulders sag with defeat. Guilt sets me on fire. I fucked up. *Don't be sad, Angel.* I plead for her to say something, change the subject, do anything other than be sad. I don't know how to handle her, much less if she starts crying. Fuck. What do I do?

"He must have been a real catch," I tell her. If she's mad, she won't be sad anymore. How could someone like her sit here and cry over anyone? Doesn't she deserve the world and shit? That's what her friends and family would be telling her if they were sitting in my seat. Her brown eyes flicker to me, holding mine again with a little more life in them as I annoy her.

I see it then—the tear streaks that have smeared makeup under her eyes and down her soft cheek. Her eyes are pink and swollen, but I can't tell if she wants to cry now or if she was crying on the road. That would explain why she didn't respond earlier at the light. I feel like shit. The girl was being cornered and saw me as an escape, of all people. Sure, she used me, but it must have been a real shit show back there to run off with someone she doesn't even know.

Maybe she's only telling me part of the story, but I need to back off. Not everyone is ready to open up about shit to people right when it happens. "Sorry," I mutter, gritting my teeth as the words leave my mouth. I sigh, hearing myself try to apologize. She deserves better than this. I clear my throat to try again, but the damned waitress can't read the room.

"What can I get you, babes?" She pops her gum as she asks for our order.

"Give me the star-bangled breakfast," I don't hesitate. This place is a shit hole, but they have waffles that can cure anything. Breakups, hangovers, and family matters included.

"Same for me," the angel across from me chimes in. The waitress and I exchange a glance. There's no way she's going to eat all that food. Hell, I can barely finish it myself.

"Are you sure?" I ask. She shrugs in response. The waitress saunters off to put in our order, leaving us to pick up the conversation, but that moment of tenderness is gone.

"What do you do for work?" she asks. I scratch my thumb across the stubble that's come in since my shave this morning, unsure how to respond; owning the shop isn't what I like to tell people. It's just not what I had in mind for myself, but it has to be done, and that answer usually brings on more questions than I can stand to answer. As she sits across from me with those tear-streaked cheeks, I can't help but feel this nagging inside me to get to know her.

"I own a mechanic shop. Cars and shit," I spit it out quickly. The words are bitter, but maybe she is who I need to vent to. This week has been a disaster. John and Tracy fight nonfuckingstop and I'm at my wit's end trying to get them to calm down. I need them both more than ever; I've managed to pull the shop out of debt early last year, but it's been hard. I've worked damn near around the clock to make it happen, and now that people know that my brother and father are nowhere around the place, business is starting to pick up daily. I wipe my face with both my hands, trying to get some of the stress off me. Tonight was supposed to be an easy night, but here I am thinking about all the shit that's going on.

Glancing back at her is a mistake. She's sitting there with sex written across her face again, cheeks flushed with her mouth parted like she's going to start panting any second. I sit back, wondering what I did to get her so hot and heavy all of a sudden. I can't help but smile at her. Does she know how easy it is to read what she's thinking when she looks like that?

I clear my throat, trying to keep from having to beat her off of me with a stick, but thoughts of her under me have started to take over my mind. "So, uh. What about you? Work?"

"Oh, I was working at a boutique for the last few years, but today they closed for good. The owner was a friend of my parents, and she passed away. I guess technically I'm unemployed now," she says as she waves her hands around.

That's pretty fucking cute. My girl is basically a freeloader.

The longer we talk, the more he smiles at me. I've got to admit, it feels good to have someone to talk to who isn't focused on someone else or their problems. All my life, I've heard about people's issues, but nobody ever offers solutions; they just sit around gossiping. The longer we talk, the lighter I feel, as if a weight has been lifted from my shoulders. Our conversation flows effortlessly as we patiently wait for the waitress to come back with our food.

We've also moved away from my dating issues, which is refreshing because it's all I've been able to think about for so long. Two years of complaining and negativity can wear down even the strongest person, and I'm starting to feel like myself again. I say something that must be funny because he responds with a blinding smile. I wonder if it's genuine, but the crinkles around his eyes chase the thought away.

This man is nothing like Sebastian, even though I don't know him or his name. Oh shit. "What's your name, motorcycle man?"

He looks at me, puzzled but amused. Those beautiful eyes. "Kellan. What's your name, Angel?" he stares into me.

Angel. My heart squeezes in my chest. I could get used to that. "Okay, kids. Two star-spangled breakfast plates. Anything else I can get for you?" the waitress asks as she places six plates down in front of us. I shake my head, wanting her to leave quickly. Kellan is the first to dig in, scarfing down his portion of scrambled eggs and hash browns before I can pour syrup over my oversized waffle. He looks up at me, fork frozen mid-air.

"You hungry?" I ask, teasing. I know I'm hungry, but not for food. He clears his throat and sits up a little straighter. "Oh, I was just kidding. I didn't mean to embarrass you. I'm sorry." I ramble, feeling like a fool. I should stuff my face and stop talking. The alcohol in me has started to fade, but I'm at that point where anything could come out of my mouth. It's a dangerous game.

I watch as he starts to eat again, slowly this time. I didn't know watching a man eat could be erotic. I wiggle in my seat, trying to think about the food in front of me, but I can't focus on anything but his mouth. If I were to pour syrup on me, would he? Jesus. *Pull yourself together.*

Ten

Kellan

I force myself to eat, but I'm not quite as hungry as I was before. Food is the last thing on my mind right now. I dig into the greasy hashbrowns, swallowing them down quickly to avoid saying something stupid.

"You hungry?" she asks. Something about the way she says it makes me think she doesn't mean the food. Oh, darlin', you got no clue. I'd eat you until you can't walk. I sit up straighter, grabbing my jeans at the knee to tug them down a little. If she looks at me like that again, I'll be pitching a tent under this table.

"Starving," I reply, gazing directly into those brown eyes. Her face flushes, and I can tell she caught my double meaning. *Don't back down, angel. You started this.* I watch as she carefully cuts her waffle into small pieces before taking tiny bites.

Crunching into my bacon, I sit back and watch her eat. There's no way she will finish all that food, but I'm going to enjoy watching her try. One small bite after another, she works her way through the damn thing but gives up halfway, opting for her eggs next. She cuts it into tiny pieces, as if it might choke her if it's larger than a dime. That's kind of strange, but okay.

Grabbing the syrup, I pour a heaping amount over my waffle, fold it in half, and eat it taco-style. She looks at me with a horrified expression. I give her a grin, hoping to break the silence that has settled here, even if it's at my expense. "You never answered my question," I remind her. No way I'm going to sit here and let her drool over me without knowing her name.

"Ava," she says softly.

"Where do you live, Ava?" I gotta know more about her.

"In an apartment," she answers. I cringe a little as she looks around. I realize that wasn't the best thing to ask someone you hardly know. What a dumbass. I should keep the conversation moving.

"Sometimes, I stay at the shop," I tell her. "Just don't want to go home, I guess," I shrug. "Last year, I was too busy to keep making the trip home, so I had the building extended and added a makeshift apartment." I over-explain to her.

"Where's your shop at?" she asks, eyes down low. What does that mean?

"Downtown, it's not in the best area, but we get a lot of business, and no one messes with us." I could elaborate more, but when she looks up at me, I lose my train of thought. Shit. My dick twitches in my jeans; how is she doing this to me? Her eyes search my face. What's she thinking? "You want me to take you back to your friends?" I ask, not wanting my time with her to end, but not wanting to scare her off either.

After a minute, she slowly shakes her head, and I let out a sigh of relief. But where do I take her from here? Is she trying to work up the courage to ask me to take her to the fucking shop? I mean, I considered it, but there's no way I could. Right? No, I think she deserves a little more than that. She isn't like Crazy Bethany. Hell, they aren't even built the same. Ava is soft and innocent. I don't even see a hint of a scar anywhere on her pale skin. Her light brown hair curls around her face and slender shoulders in thick waves; I bet it feels like silk between my fingers.

I lean back, putting my hands in my lap, before I can reach across the table and give in to the caveman inside of me. I want to pull her hair, not hard enough to cause her any pain, just enough to get her hot and bothered. Just enough to get her to open her mouth and let me in. I close my eyes, battling with myself. I could take her to the shop and show her how she should be treated. I shouldn't. But fuck, I want to. Looking back at her, she's eating again but staring out the window with wide eyes. The sound of bikes rumbling sets my heart racing.

I wasn't expecting them to find me so soon. And just when the night was starting to get interesting.

Eleven
Ava

Kellan is staring at me, drinking me in like I'm a cold glass of water in a hot desert. His eyes roam over my face, my hair, shoulders, then back up again. My blood heats under his gaze. Something about how he looks at me makes me nearly irrational. I want to climb across this table and claim him as mine.

I'm two seconds from asking him to take me back to his place when a familiar sound outside catches my attention. Looking back at Kellan, his eyes are closed, too deep in his own thoughts to hear the noise coming up quick. Two motorcycles pull in and park beside him; the larger rider takes off his helmet and lights a cigarette with one hand. I recognize him immediately. He's the same guy who tried talking to Amber and me at her house before the shit hit the fan.

The other rider is built significantly smaller; they take their time taking off their helmet, and to my surprise, it's a woman. Jealousy rears its ugly head inside me. Kellen's eyes pop open, and he glares outside at his friends. The big, burly man waves, imitating a small child excited to see a parent, but Kellen isn't as happy to see him. He holds a middle finger up to the window, but the guy outside catches it like a kiss being blown in his direction. I try not to laugh at them, but it's adorable. Earlier tonight, I was almost scared of the guy, but now I feel comforted by just seeing a glimpse into their friendship.

"Are you done?" he asks me. Excitement runs through me. Where will we go?

"Yes," I say, a little breathless. He pulls his wallet from his back pocket as he stands.

"Oh, I got it," I say quickly, grabbing for my cross-body clutch. It's the least I could do, considering I hijacked his night.

"My ass you do," he states. I'm shocked at his words, and a little confused. He throws four twenties on the table. I don't know how much the ticket is, but that seems generous. He grabs the helmet from the booth and walks quickly towards the door. Now that I've eaten, my drunken state has dissipated, but the buzz is still there. Once outside on the broken parking lot, I wobble. The winter air bites at my bare legs, and I regret not wearing jeans tonight.

"What the fuck are you doing here?" Kellen barks out at them. The man stares past him, looking me up and down.

"Nice jacket," he says with a smile, but his tone isn't as friendly as it was earlier tonight. He looks Kellan over, eyes lingering on the helmet in his hands.

"What the fuck do I look like? Charity?" he flicks his cigarette onto the ground and then starts his motorcycle, cutting off any response that would have come from either of us. I shiver as I stand behind Kellan. Obviously, this isn't how he wanted his night to go; I feel responsible for their argument, but what can I do? Taking a step closer, I decide it's best if I go back to Amber's house. Starting drama between a group of friends isn't something I want to do, and I already have enough drama of my own to handle. Sensing me behind him, Kellan reaches for me without turning around. His calloused fingers lace into mine, causing heat to travel up my arm. His hand is rough, but I don't dare pull away. His rough hands feel delightful on my skin, like warm sand on a beach. Holy shit. Okay, I'll stay here all night if I get to keep his hands on me.

Images of us tangled in sheets flash in my mind, waking a fire deep inside my lower belly. I want those rough hands on my body. Ice is poured down my back as I look up, meeting the glare of the woman still sitting with her helmet off. She stares at me with anger and disgust. It's hard to hold her gaze. I thought I was scared of the man earlier, but I'm terrified of her.

Twelve
Kellan

I stare back at Tracy as she looks at Ava with anger in her eyes. If she and John are in a bad mood, it's their own fault, and all be damned if she's thinking of taking out their frustration on me or anyone near me. Whatever the fuck they have going on between them is their business. I reach back and take Ava's hand, sensing her behind me.

I glare at the woman across from us, silently pleading for her to back down. What the fuck is her problem? She didn't care about John earlier today; why would she care that I bailed from the party and didn't tell him? The nerve she has to act protective of either of us is staggering. I'm not going to deal with this jealous behavior from her. She's an employee and a friend, nothing more will ever happen between the two of us, and I had assured John weeks ago that I wanted nothing to do with her. I also pleaded for him to keep it professional between them, but he hardly ever listens.

She finally meets my gaze and flinches before she pulling her helmet on and starting her bike. In the blink of an eye, she darts off, chasing after John. They are undoubtedly headed to his friend's bar across town to lick their wounds. Wounds they have created themselves by acting like lost puppies and following me around town. I couldn't care less what they do for the rest of the night. I'm not their damn keeper; they are free to come and go as they like. Some days I do feel like we are family, but nights like tonight, they just piss me off.

I tug Ava closer to me. She must be freezing in that skirt; I hope the jacket is enough to keep her from being miserable. I did have some kind of hope that I'd have someone to share a drink with tonight, but I didn't have a clear plan in place and things like this hardly ever happen. I'm not that interested in one-night stands like I used to be, but as I stand here trying to figure out where to go, I'm realizing a little too late that I'm less prepared to take someone home with me than I had thought. Or maybe it's the type of woman I've managed to slip off with.

Crazy Bethany never cared if my sheets had oil stains or how dirty the shop was, she would show up and crash then leave with some cash later in the day with barely a word spoken. I once imagined where she lived and shuddered at the thought of my place being the best she had. I push all thoughts of her from my mind and focus on my current situation.

Where the hell do I take Ava? She was running away from the party; there's no way she would want to go back. Would she? I can't take her to my house. It's too far out of the way, not to mention not even my own mother knows I have it.

There's no way in hell I'm going to ask if she wants to go back to her place. I feel pathetic at even considering it an option. I glance down at our fingers laced together, the sight sending some caveman-like urges through my body. There are only a few options here, and I have no way to decide which one is the best. I sigh. Fuck it, let's just go.

Thirteen

Ava

The low fire that has been building inside my lower belly bursts into roaring flames as Kellan gently tugs me toward the lone motorcycle in the parking lot. I take a deep breath and fall into step beside him. I've never been this excited for anything in my life, and I silently cross my fingers in hopes that he will take me... anywhere. Anywhere. I don't care where he lives; I don't care what the place is or where it's at. In the past two hours, I have been treated better than I have been by Sebastian since I've known him.

I hardly know Kellan at all, but he hasn't mistreated me in the slightest since I've thrown myself into his life. He could have turned me away, he could have done several things to me by now, but he hasn't once even slightly crossed the line or raised his voice at me. I let him pull me close and shove the helmet onto my head. Standing still for him to buckle the strap under my chin, I press my knees together tightly, stifling a low moan as his warm fingers brush softly against my neck. I'm surprised by my body's physical reaction to him barely brushing over my skin; if I don't pull myself together soon, I'm going to break into a million pieces in front of this gorgeous, devilish man.

I take a deep breath, praying that I won't hurl myself over the line before the night is over. I don't want to embarrass myself. As he takes his time buckling the helmet onto me, my insides begin to scream for him to make a move silently. His eyes dart around, taking in my expression before looking back at his hands and letting me go, throwing a leg over to straddle the bike and standing it up before holding his hand out for me; I take it and allow him to help me sit behind him with a huff of frustration. When I have trouble finding where to place my foot, his rough hand finds the back of my knee before traveling down my leg to lift it slightly and find the peg for my foot.

My breath hitches as his touch sends a warm bolt of lightning through my body. I grab the back of his hoodie with tight fists, praying for him to use those heavy hands on the rest of me. My body feels hot, even in the frigid winter air. The burning desire travels from where he has touched my bare skin, up my leg, down the other, and is now threatening to climb up my throat. I quietly groan with need before feeling my face flush with embarrassment. If he heard me, he doesn't let it show. He walks the bike backwards and revs the engine loudly. Several people inside the dinner watch us from the windows, and I feel exposed, as if they all know what I could be thinking, dressed like this as I sit behind him.

I look away and pull down the tinted plastic on the helmet, shielding my eyes from the judgmental crowd inside. Their gazes did nothing to extinguish the fire that had been lit inside me. As we speed down the empty highway, I can't help but appreciate the way Kellan feels in front of me. His hard, muscular back presses into my chest as I lean forward, placing my hands where he told me to earlier. His scent invades my senses, overriding any and all logic I have.

We slow down for a traffic light, and I silently thank whoever decided it was a good idea to place it here. My fingers are starting to go numb from the wind. I need gloves. I suddenly have a strong urge to see how far he would let me go with him. It isn't a very good idea to put frozen hands on someone's skin as they drive. I'd jump out of my skin even if we weren't on the road, but maybe I could put them somewhere else. My heart threatens to beat out of my chest at the thought of touching this man while we race down a road, but what if he lets me?

Could I go through with it? I glance up at the back of his helmet, then look around to see that we're still on the outskirts of town, but where are we headed? I clench my hands into fists, trying to get blood pumping through them. I decide to go for it, I can't sit here any longer and suffer. I slip my hands into the front pocket of his hoodie, spreading my hands flat against his hard stomach; he tenses beneath my touch and looks down at where I have placed my hands, but I don't take them out of the pocket. The warmth is just too good. *Ah, this heat feels amazing.*

Time freezes as I sit, waiting for him to push my hands away. The light turns green, but he stays frozen in place, still looking down as if he knows what I intend to do once I have feeling in my hands again. Eventually, headlights creep up behind us before a car honks a few times and passes by. Kellan shifts, and we shoot off like a rocket. I grab onto him tighter as the wind picks up and blows around us almost violently.

In a matter of seconds, the cold air has taken away any warmth from my legs, and I begin to shiver. I pull myself closer to Kellan, closing the gap between us completely before curling in behind him as close as I possibly can. He slows us down as the road begins to twist and turn, and I let out a sigh of relief. I don't think I've ever gone over the speed limit in a car before, and I'm afraid to ask what our speed was before we slowed.

Kellan leans with the bike as we make a turn and climb up a steep hill. My body follows his, as if I'm the shell of a turtle. I close my eyes, absorbing the way his body feels as it moves against the front of mine, and dark, feral thoughts spring into my mind. His hand slides across one of mine, and for a moment, I think he may be trying to guide me to go lower. I open my eyes and see we are slowly coasting next to the river.

Boat lights twinkle across the water like stars; in the distance, I can make out the silhouette of a large barge with several people wearing headlamps running from one end to another. Suddenly, fireworks shoot into the sky, their loud booms fill the air in unison, before lighting up the area in various colors. Cheers erupt from the boats on the water before being drowned out by more explosions.

I take in the view and open the helmet's visor to see more fireworks shooting into the sky. This has to be the best New Year's celebration I have ever been to. My emotions ball up in my chest, and I continue watching as one burst of color showers after another, and hot tears slowly fall from my eyes.

I pull us up to the levee, taking the sidewalk to see everything happening on the water and coast along. The shop is just a block away, but I gotta work up the nerve to take her there. She doesn't seem like the type of girl to be happy with something like that, and I know she damn sure isn't the one-night type. I try not to laugh at that, seeing how she was just warming her hands an inch from my dick. For a second, I was starting to worry that she was going to pull it out in traffic. The girl sure knows how to get someone riled up; that's for damn sure.

I sigh. John and Tracy really fucked up the mood there for a minute, but I'm glad; it got me out of that gotta-fuck headspace and set me back on track. Unfortunately, Ava is dragging me right back to it. I'm trying to be some kind of fucking gentleman while she keeps moving her hands around in the pocket of my hoodie, and I can't tell if it's deliberate or if she's just not paying attention to where her hands are. If she is doing it on purpose, she's got another thing coming.

Fuck.

Her hands move lower, pulling the front of my jacket down far enough that I feel the wind on my neck. I look down and see her fidgeting inside the pocket. What the fuck is she doing? I snake one of my hands inside and feel for her, realizing she's picking at the nail on her thumb. Jesus Christ. I've got to get it together.

We come to the end of the sidewalk on top of the levee; I stop and let her watch for a few minutes before turning to look at her over my shoulder. She finally leans over to meet my stare, and I see it then. Her eyelashes are wet, and her nose is red; it's obvious she's been crying. Maybe the shop isn't such a good idea.

"You ready to go?" I'm going to drop her off at the house party, at least then she can cry to her friends and the people she knows.

"Yeah, where to?" Her voice sounds happy, almost excited. Where to? She's sitting here crying her eyes out and now wants to know where we're going? I shake my head. Oh, she's got some baggage. Maybe she is my type.

Fifteen

Ava

I nervously pick at the side of my thumb, desperately wishing I could bite the sliver of nail I have managed to break away from my nailbed. I take a deep breath and exhale slowly to regain composure and bravery. We descend down the hill and pull back onto the road before cruising at a steady pace, much slower than before. Loud booms erupt from the water I can no longer see, then the sky is filled with bright colors again. I stare in amazement as more fireworks light up the night.

Eventually, we approach a locked gate at the back of a metal building. My heart beats rapidly in my chest as I think back to what little I know about bikers. I draw a blank, never having the opportunity to be around anyone like Kellan before. He leans the motorcycle to the side, propping its weight up but leaving it idling loudly. Then, he walks to the gate to open it. I wonder if I should follow him, but he returns to drive us through the parking lot.

I look around, eyeing the gate with barbed wire across the top, wondering if this is what a prison yard looks like. There are more motorcycles parked along the fence line, shining in the dim streetlight. My heart threatens to climb up my throat at the sight. Is this a clubhouse or something? More bikes mean more bikers, and while my time with Kellan hasn't been the worst, that doesn't mean I am willing to greet more of them with open arms.

I sit on my hands, warming my fingers now that I don't have Kellan's jacket to shield them from the cold, and stay silent as he parks under an awning and holds his hand out for me. For a moment, I sit, unmoving. I don't know where we are, who is inside, or what we are doing here. He leans his helmet close to mine, barely bumping them together. I can't see his eyes, but this tiny movement calms my nerves significantly.

I place a hand on his shoulder and swing a leg over the seat, careful not to touch the long pipe radiating heat below me. As I glance down at my shoes, I can't help but notice how he is now standing between my legs. My face flushes beneath the face shield, and I pray no one walks out here to see us like this. The last thing I need is for someone to see me spread-eagled on a motorcycle in a parking lot. My heart thuds in my chest at our proximity; I could get used to this. I just need to know what's inside that building before I commit to anything. I'm battling with myself, trying to fight off the fear of the unknown, just to spend time with this stranger. This is definitely a new me; I would have never done anything like this before.

He steps back, holding both my hands gently, as if cradling a wild animal. I hesitantly stand, taking a small step towards him; I was pretty ballsy earlier, but now I feel far out of my comfort zone. Is this how people get kidnapped? Because the trust that I'm putting into this stranger is mind-numbingly stupid.

I sigh, letting him lead me inside the metal door, where I'm suddenly hit with an overpowering smell I have never experienced before. I try to cover my mouth and nose with the long leather sleeve, but the helmet blocks my movement. Kellan's hands fumble on the wall before a row of lights overhead buzz to life, illuminating engines and parts scattered across ugly wooden shelves. Clear plastic packages filled with pieces of what look like the gears inside a clock hang from pegboards along the wall. Photos of women and motorcycles line the door behind me, and a metal rack holds several larger pieces of engines in the corner.

I look down and gasp. I'm standing in the middle of a giant, black puddle. Oh God. My shoes! I flail my arms around as I begin to slip on the floor, tugging on the calloused hand that has led me here.

"Fuck. I'm sorry. Shit, I thought I emptied that before I left. Hold on," Kellan lets out a frustrated sigh before he scoops me up and carries me through the room. I try my best to breathe through my mouth and watch as dark brown oil trails after us as we walk through the rest of the building. He sits me on a high counter that is littered with papers and receipts, then starts fumbling with the buckles of my heels. My skin feels alive everywhere he touches as he gently removes one of my shoes from my foot. My toes are still freezing, but the warmth coming from him feels amazing.

I wait patiently for him to slip the other shoe from my foot and set them both on top of a box with blue paper towels coming from the top of it. He stands tall before working on the strap under my chin. I sit as still as I possibly can, letting his fingers brush my neck over and over again as he feeds the long fabric through the rings under my cheek.

Glancing up at him, I want to scream in frustration. He's still hidden away behind his visor. I unsnap the strap on his helmet and feed it through the loop, understanding how it works now that I see it on him, and enjoy how his rough stubble scrapes across my knuckles. We pull the gear off simultaneously, and I revel in his ice blue gaze once again.

A smile spreads across my face. He's just too damn hot for his own good. I hand his helmet to him, not sure where he keeps his stuff, and watch as his long, rough hands take it from mine. How do I get those hands on me again? I look at my leg, wanting to wrap it around his to pull him closer, but hesitate. Would that be too direct? My face heats as I consider it and what his reaction would be. I don't even know if he's interested in going further with me. This could just be him being nice; it isn't like I've had too many instances where someone has shown me even the kindest of decency. I could be reading too far into this situation.

Shit. What if I am making up the tension between us? I meet his gaze, deciding on what to do. I'm not usually interested in the whole one-night-stand thing like some of my friends are, but now is my chance. Maybe this could really kick off my new year, new me way of life.

Sixteen
Kellen

I swear if she gives me those kiss-me eyes one more time, I won't hold myself back. Yeah, I finally brought her here, but there's some shit I need to know before we go any further. Considering where she was when she jumped me, I'd say she knows someone high up that food chain, or she is up there herself. The last thing I need is cops pounding at my door because their daughter was seen with me and they press charges for shit I didn't do.

"Alright, Ava," I clear my throat and toss my gear to the side. "Let's get into it. Cause last thing I need is someone putting out a message saying you've been taken against your will or some random dude showing up here threatening to beat my ass." I smirk. Yeah, threaten is about all those shit stains could manage to do to me, but she gets the picture.

"Oh. Um," she stutters, pulling her phone from the tiny bag on her hip. "No, nobody is looking for me. I told my friend I would talk to her later, but she's probably dealing with a lot right now, so she hasn't responded. We track each other, though, so she knows where I am."

Well, thank fuck for that. Now her friends know she's alive, that's a relief. I sigh, watching her perfect legs swing from the counter; even her painted toes are pretty. I take in the color of them, turning red from being cold for so long, only to walk into the heat of the shop. I push off the counter, grab two beers from the fridge, and set one down next to her, but I'd be surprised if she drinks it. I take her foot in my hand, her cold skin nearly burning me. She's still frozen.

"So, you told your friend, but not the boyfriend?" The question hangs in the air between us, so help me God, if she says boyfriend, I'm rioting in the street.

"My friend." She sets her gaze on me, turning red in the face. There's that fire, that hint of anger on her angelic face that I like so much. I smile at her. "I think he more than got the hint that we aren't together anymore, and so did I. So there's no reason to tell him anything." Her eyes close slightly, squinting at me like she wishes they were daggers. Yeah, angel. Show me those sharp little teeth.

"And you left him cause he was kissing some bitch?" I don't mean to sound harsh, but the truth hurts, and I need her to be honest with me. I know she didn't want to keep talking about it earlier, but if her story is still the same, then I'll back off and accept it. She clears her throat and leans back on the counter, resting her arm on the box of shop rags before grabbing the beer.

"Is that what you call women?" She tosses her hair over her shoulder, showing off perfectly smooth skin. The sight of more of her causes my dick to jump in my jeans. I need to rein myself in.

"Hey, don't be mad at me. They were the ones sucking face. Where do you live?" I'm going to take her answer as confirmation, but there's still the problem of who she knows back there.

"On the west side of town," she states. Oh, she's annoyed with me. The thought of her releasing her wrath on me is comical. She can be irritated all she wants, but at the end of the night, it's my ass that's on the line if she isn't safe.

"Yeah, no shit on the west side of town. Show me," I spin the laptop around to her and open it for her to type in the address. Anyone who looks at her can see she's in a different tax bracket. She doesn't need a job; hell, she isn't a freeloader at all. I said that shit as a joke. She comes from money and probably won't have to work a day in her life if she doesn't want to, and I bet the house matches the income.

Her face reddens again, and I can tell that one struck a nerve. Maybe I should ease up a bit, but I need to know who's been backpacking with me for the last two hours before I get into some shit that even the best lawyer I've got can't get me out of. "Look, angel, I just want to make sure the FBI isn't about to come kick my door in because daddy doesn't approve of where you went or you didn't take security." I sigh. I know the type of money those people have; the last thing I want to do is end up in jail for giving someone a ride or two. My dick stirs again as she stares back at me with fire in her eyes. *Or three.*

She rolls her eyes and types in her address, drops down on street view, and sits back with a huff. I'd be lying if I said the attitude doesn't turn me on. I want to bend her over right here and now, but I can wait.

I look the house over, then copy the address and search tax records for her parents. There's no way in hell she bought that with inheritance.

"Are you happy now?" She takes a long pull from her beer, and it's the cutest fucking thing I've ever seen. I look back at the screen, copying the names on the tax information and pasting them into the search bar.

She leans the screen back to see what I'm doing and scoffs. "How did you look up my parents' information like that?"

"Hell no, I'm not happy. Your mom is some high-end realtor, and dad owns more companies than there are grocery stores in this state, and you're gonna sit here and tell me they let you go off with whoever you want to? I thought you said you live in an apartment anyway." I wave my hand at the screen, "Tax Accessor websites are available to the public as long as you know how to use the shit." I glance over my shoulder and see she's biting her nail. The last thing I want is for her to have a full-on panic attack here in the shop. "Alright, I'm sorry. I won't pry anymore. But you lied." I tell her.

"What about you, Kellan? Where do you live? What do your parents do for a living? Do you run this whole shop by yourself? What else do you have in the garage?" A smile takes over her face when she says my name, but it disappears as she rapid-fires her questions at me. I stare at her in awe, still caught up on the way my name sounds coming from her pretty mouth. I like the way it rolls off her tongue.

"I already told you where I live, but if you want me to be more specific, I live here, too. My dad passed away about eight years ago, and my mom is retired." I finish my beer and toss the bottle into the can before grabbing hers and downing it. I don't know why she's pressing me so hard. I'm not the one lying about where I live to be more relatable.

"Well, if it's any less concerning, I do live in an apartment. I moved out when I turned nineteen because I couldn't bear not having my own space anymore and living how I want." She bites back at me. Her admission is pretty cute; I try to think back to where I was living at nineteen and shudder at the memory of my mom's apartment when she was let go of her job and went through a deep depression.

"You didn't have enough space in a fucking mansion?" I jab at her. I realize my mistake as soon as I speak the words, shit. This night just took a turn for the worse. We stare at each other, tension filling the room so thick you could cut it with a knife. She's the first to break and look away. The muscles in her jaw tighten, sending guilt shooting through my chest.

Seventeen

Ava

"I'm sorry. I didn't mean to bring up something so sensitive." My voice sounds weak and small, but his reaction to my questions struck a chord in him.

"What?" He sounds confused.

"About your dad," I tell him.

"Why are you sorry? Were you the one who killed him?" My eyes nearly pop out of my head at his question.

"He was murdered?" I ask, completely shocked. He laughs at my reaction and grabs the case of beer from the fridge.

"Hell, I don't know. It was a long time ago, and he wasn't that great a person. The only good thing he ever did was leave this place to me, and it was deep in debt when he did that. I just wanted to see your reaction." He sets the beer onto the counter before walking away., disappearing from my sight completely. When he comes back, he's holding a bundle of wool.

I crinkle my nose when he lifts my leg, wanting to put the socks on me. I tug my leg free before he rips the socks apart, breaking the thin plastic that keeps them together. I hadn't realized they were new. He pulls them apart and reaches for my leg again, warming my feet with his hands before sliding the itchy material onto my bare foot. He's so warm, I want to burrow into him. He does the same with my other foot, warming it between his hands and traveling up my calf until he pulls up the sock and moves away.

I pout at him, wishing he would let me warm my feet on his body. He takes my hand and pulls me from the counter, making sure to hold me steady on my feet. I don't argue when he leads me further into the building. The tension was getting a little high. He pulls me through a maze of parts sitting haphazardly in the open shop, and I sidestep parts and pieces before stopping short.

"What's the matter?" He asks as he turns to face me, unaware that he is standing in another giant black puddle.

"What is that?" I ask, tilting my head down to point with my chin.

"It's oil that spilled out of the pan when we changed it from one of the bikes. John usually cleans up after himself, but he's been a little out of it lately. Hold on." He wanders off, and I am left standing in what feels like a tool warehouse filled with machines I'll never understand. When he comes back, he's carrying a box of cat litter. I'm not sure how they usually clean up things like oil spills, but a box of cat litter was the last thing I expected him to use. He shakes the litter over the puddle and throws the empty box next to a large trash can against the wall.

"I'll let it soak up and clean the rest in the morning. Let's go this way," he says, taking my hand and leading me around an overflowing black tub on the floor. I'd say the guy was more in a hurry than out of it, because that looks like it was pushed aside and forgotten. Once we reach the back door, I stand off to the side while he props it open with a crooked metal bar. Eventually, we make it outside and begin climbing up old, rusty stairs. I take each step hesitantly, sure that any second, they will come crashing down under our weight and throw us onto the pavement below. A loud boom erupts around us, pulling a scream from my lungs. I drop to my knees in a panic before the sky is illuminated in an array of beautiful colors. I grab my chest, feeling my heart quicken, and gasp for air.

Kellan bursts into laughter at my side, obviously enjoying seeing me nearing a heart attack. I slap his leg. How dare he laugh at me when I thought I was seconds from dying? The firework display continues, sending waves of noise and colors into the air rapidly. I look up, shooting daggers at him, but soften when I see his face. His smile is wide, showing off his nearly perfect teeth as he leans down to me and offers his hand.

"What you so scared of?" he asks.

"I thought that was a gunshot or something," I answer, but as I say the words, I feel embarrassed. Looking into his eyes, I doubt he would willingly put anyone in danger. I grab his hand, putting all my trust in his palm as I pull myself to stand. He keeps smiling, as if he understands. The longer we stand here, staring at each other, the more lost I become. His smile is comforting and mesmerizing. My insides do a flip, and the possibilities of the night flash in my mind. For the millionth time tonight, the same question echoes in my mind: How do I get those hands on me again? I take a deep breath and look back up at him again. Am I really about to do this?

Eighteen
Kellan

There's something in her eyes that clicks into place as she looks up at me, like she seems to realize I won't risk anything happening to her. Seeing her on her knees in front of me sends my mind into overdrive. Images of all the things I'd like her to do race through my head until the tension between us is so thick it presses down onto us. A dark look flashes across her face as her eyes drink me in, looking me up and down like I'm her own personal eye candy. I feed into it, wanting her to tell me exactly what she wants, and just maybe I will give it to her.

"Good girl," I say as she slowly stands in front of me. Her cheeks flush a soft pink, the words flustering her. I can't help but wonder, what else could get her blood rushing like that?

"Do you want-" I try to offer her another beer, but my question is cut off as her soft hand runs up my arm to lightly squeeze my bicep. She bites her bottom lip as her gaze shifts down my body before looking up at me again. What the fuck is this? Where did the shy little angel go? I'm not complaining at all, but what a sudden turn of events. Is she still drunk? "Ava. I – are you -?" I don't know what I'm trying to say or ask anymore. She has completely surprised and disarmed me.

"Oh, I'm sorry. I'm so sorry." She starts apologizing, tripping over her words as she looks around frantically, but it pisses me off. What does she mean by she's sorry? She rambles more, but I tune her out. Does she think I'm not interested? I look back down at her, and without warning, press my mouth down on hers.

I kiss her hard, pulling her into me by the back of her neck and wrapping her hair around my fingers and wrists. There's only one way she's going to pull away from me, and that's if I allow it. Maybe I'm being a little too aggressive, but what the fuck does she mean by 'she's sorry'? Why do something like that and apologize? I slip my tongue into her mouth, pulling a moan from her, and feel her press her body against me. She gives in to the kiss completely, slowly bringing her arms up to wrap around my neck until I feel like I'm holding up most of her weight.

That's right, sweetheart. Melt into me. Once I can feel her breath become ragged, I pull away to let her suck in air before diving right back into her mouth again. Fireworks ring out around us, exploding one after another, and if I weren't taking my anger out on her mouth, I'd say the scene could be romantic, but who the fuck cares?

I'm still stuck on her reaction to me. Why apologize? Her hands claw at my neck, but I can't tell if she wants me to pull back or press forward. There's only one way to find out. I break away from her and look around. I'm not going to lie her down on the nasty couch up here, and the chairs aren't big enough to hold us both. Fuck it, we're going back inside. I pick her up and wrap her legs around my waist, and try not to take the stairs three at a time. I've never been more aware of the creaks and moans of the rusted metal before as I carry her back down and kick the door open. I need to be careful.

Thank God the staircase didn't cave in under the weight of us both, but hey, if they can hold John, they can handle the two of us.

"So, no girlfriend then?" She whispers in my ear.

"No. No girlfriend," I'm not going to explain Crazy Bethany at a time like this. She definitely isn't a girlfriend; the bitch should be in jail. If I got the call tomorrow that she was locked up, I'd do a celebration dance and tell them to throw away the key. Is that why she apologized? I almost want to laugh at her timing, but I hold myself back. Her soft fingers pull at the neck of my hoodie, pulling the fabric down to give her more skin to trace. I kick shit out of my way to take her to the kitchen, pissed that it's closer than my bedroom. There's no way I'll be able to hold either of us off long enough to make it there.

Nineteen

Ava

Kellan's strength surprised me when he carried me down the stairs and through the dimly lit shop. I don't know where he plans on taking me, but I don't care. I keep my ankles locked at his lower back while I work on his neck, kissing and trailing my way down as he stomps through one door into another.

I didn't mean to wait until now to get a solid answer on the girlfriend situation, but there didn't seem to be the right time, and I was tired of waiting. I didn't want us to spend the night watching fireworks and then have some awkward goodbye later on because neither of us wants to paint him in a bad light. This is what I want, and yeah, it may seem fast, but when will I ever feel this alive again?

Once I have the fabric of his jacket pulled out of the way, I bite down on his exposed skin, pulling a groan from him. The sound sets my body on fire, spurring me on. I lick and suck, reveling in the taste of his slightly salty skin. He smells amazing, like pine trees and laundry detergent; I want to wrap myself around him completely. I feel my skirt shift before a cold, solid surface presses onto the back of my legs, surprised that he didn't take me to the apartment add-on of the shop he was telling me about earlier.

He reaches behind his head and lifts his jacket completely, and in that brief moment, time stands still. My mouth pops open once he stands before me in just his jeans. His chest is chiseled to perfection, tattoos blend into one another with dark lines, splashes of color breaking the pieces of art up. The images pull my eyes in every direction, helping me study his body in a way that's borderline illegal. The sight of him makes me feel almost giddy. Emily can suck my ass. I won by miles.

I bite my lip to fight back a smile as I take in the sight of him half-naked in front of me. His stomach is flat and toned, but not perfect. I silently thank whatever God is listening that he isn't one of those people who has completely shredded abs; not that it's a bad thing to be fit, but if the guy was going to talk me into going to the gym with him, this wasn't going to work out. The tattoos that frame his sides grab and hold my attention the most; they aren't faded like the rest on his body. I've never seen anyone with tattoos like this before, but I'd say the ones on his sides are somewhat new.

I can't make out exactly what they are in dim lighting, but now that his shirt is above his head, I reach out to touch the colorful skin. I trace the bold lines, shocked that the art feels like any other skin on a person, except for a few places that are raised like the ink bubbled and had nowhere to go. I trace the deep scar with my fingertips, testing how far he will let me go. The ink obviously extends below his belt, but how far will he let me go? He finally throws his black hoodie and shirt across the room, standing still and watching as my fingers turn back up to travel across his chest. I remember the way the hood of his jacket was pulled down earlier and know without a doubt that he has just as many pieces on his back as he does on his front. The idea of letting this man claim every inch of me sends a shiver down my spine. He's like no one I've ever met in my life, and it thrills me. I can only imagine what my friends would think of him, but that's fine by me.

He grabs my legs and pushes them further apart to stand between my knees; the cold that has settled into me slowly fades as his body heat threatens to smother me. Grabbing the back of his neck, I pull myself closer to him, wrapping my legs around his waist to pin us together. He kisses the side of my neck, lighting a roaring fire inside of me. Those rough hands I've been thinking of all night push up my thighs, threatening to go into territory that I hardly allow anyone access to.

"What do you want, Ava?" He blows against my skin, causing me to shiver in response. This is usually the time when I'd tell Sebastian to shut the fuck up because I'm trying to focus, but something about Kellan's deep voice pulls me deeper into my dark thoughts. I twist my fingers in his hair and pull him into my neck. I want him to keep his mouth on me. Is that too much to ask for? I want him to take me right here on this kitchen counter. I want to be his for the night. I want to carry this memory with me forever, and when anyone asks what happened to me, I want to smile and say that I lived.

He bites my neck hard, sending my eyes rolling into the back of my head. My hands are yanked from his hair and pinned against the cabinets above my head faster than I can comprehend. "Answer me, angel." He nips at the soft skin on the back of my arm, and I squeal with excitement. His voice is dangerous, even if his warning is playful. He pulls back and stares into my eyes, waiting for my response. Embarrassment creeps into me; I thought this was a mutual thing? I thought he wanted to do this, too. Does he want me to say this aloud so he can laugh at me?

"What do you want, Kellan?" I ask and look away, fearing he may be backing out of this. Was I too forward, and now he's no longer interested in me?

"We both know what I want," he pulls me by the back of my knees until I collide with his belt. The bare skin of my thighs smacks against his bare stomach, closing the small gap that has formed between us. He presses his pelvis into mine, pulling a gasp from me as I feel every inch he has to offer. My eyes widen as I look down between us, noticing the prominent bulge covered by his jeans. I try to pull my hands down to cover my mouth, but his grip tightens around my wrists.

"You gotta say it for me, angel. What do you want?" We stare into each other, my embarrassment being replaced by lust so strong that I struggle to breathe. My back arches as I try to create some friction between our bodies. I'm so close to getting what I want; all I need is a little room to move.

He watches me wiggle and grind against him, lifting my shirt with his other hand to see more of my body. I look up at the ceiling, feeling like a goddess as I try to chase the release my body craves. "So needy, but not needy enough," I hear him say as he takes a step back. I let out a frustrated groan when his body is no longer pressing into me. My shirt falls, covering my body once again. My mood plummets; I don't like this game he's playing with me anymore.

Twenty

Kellan

If she really thinks she can come in here and use me as her personal dildo to get off, she's got another thing coming. I'm not one of those little rich pricks from that house party she was running from. I know how to please a woman. Even if I've only been with two women in the last three years, I still understand what they need and how to deliver.

I hold myself back, refusing to give in and fuck her brains out. I'm not going to give in until she tells me she wants this as bad as I do. Consent. I need her to be willing to do this because, at this point, I may leave bruises on her beautiful skin. She wraps her legs around me, trying to pull me towards her again, but I refuse to give her what she wants. I need to hear the words leave her pretty little mouth.

Tightening my grip on her wrists, I pin her against the cabinet doors again. "Do you want me to stop?" I ask her, praying she wants me to keep going. She shakes her head but sits quietly. Fine. Let's see how quiet she can be.

Her skin is soft under my touch, like silk slipping under all the calluses on my hands that have built up over the years. Starting behind her knee, I slide my hand up and around to push her skirt up as far as it can go. White and silver panties stare back at me. I glance over at the shoes she was wearing earlier. All be damned, she matches. I slowly flatten out the thin straps that wrap around her hips, toying with her, letting her think I'm giving in. A devilish grin takes over as I consider all the ways to have her begging for me.

My fingers trace the patterned lace that lies perfectly flat against her skin, and I watch as her breath hitches in her chest. I move to the outer edges of the material, sliding the backs of my fingers along her skin in the crease of her leg, and watch as she tries to move so my fingers will dip further inside. I strain inside my jeans but hold myself back, still denying her. She lets out a soft whimper as I apply more pressure to her hands.

I tell myself to keep calm, repeating the words in my head before I tear her clothes off. Just wait her out; she'll either give in or tell me to stop. Just breathe. She inhales deeply, looking at our hands above her head, and lets out a frustrated groan.

"What is it, Ava? Have you decided on what you want?" I smirk as I ask. I hope she stays silent. To my surprise, she finally hooks a leg around my waist and pulls me forward. I bow my hips, not allowing her to rub against me. Instead, I take a thumb and press it against her clit, feeling how slick she is already. A groan escapes her, loud and animalistic; I'm so fucking glad the shop is empty, or else everyone here would have heard her.

I freeze, letting her make up her mind on how long she will torture us both. I'm in agony, all the blood in my body feels like it is draining from my head, and my zipper may bust if this goes on any longer.

"Please," she whispers. Fuck's sake.

"Please, what, angel?" She doesn't respond. I slide my thumb lower, feeling her legs and body shake as she takes in the feeling of me teasing her. She's so god-damned wet I could swim in her for days, and yet still won't give in.

I dip my thumb inside, just barely to the knuckle, and pull back out before sliding up to her clit and circling. She bucks under me, and I know she's close to caving in.

"Please, what? What do you want?" She pauses, as if she doesn't know how to say the words. Finally, they fall from her mouth.

"You. I want you." Her words crash into me. That's all I needed to hear.

Twenty-One

Ava

Holy Shit. I said it. I didn't think I'd ever be able to get the words out, but I finally did. I tried so hard to force myself to say it, but how could I when I was fighting back an orgasm with every fiber of my body?

I'm fucking embarrassed at how wet I am. If I didn't know any better, I'd swear this counter is dripping as badly as I am. But what can I expect from myself? When was the last time I felt this way? When was the last time someone truly got me off, and I didn't have to finish after they fell asleep?

My legs shake as he slides a finger inside me, twisting and massaging. I feel his finger slightly curl and nearly come off the counter. Jesus. How did he do that?

If I were to die, this is the best heaven I could imagine myself in. Pure bliss has taken over my body, sending waves of heat pulsing through my veins. I want to be quiet, I really do. But the way this man has me spread open has me panting like a dog.

Another finger slides inside, forcing me open wider, and I can't prepare myself quickly enough. An orgasm rips through me so hard and suddenly, I fear my soul has left my body. Great. Just great. We've barely started, and I've finished in his hand. I'm so embarrassed.

I ride out the waves of pleasure until a horrible thought comes to mind: if this is the foreplay, what does the rest of the night entail? Good Lord. What have I gotten myself into?

"You're beautiful when you're flushed," I hear him whisper before he releases my hands.

Oh. I wasn't expecting to hear anything like that. Do one-night stands usually call people beautiful? He grips my thighs and lifts me from the counter to carry me out of the kitchen. I can't help but feel as if I've bit off more than I can chew, especially now that he has found his way under my skirt again.

I lock my ankles around his waist to keep from falling and revel in the feel of his rough hands roaming on my body. It takes every ounce of strength I have to keep myself from tilting my head back and letting my moans escape from me. His fingers tease me relentlessly, sliding over my clit slowly before slipping back inside me. He carries me down a black hallway, his heavy footsteps causing me to bounce on his fingers. I can't imagine where we could be going, but I don't care.

We pass two doors before he stops and gently presses me against the wall and grinds into me. My legs spread so far apart that my hips ache. I soak in the pain and push past it to absorb the feeling of his pelvis grinding into me as much as his jeans will allow.

All I can think about is the possibilities, the promises he makes without saying a single word. My body is on fire as I drink in the feel of his bare chest under my fingertips, the thick arms with rippling muscles as he holds me up and struggles to open the door beside us. His mouth comes down on my neck, kissing and biting at my flesh. I roll my head to the side to give him more room as he works his way back up, leaving a stinging heat behind everywhere his mouth was.

I press against him, needing to feel the friction. I need this. The door finally swings open beside us. I freeze when I peer into the room.

Oh shit. Panic sets in so quickly, it's as if ice water has been poured over my body. Oh my God. Am I really about to have sex with a guy that I barely know? I've only met him hours ago, and we're ripping each other's clothes off. There's no way this can happen. I lock up, unsure what to do. How do we handle this when it's over? Are we just going to go our separate ways and never talk again? Do I call an Uber when we're done? Fuck, that's going to be embarrassing. I don't think I can go through with this.

As he carries me into the room, the faded scent of cologne lingers in the air. There are dirty uniforms in the corner and a messy bed with grey sheets pushed against the furthest wall. A dresser is on the other wall, complete with the largest TV I've ever seen, with two empty energy drink cans sitting under it. It isn't the cleanest room in the world, but it also isn't the dirtiest. I have more clothes than this piled so high you can't see the chair underneath; I have no room to judge this man. Everything seems to have a place here, more so than in my entire apartment.

"Are you okay?" He whispers in my ear. I shake my head, admitting that I'm having second thoughts. But what do I say now? Will he be angry when I tell him I can't do this? Sebastian would be furious when I turned him down; he even threw me out of his apartment once before. Kellan sets me down slowly but doesn't back away.

"I'm sorry, I know this isn't exactly the cleanest, but I stay here a few days out of the week when I don't want to go home. We can go, if you don't want to be here." He tilts my chin up so he can look at me as he speaks. Our eyes lock, sending a million emotions racing through me. Relief because he isn't angry; sadness because he thinks this isn't good enough, and desire because, for once in my life, a man hasn't thrown a tantrum for me wanting to slow down.

I hadn't realized that it was such a turn-off before. It's amazing how this guy has shown me more kindness and respect tonight than I have been given my whole life. Fuck, that's hot. As he stares into my eyes, I can see the fire slowly fading from him and worry creeping in. He is truly backing out of this. Oh, I may have fucked up. He pushes my hair over my shoulder and sighs, accepting that I have put a stop to us going too far, too quickly.

"Come on, we can go anywhere you want. Just tell me where," he says as he reaches down for my hand.

"I'm not on birth control," I blurt out. How embarrassing. Why would I say that?

"Neither am I," he says. Silence rings loud in the room for a moment before we both burst into laughter, and oh man, does his smile amaze me. My heart flutters in my chest as I watch him laugh. He's probably the most perfect man I will ever lay my eyes on.

I definitely messed up.

Twenty-Two
Kellan

I laugh so hard my side starts to hurt. Damn, that delivery was perfect. Her laughter fades, and tension fills the air around us. I wish she would tell me what she wants, where to go from here, because I honestly don't know.

Seeing the panic in her eyes once we walked in was awful. I'm not saying that I know what women want all the time, but when she changes her mind, it's pretty fucking obvious. I'm not about to sit here and force her into this just because my dick is aching. But does she not think condoms are a real thing? Is that what her concern is? Another sickening thought crosses my mind, but I push it away before I can dwell on it too much.

My girl panicked and wanted out, and the last thing I want is for her to feel pressured into anything around me. I need to get her out of here, need her to see that I won't press this situation, and she can always believe that she is safe with me. I grab her hand again, looking around for a shirt to cover my body, but she pulls away.

Fuck.

"I'm sorry," I say as I walk towards my dresser. Where the fuck are my clothes?

"For what?" Her voice rings out, no trace of fear in her tone. Turning back to face her, I watch as she lifts her shirt over her head and walks towards me.

That wasn't what I was expecting, and I can't stop myself as I reach for her. God, she's so soft. Everywhere I touch is like silk; her hair, her skin, her bare ass that's barely covered by that skirt. Once I have my arm around her waist, I know this is it. There's no turning back for either of us now. She's all in, and so am I.

Twenty-Three

Ava

There's just something about the way he backed down that did it for me. Something that brought back all of the intensity and poured gas on the burning fire inside my core. This man knew exactly what he wanted, but backed down the moment I showed how hesitant I was, then eased my mind with a joke like I didn't just torture us both.

I want this. I want him more in this moment than I did before, when he had a hand between my legs. I clench my thighs together as I slowly walk towards him, remembering the way he made me feel in the kitchen. I want to know what else he can do to me; how high he can take me.

Once I'm within his grasp, he snakes an arm around me and pulls me against his bare chest. He pushes my bra down, exposing my chest to him, and takes one of my nipples in his mouth. I nearly scream as pleasure washes over me. He swirls his tongue around my nipple before switching to the other side to do the same, palming the other and squeezing just enough to cause the right amount of pain. Pain that I didn't know I was into until now.

With each pass of his tongue, my heart beats harder in my chest. God, he's good at this. His teeth come down slightly, causing me to yelp in surprise, but it doesn't hurt at all. His strong hands grip both of my hips so hard that I may bruise tomorrow, but I don't care. I want this. I grab his shoulders to steady myself and tilt my head back. Allowing him to claim more of me freely.

Rough hands glide over my skin, traveling up my body until they cup both of my breasts. A shock wave takes hold of my body as each of my nipples is pinched between his knuckles. The pressure comes and goes as he squeezes and loosens them in sync. I cover my mouth as I moan, afraid that the sound will be loud enough to burst our eardrums. His breath comes out quickly, breathing like he's gasping for air.

Holy shit, that feels good. My pussy throbs between my legs, my insides begging for release. But he continues to knead my nipples, pulling moans and groans from me that I've never heard myself make before. One of his hands slides up and barely clenches around my throat, and I nearly explode at the sensation. He lightly squeezes before pulling his mouth away from me and steering me backwards by my neck.

I hold onto his wrist as I walk, and feel the muscles flex under my touch. What is that such a turn-on? He forcefully pushes me backward, letting go of me completely, and for a moment, I think he has just shoved me onto the floor. My heart nearly explodes in my chest before soft blankets and pillows surround me.

"Kellan!" I scream, ready to call him every name in the book. My outburst fades when he presses his mouth onto mine. The kiss is soft but demanding. I open my lips, reading to invade his mouth, but close them quickly. I've never actually tongue-kissed anyone in my life.

I decide to go for it, mimicking the way he kissed me when we were on the roof earlier. His tongue laps back at mine until we are moaning into each other. His body weight presses me deeper into the mattress, and I wrap my hands around him to deepen the kiss. I lick at him until I can no longer breathe before having to break away to suck in air.

"Dirty girl," he whispers in my ear before trailing kisses down my body. Why does that make me want to finish right here on this bed? My back bows off the bed once his mouth reaches the hem of my skirt. I feel his mouth bite down on the fabric and drag it up my body, exposing my panties.

Oh, wait. Is he about to do what I think he is? "Wait! Wait. Wait. Wait." I nearly yell. I've only had this done once before, and it was the worst experience of my life. It was painful, and I swear I was raw for days. He grabs hold of my thighs and pins me down, staring into my eyes as he slowly takes the elastic band of my thong between his teeth and stretches it down my thigh. The sight causes my breathing to hitch.

I can't watch this, but I can't take my eyes off of him either. Now the right side. Oh, God. His teeth come down on my hip, and I flex my toes as he grazes them against my skin. He's going to hurt me, I know it.

"Ava. Relax before you take my head off. I'm not going to hurt you." His voice sounds deep and gravely. I can't help but sigh and release the tension from my body. How does he do that? How does he tell me what to do, and my body just accepts it?

I feel the elastic band snap against me. Great. Now, what will I have to wear when all of this is said and done? I throw my head back onto the bed and watch as a tiny feather flies into the air above me. Just trust him.

He kisses me softly below my belly button and trails down to where my panties lie broken on top of me before pushing them down until I am completely exposed to him. I brace myself for the pain, but feel nothing until his tongue begins tracing patterns across my pelvis. He slowly starts to go lower before sliding his tongue in. He starts above my clit and heads straight down, the movement parting me open for him. I nearly come off the bed completely. What the fuck is this?

"Easy, baby," he whispers against my leg before pulling me to the edge of the bed.

Is that what it's supposed to feel like? He hooks his elbows behind my knees and spreads my legs open, looking at my pussy like it's a feast and he's a starved man. I attempt to close my legs, but he is too strong.

"Uh-uh. Don't hide from me now," he says as he pulls my legs apart even more and dips down between them again. My skin is painted again. As he swirls around and around, from one hip to another, I feel like I'm in heaven.

"But, why?" I whisper.

"I'm just writing my name," he says as he plants a kiss on my hip and slowly makes his way further down. My face reddens as cold air blows across my body. I can't bring myself to look down and see what he has done with his mouth. It's too embarrassing. His tongue widens again and glides down until it meets my clit once more.

"Oh, fuck." I scream out as all the nerves in my body are suddenly electrocuted, and his mouth is the live wire. I feel everything he is doing with his mouth with hyper awareness.

He flicks his tongue once, twice, and a third time. I can't take it. It's too much. Fisting the sheets under me, I bear down and try to close my legs. His strong arms push them further apart, allowing him to dive deeper into me. He licks across my opening slowly before pressing his tongue in as far as he can, and I lose my mind.

"Kellan!" I scream and fist my hands into his hair, holding on for dear life. How does anyone survive this? He could be stealing my soul right now, and I wouldn't even care, as long as he kept going.

Twenty-Four

Kellan

I could eat her all night. She tastes so good, but I don't think it's going to last much longer. I'm barely putting any effort into this, and she's nearly coming apart underneath me. I can't imagine what would happen if I were to do much else. She must not experience this very often; something about that thought makes me smile. I'm bringing her pleasure that no one else can- or has.

She fists her hands in my hair, and I know she's nearing climax, but this is nowhere near the end for either of us. I plan on wringing out as many as I can from her from now until dawn. I take her in my mouth and lap up everything she has to offer, separating her tight cunt to roll my tongue through it like soft bubblegum. I pull out of her to tease her clit until her legs shake.

That's my girl. My name pours from her lips repeatedly, a whimper, a scream, a moan. Every sound from her causes my dick to pulse in my jeans; I need more room before circulation is cut off completely. I throw her leg over my shoulder to free up my hand, making quick work of my zipper without ever taking my mouth from her, but it isn't enough. I need to be inside of her.

I need to feel her walls wrap around my cock and quake until she collapses with exhaustion. But I need her to come in my mouth first. Reaching up, I take her nipple between my fingers, rolling it around before pinching it between my knuckles. Her tit's are perfect and heavy. They're large enough that I can barely hold one in my hand. She's fucking perfect.

I switch to the other nipple and sync my hand to my tongue, flicking her clit while rolling that sweet nipple around. Her back bows off the mattress again as her pussy leaks and squirts into my waiting mouth; I lick it up as quick as I can and stick my tongue inside her tight cunt one last time.

A shiver takes over her body as she rides out the high. I take the time to roll a condom on, smiling at the memory of her horrified confession earlier. Fucking birth control. As if I'd expect her to saddle all the responsibility when we're both here for this.

"Oh, my God," she whispers repeatedly.

"You praying, baby?" I ask, grinning from the floor where I still kneel between her legs. Her pussy glistens with my spit and her sweet juices. I suck in my bottom lip with anticipation, tasting her on me. She lifts her head, looking down at me with excitement shining in her eyes.

Shit, I might be in love.

Twenty-Five

Ava

"Oh, my God." It's all I can say. All my brain knows in this moment. If that wasn't the best thing I've ever felt in my life, I don't know what is. I lay still, riding out the waves of pleasure as my heart tries to slow in my chest. I'm a soaked mess, covered in sweat and everything else that has come from me, but I couldn't care less. My arms and legs feel like jelly, but for once in my life, it isn't from a treadmill.

The familiar sound of a condom package brings me back to the present. My insides clench in preparation. I don't try to close my legs in embarrassment; if he can make me feel like that with only his mouth, I can only imagine what comes next. I sit up, needing to see him fully. I need to see what I'm about to feel inside me. My pussy is soaking with his spit, but I don't dare try to clean it off. As he rises from the floor, I come face-to-face with his dick. One of his hands finishes rolling on the condom, the other strokes the monster he's been concealing all night.

My breath catches in my throat as I watch him crawl onto the bed, knocking my knees further apart with his elbows. There's no way he's going to fit inside me. I remember the time Amber snuck me into her house when her parents were asleep, and we bought that filthy porn movie. That guy had the biggest thing I had ever seen. Now I can say I've seen it in real life. Jesus. He's not going to fit inside me.

I feel myself throbbing, leaking onto the bed where he's finished me before we've even started. My breathing is uneven. I've never wanted someone so badly before. For a moment, I wonder who the hell I am. I've never been this filthy. I've never even really called my vagina that p word before tonight. What the hell has gotten into me? I watch him with excitement, knowing the answer. New year, new me.

I snake my arm around his neck, bringing his mouth onto mine and tasting myself on him. I don't know how many times someone can orgasm in a single night, but I can count on a single hand how many times I've gotten off in my life. Tonight, that number is about to double.

He groans into my mouth as I twist my tongue around his, the sound of him needing me sends fire through my veins. Why is it such a turn-on to hear that noise come from him? The sound alone brings back my desire tenfold. I have to break away from his mouth to drag fresh air into my lungs.

"Fuck me, Kellan," I groan under him and press against his cock. Heat rushes to my cheeks as I realize the words that have come from my mouth. His head slips against my clit before he grabs himself and rubs it through my pulsing lips, smearing my cum on the condom.

"Fuck you? No baby, not yet." He plants a kiss under my ear as he whispers to me. We groan together as he holds his cock in his hand, pressing his thick head into me before pulling it out to rub against my clit again and again.

Each time he goes deeper than the last, and I can feel him stretching me open more each time. I thrash under him, feeling as if I will lose my mind if he doesn't speed up and give me what I want. I grab onto his arms, trying my hardest to pull him into me, but he is a brick wall. He keeps up his torturous rhythm until he finally releases himself and pushes into me slowly.

Inch by inch, I take him, feeling myself stretch around his girth until I can't hold back anymore. Moans spill from my mouth as pleasure rips through me. I try desperately to hold onto him, but we are both slick with sweat. He grabs one of my legs, pulling it up to his hip and grinding as deep as he possibly can into me before slowly pulling out. He presses into me again, then waits for me to calm down. I let out a breath, finally used to being spread so wide. He picks up the pace, causing our skin to slap together as our bodies collide over and over again.

Yes, this is exactly what I want. He hits that spot inside me perfectly, somewhere that has never been touched before, and I fucking love it. I lose my mind, nearly screaming from being driven wild. How the fuck did he know that was there?

"You okay, angel?" I hear him, but his voice sounds like it's underwater. I nod in response, praying that he doesn't stop. He rams into me, sending a shock wave through me that takes my breath away. I writhe underneath him as he pushes and pulls into me—my god. I've definitely died and gone to heaven. I feel every inch of him over and over again. Even his thick head as it slides into me to make room for the rest of him.

My body is on fire as he slowly works me over. He pushes up onto his hands, watching me as I grab onto the sheets above my head with a death grip. His hand snakes around my throat, applying barely any pressure but still enough to send me spiraling. My legs begin to shake violently when I try wrapping them around his hips. I clench down to try my best to hide how close I am to another orgasm, but lose all grip on reality when he groans loudly.

"Fuck. Don't do that, Angel." Holy fuck, what did I do to make him say that? Does he not want to get off, too? Wicked thoughts course through me as I get the strongest urge to feel him burst inside me. I clench down again, imagining myself sucking him inside me. His fist closes down on my throat a little tighter, and I revel in the feel of it.

"Ava," his voice deepens. Oh, he's warning me. I don't release the muscles inside me, and feel his rhythm change as he tries to pull out, then pushes deeper inside. I swear I feel him hit a wall inside of me, and a string of groans burns my throat as the sensation runs through me. He pulls out of me, further this time, before sliding the head of his dick up to my clit, then slowly pushing back inside. He picks up the pace, and I nearly scream with madness. How can he do so many things to me at once? This is a form of torture.

He pounds into me while pushing me into the mattress harshly, but I love it. I've never had anyone be this rough before. I claw at his wrist. I want to feel the pain of his fingers digging into me. He groans as I finally release my muscles to free him and push my hips off the bed to meet each of his thrusts with my own. My hips begin to ache as I fuck him in return, but the need to feel him explode inside me has grown; I can't stop.

"Harder. Please," if my voice weren't so hoarse, I'd be screaming. I need him to get off. I need to feel him hit that spot inside of me again. He picks up the pace, slamming me into the mattress until I feel the bed shake under us and rock against the wall. This is how I want it. "Come on, Kellan. Fill me up."

He rips his hand from my throat and covers my mouth tightly before pulling his face back to look at me. His eyes burn into mine, and I can tell he's losing his mind. A crazed expression takes over his face as he flips me around and pulls me up on all fours—holy...shit.

He presses down between my shoulder blades until my chest presses into the mattress. Once he's satisfied, a sharp slap echoes off the walls. I don't feel the pain at first, not until another slap rings out and I yelp—my ass tingles where his palm landed on both of my bare cheeks. I try to wiggle away as he traces the outlines of his hands that are forming on my skin and slaps again. I yelp, feeling how his punishment causes me to pulsate. The feeling makes me realize how empty I am, and I nearly start begging.

He grabs me by my hips, pulling me higher into the air to stand tall on my knees. The way he throws me around like a ragdoll has me aching. I've never in my life been so turned on by being handled this way.

"Look at you, Ava. Dripping down your legs," he growls as he leans over my back to press my shoulders again. Satisfied, I'm still face down, he straightens. I feel his dick hitting the back of my legs as he positions himself behind me. His fingers trail up my thighs, where my cum has run down to my knees. He kneels behind me, and I brace in anticipation for what comes next, arching my back to give him better access to me. If he doesn't dive into me, I may explode.

I part my legs slightly, steadying myself and shifting my weight so I won't be pushed forward by the force I expect him to use. Instead, he drags his fingers across my clit, then down to my opening, widening his fingers to part me. I take a deep breath, surprised that I am this comfortable being so vulnerable with this man. I feel the tip of his dick pressing against me, sliding up and down to spread my wetness around.

"You're going to need a shower when I'm done with you, Angel." His words come out as a harsh whisper, his voice sounding strained. I feel myself throb against the pressure he is applying between my legs, and turn my head slightly to bite the comforter underneath me, but even with the mouthful of fabric, a moan fills the quiet room.

He continues to tease me, slapping himself against my pussy until the smacking wet sounds are all I can focus on. When have I ever been this wet in my life?

".Jesus Christ," I spit out, pushing the blanket away from me to take in a ragged breath. I'm beginning to ache, and he just keeps torturing me.

"No, not yet," he slaps my ass again and presses into me slowly. He still holds my open with his thumbs as he presses deeper. I feel his thick head pressing further in, and I can't take it any longer. I push back onto him, wanting to take him all at once and feel him hit the end of me again. I want to feel the ache inside me when he touches my cervix. At first, it was slightly painful, but now there's a longing there that only he can fill. He grabs onto my hips and holds me tightly in place, pushing me away from him, and pulls out almost entirely.

"No!" I scream at him. How could he deny giving me what I want? This hateful man.

"I know what you want, baby. I'm just going to take my time giving it to you, or we won't last as long as I want it to," He whispers against my back before straightening. Opening me with his fingertips again, I feel his dick jump with excitement as he positions himself and once again presses slowly into me.

"Please, Kellan. Please." I beg him, but my pleas fall on deaf ears. Once he has pumped into me a few torturous times, I feel the back of his hand come between us. Not knowing what he is doing, I wait in anticipation; he grabs himself and tries to lift his dick up and down in a slapping motion, but he is too far inside. The sensation causes my eyes to roll involuntarily. I swear to God, this man is just making shit up at this point. There's no way this is a real thing to do to someone.

He does it again, and I moan loudly. How the fuck does he know to do that? My pussy stretches one way, then another as he moves his dick up and down while still inside me, in, then out again.

"You take that good, Ava," he groans to the ceiling. His words set me on fire, and my insides tighten again, threatening another orgasm. Fuck. I'm ruined. There's no way I will ever be with anyone like this ever again. No one will ever be able to compare to this night.

Twenty-Six

Kellan

I told myself that I would get her off at least one more time before I finish, but she just feels too damn good to stop. I've been more than ready to bust, and she almost had me when she was begging me to fill her up. God damn, those words coming from those pretty lips really had me fighting for my life, but I can't give in that easily. Especially when she's ass up like this, letting me wallow her out.

She's taking me so fucking good, but I shouldn't have told her. I can feel her tightening around me again, and I know she needs a break after this one. I'm not exactly the biggest dick in the world, but she's so damn tight. I know she's going to be sore after this. My balls tighten almost painfully, ready to release, but I won't be truly satisfied until I feel her buck underneath me.

I grab onto her soft hips one more time and fucking ram into her until her ass bounces her off me. Her scream sounds like music to my ears, filled with pleasure, surprise, and pain.

"Is that what you want, Ava?" There's no sense in asking her. I know she does, but I want to hear her beg again. I pound into her two more times, letting her bounce away from me each time. She doesn't say anything, just gurgles and moans into the mattress.

"Tell me, Ava. Is that what you want?" I ask her again, but pick up my pace and fuck her until she can't make a sound at all. I pound into her relentlessly, angrily. She's going to take it as rough as I can give it to her, since she wants to beg so much instead of being patient. Who knew this sweet, shy woman was hiding such a filthy mouth underneath?

The muscles in my back begin to ache as I drive into her, and I know I don't have much more in me, but damn it, she feels too good to stop. I have to find a way to keep going. I grip her hips tightly and lift as much of her weight as I can before slamming her against my dick.

Yeah, that'll work. She isn't heavy, but I'd say that about a lot of women if I were to compare them to the shit I usually have to throw around in this shop. I keep holding her up, slamming her onto me. I fucking love the way she cries out when I keep her from recoiling off me. I take hold of her hips and thrust her onto me, moving her like she's my own private pocket pussy.

"Kellan!" she screams my name, tightening around my cock. Yeah, that's it, baby. Cum all over me. Her pussy is like a vice, clamping down on me so hard I can barely move inside her. I look down, where we are joined, and see nothing but her sweet juices covering the front of my thighs, and I lose it.

My muscles fight through the strain, and I ram into her as hard as I can, busting into the condom, pushing as far into her as I can go.

Holy Shit. Kellan finally came, and I felt it all. Some twisted side of me wanted him to get off without the condom, but God, did I love feeling him pump into me until there was nothing left in him.

As he lowers my legs, my knees finally touch the mattress again. I fall to the side, exhausted. Kellan face plants, landing on the bed beside me. For a second, I worry he died.

"What the hell was that, Ava?" he mumbles into the sheets.

"What?" I ask, massaging the life back into my arms. He lifts his head slightly, turning to find my face that reddens as his beautiful blue eyes meet mine. He props up on his elbows to take in the sight of me fully naked, and suddenly I feel all too exposed.

"You know damn well what I'm talking about," he says as his eyes find mine again. I grab the blanket, attempting to cover myself, but he is lying on the rest of it, and much too heavy for me to move so I cover my chest with my hands and scoot away from him until my back presses against the wall.

"Hey, I'm just kidding. Come back, please?" He pleads and reaches across the bed to grab my ankle. A wicked grin spreads across his face. In a flash, he pulls me down onto the bed and presses his body weight onto me. I squeal and try to wiggle away from him, but he is too strong. Huffing in defeat, I stare up at him.

"What Kell-" I try to complain, but he brushes his lips softly against mine.

"Don't crawl away from me, Ava. I was just trying to lighten the mood. I'm sorry. I didn't mean to upset you," He says, staring down at me with a soft expression. I nod in response, but shame has crept in. "You just caught me by surprise, is all. I didn't expect to hear anything like that. He grabs my thigh and wraps my leg around his waist as he talks.

"I'm sorry," I mumble. Not sure what else to say. His fingers trace random patterns on my leg as he stares down at me.

"Don't be sorry, Angel," he says. My insides begin to melt, and I feel my body relaxing as I forgive him, yet something inside me hardens as I accept his words. I apologize to people too often for things that are beyond my control or things that others have done. It dawns on me then that I have been put in far too many shitty situations by taking responsibility for other people's issues, and no one ever apologizes to me.

I nod my head once and silently vow to stop letting people take advantage of me. Kellan stares at me, as if he can read my thoughts as they pop into my head; a grin slowly growing into a broad smile on his face, the longer we lie here.

"What is it?" I ask.

"I've never seen someone with so much conflict in their pretty little head before."

"The only conflict I have right now is how uncomfortable I'm going to be on the ride home with no panties while wearing a skirt," I respond. Even if I were to find them, I know they will be soaking wet, and that's not something I want to put back on my body.

He taps the end of my nose. "I'll drive you."

I open my mouth to respond, but between his fingers drawing patterns on my bare leg, and the growing hardness that begins to press into me, all thoughts fade quickly from my mind.

Wrapping my arms around his neck, I pull him closer as the embers inside me begin sparking to life. Our lips brush softly against one another once before passion consumes us both; I don't let him pull away until my lips feel raw, my skin suffering from the rugged stubble that has grown on him throughout the day.

His rock-hard cock presses against me lightly, but I don't want to wait, and I begin to grind against it.

"Wait, wait, wait," he mumbles against my neck.

"What?" I huff, impatient.

"I don't have any more condoms here."

My head spins around so quickly, I hear the bones pop. Who the hell brings a girl back to their – whatever this place is – and only has one condom?

My face must give my thoughts away, because he quickly explains.

"It's just been a while since I've been with anyone, and I don't usually bring women here, but I can't remember the last time I was at my apartment; there's no telling what condition it's in if I'm being honest." He's rambling, scratching the side of his cheek before placing his forehead lightly on my shoulder.

I feel bad for judging him, but that was kind of a dumb move. I shrug as the fire inside me dies down slightly and feel his face shift with my movement.

"You look exhausted," I whisper.

"Nah," he whispers back before drawing circles on my thigh again. This time his touch is softer, causing my skin to prickle under his fingertips.

I wiggle away, feeling ticklish, but he grabs my leg to pull me towards him. I squeal as he brushes his fingers down my side, lightly probing between my ribs as he makes his way down to my hip, but stops abruptly.

He sits up, turning his head to listen as a low rumble slowly grows audible until it's loud enough that the room feels like it is shaking.

"Fuck." Kellan grumbles as he stands from the bed and pulls his jeans up his legs.

I scramble to find my clothes but give up when voices echo down the hallway. I dive back onto the bed and wrap the sheet around my chest, watching wide-eyed as Kellan pulls his shirt over his head.

He opens the door and stands in the hallway, listening to the argument, when a loud crash suddenly ends it.

"Hey!" Kellan takes off, and the yelling picks up again.

I strain my ears to hear what they are saying when the sound of metal clangs against the floor several times, followed by grunts. The sound of fists meeting flesh rings out, and I jump up to search for my clothes once again.

I don't know who could possibly be here, fighting nonetheless, but I won't stick around long enough to ask questions. I find my bra and shirt, but my skirt is nowhere to be seen. I squat down to look under the bed when Kellan begins yelling for everyone to leave.

The door swings open, and Kellan comes barreling in, the sound of grunts and yelling still coming from the shop area. I freeze on the spot, feeling guilty for being caught in the act of trying to leave.

Kellan stares down at me, panic replacing the anger on his face as he realizes what I'm doing. He stomps over to the dresser and takes out a pair of sweatpants, holding them out for me. As he stands there, staring down at me, his face falls more every second.

I stand to take the sweatpants, not sure what to say.

"I'm sorry," he says while I slip the pants on.

"It's alright," I respond, rolling the waistband a few times. When I look up, he is grinning down at me.

"What?" I ask, confused by his sudden change of mood.

"Nothing," he shakes his head and pulls a black shirt over his head before grabbing a small set of keys from his dresser.

"I got the car parked around the back, we can go down the hall here," he says as he opens the door and stands to the side to let me pass.

I'm barefoot and holding the thin chain of my purse in one hand and my skirt in the other. I have no clue where my panties or shoes are; Kellan must realize I'm leaving without them because he stops us and looks down at my feet.

"Wait right here, I'll grab everything for you, doll."

He walks the other way, turning the corner where the small kitchen is. Silence consumes me in the hallway, and I take the time to calm myself. Whoever was fighting has left, or at least taken their party outside, but I feel as if my night was taken from me.

It isn't every day that I do something like this, and now that it has been abruptly interrupted, I may never have this experience again. Kellan's heavy boots thud against the concrete floors as he comes jogging in my direction with a huge smile on his face.

My face heats at the sight of him, wearing my panties on his head. He slows down and spins in a circle, opening his arms like he is showing off the most fabulous outfit he owns. The thong's string runs down the back of his head, parting his hair in the middle; the waistband stretched across his forehead and ears.

"Oh, my word. My panties!" I screech as I reach to snatch them from his head.

He's too fast, dodging my hand and taking a step back before darting out the door.

"I like these," he says as he darts past me.

I chase after him, running through the parking lot even though I have no shoes on my feet. Small flashes of light flicker from the sky above us, the explosions making popping noises in the distance.

I slowly close the gap between us, determined to get my panties from his head when I stop abruptly in my steps to take in the sight of the car that has come into view.

It's old, an obvious classic, and the bright blue color twinkles under the lights that flicker above us. The color is gorgeous, and the two broad, white stripes on the hood really make the color pop even more. Everything that isn't blue or white is solid chrome; I don't usually think chrome looks good on anything, often finding it tacky, but this car is the most beautiful thing I've ever seen.

"Whoa," I say as I take in the sight of the muscle car.

"What?" Kellan asks as he walks towards me.

"We're driving that?"

"Well, I'm driving that," he responds, jokingly. I walk around the car, taking in the sight of it, and read the cursive emblem on the side.

"I've never seen a car like this before. How old is it? A Chevelle; what's that mean?" Questions flow from me, but I can't hold them back. Curiosity has bitten me.

Kellen's eyes twinkle across the hood as he watches me, a wicked smile spreading across his face before he clears his throat. "It's a 1977 Chevy Chevelle. A first-generation model; some people think these were the most problematic year models they ever made, but I've rebuilt it and drive it now and then."

"I love this color, I didn't know blue could be so pretty," I say as I squat down to get a closer look.

"Originally, it was blue, but the paint was chipping and scratched, so I got it repainted in this shade."

I make my way to the passenger side, but freeze, afraid that I will smear my fingerprints if I touch it in any way.

Kellan gets into the driver's seat and leans across to open the door for me. Opening my door, I peer inside to see the seats are a creamy, off white leather, as well as the dash and door panels. The carpet on the floor matches the blue exterior paint; all the dash trim pieces and knobs are a shiny, chrome finish.

I gently sit down, too scared to touch anything. I stack my phone, purse, and shoes in my lap before shoving my hands under my thighs to help fight the urge to run my hands across the soft leather dash.

Kellan starts the car, and to my absolute shock, it sounds like it literally growls. I smile widely, feeling the vibration run up my legs and core. This is definitely the best night of my life.

Glancing over at Kellan, he is already smiling at me, which does nothing to help knock the grin off my face.

"You like it?" He asks, showing off his perfect smile,

"I had no idea this was even a thing. I love it!" I feel giddy, which surprises me.

He laughs softly, then puts on his seat belt; I follow his lead and buckle in, thrilled to be riding along in this man's car. We slowly crawl forward, and I watch as he grabs the metal bar from the floor and moves it towards him, then forward.

"What is that?" I ask.

"This is how you shift," he pushes the bar back and shakes it. "I got it in neutral now. I forgot something."

I watch, in absolute horror, as he pulls my panties from his lap and stretches the material across his rearview mirror.

"Kellan!" I exclaim, feeling my face turn red.

"What? They match the seats," he smiles at me.

"You can't be serious. People will see those!"

"Yeah, that's the point." He laughs and steers us out of the parking lot.

"No, no, no, no. No." I reach for them, but the car lurches forward, sending me into the back of the seat before slowing down.

"If you can get them, you can have them," he says as he grins over at me. A challenge.

I reach for the rearview mirror at lightning speed, but the car lurches forward and pins me to the seat again. I stretch my arms out, trying my best to reach forward, but Kellan speeds up. I feel like I've become an astronaut, blasting off to the moon; if only the rocket were as pretty as this car.

"Alright! I give," I throw my hands in the air in defeat.

Kellan smiles over at me smugly, but instead of wanting to slap the look off his face, I can't help but smile back at him. This is how banter should be between two people; my heart sinks as memories of Sebastian and his hateful comments flood me.

I look at my feet, seeing my phone sliding around on the floor for the second time tonight, and feel the tears burn my eyes.

Fingertips brush my elbow, pulling me out of the trance that has taken over me, but I don't want to look at who they belong to. I feel guilty for using him to escape the torment that had taken over my life, but I sit here next to him and let it consume me all over again.

"Slide over here, angel." Kellan's voice is low and soft, comforting me.

I slide across the seat, careful not to bump the thing sticking up from the floor, but there's no way to sit comfortably unless I spread my knees.

"So, you've never driven a manual?"

I shake my head in response. I don't even know what that means. All of my life, I have been driven around by someone else.

"I don't even have my license," I whisper, shame creeping into me.

"Ain't nothing wrong with that. Look at this. This is the shifter, see these lines and numbers?" He points to the top of the ball, and I nod. "These numbers are the gear you're in. When you need to slow down, you shift to the lower number or put it in neutral to coast. When you need to go faster, you shift to a higher number. Does that make sense?"

I blink the tears from my eyes and lean closer to see the numbers, then nod.

"Alright, so they call this the H pattern because of the way it's set up and moves, feel this." He says as he grabs my hand and places it on the top of the shifter.

He pulls it towards me, and I feel some resistance, but Kellan's hand on mine holds the shifter in place until it clicks, and we speed up. The car's engine grows louder, and Kellan presses my hand and the ball of the shifter forward, then slightly to the right.

It feels like there is something in the way, on the other end that I can't see, but it has a way of guiding you into the next gear.

"Okay, we're in fourth now. The speed limit is forty, so we're going to stay right here for a minute."

I check the dashboard and see we are speeding, but the car is driving so smoothly, it feels like we are going much slower.

"How fast can you go when you're over here?" I ask and point to the number six on the shiny ball.

Kellan smiles over at me, his eyes twinkling under each street light. Maybe I've asked a stupid question, but the way he looks at me is almost in adoration. A comfortable silence settles in the car as we glide through town. Kellan helps me shift gears as we slow to turn and speed up to run through lights. I swear we have driven down every road at least twice when he finally starts talking again.

"So, you've never driven a car before at all?" His tone is curious, not judgmental in the slightest.

"Yeah, I've driven before. I can drive, I just choose not to. It's just, I don't have a car of my own, so there's really no point in my having a license," I shrug.

"Sure, there is," he looks over at me as if what he is saying has more meaning.

I shrug again, then yawn. I don't know what time it is, and I'm not about to turn my phone on to check, but if I had to guess, the sun should be rising soon. The fireworks died down a long time ago, and more cars are on the road with us now.

I realize the houses we pass are starting to look more familiar, and a sadness washes over me. I knew the night had to end, but I wanted it to last a while longer.

Sighing, I pull myself to the passenger seat and grab all my junk from the floor, setting it all in my lap once again. Kellan reaches over, grabbing my phone. He gives me a questionable look when he sees it's off and hands it to me, followed by his own.

I stare at the photo background, smiling like an idiot. Of course, it's his motorcycle parked in front of the mechanic shop. I'm not sure what I expected, but that's fitting for him.

"Smith & Son's, that's the name of your shop?" I ask, looking closer at the photo.

"Yeah, that's what my dad named it before we were ever born. Good thing we weren't girls."

The car slows in front of my apartment building, sending my heart racing. What do I do now? Should I invite him in?

"Ava," his voice is deep and gravely again, sending a shiver up my spine. "Look, I don't do this too often, but I'm going to need your number. Let me take you somewhere other than a ratty shop. That," he pauses long enough that I look around to see if there is something happening.

"That wasn't something that I want to take you back to. You deserved better than that, I'm sorry."

"What? No, this was the best night of my life. Don't apologize for anything. I had fun. I think this is the first time in my life I've ever had this much fun. You don't have anything to be sorry for," I finish with a huff, feeling annoyed. Of course, my parents' social status would come back to haunt me, making anyone I associate with feel like they aren't good enough for me.

Sighing, I put my number into his phone and save the contact, then call myself. Of course, the call goes straight to voicemail, but I still don't want to turn my phone on. Just thinking about the shit that will be said to me has my insides in knots.

I don't regret leaving with Kellan, but maybe I should have at least given Amber some kind of information so she wouldn't worry about me.

Kellan looks tired, concern written on his face as I give his phone back.

"What do you have in mind?" I want to keep talking to him. I want to drag this conversation out and stay in this car with him for the rest of the day, but I know that isn't possible. Eventually, I will have to face everyone in my life, and he does have a business to run.

His slow smile is contagious: "I guess you're just going to have to wait and see."

His words are sweet and playful, pulling at something inside me, and I realize, this is how dating should be. Sliding towards him, for the second time tonight, I kiss him.

I kiss him like my life depends on it, crushing my lips to his as I wrap my arms around his neck to keep him from pulling away from me. His arms wrap around my waist, and I feel those strong muscles flex before he crushes me against his chest so tightly that my chest aches.

He kisses me back, softly at first, but something inside us takes over completely. Before I know it, his calloused hands are under my shirt, and I've fisted his hair so tightly that my nails bite into my palms.

As his hands roam freely under my shirt, my skin heats. He moves down my neck, kissing and softly biting until I'm panting and straddling him on the seat.

"Come inside with me," I plead.

He pulls away from my neck, twisting one of my nipples until I moan and grind into his lap.

"Please," I beg him.

"Not until we go out again. I can't be putting out on the first date, angel."

He nips at my jaw and releases his grip on me to pull my shirt back into place. I feel rejected, but his smug smile eases the pain.

"I think you have company anyway," he says and points behind us.

I never saw the car pull in behind us, but I know it's Amber. She is the only person I know who drives a white SUV with pink eyelashes on the front headlights. The car is off, which means she is already in the building, probably banging on my door.

"Is that your friend, or someone we need to run away from again?"

I smile down at him, happy that he won't hold any resentment towards me for jumping onto his bike and hijacking his whole night.

"That's the best friend," I say.

"Oh, so you're in trouble," he jokes, but his words couldn't be more true.

"Yeah, I'm probably in it deep. I won't find out how deep until I get in there."

"Is that why your phone is off?" He questions, but the words sting.

"One of the reasons, but it was going to die anyway. I told her I was okay, she's just overreacting because she doesn't know why I left to begin with." It's the truth, but as I say the words aloud, I can't help but feel guilty leaving her in the dark with everyone else at her house.

"You'll have to tell me about that sometime."

"I will," I promise as I slip off his lap and gather my belongings for the last time.

Glancing at the rearview mirror, I smile at the piece of me that I'm leaving behind. A part of me hopes he leaves my thong there for everyone to see, but another part of me is too embarrassed to admit it's mine.

"I'll see you later," his tone sounds more questioning than promising.

"You know where to find me," I tell him as I close the door and walk away.

Twenty-Eight
Ava

The concrete was so cold on my bare feet that I chose to take the stairs to get my blood circulating through my body faster to keep warm. I should have taken the elevator to my floor; it certainly would have been faster, but I'm also buying myself time. The last thing I want to deal with is an angry Amber, but time has run out, and I can't put the situation off any longer.

Coming around the corner, she is the first thing I see. She's sitting on the floor with the back of her head leaning against the door of my apartment. I slow down, careful not to startle her too badly, but she senses me immediately.

"Ava! Jesus Christ, are you insane? I've been calling you all night. Who the fuck did you leave with?" She's screaming, and I can't blame her, but the last thing we need is for my neighbor to come out here.

"I can explain it all, okay? Just come inside first before the old lady hag down there starts some shit."

"Oh, fuck her! You've been missing all night, and no one has been able to get in touch with you. I thought you were dead," she screams.

As soon as my door is unlocked, I push her inside, readying myself for the rest of her wrath, but it doesn't come. She quiets down once we are face to face, then throws herself at me.

"I thought you were dead," she sobs into my hair.

I feel awful, but confused. "Why would I be dead?"

"Oh my God, Ava. Don't you know who those people are? That's like a biker gang or something, and you just jumped on with that guy and left with them!"

I can't fight the smile as it spreads across my face. If Amber and everyone else think Kellan is in a gang, that's the best thing I've ever heard. I can't imagine what everyone has to say about me now.

She notices my silence and pushes away from me, "What the hell is so funny?"

"You think I ran off to join a gang? That's hilarious."

"Ava, this is serious! You could have been killed!" She isn't screaming, but her face is turning red again.

"Amber. Do you really think I would put myself in harm's way just to get out of a party? You be serious. Since when have I ever been a risk taker?" I quiz her, trying to make her realize her flawed logic.

"Okay, so then what happened?"

I take my time giving her the rundown on Sebastian and how he has treated me in private for the last several months, and how it only got worse as time went on.

I explained to her how everything unfolded with Emily the first time, and how I felt about her once she admitted to starting the rumor, and how I always felt like she was making me a target. I even told her about my parents loaning Emily's family money, and that is why she played nice for so long. Amber sat quietly, listening to everything and never flinching at my harsh words aimed towards one of her friends.

Eventually, I have to stop. There are things Sebastian did and said to me that are still too raw for me to put into words, and to keep myself from becoming an even more emotional wreck, I sigh and tell her that's something to discuss another time.

By the time I've aired out everything, I can see the sun shining through my curtains. I take a deep breath to ready myself. This is where she will lose her mind. I had such an amazing night, and no matter what she tries to say or do, she won't take this away from me.

"I already made up my mind that I was leaving Sebastian. I couldn't take another day with him; it was unbearable. Then we were all at your house, and I saw Emily come downstairs, and she was still straightening her clothes. I mean, she looked like she had rolled out of someone's bed and came back to the party without taking a breath in between. I don't know where Sebastian was. I ignored him, but he appeared not long after that."

"That doesn't mean they were together, Ava. Don't let her get into your head like that," Amber's words are a whisper, pity and sadness laced through them.

"Not long after that, they kissed in the hallway. Right in front of me, that was when I knew that it had been going on way longer than I ever suspected." I stare into her eyes when I say it, pleading with her to understand that was my way out.

She sits still, processing my words, and I fear that she may try to make another excuse for one of them, but to my surprise, she doesn't.

"I'm so sorry, Ava. Thinking about it, that explains a lot of situations."

"When I saw them together, it just pieced so much together, and I knew that was the nail in the coffin. I just didn't expect either of them to supply it. Then I wanted to leave, and Kellan was there,"

She cuts me off, "Who?"

"The guy on the motorcycle, his name is Kellan." I explain before continuing, "He was parked right at your front door and I knew that no one would chase after me if I went with him. At first, I was going to tell him to take me home, but then he gave me a jacket and a helmet, and I just went with it."

"Holy shit! Weren't you scared?" Her eyes are wide, as if she's imagining the worst.

"I mean, for a minute. I was worried when we pulled up to the house because I had no idea where we were, but he left the bike running, and I could still see him the whole time, so I didn't feel like I was unsafe." I shrug and think back to that guy's face when he saw me wearing that jacket. I wanted to crawl out of my skin and hide forever.

"Earth to Ava," she snaps a couple of times in my face to bring me back to the present.

"Sorry, it's been a long night. Um, after that, he must have realized I was drunk, so he took me to a dinner to eat, and we stayed there for a long time." I stop, wondering if I should tell her the rest. I could lie and tell her we stayed there most of the night, but that's wrong. Her eyes are still wide, but nothing like earlier. How would she react if I told her we had sex? What will she do if I tell her that was the best sex of my life?

"So, you got to know him?"

I pause, thinking about the tattoos he had hidden under his shirt and the way his hands felt like sandpaper on my skin, but in the best possible way. "Yeah, I did."

She studies my face, looking for answers to questions she hasn't asked yet.

"I don't know, Ava. I mean, you can't spend a couple of hours with someone and say that you know them. He could still be a killer. Just because he was nice to you for a little while doesn't mean anything."

I lean back onto the couch, curling into the soft cushions, and sigh.

"He isn't a murderer, Amber. He owns his own business, he's got cars and an apartment -"

"You went home with him?" Her voice jumps an octave, sending my eyes wide open.

"No, but he told me where. And I went to his shop for," I pause. What? What do I say? "...an afterparty."

Her mouth hangs open, like she can't believe what I've said. "Jesus, Ava. When I grow up, I want to be as brave as you."

I smile at her words, my eyes getting heavier by the second.

"So, what happened to your clothes?" Her voice is a whisper, and that's a question I'm going to have to sleep on.

I don't know where to go from here. I've sat in the parking lot behind the shop until the sun blinded me, trying to figure out what to do, but I have no clue. I haven't been on a date with a woman in years; all Crazy Bethany ever did was show up and hang around, but I never told people we were together; they all just assumed, and I went along with it.

All she ever wanted from me was money and a place to stay. I haven't seen her in weeks. If I'm being honest with myself, I think she's in jail, and I'm fine with that. Does that make me a bad person if I don't care where she is or even bother looking for her?

I told John and Tracy they could have the day off, but looking at the tools scattered everywhere, I might call them in. The shit they pulled last night was stupid, and seeing everything knocked over pisses me off. I lock all the doors in case they show up; they probably won't, but if they do, the message will be clear.

Walking past the kitchen, I can't help but stop and stare at the place I had Ava pinned earlier. Damn, she felt good when I fingered her on that counter. My dick jumps in my jeans as the memories come back to me. I should probably clean in here too, but I'm too damn tired.

Opening the door to my half assed apartment, the smell of sex lingers. I inhale deeply, feeling some primal urge to take her again, just as rough as I did earlier. A part of me can't believe it happened at all, but the evidence hangs in the air and invades my senses.

The way she moaned and dripped for me was better than any drug I've ever experienced. Stripping the clothes off my body, I finally lay in bed and wrap myself in the scent of her that still lingers behind.

As I close my eyes, a sense of dread washes over me. I might be in over my head with her; I don't think there are books or videos on how to date women out of your league. Is there?

Thirty
Kellan

It's been ten minutes of constant banging on the back door. I'm starting to wonder who it could be; John wouldn't still be out there. He would have walked away when he realized it was locked. I was sleeping good for the first time in months. Whoever is out there is going to get the beating of a lifetime if they don't shut the fuck up. My phone says it's one in the afternoon, and I should be up working, but fuck it. It's the weekend, and tomorrow is for overtime. Perks of being the owner, I can work when I want and there ain't shit out there on the floor that I can't fix in half a day or less.

The banging eventually stops, and I turn over to grab the remote, flipping to the camera feed on the TV to see who is out there and where they are headed. To my surprise, it's Tracy. She walks away from the back entry and heads to the front. Sighing, I get up and pull on some pants. If I had to guess, she's either here to work the rest of the day or coming to clean up the mess she made last night. Either way, I have to let her in.

I track through the shop with my bare feet smacking the pavement, cursing her under my breath for waking me, then press the latch to release the door. It creaks loudly as I raise it a foot off the ground before heading back to my room. If she wants to come in, she can raise it herself.

Once in my room, I hear the door roll to the ceiling and know that I won't be able to go back to sleep. Tracy is going to be throwing shit around left and right for the rest of the day. She's too loud when she works, but even louder when she cleans.

I throw on some clothes and head out. I'm not trying to ignore her, but bringing someone here in the middle of the night was stupid. She has her own place, and so does John. Whatever they were up to, they can solve it away from here.

There's a new coffee shop uptown that John has been raving about for a while. I think he's told damn near everybody about it. For a minute, I consider taking the Chevelle, but choose the bike instead. I don't feel like being caged in today, not after the night I had. I know the wind is going to bite, but I don't care. I gotta give Ava props for riding in that mini skirt of hers last night, cause that wind chill was eating through my jeans.

Ava. The thought of her brings a smile to my face. I wish I could see her storming out of that house again. The look of determination when she bolted out of that front door was something else; she was hell bent on leaving. I'm just glad she chose me instead of John. I probably would have beat the shit out of him if he even looked in her direction.

I start daydreaming of her throwing those pretty legs over the seat of my bike and realize she probably doesn't have a clue what road rash is. I want her to ride with me again so it probably isn't a bad idea to get her some gear. The mention of road rash makes my skin crawl. I don't plan on laying my bike down, but it's best to be prepared. People can't fucking drive these days, and I've broken my fair share of side mirrors for being run onto the shoulder or into ditches.

Hope blooms inside me when I think of her beautiful face agreeing to see me again. I don't think last night was something either of us planned on. I sit for a minute, thinking back on how shy she was before and after I had her in my bed. She's definitely never gone home with a man before. A surge of pride fills me the longer I think on it. I'm willing to bet I was her first for a lot of shit last night. I head out the back, slamming the door behind me loud enough that Tracy knows she's on her own for a while. Even with the shop being downtown, there's nobody stupid enough around that will walk up here to start some shit, but she should know to watch her back.

Pulling into the coffee shop's parking lot, I immediately find a Sportster Model S and pull in beside him. The bike is clean. I'll admit that I've considered owning one myself, but I already have the Springfield. Lately, I've been taking the V-Max. Even though I'm not a huge Yamaha guy, this bike has grown to be one of my favorites. Ava didn't seem to mind it either, since she jumped on the back of it.

The coffee shop is packed, so I take the time to do some online shopping. Some of the things she needs are basic. I don't know what her jeans sizes are, but I can still get the rest. The memory of her soft skin enveloping my body as she wrapped her arms around me takes over my mind. She needs silk. I purchase everything she needs to be safe on the road, then switch to another website. I want to get her everything that shows up on my screen, but I know she isn't experienced enough for some of the shit. Hell, neither am I. But the idea of testing her limits with me is too tempting. I smile down at my phone like a moron, adding shit to my cart that will make her pretty cheeks blush when she sees it.

A New Year's Ride

"Excuse me, sir. I can take your order." The barista startles me. Her voice bringing me out of my dark thoughts quickly. I place my order, then sit to watch the people who come and go from the coffee shop. Is this the type of shit Ava likes to do in her downtime? I bet she's come here already. I take in the looks of everyone around, trying to compare them to her. I could see this being her crowd. Several people work on laptops in silence, a couple of suits talk business in the corner, but it's the couples that I take an interest in.

I've convinced myself that I don't know how to be the boyfriend type, but from the outside looking in, I'd say I'm a hell of a lot better than the piece of shit Ava was with. All this time, I've felt as if something were wrong with me, and maybe there is, but at thirty-six years old, I figured I would be settled down by now. Every relationship I have ever been in has ended on the rocky side for one reason or another. I eventually gave up and aimed for the short term, one night side of things, until I gave up on that too. That's not what I want to happen with Ava, even if it did start that way.

I watch as a couple takes pictures of their coffees together, wondering if that's something Ava would do if we were here together. I pull my phone out to snap a picture of the cup before texting her.

Do you like this place

Omg i haven't been there yet but i want to go!

I smile at how quickly she responded. Was she waiting to hear from me? She sends another message, just as fast as the first. Jesus. How fast can she type?

What did you get? Is it good?

I got a hot cappuccino. It was alright

Ew hot coffee

Coffee is always hot Angel

Not when you get it iced

Now it's my turn to be disgusted. No wonder she didn't drink the coffee from the diner.

Cold coffee sounds like it came from hell
John wouldnt shut up about the place so here I am

Is John the big scary guy?
I didn't think he would be the type.

Big scary guy?

Yeah, the bald one.

Yeah that is john

I laugh loudly, reading her description again. He would punch me right now if he knew I was getting such a kick out of this. I look up from my phone and meet the stares of everyone around. I guess I laughed a little too loud for these folks. I down the rest of my cup and toss it in the trash when I walk past. I should head back to the shop anyway. I need to keep my hands busy for the rest of the day, or I'm going to be texting her back-to-back.

"Hey man," I hear someone call out to me from the front of the building. Turning around, it's a guy my age wearing ripped black jeans and a thick blue plaid jacket.

"Yeah?" Who the fuck is this?

"Are you the owner of Smith's?" He looks me up and down as he asks. I don't appreciate being sized up. If this fucker is planning something, I've got the time.

"I am." I set my eyes on him. He doesn't look like trouble but considering the part of town we are in right now, he sticks out like a sore thumb. A little voice in my head tells me I stick out the same way he does, and to anyone passing by, they probably think we know each other already.

He sticks his hand out, "Thomas Lyles."

"Kellan Smith," I take his hand and shake it firmly. "You on the Sportster?"

"I am. That your Yamaha?"

"It is." The guy doesn't seem like a total piece of shit if he's got something like that sitting in his garage, but I don't have all day to stand around and get to know him. "What can I do for you, brother? She looks like she runs great."

"It ain't really the bike I got problems with, man." He looks embarrassed but walks further into the parking lot. What the fuck is this? I glance around, wondering if I'm in some kind of twilight zone or maybe dreaming. Does this happen to normal people? He props his arm up on the clutch of his bike and drops his voice. I almost have to lean in to listen to him. "There's a girl in there," he starts.

"Aw, hell," I shake my head in disbelief. "There's always a girl, man. You just have to give it a go and figure it out like the rest of us." I sit down, ready to get away from this fucking idiot.

"No. It ain't like that. She's got something going on. I think she's got two kids living with her."

"So, send her to rehab and feed the kids for a while." I don't know what I expected from a stranger standing on the sidewalk, but this was the last thing I thought it would be.

"It isn't like that either. Look, man. I know you don't know me, and I don't know you. Honestly, I don't know her either, but she's a kid, and her mom ran off. She's my neighbor." He sounds defeated.

"Okay, so what am I supposed to do? What are you asking from me?" I'm not interested in raising someone else's kids. Hell, I don't even have kids of my own.

"We live in a trailer park, off Rose." My eyes widen at the street name. I've pulled my brother out of there more times than I want to remember. Everyone knows what goes on there. It ain't kid-friendly by any means, and the meth lab that was found in one of the mobile homes killed at least three people when it blew up last year.

He stares back at me, and it dawns on me. He knows my brother; he's seen me there before. Rage fills me, and before I can stop myself, my hands grip his shirt. I yank him into me so hard that he trips over his own feet. "I ain't my brother. I don't mess with that shit," I keep my voice low, but there are still people staring from their cars.

"I know that! Everyone out there knows what happened. Everybody saw how you handled it." He pulls out of my grasp, "I'm just one guy, I can't afford to take on three kids and patch up a run-down trailer. Nobody around there can afford it either. How the hell do you think they got in that situation to start with?"

"I know damn well how they got there, boy." He may look older, but now that we're up close, I can tell he might be in his mid-twenties. There's just something about a hard life that ages someone physically. It ages them when they see shit too young. I see it in my older brother, the same as I see it in this kid, too. I let my anger fade, thinking about how my life turned out so much different than anyone else in my family. "Alright, let's go." If I can help some kids get out of a bad situation, I will. Shaking my head, I could fucking kick myself. When did I sign up to be a charity? Great. Now I sound like John.

After Kellan dropped me off and Amber left, I slept the best I have in so long. I felt refreshed and cleaned my apartment until I ran out of steam. Now, I lay around and replay my night with him. I'm sore in places that I didn't know could be sore. My insecurities kicked into overdrive when he text me this morning. I can't help but wonder who he was with and why. That seems out of the norm for him, but I shouldn't make that leap because I honestly don't know enough about him to say that.

Regardless, I've kept my phone charged every second of the day, jumping at any notification that comes through, but I'm let down every time. I know that he owns a mechanic shop, and I try to remind myself that he is busy. I just thought he would have responded by now. I try to push him from my mind by getting up to clean and start my day, even though it's well into the afternoon.

I have more important things to worry about, like getting another job now that the boutique has closed. It's a shame that Mrs. Parker passed away and none of her kids want to take over the business, but I guess that's how family goes. There's also the Sebastian situation with my parents; I don't know how much of the situation they have heard, but I've talked to my mom a little. She honestly doesn't seem to know anything, and if she does, she isn't saying much about it.

I've downloaded an app on my phone to help me look for a job, but I don't have any experience to apply for the things I want to do. My parents always had opportunities for me, but I want to do something on my own for once in my life. Becoming an accountant seems like the best fit for me. I've always loved numbers. I hit apply, read the requirements, and then close the app completely. I don't have a degree in anything, I have no prior experience, and no way to get to work unless I take a cab every day, which will get expensive.

I crawl back into bed, feeling hopeless and lost. Amber stayed most of Friday with me before she had to go home so her door could be replaced, which she blames Kellan for completely, but we all know it was ruined by the group of guys that fought earlier in the night. She has texted me a few times since then, but they aren't her usual happy texts. I know she is mad at me for leaving, but that was nothing compared to how upset she was when I told her about the kiss when Kellan dropped me off.

A New Year's Ride

I didn't bother telling her that it went farther than that; she would have lost her mind completely if she knew the rest of the story. Shifting my legs, the lingering soreness causes my insides to flip a little. I know, without a doubt, that was the best sex of my life. If I don't see Kellan ever again, I will chase after a high like that until I die. It wasn't just the sex that meant something to me, though; he treated me like a person. Not a trophy like my parents do, or someone to own the way Sebastian did. Kellan made me feel everything that a person should feel. And who in my life has ever taken the time to teach me about driving a car? For the first time ever, I felt like I was living.

My phone pings from the floor, but I couldn't care less. I leave it lying there until several more notifications roll through. Someone is obviously texting me, but they can wait; I'm comfortable. It goes off one more time, and I fly off the bed. Surely there is nothing that damn important to text someone repeatedly until they answer. I immediately stop, then jump in the air, squealing. I sit on my bed, kicking my feet as they dangle above the plush carpet.

Hey angel
Sorry I got tied up
How has your day been
You miss me yet
That was a joke
I think im sending too many messages
Okay ill stop now

I stare at my phone like an idiot. He must not text people often, but his attempt is adorable.

Hey stranger.
I thought you forgot about me
:)

How could i forget about you woman

The muscles in my cheeks begin to burn from the strain of smiling for so long. He's admitting to thinking of me all this time. The thought of him working around in the shop with me on his mind makes me giddy. I feel like a teenager with a crush who's acknowledging her existence.

> *Do you like movies*

> *Depends*

> *On what*

> *Are you asking if I like going to watch movies? Or my favorite type of movie to watch?*

> *I don't know. both*
> *do you like scary movies?*

I laugh out loud as I consider quoting some one-liners from horror movies to test his knowledge of all my favorites. No one in my friend's circle has ever liked the slasher films I always suggested, but they are my secret obsession. Finding someone to share my interest would be amazing.

> *Whats your favorite scary movie?*

> *I don't watch that shit*

I frown at my phone. Of course, he wouldn't like horror movies; nobody I know does. I must be a freak or something. The screen in my hand fades as my heart sinks. I don't know why I let my hopes get that high anyway. A new message comes through before the screen turns off completely.

> *Please, don't kill me. I wanna be in the sequel.*

Excitement floods me. How did I not realize he was playing along? Finally, someone who has watched a classic! Before I have time to respond, he texts again.

A New Year's Ride

> *Okay idea*
> *Lets watch horror movies together*

> *Okay :) When?*

> *How about tonight*
> *I can come get you*

> *What are you going to drive?*

> *What do you want me to drive*

> *I was just making sure*
> *I'd be dressed properly*

I wait for a response, but it never comes. Eventually, I give up and toss my phone behind me to stare into my closet. I don't remember the last time I wore jeans, but I know I have plenty. If I have to get on a motorcycle again, I need jeans and a thick jacket. I could match him if I find the boots I bought for a music festival last year, but I know I don't have any kind of leather jacket. I tap my fingers on my cheek, considering all the options I have for the night and jump up to sort through everything I own. After hours of picking out clothes just to toss them onto my bed, I finally throw my hands in the air. I give in. I have nothing that screams for me to put it on, and I know I've been at this for far too long.

I decide on a pair of dark denim jeans with rhinestones sewn down the length of the leg with a plain black undershirt. The boots give me a few inches of height, but I will still be a foot shorter than Kellan. A black ripped jean jacket won't keep me warm at all, but it ties my look together better than I thought it would. I have no idea where it came from, but it never left my apartment. It isn't something that I would buy for myself, so I assume it's Amber's and she hasn't missed it enough to take it back.

After I've overanalyzed my outfit to the point of hating it completely, my phone chimes. We never really said what time he would show up because he never answered me, but we must have read each other's minds because apparently he is waiting at the front of my building. I take one last look at myself over my shoulder and leave for the night. A part of me is in complete disbelief that I am seeing him again, and I worry about what Amber will say if she finds out. I can't dwell on her opinion too much, though. She has done wild shit for as long as I've known her, like going to a private island with some guy that said he knew her parents. Then once she got back, they had no idea who he was. She was there with him for eight whole days before anyone found out and her mom flipped her shit.

Once outside, I'm slightly disappointed to see Kellan leaning against the hood of his shiny blue car, but it still sends excitement through my veins. No one in my friend's group would ever drive something like this; not that I'm tallying up reasons to be with him or anything. I had hopes of him driving me off into the sunset on the back of his motorcycle again, but the car will totally suffice. My disappointment doesn't last long. I take in the sight of him and feel my insides do a cartwheel. I swear he could be a model, even with the tattoos peeking out from under his collar and covering his arms, but maybe my opinion is a little biased.

He must feel me staring because he looks up and locks eyes with me. Our smiles grow as we stand there, taking in the sight of each other. His eyes crinkle at the corners, but he looks so relaxed and calm it gives him a much younger, carefree expression. He eventually steps forward, so I walk down the few steps that separate us.

"Hey, angel." His voice is soft as he greets me, but his expression darken the longer he stares.

"Hello, handsome," I respond before stepping into his open arms. He wraps around me, pulling me tight against his chest and body. I melt into him and let the smell of his cologne invade my senses. There's something else that lingers there, too. I think it's the same motor oil smell from the shop; the scent is masculine and comforting.

"After you," he says as he opens the car door for me. My insides flutter as he walks around the vehicle, muscles ripping under a short-sleeved shirt, black and grey tattoos on full display for the world to see. How is he not freezing? The car rumbles to life before Kellan pulls us into traffic with ease. Several people on the sidewalk stop to stare as we pass by in his flashy old car. I hadn't realized a vehicle like this would cause such a commotion. Something about the experience feels familiar to me, but I'm not sure why.

"Do people always stare at you like this?" I ask as someone stumbles in the crosswalk in front of us.

"Mostly, they just look at the car and appreciate it. It's technically an antique, but the color and exhaust make it stick out like a sore thumb," he explains. His words pull on some memory in my head, but I can't quite put my finger on it. I look around us, seeing all of the white and grey vehicles sitting on the street side.

"Why do most cars only come in standard colors now?" I ask. Deja Vu hits me hard, but I know I haven't asked him this before.

"Companies can pump more cars out faster if they have fewer colors," he glances over at me, studying my face. "Make more money if you have more cars ready to sell. Also, preference. Not many people want oddball colors anymore." I nod along, taking in the information that I never thought of before. Interesting how one night out with Kellan and my mind seems to be starving for knowledge about things that have piqued my interest suddenly. But still, something is lingering there; some distant memory that tells me this isn't the first time I have been interested in cars. Something that tells me I have always been interested. I close my eyes, trying to piece together puzzle pieces in my mind that I can't see. The memories never resurface, and no matter how hard I try to reminisce, the thoughts just won't come to light. Giving up, I change the subject.

"Do you have any hobbies?" The question surprises him, causing him to glance over at me with a questionable look again.

He seems to think about it for several minutes before answering, "I'm not sure what a hobby is anymore. I don't have time for much else outside of the shop. I have interests that take up time, things that are fun to do."

I laugh, "That's the definition of a hobby, Kellan."

"Well, if that's the case, then you are becoming my favorite hobby." His eyes darken for the second time tonight as he looks over at me once again, and I feel the flush creep across my cheeks. "What are your hobbies?"

I clear my throat, trying to hide the way my body reacted to his confession before answering. "I don't know anymore either. Amber and I used to travel together before her dad said it was getting out of hand. We used to go to a lot of music festivals, too. I guess I started working at the boutique, and that took up a lot of my time. Sometimes, I would go to the pageants to see the dresses that the kids would wear because they were so excited to come try them on. Oh! I like to read."

"So, you like reading and you like horror movies, traveling, and music festivals." He tries to sum me up, but I crinkle my nose with disapproval.

"I never said I liked traveling or going to music festivals. I just said it's what we used to do. I mean, they were fun and we have good memories, but there were some events we went to that were awful. It gets too hot, and the bathrooms are terrible. I also don't like sleeping in tents or those buses very much." I imitate a look of disgust as I remember the last time Amber and I went to a festival. She had paid for us to travel with a guy she met from California, and he was going to let us sleep in his bus. Before we knew it, he had invited at least a dozen people to stay with us. I woke up to someone standing over me touching himself and shudder at the memory. He studies me, amusement flickering across his face.

"I thought hobbies were the things we enjoyed?" He says while covering up a laugh, I shrug, realizing that I only enjoyed spending time with my friends, no matter what we were doing.

"So you like driving around in shiny cars and going fast on two wheels?" I poke his side as I joke with him.

He picks up on my lighthearted shot, smiling over at me before responding. "Going fast, no matter what, is fun. Doesn't matter how many wheels." We pull into a small parking lot, and I realize we are downtown, where several of the old buildings have been renovated, but they are obviously holding onto that antique charm. All the stores around us have the same antique brick exterior, with plants and chalkboard signs lining the sidewalk. The area feels cozy and inviting, but my parents would lose their minds if they knew I set foot on this side of town.

The smell of fresh bread fills the air as we round the corner; the cafe has its two glass doors propped open, the cashier smiling widely as she hands over a large white box to someone at the counter. I inhale deeply, suddenly craving the sweetness from the large cupcake sitting in the display case.

"Oh man. That looks so good." My mouth waters when I realize there's a large variety of flavors to choose from.

"You got a sweet tooth?" He asks as he walks beside me.

"Not really for candies, but cakes, yes." We fall silent as we continue to stroll through town. People come and go out of the stores, bumping into each other as they hurry away with smiles on their faces.

Their joy is contagious, and I'll admit that I want to come here more often by just experiencing their hustle and bustle. I want to visit all the stores and see what each of them has to offer and spend my money in these adorable small-scale shops.

As we make our way down the sidewalk, I find myself falling in love with the city that I have lived in all my life but never had the chance to truly experience. One large storefront has several vinyl records on display, a couple of guitars propped up to showcase their products. Across the street, large bay doors are open, revealing a bar seating area where people eat and watch large TVs hanging overhead. The smell of BBQ fills the air, causing my stomach to loudly protest as I realize how little I've eaten all day. A barber shop has one of the classic twirling poles by its window, sitting beside a bench made from the back of an old pickup truck.

If I wouldn't feel so silly, I could spin in a circle and skip down the sidewalk. The place feels like a step back in time, somewhere to spend a whole evening getting to know one another. This is much better than sitting around, listening to a man-child complain about his wealthy father cutting his allowance down to three thousand a week - or whatever it was Sebastian always said. I roll my eyes at the memory, realizing how much of life I have been missing out on.

Before I know it, we are walking under an enormous sign with the word Theatre written in blinking light bulbs. I smile up at Kellan, knowing how cliché it is for our first real date to be at a movie downtown, but I couldn't imagine it any other way. He opens the door for me, and I step inside. Immediately, I'm met with the overwhelming, delicious smell of fresh popcorn and candy. The walls are all black with large canvas photos of Broadway and the first theatres in black and white prints. A large concession sign hangs on the wall in front of us, lighting up the dimly lit entrance. A teenager stands behind the counter, looking like she would rather be anywhere else, but perks up when she sees us. She yells over her shoulder for someone, and the door swings open so hard it slaps against the popcorn machine with a loud pop that takes me by surprise.

An older man walks out, grinning as he makes his way from the backroom to greet us. I swear he must be the tallest man alive, and the roundest too. Kellan laces his fingers into mine and offers his other hand to the stranger once we've finally make it to the counter.

"How you been, son?" They shake hands, both letting out some grunts when their palms connect.

"I've been doing fine, old man. How are you?" Kellan chuckles as he insults the guy. I stand in silence to watch their interaction, unsure how to react to Kellan throwing out insults.

"You still got that damned Yamaha?" The grey-bearded man asks. His voice is laced with disapproval, but Kellan brushes it off.

He nods, then tilts his head in my direction, "Hell yeah, I do, how do you think I impressed her?" They both turn to look at me, and my cheeks redden as I become the center of their attention.

"Um, hello. I'm Ava," I stretch my hand out to introduce myself, but the man doesn't take it. Instead, he leans across the counter and lightly hugs my shoulders.

"Nice to meet you, Ava. I'm Kelly's uncle, Duncan LeCass." He waves his hand to the girl standing off to the side, "This is my youngest daughter, Steph." The girl looks at us over her shoulder and smiles for a second before going back to scrolling on her phone.

Kellan and I share a glance for a second over his nickname before he turns back to Duncan. "I hope it wasn't too much trouble to get everything set up, Dunk."

Duncan waves his hand in the air and grabs a large tub, filling it with popcorn before setting it inside a plastic crate. He pulls out several boxes of candy and stacks them on their side. "It ain't a problem, son. Tell me how the shop is running."

"It's going real good. I'm thinking of hiring another mechanic and someone to do the desk part of it too, just getting too busy and can't do it all on my own anymore."

"That's good. I'm proud of you." Duncan's smile doesn't meet his eyes, but there is honesty behind his words, even though something else lingers between them. He takes two large cups and fills them with ice before setting them under a drink machine. "I heard from your brother last week."

"Yeah?" Kellan tries to keep his voice in the same tone, but I see his jaw tense.

"Gonna be coming home soon, is what it sounds like." Duncan sets the drinks into the carrier, then stuffs too many napkins between the cups. He moves around behind the counter, keeping his eyes and hands busy to keep from meeting Kellan's stare that has turned into daggers.

"Guess we will find out," Kellan says as he releases my hand to pick up the crate filled with enough snacks for at least ten people. Neither of them says another word as we silently walk away. Kellan leads us through the doorway off to the side while I sense the tension rolling off of him but decide it's best not to ask.

Once the door closes behind us, we are plunged into darkness. The large screen eventually illuminates the empty room, and I'm glad to see Kellan is still standing in front of me. He leads us to the very top of the steep stairs, then chooses two seats directly in the middle of the row. Once seated, he pushes up the armrest between the two of us and hands me one of the large cups.

"So, what movie is this?" I ask him.

"One of the best. An oldie, but a good one," he says as he pulls out the boxes of candy, offering them to me. I choose a roll of sour candies and lean back to settle in, wondering how many people come to see an older movie that they can watch at home whenever they want.

"Are they coming to watch too, your uncle and Steph, I mean?"

"Nah, he probably locked up and took her home." He says as he tries to balance the crate in his lap.

"What do you mean, he locked up?"

"I mean, he closed it down just for us. Nobody can get in," he throws some popcorn in the air and tries to catch it in his mouth, but it rains down on us instead. I stare up at him through my lashes, trying to keep my breathing even. I'm alone in a dark theater with this man, and no one else will be here but the two of us. My heart rate steadily climbs as dark ideas begin to race through my mind.

Oblivious to my racing ideas of straddling him right here and now, he twists and turns the crate in his lap before giving up on trying to hold it all and sets the entire thing in the seat beside him. The muscles in his arms flex as he picks up the plastic box, and I half suspect he did that on purpose to show off but I can't be too sure.

I fix my eyes on the screen once he has the snacks arranged beside him, and kick myself for wearing a jacket. It's already warm in the building, but the heat radiating off him has me nearly fanning myself. He slides his arm around the back of my chair, and I feel the nerves inside me gather in my stomach. What do people do on dates when they see movies? I shove a couple of the tarts in my mouth and chew them, hoping to focus more on the sour flavor instead of the world's hottest man making a move on me.

I completely zone out, realizing too late that the opening scene has already flashed across the screen and the movie has started. I haven't paid attention in the slightest to what has been in front of me, or what I've been doing with my hands, because the empty candy wrapper is balled and twisted like I've been mindlessly attempting to create some type of animal.

The screen darkens, sending the auditorium into complete darkness. I try to focus on keeping my breathing steady as the tension and heat between us rise, but I'm struggling to be as nonchalant as possible. His arm around the back of my chair has my body heat skyrocketing, and that open space between our seats looks too inviting.

I watch him out of the corner of my eye, taking in the view next to me as best I can without turning my head to be so obvious. He's leaning back, legs opened wide as he lounges comfortably in the leather chair. I can't see his face, but I can tell he's watching me too. I bite my lip, knowing what's hiding under that black shirt that hugs his midsection in the best kind of way.

Leaning forward, I shrug my jacket off and toss it on the chair beside me. When I sit back, I feel his eyes on me, questioning what I'm doing without uttering a word. "It's hot in here," I admit. His grin says something else entirely, and I swallow hard. Why is my body betraying me like this?

"Is it?" His eyes roll over my body, causing my breath to hitch. I face him directly, confidence surging inside me as I catch him staring at what my jacket no longer conceals. That low-burning fire that he left me with days ago crackles to life deep inside me. I grab onto the sides of my seat and squeeze it harshly to keep my hands to myself.

His eyes drink me in, watching my hands as they tighten on the leather beside my thighs, fighting to stay near me and not roam over him. When he finally meets my stare, his eyes have darkened completely. His expression does me in, and in a heartbeat, I'm stretching across him as he continues to lie back, completely composed. I take a deep breath and hold it before pressing my lips against his.

His mouth responds to mine immediately, kissing me back hungrily until our breaths are heavy with want and need. He sucks my bottom lip between his teeth, biting softly, then slips his tongue against mine. Memories of the previous night with him flood me, and I wonder if he will kiss me like this every time.

I kiss him back before coming up for air, inhaling as I bite his lip, taking it between my teeth, and rolling it against my tongue. I'm so proud of myself for making the first move and where it has led us, but I don't know how long Duncan will leave us alone here. With regret filling me, I decide it's best to stop while we're ahead and leave the promise of more dangling between us.

I try to pull away, try to end the kiss before we go any further or risk his uncle walking in on us, but the low groan that escapes him as my teeth release his lip fuels me. I suck it back into my mouth and roll my tongue across the soft skin before letting it go again and silently celebrate as he lets out another low groan. His hands fist into my hair, using the hold on me to bring me closer to him, giving him room to take my neck into his mouth.

He kisses and bites at me until I feel raw, pulling soft gasps from me each time he moves to a new spot until the collar of my shirt stops him from going any lower. He yanks the fabric down to give him more access to my skin, but the material doesn't stretch enough. He's left with only a small section of unexplored area to work with.

The loud sound effects from the movie startle me, and I break away to look around. We're still alone; not even a shadow moves upstairs in the projector room above us. Kellan brings me back to the present by pulling me into his lap and sitting up, so we face each other. I stare down at him, sucking in air and trying to find the courage to take this where I want it to go now.

Rough hands travel under my shirt until he reaches my bra and pulls both cups down, spilling my breasts into his hands. I slide closer to him, my body begging to feel his mouth on me. The fabric of our jeans rubs against each other, keeping me from feeling what I'm truly after. I struggle to grind against him, feeling my knees press into the harsh metal frame of the chair and give up before I hurt myself.

Once I still, he takes both of my nipples between his knuckles, rolling them until a moan escapes me. I grab the back of his chair to steady myself and let my head roll back. One of his hands continues its slow, delicious torture on my nipple while he explores the rest of me with the other. His rough touch travels down to my hip and rocks me against him as he slides further down the seat, sending bolts of pleasure through me as my clit bounces onto him.

With my knees no longer pressing into the chair, I continue to rock against him, all too aware of the growing damp spot I've created on my jeans. His fingers dig into my hip, trying to slow me down before I get too carried away. I try to fight against him and take what I want, but his grip is unshakable; if I keep going, I'll have bruises tomorrow.

God, I'd give anything to have his mouth working between my legs right now, to feel his tongue darting into me like he did before. Oh, I need to pay him back for that. Groaning in frustration, I slowly untangle myself from him, planting a kiss on his mouth before he can argue, then lower myself to the floor. The concrete is hard on my knees, but I don't care.

He looks down at me as I make quick work of his belt, slowing down to focus on the button holding him back. Once I've set him free, he raises himself above the seat just enough for me to pull his boxers and jeans down his legs. Immediately, he's freed and bouncing about, smacking against his lower stomach. The sight of him surprises me; It's been a long time since I've come face to face with someone else's most private parts.

Now that I've pushed passed my surprise and I'm staring directly at his thick cock, panic courses through me. I've only done this a couple of times and I'm not even sure if I'm that good at doing this. I exhale, then grab it in my hand, stroking him lightly before leaning in to lick the length of him.

A half sigh, half moan leaves his parted lips. The way he sounds adds fuel to the slow building fire inside of me. I suddenly want to please this man like he has never been pleased before in his life. Slowly, I wrap my lips around the tip of him and swirl my tongue around and around, soaking his flesh to help him glide further into my mouth. He grips the armrest and edge of his seat as I push my mouth lower, then come back to his head.

Inhaling through my nose, I bob down on him several more times, swirling my tongue around as I go, then suck hard as I come back up for air. I keep up my movements until my jaw aches, wondering how I could change up my rhythm to ease the pain that has started to set in.

I pull back slowly, trying to keep from gagging on his length but the leather cushion beneath him groans as he lifts, following my mouth to stay inside. I grab the top of his thighs with both hands and ready myself before taking as much of him into my mouth as I can and gag loudly. I'm not used to having my mouth and throat so full like this, but I need to try.

Inhaling through my nose, I try again.

The taste of precum coats my mouth, causing me to moan. I swallow, using my tongue to lick the tip until it's clean, then take his full length. My eyes water as I force my throat to relax to take as much of him as I possibly can. I work my neck and head, forcing him to fuck my throat until I can't hold my breath anymore.

"Ava. Slow down," he warns me through moans.

I come up for air, gasping as I stroke him with both hands to give myself a moment to pull myself back together. Angling my head, I open my mouth just wide enough to fit him between my teeth, then rub his thick head on the inside of my cheek. He groans, sending more precum in my mouth. I feel how wet my panties are, how turned on I am by pleasuring him, but I can't stop. I need him to fuck my mouth again. I need him to fill my mouth and claim it as his.

Switching sides, I open my mouth again to do the same thing. His dick presses to the inside of my cheek, stretching my skin tight as he takes up all of the room. I use my tongue to stroke him, eyes shining as he reaches over and takes my face in his hands.

He presses a thumb on my cheek, feeling how full the inside of my mouth is before brushing my hair over my shoulder so he can see what he's doing to me. I glance up at him before pulling off completely and take a deep breath. His eyes lock onto mine as he looks down and exhales slowly but we aren't done.

I grab his hand and force it into my hair before easing down on him, sucking hard. His fingers dig into my scalp as he lets out a loud groan. I bob up and down on his cock, hollowing my cheeks as I go.

"Ava," he moans again. "Oh. Fuck." Kellan fists my hair with both hands, slamming me down onto him repeatedly as he loses control. I press my knees together, feeling my rapid heartbeat between my legs as he violently fucks my mouth and throat until his hot cum shoots into my mouth and throat.

He slows his rhythm, still moving inside me while I try to swallow everything he pumps out. I keep sucking until the last drop, until he relaxes completely and pulls me up from the floor.

"You're greedy." He says as his eyes swirl with lust. I smile down at him, a sense of pride filling me as he struggles to pull his pants up with shaking hands. I sit down and sip the soda next to me, wondering how the hell I'm going to make it the rest of the night with soaked panties.

"I don't think so," he says.

"What?" I ask, glancing over at him.

He takes my hand and leads me out the other end of the row of chairs. We take the stairs quickly before exiting through a door next to the screen. We step into a long hallway and make our way to the exit sign before coming out on the side of the building. A dark alley greets us, sending the hair on the back of my neck standing on end. I'm not one for hanging out in dark places like this, no matter who I'm with.

Kellan picks up on my unease and navigates us to the sidewalk quickly, my legs struggling to keep up with his long strides. I slow my pace once we pass the music store, feeling more in the open and safe with the streetlights coming on. He slows his pace, falling in step with me. The sun is setting now, and the only cars on the street are parallel parked in front of shops that are closing for the evening.

Our car is the only one left in the parking lot once we make it there. Kellan opens the driver's door for me and waits patiently as I fold my body into the seat. I watch as he closes the door and crosses over to the passenger side.

"Kellan, I don't know how to drive this-" My words are cut off as he grabs my knee and pulls me across the seat. My heart races in my chest as he smiles over at me before pushing me to lie down. I do as I'm told, suddenly excited to see just how far we can go while parked in such an open area.

I glance out the window as he yanks my jeans down my legs, stretching me across the car before taking my boots off and throwing them into the backseat. He wastes no time, kneeling between my knees to lick the wetness that has spread down my thighs. I close my eyes and grip the steering wheel with one hand and cover my mouth with the other.

"Keep an eye out, Ava. Don't let us get caught." My eyes fly open, but I've slipped too far down the seat to see out of the windows.

"Kellan," I breathe out to argue, but my words fail me. His tongue darts out of his mouth, fucking and licking my pussy relentlessly. My back arches off the seat, causing me to press my shoulders into the door.

"Oh, God." I cry out when he presses a thumb to my clit, sending me catapulting towards climaxing almost immediately. I knew I was turned on and ready for this man, but holy shit. This is almost embarrassing. He runs his thumb down, pressing it inside me, then thrusts several times before pulling out to hold it to my bottom lip.

"Taste yourself, you greedy girl." He hooks his thumb into my mouth, rubbing it on my tongue as I pant and moan. I suck his finger, cleaning it with my tongue until I taste nothing but his skin. Once satisfied with the work I've done, he pulls his finger from my mouth just to push it back inside me again.

My shoulders scream in pain as I push against the door, fighting to stay in this position for as long as possible. His tongue darts out, spreading my lips on either side before focusing on my clit. He circles it several times, then sucks it quickly, causing my legs to shake uncontrollably.

I release the steering wheel to fist my hand in his hair to pull him even closer. My body takes over as I grind into his face, an orgasm like never before threatening to consume me entirely, begging for him to keep going.

He takes my leg and throws it over his shoulder, giving me the leverage I need to pull him into me. I hook the back of my knee onto his neck and shoulder, using the position to ride his face from the bottom, gaining the friction I need against his tongue. He snakes his arm up my body, finding a way under my bra to cup my breast; the warmth of his skin lights me on fire everywhere he touches.

I grab onto his arm with my other hand, letting out a loud moan as he finds my nipple and takes it between his fingers, sending me squealing as I finally reach my peak.

"I'm coming!" I scream out, gripping him as tightly as I can. My toes curl, my legs shake, but he continues to dip that long, wet tongue inside of me. He sucks and licks at me until I can do nothing but moan, grinding against him so hard that the back of my thigh bruises on his shoulder. "Kellan. Don't stop. Please. Fuck. Don't stop."

A flash of lightning rips through my body as I finally finish in his mouth while he kisses and licks me clean. My vision blurs as I buck and writhe under him, pulling in ragged, loud breaths and letting them leave me in guttural groans. My clit is so sensitive now, but fuck, that was amazing. His face is slick against my thighs as he pulls away, gently folding my shaking legs to the side.

I place a hand over my chest, feeling my heart pound as I try to slow my breathing. I can't believe that just happened, but I refuse to be embarrassed. A part of me wishes I could have been experiencing this my whole life, while another part of me is ecstatic that only Kellan has been the one to give me this kind of pleasure. The thought of another man being between my legs nearly causes me to gag when I feel him plant a kiss on my bare hip.

My eyes fly open when I suddenly remember I'm lying naked in his car, in an open parking lot. I watch in horror as he steps out of the passenger door, closing it quickly, then comes back. I pull myself upright and reach for the jeans in the backseat, but he stops me. I look at him, confused. Surely he doesn't want me riding in the car with no clothes on. He nods over my shoulder, pointing out the car passing by.

We watch as it crawls by without stopping, letting out a sigh once the taillights are out of sight. He turns to gather my clothes from the backseat, and I use the brief moment of privacy to clean myself with a plain black shirt he's given me before fighting to put my pants on in such a confined space.

My arms and legs are still shaky as I struggle to pull the denim up my legs that have become slick with sweat... and something else that I refuse to say. Kellan watches with a smile as I shove my feet into my boots and turn to face him.

"Now, who's greedy?" I poke at him, surprised that we weren't caught from his very public act of service.

"I'd say we both are." He smirks at me, unfazed by my annoyed tone. I can't even imagine what I would have done if we had been caught doing that. My face flushes at the thought of a stranger seeing us and having to call the police. A horrible thought crosses my mind, then: What if it were Duncan who saw us? He should be coming back to check on us to make sure we locked the door; wouldn't he? Oh, shit.

"I'm sorry I ruined the movie." His expression turns to one of surprise before he chuckles.

"Ruined?" He grunts. "Is that what we are calling that?" My face heats more as I think of what I've done in there. He doesn't give me time to respond before he jumps out and comes around to the driver's side of the car, scooting me over slightly so he can start the vehicle.

Thirty-Two
Kellan

I can hardly focus on the road as I drive us across town to the restaurant. My eyes keep shifting back to Ava, taking in how red and swollen her lips are after she damn near sucked the soul out of my body through my dick. I felt bad, leaving her begging when I dropped her off at home the last time we saw each other. I've fucked my hand twice since then, replaying that memory of her pleading to come inside with her to put her out of her misery.

My dick twitches at the idea of her playing with herself, finally coming back to life since spurting into her hot mouth not even half an hour ago. I look over at her again, finding her already staring at me, and can't help the smile that spreads across my face. It's a good thing she can't read my thoughts, or I'd be in serious trouble.

"Where are we going?" Her voice is nearly a whisper beside me, her throat probably sore from screaming her pleasure loud enough for everyone in the city to hear.

"A place called Romero's," I respond. "It's just up ahead." Out of the corner of my eye, I see her clutch her stomach. I open the car up a little more, speeding down the street to get us there quickly, knowing how hungry she must be after the fun we just had. My stomach growls in agreement, no longer satisfied by the handfuls of popcorn from earlier. "This place has been open for a while now. I've had my eye on it, but never got the chance to come try it out. I love Italian food." I feel like I'm rambling and realize I'm nervous but I have no idea why.

"I like Italian food too." She says as she looks out the window to see the front of the restaurant. We pull into the crowded parking lot and head to the back. She takes my hand once I open the door for her, and I can't help but notice how quiet she is. We walk to the door in silence, but it isn't as comfortable as it was earlier today. What could she be thinking about?

"What did you do today?" I ask her, curious to see how she spent her free time.

"My day was pretty uneventful. I spent the majority of it looking for a job, but..." she trails off, then shrugs.

"I remember you saying the place you worked at closed. Did you like it there?" Could this be what's bothering her so much tonight? I rack my brain, replaying everything I've said to her so far, and come up with nothing that could have been offensive.

She nods her head in response, but there's sadness there and it pains me. I thought her parents were loaded. Are they going to sit by and let her struggle? I can't have my girl sitting here worrying all night that she won't find a job when I need help running the business side of the shop. I watch as she stares off into the distance, taking in the building and people milling about. She looks lost and a bit hopeless.

"You could come work with me," I tell her. The words spill out of me in a rush. She looks up quickly, mouth hanging open in surprise, before a small laugh escapes her.

"I wish, but I don't know how to work on stuff." Her voice is soft, drawing me into her as we walk inside. I hope the door for her, lacing my fingers into hers when she passes by.

"No, Angel. Just work the desk side of it for me, I can't keep up with what goes on anymore." Her eyes shift to the wall in front of her to stare in silence at the painting until the hostess comes to take us to our table. I give them the reservation information and gently tug Ava's hand to lead us to the back of the restaurant. Once alone again, our eyes lock and the chemistry between us comes to life.

"Do you think that's a good idea for you to be my boss and my boyfriend?" Boyfriend. The word kicks me in the chest while scrambling my brain. I search her face, trying like hell to read her intentions. Should I tell her that I have no idea how to do this? I clear my throat, but when my lips move, nothing comes out. Her brows rise as I struggle to speak, to say anything at all. Sitting back in my chair, I try again. Using sarcasm to communicate instead of the full truth.

"I think I'm a little old to be a boyfriend." There. Now we can be on the same page. I think. Her eyes sparkle with amusement, like she didn't just sit there and watch me have an identity crisis over a simple word.

"And just how old are you?" She smiles as she leans across the table.

"Thirty-six," I tell her. I know better than to ask her age, so I remain silent. My mama would slap the eyes out of my head if I dared to even think of asking her such a thing.

"I don't know if I should point out that you aren't much older than I am, or start calling you old man," her lips twitch as she meets my sense of humor with her own before moving the conversation on. "How was your day?"

"It's looking better by the second," I admit. "I'm a little sore, though. Some kid twisted my arm into helping him fix up a run-down house for his neighbor yesterday. I've been swinging a hammer nonstop and eventually told him I've done all I could, or he would have asked me to stay well into the week."

"You mean like a renovation?" She looks puzzled.

"Mostly repairs that piled up over time, and no one was around who could fix them, so things were going downhill fast. I don't know them personally, just a couple of kids. Their mom ran off, and their teenage sister has been raising her two younger brothers." I explain the situation, feeling the night taking a depressive turn, but I don't know how to get it back on track.

"So, you both fixed up their house and did repairs, but is there anything else they need?" Her eyes are soft and caring, adding to the list of reasons I call her Angel.

"I'm not sure, but we can find out." The splinters in my hand argue with me that I've done enough, but the way she looks at me with pleading eyes convinces me that I could do more. I realize then, she's the type of person to think of herself last. She doesn't know anything about these kids, but she is ready to provide anything she can to help them. I feel a sense of pride swelling inside my chest; it mixes with the guilt I have, knowing that I won't ever be good enough for her, but I'm determined to be the best I can be from here on out.

If someone had told me a few weeks ago that I would be willing to change for a woman, I would have laughed in their face. I would have told them there is nothing wrong with the way I live my life and they could stick it up their ass because I'm not changing what ain't broken. But now I sit here, having dinner with Ava, and I'm willing to do what it takes to make her happy, and for what? It isn't like I know her that well, but I want to.

I want to know everything about her; her hopes, dreams. I want to know who she was as a child and where she sees herself in the future. I want to know all the small things and memorize them, like her favorite color. Then I want to know all of her big life moments and create more with her. I want to obsess over all the things that make her happy and find joy in them, just as she does. I clear my throat, surprised by my own thoughts. I've never wanted something like this before, and I have no idea how to tell her any of this.

"Think you're ready to drive the Chevelle?"

Thirty-Three

Ava

My sides hurt from laughing too hard for so long tonight, but I'm having such a good time. I grab at my ribs as the pain shoots through me but I can't stop the burst of giggles that has taken over me for the third time. Kellan was dead set on teaching me how to drive his car, but I think he is having second thoughts now. I've never heard a man yell in lowercase before tonight, but that was the funniest thing I've ever experienced in my life. The sound that came out of him when the car lurched forward, nearly hitting a fence, was hilarious. I wipe a tear from my cheek as the giggles die down and blow a breath out of my lips to try to settle myself.

Once again, I try to find neutral before starting the car, then glance at Kellan to gauge his reaction. I bite my lip to keep from laughing. He has his seatbelt on, one hand on the dashboard, and one hand on the seat, bracing for impact or maybe another lurch forward when I stall again.

"I swear, I'm not doing this on purpose," I admit to him. He just nods while giving me a tight, nervous smile. I shift the car into first and ease off the clutch while lightly pressing the gas. The car moves forward, faster than I'd like, but I don't attempt to slow up down.

"There you go, that's good." He cheers me on but the unease is still lingering in his tone. I let off the clutch completely while pressing the gas a little more. Excitement runs through me as we launch forward. I'm driving! It's an empty parking lot, but I'm still driving. "Alright, go into second just like I showed you. Clutch first, then shift."

I press the pedal in and shift, feeling that small window of gliding before the car catches and launches forward once I find the gear. I release my breath, glad that I didn't grind my way through the gears like I did earlier. That noise alone made me flinch earlier.

Kellan explained to me how the transmission and engine disengage when I press the clutch in, but I have no idea what gear ratios are or how it physically works. To me, it feels like driving a train, or even a plane, and that's something I simply don't know how to do. Press this, pull that, it goes when you do it right. I tuned most of his explanation out earlier when he went into depth on the whole mechanic side of it.

"There you go. Okay, once we get to the end, let's slow down and turn to go again." We've been out here for an hour already, my neck hurts from being jerked forward and backward too many times, but I do as he says and pick my foot up to let the car slow down. The car shudders as I realize my mistake, and I stomp on the gas pedal to keep from stalling again, but I am still turning the wheel.

"Oh shit!" I scream as we spin around too quickly. I panic and try to steer us straight, but the back of the car feels like it is sliding as we race across the pavement. I turn the wheel again, spinning us the other way and scream. I'm no longer in control of the vehicle. "Kellan! What do I do?"

He laughs as the car begins to turn the other direction. "Clutch and let off. Down shift!" We slide sideways and I continue to scream, terrified that I've just ruined his vehicle. I press my full weight into the clutch, holding on to the steering wheel for dear life. I stomp on the brake, bringing us to an abrupt stop. My neck feels like it may break from the sudden stop, but thank God we have finally come to a standstill. The car continues to softly rock from side to side but I wish it wouldn't; I fear I may vomit from the wild ride that I just sent us on.

Kellan's laughter dies down when he turns to look out the passenger window. "Well, there goes my set of tires."

"Wh-what?" My voice cracks and my limbs are shaking from the surge of panic and adrenaline. I release the steering wheel and find neutral before pulling up the parking brake and turning the car off. My legs are like Jello, and I'm certain that the palms of my hands are bruised from gripping the wheel so tight.

"Yeah, look." He points at the black smudges on the grey concrete. "You did one hell of a donut. Let's get out of here before someone calls the cops."

"The cops? Why would someone call the cops?" He laughs at my question but gets out hurriedly. I slide over the seat, not trusting my legs to carry me; it isn't lost on me that this is the second time tonight I have felt weak in the knees from new experiences with this man. He starts the car and launches us onto the road, making the tires squeal loudly as we leave the scene. I look behind us to see the perfect black figure eight I left behind and wonder when I will ever be able to do something like that again.

We weave through town before I notice we have circled around a few of these blocks a few times and I wonder if he's stalling or just taking me for a joy ride. I watch him as he shifts gears and steers around the curves, his arms flexing each time he grabs onto the shifter to push or pull it into place. I decide I'm completely happy with him taking me around town, and I'd be fine if we were to do this for the rest of the night.

When I finally look back at the road in front of us, we are on a twisting road headed out of town before eventually turning into a neighborhood. Once again, I'm in a part of town that I never knew existed, but the houses that are coming into view are beautiful. "Where are we going?" I ask.

"My place." Butterflies erupt in my stomach at his response. I understand now why he was taking his time before bringing me out here. I feel giddy as we pull up to an iron gate, watching as it slowly swings open to allow us in. There are several side roads to the left and right of us, but we continue to drive straight.

The houses here are big and old, but well-maintained. Twinkling lights shine from privately fenced-in backyards as we pass by. The further into the neighborhood we go, the older and larger the houses get, until we come to a dead-end sign. Where the pavement ends, a concrete driveway begins. It's longer than the ones from the neighborhood we drove through, with plenty of tree coverage to hide the two-story home that comes into view once we pass under the trees.

If I had to imagine where Kellan would live, it wouldn't be anything like this. I turn to look at him, wondering how he could live in something that is from the cover of a magazine. Even during this time of year, the trees hold onto green leaves; not as full as they will be in the spring or summer months, but still full enough to provide him with privacy.

"You didn't tell me you owned a mini mansion," I try to joke, but my tone is nothing short of impressed. Why would he take me to the shop that first night when he has all of this?

"No one knows this is where I live; they think I stay at the shop or at an apartment downtown." His ability to suddenly read my mind surprises me but I keep quiet, too amazed by the beauty of the place he calls home.

"Why would they think you live in an apartment?" I question, seeing the red flags begin to wave.

"Because my mother has lived there for so long, she can't see herself anywhere else. That's where she raised me and my brother, after my dad gambled everything away. There are too many memories in that place, and she can't pack them up and bring them with her." I study him as he steers the car down the driveway, never taking his eyes from the pavement as he opens up to me about his parents. We pull into a garage and I'm just as taken aback by the size and organization. If I had to guess the square footage, I'd say it's just as large as the first floor of the house it sits next to.

Dim lights automatically turn on as the door closes behind us, revealing two more sports cars and another motorcycle that is different from the one he first rode so many nights ago. Large black and orange toolboxes line the walls around us, with spare tires sitting on metal racks in a corner. Several sets of rims hang from various places, twinkling from the dim lights that shine from above. Equipment is spread out along the wall and pushed under worktables that are cluttered with parts of all shapes and sizes. I smirk at the sight of the place; this is who Kellan is, and now I'm in his home.

"Wow, this place goes on forever. I'd love it here," I pause, realizing what I said. "If I were your mom, I mean." My cheeks flush. That came out all wrong. "That's not how that was supposed to sound." I shake my head, then throw my hands in the air. "Whatever."

"Good thing you aren't my mom, or this would be super weird." He jokes but cringes just as I did.

In a way to get past my embarrassment, I keep the conversation focused on her. "Does she come visit often?"

Kellan tries to hide a smile as he exits the car, but I see it before he's completely out of sight. I chase after him, curious for more information. "No. This place was left to her by her father, but she hated him. When he passed away, he left it to her as a way to apologize for leaving her behind when she was a child. No one knew he had this house before he died, so she felt it was just another slap in the face. It's a reminder that she didn't know who he was. She came out here to see it after he passed away, then put it up for sale."

"So you bought it to keep it in the family?" I ask, puzzled by the situation. If my father had left me a house, I would live in it, no matter the life he lived before.

"That wasn't my intention at the time, but it did work out that way. My mother, as strong as she is, couldn't stand walking through the whole house, so she didn't see what I had found. After I did some digging, I found that there was more to it than just a house and some land. It turns out that Grandad was an architect and also owned a construction company. He owned all the land where this neighborhood was built and made a fortune designing every place that was built and having all of the plots surveyed to sell them off. This was the first house he ever designed. It was meant to be their family home until he had an affair with his secretary and she got pregnant; she blackmailed him into leaving my grandma. This place was supposed to be for her; it was where my mother and all her siblings were supposed to grow up but never got the chance." My mouth hangs open as I listen to his story, saddened by the happy ending that didn't happen.

"After that, I bought it out of spite. To keep that woman or her kids from living here." He looks down at me, eyes shining with mischief. "I knew that she would find out about it if it was to go on the market. The woman has made my family's lives hell because she believes she's entitled to everything that was my grandfather's."

"Did you tell your mom about her?" I ask.

"I did. When I walked through the house, I found a letter her father had written to her. He explained the situation and admitted he had made a mistake in his life that cost him everything. He loved his family and wished he could go back in time, but the damage was done, and how it was handled was awful of him. She said she wanted to burn the house to the ground after that, so it would always be a reminder of what was taken from her. I thought she would come around, but she still hates him and still refuses to come see what I've done to the place."

I nod, understanding her reasoning, but my heart breaks for her. We walk through the breezeway that connects the shop to the house in silence, our hands brushing together as we walk side by side. We eventually make our way to the wide porch that wraps around to the front of the house and enter through a heavy wooden door with windows on each side. The smell of cedar hangs faintly in the warm air that brushes my face as I move further into the mud room. The leather soles of my boots are so slick on the polished hardwood floors. One wrong move could send me slipping and sliding as if walking on a sheet of black ice. I kick my shoes off and push them to the side, then stare up at Kellan in surprise.

The floor is heated!

He grins down at me, knowingly. "The house is old, but I've had some modifications added over the years."

"And a heated floor was the highest of priorities." I laugh, but it feels wonderful on my frozen toes.

Around the corner, I come to a sudden stop at the sight of his kitchen. A large island with a light grey stone countertop houses a deep barn house style sink, and the cabinets underneath are a beautiful dark wood stain. Several plush cushioned bar stools line one side of the island as pendant lights dangle like ornaments overhead. White cabinets stretch across the walls, framing shiny appliances that look barely used. An arched niche holds an electric fireplace that crackles quietly. My eyes travel up the tall white brick walls to appreciate the wooden ceiling beams that break up the white shiplap ceiling, offering more color and height to the space. On the opposite wall, a TV hangs beside a hideaway door leading to an oversized walk-in pantry.

"Wow," I whisper.

I race to keep up with him as he continues through the house, oblivious to my reaction. We make our way up a narrow but steep staircase before stepping into an open game room. The same polished wooden floor from below stretches across the space, light from small lamps reflect on the glossy finish, but it's the wooden cathedral-style ceiling that comes down the walls in each corner that defines the space. The natural wood draw my eyes up to show off the steep pitch and exposed beams. Elegant ceiling fans with integrated lights spin slowly as they hang from long pipes to keep them in place.

"The ceiling goes on forever," I can't help but point out the obvious. To my surprise, the room doesn't echo at all.

An enormous stone fireplace anchored to the furthest wall catches my attention, it must be at least twelve feet wide. Two deep green sofas sit side by side in the center of the room, surrounding an iron-legged wooden coffee table that looks as if it were dragged directly from the woods and assembled in the very spot it occupies. On the left side of the stairs, a small shuffleboard table surprises me. I didn't take Kellan as a shuffleboard kind of person. Opposite the game table, an office desk and chair is tucked between two expansive windows, offering a quiet nook for reading or writing.

Several mounted deer heads and antlers adorn the walls around us, reminding me of a cabin hidden deep in the side of a mountain instead of this old school manor off the edge of town. I make my way to one of the velvet couches, surprised to see a fully stocked bar tucked out of view from the stairs' landing. The high countertop is long enough for five leather bar stools that swivel at the base, with a TV hanging from the wall behind it. Bottles of alcohol line the shelves beneath the black screen, mounted ducks with wings spread wide hang from the vaulted ceiling on either side of the hidden drinking area. The space as a whole is very outdoorsy and masculine.

Kellan seems nervous as he watches me take a seat, shifting his weight from one foot to another in anticipation. I bite my lip to keep from smiling, as his words play back in my head. No one knows he lives here. I'm the first person he has allowed into his home – he's let his guard down for me, and a part of me wants to do the same.

"If I were you, I'd never leave this place," I say in an attempt to ease him. I watch as he makes his way to the bar and pulls some bottles from a small refrigerator that I can't see.

"Yeah, I'd love to be here more. It's peaceful, but the shop feels like home." His words fill me with sadness as I realize what he truly means. It's lonely here. He obviously spent time and money to make this house more comfortable for his mom, but she still turned her nose up at the idea of this house belonging to her, and it's too big to be here alone.

"Why do you feel that way about the shop?" I ask, taking a beer from his hand.

"Because it's where I spent my time as a kid when I wasn't cooped up in a tiny two-bedroom apartment with my brother, and all I really need is a bed." He tosses our caps into a large bowl on the table before taking a seat next to me, releasing a deep sigh when the couch sinks beneath his weight.

"That makes sense." I nod as butterflies erupt inside of me again when our arms brush against each other. He only needs a bed big enough for him because he doesn't have anyone to share it with. I feel giddy knowing that this man could be all mine for as long as I want. No Emily in sight to hunt him down. "So, shuffleboard?" I question, biting down on my lip to hide my smile.

"I am a fucking shuffleboard champion, I have you know," he brags, but his tone is a little too suspicious for me to believe he's telling the truth.

"Show me then."

He scoffs at my challenge, "I thought we came here to find out your favorite scary movie."

"Well, that mystery could have been solved a long time ago," I roll my eyes at him.

"Let's hear it then," he leans in with his hand cupping his ear as if we are sharing a secret. I lean in to answer, ready to tell him my all-time favorite, but I hesitate. Should I whisper something sexy instead? The thought sends me into a fit of giggles before I utter a word. He looks to the ceiling, exasperated but grinning.

"I'm sorry, I'm sorry. I thought of something funny. Okay, I like 'em all. I like horror movies. My friends all make fun of me for it and refuse to watch any of them." I bite my lip to keep from laughing more.

He groans, "You're insufferable."

I elbow him in the ribs, "I am not, I just don't want to single out one and hurt the other's feelings."

"You're going to hurt my feelings by not telling me," he says as he grabs me above the elbow. Those damn butterflies come back with a vengeance as his firm grip holds me in place so he can look me in my eyes pleadingly.

"You'll survive," I say, breathlessly.

"Guess I'll have to hear you scream on a different night then," he releases my arm to stand. I watch as the muscles in his arms work to pull open the trash and toss his empty bottle. I cock my eyebrow as he pulls two more bottles from the fridge. If he wants me drunk, he should have started with something stronger than beer, but I'll keep that idea to myself.

"I think you already heard me scream once tonight," I grin before knocking my beer back and looking away. *Checkmate.* My skin heats as I remember the way he ripped my jeans from my body to fit his head between my legs. I press my thighs together, trying to hide how the memory is affecting me, but his eyes see it all. His lips twitch as I bring my legs up to cross them under me – better to sit on them to keep them from wrapping around him again too soon into the night.

"Is it hot in here?" He asks, leaning closer into me, repeating the words I had whispered minutes before being on my knees for him. The taste of him has been on my tongue all night and I can't stop thinking about doing it again. Every time I've gone down on a guy, it always made me feel pressured into doing it but experiencing it with Kellan was different. I felt like we both enjoyed it, which makes me want to do it that much more.

I inhale to clear my head, trying to stop thinking about sucking him off again, but his scent sends me spiraling. "Not at all," I lie – I'm practically melting but I doubt it's from the warm air circulating through the house. "In fact, I want to see your shuffleboard skills." He grins, eyes traveling slowly to my lips before standing and offering me his hand.

"Okay, Ava." His voice is soft, sending a heat wave through me. How can he make such a simple statement sound so dirty? We cross the room to the ten-foot-long table, tension crackling between us but he never makes a move to come onto me. I half pout, wishing he would close the space between us, even if it's just for a quick kiss.

He moves gracefully, taking his time to shake some powder onto the playing field before picking up several pucks from the gutter surrounding it. Then presses a button on the side of the table to turn on the soft purple lights, illuminating the acrylic numbers and lines on the board. I try to look more interested in the game, but watching him set up everything is far more entertaining and I realize a little too late that I've begun to twirl my hair around my fingers as he pulls the table away from the wall. The grin on his face tells me that he spotted me daydreaming, but I can't help it.

"Have you ever played before?" He asks.

I shake my head. "I've only ever watched."

"Pick your color," he offers me two pucks.

"I choose black." His lips twitch before he nods and hands it over. I test the weight of it, surprised that it's so heavy.

"We each get four pucks and take turns sliding them across the board. If your puck doesn't make it out of the dish in the center, it's out. If it slides into the gutter, it's out. You can knock my pucks off, I can knock yours off." He explains as he gathers up the white pucks and places them at the end of the table.

"How do you know who wins?" I ask.

He smiles widely at me, "Doesn't matter."

I scoff. "It does so. I want to know when I beat you."

"You aren't going to win." He says in a matter-of-fact tone.

"I bet I will." I challenge him.

"What's the bet?"

I size him up, then step forward, poking his chest. "Tell me how scoring works, Kellan."

He sucks his bottom lip between his teeth, glancing down at my finger digging into his chest. "Whoever has their pucks furthest down the board without falling off gains points. If it's in the zone labeled three, you gain three points. Highest score wins." I gather my remaining pucks and stand at the corner of the table beside him, ready for my first game.

"Do you want to go first, or do you want the hammer?" I don't know what the hammer is, but it sounds like I play second. I weigh my options before deciding to let him lead the game. I need to mimic his moves, and possibly knock him off the board.

"I'll take the hammer," I smile up at him sweetly. He slides his puck across the table, stopping dead center in the third zone. I hear him take a deep inhale as I slightly lean over the table for my turn and shove my puck forward. It hits the side of his puck, sending it straight into the gutter. I clap my hands in celebration before moving to the side so he can take his turn.

He leans forward and flicks the white piece across the board. It lands further down than his first one. He opens his arms out, as if waiting for my praise. Rolling my eyes at him, I step closer before leaning down to line up my shot. I flick my wrist just as he did, sending my piece down to bump into his.

"Another gutter," I tease.

"Oh, really? I thought you had never played before. You hustling me?" He pokes his finger into my chest lightly before clicking his tongue at me in disapproval, then glances at the board. He looks back at me and pushes his third puck across the table. It clicks into mine loudly, sending it flying into the surrounding sand, leaving his hanging over the edge. I step closer, pushing his strong body to the side, and line up my piece before releasing it. It stops as it crosses into the third zone. I breathe a sigh of relief but tally up the points in my head, realizing he is several points behind me.

Before I have the chance to stand completely, he leans over me and takes his shot, sending two of my pucks into the gutter, leaving his final one over the edge beside the other. He places my last puck in front of me before backing away. I send my piece across the board, watching as it slowly glides into the second zone.

"That's eight points for me, and how many for you?" His eyes shine with mischief as he stares down at me.

"Three and three equals six, you cheater," I say to him as I walk to the end for our pieces.

"A hangar is worth four points, and I have two hangars. Hustler," he looks me up and down.

"It was just beginner's luck, and you didn't tell me anything about a hangar. What is that?" I slide his pucks to him while I fish mine from the sand.

"A hangar is when it hangs over the edge without falling from the board. Now what was the bet?" I swallow, weighing my options. He could easily turn the game to favor either of us, and no matter how I play, I won't be able to beat him. I've never played this before tonight and there are obviously more rules that I still don't know.

He waits patiently for me to make a decision, flipping one of his pucks around in his hand as he studies me. There's no winning for me, but I know a way to get what I want. "How about, let's play again. And if I win," I step up to his legs to lace my fingers through his front belt loops and tug on his jeans. "We both lose these." My face heats from embarrassment. I've grown to be so direct in the last few days which is very unlike me - but I like this new version of myself.

"And if I win?" He swallows as he asks.

"I'll sit on your bike."

He huffs out a laugh, "That's hardly fair for one of us."

"Naked." I finalize my deal, watching his eyes go wide as he realizes what I've just said.

He leans down, leveling his face with my own. A dangerous glint in his eye sends a shiver down my spine but I refuse to back down. "Bet."

"Bet," I mimic him.

"You first, loser." He says at he pats me on the back.

"That's rude." I flick my wrist, sending my puck skating across the top. It lands in the center of the third section. His hand grips my hip, pinning me against the table as he pushes his puck to knock mine into the sand.

"I'll show you rude, Angel." He whispers in my ear before releasing his hold on me. I slide my piece across the table, bumping it into his, but they both stay on the board. I stay in place, expecting him to grab onto me again, but he doesn't.

Instead, he stands close behind me. My breath hitches as I wait for his body to press against mine. He takes his time lining up the shot before pushing his piece hard enough to knock my piece into the gutter. I celebrate when his follows. "You're awfully cheerful for someone who's losing." He says over my shoulder. "You must want on that Indian pretty bad."

I shudder, feeling his breath tickle my skin, pushing my puck across the board, watching as it stops on the second section. Sighing with frustration, I move out of his way.

"I bet that seat is pretty cold out there." He says as he pushes the white piece across the table. It stops directly on the line between the first and second sections.

I bump my shoulder into his arm and line up my shot before flicking my wrist. My puck glides across the powdered top, clicking against his. It's momentum pushes his over the line, giving him two points instead of one while mine stays in the first section. "Fuck."

He steps up to the table, studying the board as he flips his puck around in his hands. He places it down, then sends it flying, crashing into mine. They both glide down the table, but mine stops just before falling off.

"Wow, giving me a hangar? I'm honored." I lean forward to count the points. I tally mine to six points, but frown as I count his eight points. He smacks me directly on my ass, the wave of pleasure travelling directly to my clit, then leans into my back, caging me in with those big, muscled arms.

Thirty-Four
Kellan

My girl talks a good game; I honestly can't tell if she's played before or not. If she's lying, she has some explaining to do. Her breathing catches as I press my chest into her back, the sight of her bending over the table sends blood pumping straight to my dick. Tonight isn't supposed to get too far – I told myself that I like her more than that and I want to take it slow with her. I want to get to know her, but my lower half thinks the exact opposite.

I try to let her up, even standing to give her enough room to walk away from me if she wanted, but my feet won't move away from her another inch. I stare at the space between us, making sure she doesn't feel trapped when she doesn't move away. What could she possibly be thinking?

My mind races with all the ways I could have her, all the ways I want to take her the longer she stands in front of me. She leans back on her heels, pressing her ass against me, sending my mind into overdrive. She flips her hair over her shoulder, taunting me. I know what she feels between us; I can feel her jeans rubbing against my length as it presses into her ass. Fuck the promise I made to myself earlier tonight – we already went too far anyway. What's it matter anymore?

I take her hands, placing them flat on the table in front of her so my hands can roam her body. I take my time appreciating every dip and curve she has to offer until I grab the end of her shirt and tug it over her head. The fabric falls down her arms, showing off what she's been hiding all night.

I trace patterns across her bare skin, taking my time winding her up before removing her bra. I let it fall from her arms onto the table, watching her shiver when the cool air sinks into her. I cup both her heavy breasts in my hands, appreciating the weight of them before turning my attention to her hardening nipples. Her head rolls forward to let out a quiet moan that I know she tried to hold back. I shake my head slowly, disappointed that she would even try to be quiet.

Her head snaps back a second before she tries to turn to face me, but I refuse to move. I press my hips forward, pinning her legs against the table. "No ma'am," I press down between her shoulders to force her flat onto the table. She looks damn good bent over.

Thirty-Five

Ava

I don't know how much more of this slow teasing I can take before I lose my mind. I've completely soaked through my panties from his hands on my body, something I still can't believe is possible, considering how hard I've had to work to get off with every man I've been with in my whole life. I suck in a breath, letting him slowly travel down my sides before tugging my jeans down my legs. My face flushes – I know what he's about to see.

"Kellan," I whisper. Should I tell him?

"Ava." His breath blows against the back of my thighs before pulling on my foot. I shift my weight to lift it completely, letting him remove my jeans, then shift so he can do the other. He pushes my ankles apart, forcing me to spread my legs before cupping my ass in both his hands. I'm too aware of how close his face is to the most private part of my body as he continues to kneel on the floor but I don't dare to move away.

My body tenses when his lips gently press against the back of my thigh, right above the inside of my knee. His mouth is soft and warm as he slowly moves down, up, then to the other side. Once both of my thighs have been shown equal attention, he begins tracing the same path with his tongue. I close my eyes to bask in the way he makes me feel as he finishes licking and biting his way across my skin. My breath catches in my throat when his hand slowly makes its way up my parted legs before a single finger pushes my thong aside.

I bite down on a moan when he spreads me open, sliding that single finger around until I'm slick and throbbing for more. Once he's satisfied with how wet I am, his teeth bite down on the back of my thigh as he pushes deeper. The palm of his hand flattens between my legs as he slowly presses his finger into me as far as it can go before pulling out and slowly pushing back in. His slow movements cause my legs to quake, but I'm nowhere near ready for this to end.

His teeth release my skin, then he bites down again on the opposite thigh while he continues to slowly fuck me with his finger. I silently plead for more but a part of me wants this to keep up this slow, torturous game. Eventually, he withdraws and I immediately miss the feel of him inside me.

He slides that precious finger all around, spreading more of my wetness before sliding further back. Oh. Oh, God. No. The tip of his finger presses onto my asshole and I begin to panic. My legs instinctively try to close when he swirls around. "Kellan," I whimper as he applies pressure. I don't think I can do that, I've never done anything like that before with anyone.

"Okay," he whispers. He stands slowly, while running his hands up my back, leaving a trail of kisses and marks from his teeth across my skin. I feel his zipper a second before feeling his thick cock slap me between the legs. I gasp, feeling him completely bare against me and remember just how large he is. He pushes my feet closed with before using the gap between my thighs to stroke his length, coating us both with precum and anything I have left from when his finger was deep inside me.

He moves me forward, freeing himself from my thighs, but now I have nowhere to go. The table's edge presses against my hips, biting at my skin and reminding me just how real this is. If I ever see Emily again, I'll have to thank her.

Kellan spreads my legs before stepping up behind me, letting his cock bounce between my legs freely before grabbing it to slap it on my labia. I revel in the feel of him sliding across my clit, teasing me by spreading my lips with his width just to pull and push against me until I feel my own wetness drip down my legs. My toes curl as he thrusts into me, taking me completely raw.

We groan together as he goes deeper, until I feel the front of his thighs on the back of mine. Once we've broken out into a sweat, he begins to really move inside me. Our skin collides against each other as he fucks me slowly from behind, over and over again, until he picks up the pace. The room is filled with our grunts and moans, the sound of our breath coming out in rapid pants, and our skin slapping together.

"Oh, God," I moan into the flat surface as he reaches between my legs to rub my clit. He synchronizes his thrusts, making me feel stretched and full, like I may faint from the pleasure pulsing so deep inside me that I can't speak words. Then I'm empty but writhing in ecstasy when my clit is tenderly rubbed and flicked at such a fast rate that I think he's put a vibrator between my legs. Where did this man learn to do these things?

"Harder," I breathe when he pushes into me again. Instead of giving me what I want, he pulls out almost completely. My head swims with confusion, wondering what he could possibly be doing when he dives back in. I cry out, feeling his head burrow deep inside of me until I feel like he's hit a wall. Again and again, he thrusts forward, plunging into me so hard that the table begins to scrape across the floor. I grab hold of the table's edge, using it to press into his thrusts until I feel I may lose my soul.

Something carnal inside me craves to feel him blow inside me, surprising me, but the thought sends me over the edge. If I could just feel him giving me every part of him, I would be complete. I would be – oh God. I explode around him, crying out and screaming his name repeatedly. He doesn't stop, doesn't slow down as my orgasm bursts from me. My vision blurs, my eyes roll back in my head, but he just – keeps – fucking me. "Please. Kellan," I beg.

"God damn. That's wet, baby." His words send me spiraling. I grip the board, trying to push my ass out, hoping to open myself more, wanting him, needing him, to finish.

He grips my hips, slamming me onto him as he thrusts as deep as our bodies will let him. I groan as he hits a sensitive spot inside of me just right and I buck at the sensation.

"That's it," I cry out. I want him to do that again.

"Fuck, Ava. Hold on to the table." He barks.

I do as he says, gripping the edge of the table until the wood bites into my fingers. Arching my back, I bring my ass further into the air, wanting that feeling of him bottoming out inside me again. He grips me so hard, I may have bruises tomorrow, but I don't care.

"Look, Ava. I want you to watch how you take it," he says through gritted teeth as he turns my head to the window.

I see our reflection in the glass, and want so badly to burn the memory into my brain. I watch as he drives into me, his arms straining to force me onto him as we bounce apart from the momentum. Over and over again, he fucks me on the table, occasionally looking to meet my eyes in the reflection before faltering and having to refocus. His hand comes up to my shoulder, pinning me still so he can get the right angle to dive inside of me again.

This is the best porno I've ever watched in all of my life. And the sex is better than anything I've ever experienced. The sight of him praying up at the ceiling brings me to climax again, ripping through me like lightning.

I scream as he thrusts into me, my legs shaking as everything inside me spills out onto him. I clench my insides, trying to pull him into me and hold him there forever. I bounce my ass onto his length, using the movement to force him to keep going. I fuck myself, using him until my body screams for me to stop. I'm done, I can't possibly keep going anymore.

My insides are sore, completely raw as I come down from my high. He rips out of me harshly before collapsing onto my back and I feel him reach down to jerk himself off. Hot semen shoots out onto my ass and legs and I moan. I literally fucking moan as it rains down onto me. It feels wonderful and powerful, knowing I was the one who brought him to finish and the way he's marked me is divine.

We lay on the table until our breathing evens out and I'm finally able to stand on my own. I wiggle my toes, then swing a leg back and forth, testing just how sore I am.

"Don't move," he says as he presses a kiss onto my shoulder and leaves me lying face down in a blissful state.

"Hmm," I respond. What would happen if I did? Would the evidence of what we did slide down my body until it pooled at my feet? I bite my lip at the idea, wondering what he would do if I disobeyed. I turn my head to watch him walk away from me, his nakedness making me smile. "Where did your shirt go?" I ask.

"Fuck if I know," he laughs.

Glancing around, I see our clothes are everywhere. "We made a mess."

"You started it," he says as he gently rubs a towel across my skin.

I crinkle my nose as he smears everything across my skin. I promptly take the towel from him to clean myself up. "You finished it."

His hand comes down hard on the bare skin of my ass. "And I'll do it again if you don't behave."

Pleasure ripples through me, threatening to force myself onto him again, but I couldn't possibly go that hard if we were to go for round two. The fire inside of me has died down, happy with his performance - for now.

My phone rings from somewhere on the floor but I am too comfortable to move. Kellan's bed feels like heaven, and down-filled pillows are perfect. Last night, I fell onto these sheets and let them wrap around me; they're so soft they almost feel like silk. The closed curtains do little to block out any light as the sun shines brightly from outside, letting me know that it's near noon but I want to stay here in this spot for the rest of the day.

I roll over to shield my eyes from the brightness, feeling Kellan's heavy arm wrap around my midsection. His rough hands softly slide up my back, sending a shiver up my spine as my insides squeeze. My body remembers how he felt inside of me last night and reacts to his touch with excitement.

He grabs onto my sides and flips me flat onto my back, a mischievous grin flashes across his face a second before he digs his fingers into my sides. I scream and kick under his weight, but he's too big to break away from. "Stop!" I laugh as he tickles my sides relentlessly. "Stop or I'm gonna pee on you!"

"Alright, alright." He rolls away, lying still before grabbing me again. I squeal as he tosses me around like I weigh nothing, rolling me up into the blanket to continue tickling me until I'm laughing so hard I can hardly breathe. I'm made too aware of how naked we are when he stops to yank the sheets from our bodies. I feel vulnerable when he rolls us over so I can straddle him, the room is too bright with nothing holding either of us back.

We stare at each other for a brief moment, taking in the sight from our own positions before colliding, our mouths hungrily seeking out the other's.

He thrusts his hips up, sending a ripple of pleasure radiating through me. I moan into his mouth, unashamed by how I respond to him when I feel how hard he is beneath me. His hand reaches between us to rub his thick head against my opening, sending my mind reminiscing on the first time we slept together at the shop. I feel his lips pull into a smile when he feels how wet I am already. He pulls away to lie back onto the pillow before grabbing onto my hips, forcing me higher onto my knees.

A New Year's Ride

I take his dick in my hands and watch as he comes to life from my touch – his shoulders sag a little more, his breathing changes, and the muscles in his arms flex when he clenches his fists. He's so responsive and I love it. I stroke him a few more times before angling my hips and pressing the head of his cock into me, sighing deeply when I feel myself stretch to allow him inside. He slowly pushes me down onto him, watching as I spread my legs wider to take his full length. I stay there, letting my body get used to feeling so full before rising slightly onto my knees again.

A loud groan escapes him before his eyes close, tilting his face to the ceiling. I stare down at him, watching how he reacts to my slow movements, watching how his tattooed chest rises and falls as he pulls in ragged breaths when I ride him.

His fingers dig into my flesh, holding on tightly as I torture him, dragging out my motions. I rise as high as I can until I feel nothing but the tip of him inside me, then drop down over and over again until I feel like I need more. I lean forward then let my ass fall onto him, feeling every inch burrow inside of me and shiver. If I didn't know any better, I would say his cock was created just for me.

His eyes open wide as I slam down onto him again; he tries to move me quicker, grabbing onto my hips and lifting me but I stay seated. I let him have his way last night, but this is for me now and I refuse to give up my control.

I shake my head, staring down at him before lifting again. My ass bounces as I impale myself onto him. I cry out as he hits the end of me, flooding me with that familiar feeling from last night but I'm too sore to do it again.

"Goddamnit," he slurs the words into one through gritted teeth. spurring me on. I push down on his chest and lean forward, then rock down onto him. He trusts his hips up, sending me towards the headboard but stops before I fall over completely. He lowers us onto the mattress again before grabbing my hips and holding me in place to grind into me.

"Kellan," I warn him before peeling his fingers off me. I lace our fingers together before I start to move, bouncing onto him until my legs burn and sweat beads down my back. He sets his jaw, grinding his teeth as I enjoy my ride. I lean over him, trying to give my legs a rest before continuing. He takes advantage of my pause, wrapping his arms around me before driving his hips into mine.

A New Year's Ride

I fall into him, letting him put in some work and moan into his chest as he drives into me relentlessly, rocking me so hard the bed hits against the wall. My orgasm begins to build inside me with every knock of the bed frame, threatening to spill out of me at any moment.

He releases his hold to push me into a sitting position, reaching down between my legs with one hand to rub my clit with his thumb. I bounce up and down, riding him until I gasp for air, so close to coming undone but it's still so far away. His other hand squeezes my breast, twisting my nipple between his thumbs until I scream, finding my release. My muscles clench and spasm around him so tightly that I can barely move, barely able to push him inside of me.

I ride out my orgasm, mumbling nonsense while seeing stars as he sits up, bringing my mouth to his before leaning me backwards until I lay flat on the bed. Without pulling out of me, he positions a pillow under my lower back and throws my legs onto his shoulders.

I gasp as he begins to move, feeling him reach a place inside me that he hasn't before. I claw at his arms, needing to hold on to something to keep my soul from leaving my body. My hips are elevated, resting on the top of his thighs as he plows into me and pulls my knees apart to watch, his mouth opening at the sight of me taking him.

"You've got such a greedy cunt, Angel," he groans as he picks up his pace, never taking his eyes from between my legs. My eyes roll to the back of my head, pleasure pulsing through me the closer he gets to losing control.

"Ah, that's it. Right there," I scream out as he presses his hand onto my chest, pushing me into the mattress, putting more of his weight onto me. I grab his wrist, digging my nails into his skin, and I take the pain of his heavy hand.

He tightens his grip on my thigh, yanking me roughly back onto his lap. The movement sends me over the edge and I clench around him, another orgasm ripping through me. "Kellan," I moan as I feel the pillow soak under me.

In an instant, he moves us down the bed and pulls away from me. I feel empty and sore, not used to doing so much over a short period of time. He continues shooting streams of his cum onto my stomach before falling forward onto his elbows and kissing me deeply; I sigh as deep satisfaction burrows into my chest.

Thirty-Seven
Kellan

I should have been at the shop hours ago, but I just couldn't get out of bed. How the hell could I with the view I had?

"Come on, new girl. Your boss isn't going to be too happy with you being late on the first day." I watch her eyes roll to the ceiling in response; if I were less satisfied, my dick would be twitching in my jeans at the thought of punishing her for the attitude.

"Guess I'll just have to sleep with him and ask for forgiveness."

I open the door for her to slap her ass as she walks by, "Careful, Angel. I've heard he's off the market as of late."

"Is he? Such a bummer, I've heard he's insanely attractive and quite good with his hands." She licks her bottom lip before pulling it into her mouth, giving away her thoughts of last night and this morning.

"Do we have time for me to change clothes?" She asks as we get in the Chevelle. I look her up and down, fucking loving the way she wears the same clothes from last night with no shame. I don't want her to be uncomfortable for the rest of the day, so I nod and pull out of the garage.

I smile over at her, knowing that John and Tracy are going to give me shit for showing up well into the afternoon, but I know what she's trying to hide by changing clothes. She spent the better part of the morning looking for the scrap material she called panties; little did she know that I had hidden them in my pocket before tossing my jeans into a hamper downstairs. I'll never forget her horrified expression when she saw me wearing the first pair as a hat when we left the shop. It's my mission now to take every pair she owns, and I won't stop until they are all mine.

We finally make it to her apartment despite the traffic; I wait in the car for her to run in and change clothes, deciding that we were already late enough, and if I saw her naked again, I would keep her that way. Eventually, she comes bouncing out the door wearing a pair of jeans so tight I can hardly breathe and a long-sleeved black shirt that's basically a second skin. She's all smiles as she stares back at me over the hood of the car and I fight like hell to keep my eyes on her face instead of drooling over her body like a dog waiting for a bone.

I don't fully wrap my mind around what's happening in my life at this moment but if I'm dreaming, I hope like hell I don't ever wake up.

Maybe I crashed that night on the way to the party and this is some kind of realistic shit that my brain is making up to help keep me alive. Hell, I don't know anymore. But, I know without a doubt that Ava is beautiful inside and out and she deserves the world.

We open the doors in unison before she throws a purse the size of a suitcase into the backseat but in a second I see her face fall when a voice comes from behind her on the sidewalk. The fear and panic that replaces her smile sends red-hot rage racing through me. Who the fuck is out there? I'm out of the car in an instant, stepping onto the walkway like I own the fucking city and I've got a mission.

A scrawny, piss ant of a man stares back at me with wide eyes with fear at the sight of me. His red hair is curled and fluffed on the top of his head, sides shaved down to near skin on both sides like some punk trying to impress someone with looks instead of doing anything useful with his life.

"I'm -" she pauses and looks to me as if begging to get her out of the situation, that same panicked expression from New Year's night stares at me. I take a step forward, ready to throw the guy around when her soft touch stops me in my tracks. Her face has hardened and the look of determination has replaced all other emotions on her face. I watch as she squares her shoulders and finds her words.

"I'm going to work now, and I'd appreciate it if you leave me alone. Don't come back here for any reason, I don't want to ever see you again." She turns on her heel, letting her hair blow over her shoulder before looking back to the guy still standing in place. "Goodbye, Sebastian."

Without another word, Ava yanks open the door to climb inside and slams it shut behind her. I nearly jog around the car, smiling as the prick stares in disbelief at the window tint he can't see through.

"Holy shit," she exhales as I pull the car into traffic, leaving him still standing there in confusion. I don't say a word as I burn the image of him into my brain. That's the same asshole from the party she ran from. That's the cheating boyfriend. My fingers wrap around the steering wheel so hard that the skin on my knuckles burns. Images of his face bloodied from my fists flash in my mind as some carnal instinct threatens to take over me.

"Kellan, did you hear me?" Ava's voice brings me back to reality, but my anger continues to pulse through me. I reach across the car and drag her to me by her thigh, my fingers digging into her. I've probably just left bruises on her perfect, soft skin. The idea of her being marked by me in every way possible sends a shiver down my spine.

I stop the car at the next light, stomping on the brake so hard we both rock forward. Before she has time to sit back, I grab her by the back of her head, forcing her mouth onto mine. At first, she stiffens but loosens up quickly before kissing me back. I part her lips, pushing my tongue into her mouth, staking my claim on her. If I have any kind of say in this, she won't ever be going back to that piece of shit. She's mine.

The vehicle behind us honks impatiently, but I don't give a fuck. I'll move when I'm done with Ava. I move her head to the side and bite down on her neck, sending her into a fit of moans before sucking on her skin. When I'm satisfied, I let her go, knowing the bruise will only get darker on her neck as the day goes on but I need the world to see it. I need everyone to see it and know who she belongs to.

"Put on your seatbelt, Angel." She does as she's told, making my dick twitch as she scoots across the seat quickly, not making a sound. I peel away from the light, sending her head snapping backwards as I send us catapulting through traffic.

Fucking prick has the nerve to cheat on her, then show up wanting to know where she's going? Not going to happen, not with me around. We make it to the shop in under ten minutes, barely slowing down as I make the turn and pull into the back. I throw the parking brake on and round the car before Ava has fully removed her seatbelt. Her eyes are wide as she hesitantly steps out of the vehicle and I know something is wrong.

I pull her chin up, forcing her to look at me. "Are you okay?"

"Are you mad at me?" Her voice shakes slightly. Her question confuses me. Why the hell would I be mad at her?

"No, of course not." I wrap her in my arms, realizing I had been too absorbed by my own anger to see how proud she was of herself. "I'm sorry." Her breath hitches as my words sink into her, eventually her arms wrap around me and she melts completely as she relaxes in my hold. I scared her; I fucked up and I scared her. I don't know how to fix this, but I need to get my shit together. We stand in the cold for a long time, just holding onto one another until I feel her shiver.

"Come on, new girl. Let's get you set up." I lace my fingers through hers, leading us through the back door and pray like hell that she will forgive me.

"Alright, here's the shop phone. Here's my cell, people call both throughout the day. The computer is unlocked, you can change the password on it if you want to, just make sure you write the new one down somewhere.

"Here is the clipboard; it has all the tickets on it for everything we have right now. We got parts coming for these three on top; the others we haven't gotten to yet, but it moves pretty fast. John should be finishing up on the Harley he was working on yesterday. Write down the time on the ticket when he says it's done. That's how we keep track of what to charge and what to pay him come Friday." I look over at her, worried that I've gone too fast but she's nodding along. My eyes trail to the side and I could kick myself for not at least trying to clean up a little more lately. She follows my line of sight over the desk that's cluttered with bullshit that I haven't had time to take care of.

"These are all receipts that need to be filed. Some shit, like oils, we keep on hand cause we go through it so much, but we charge it to a ticket when we use it. I'm sorry it's such a wreck."

"I've seen worse," she tells me. I snort out a laugh, feeling like she's being modest to ease my embarrassment.

"Everyone in the shop hands you a checklist when they say something is done, you can just set them all to the side so we can go over that later in the week." She nods, turning around to take it all in.

"I should probably warn you; Tracy and John get into it from time to time. They usually handle it themselves – just don't let either of them intimidate you when they start their bullshit. If you need me for anything at all, I'll be out on the floor. I think that's everything for now."

Ava's face takes on that look of determination again before she looks up at me with adoration in her eyes. It's surprising and I can't help but wonder what she could be thinking as we stand in the middle of a messy office that smells like old coffee and used oil.

"What's the password to your phone?" Her question throws me for a loop considering the way we have been standing here in silence just staring at each other like idiots.

"It doesn't have one, Angel," I tell her, watching as her face fills with confusion at my words. Maybe all she knows is secrecy from her past relationships, and maybe I won't be the best boyfriend she's ever had, but I think being open and allowing her to see anything that may be hidden will set us up for something in the future. If she finds anything in my phone at all, I'm willing to answer to it. I want to be as honest as possible with her about my life when we're both ready and I hope like hell this isn't a mistake but I need her to bet on me. I need her to choose me because I damn sure don't want to lose her just yet.

I took my time sifting through the tickets on the clipboard, trying to memorize the names of all the motorcycles and their brands. I even looked up pictures of them online to have an idea of what they would look like to help name them, but eventually, they all started to look the same. I can't help but drum my fingers on the desk and flip to the last few sheets over and over again.

These sheets are a list of cars that Tracy has lined up to work on and they keep calling to me. I look at their makes and models with stars in my eyes, feeling a pull to them. Several of the vehicles are newer with minor issues like needing an oil change, but there's a few that I can't get out of my head. I flip the pages back, looking for the details of the older cars again and again, wondering where they are hiding on the lot.

A few of the cars are much older, falling somewhere between antique and classic according to the website that I scrolled through earlier in the day. When I look up antique cars and compare them to what's here to be serviced, I crinkle my nose. They aren't what I had in mind at all. Most of them are late ninety models, far from the ones listed on the antique's site. I was hoping to see something that looked as good as Kellan's Chevelle.

I close the browser and sit back in the worn-out office chair and swivel around to look at disaster. This place needs a whole new look, but I wasn't lying when I said I've seen worse – the back office room at the boutique was awful and no matter how often I cleaned, the shit kept coming right back. I pull out my phone and begin putting in a massive order for all things office decor to make the space my own. I look around, confirming that this order will be the first of many.

The hours go by slowly and I often find myself staring out the office window to watch everyone in the shop work. Occasionally someone will go over to change the radio station which sends them all into a fit but they all go back to work quickly.

Eventually, I get a phone call and do my best to talk to the guy that claims he had been calling all day with no answer and didn't appreciate being ignored. I roll my eyes silently and put on my best customer service voice to handle him and immediately hate the whole situation. The guy becomes a total dick so I drop the charade and wait for him to stop cursing me out before setting him straight. I know damn well he hasn't called me once today, and I've scrolled through all the call logs to see if there was anything to be caught up on since Kellan and I had a late start to the day.

After his long spill of insults and slurs, he calms down enough to tell me his name again and I pat myself on the back for finding his information and letting him know that he should be getting a call soon to come pick up his precious motorcycle. I was just waiting for the ticket to be handed in by the mechanic before I could finalize it.

He called back not long after that, apologizing for his outburst and taking his frustration out on me and when he was all talked out, I went back organizing everything around me. There's so much shit stacked everywhere, it's overwhelming. Random papers, notebooks, and receipts litter every surface in the office with little organization. The clipboard was a good attempt, but I can see it being lost before long.

I lose myself in the last hour of the day, cleaning off surfaces just to stack more junk onto other piles of junk until Kellan comes in to take me home for the day. With a sigh, I throw my hands in the air and hand over his cell phone, glad to be done with my first day's work.

On the way out the door, I notice that the shop has gone silent and raise an eyebrow when we pass through the gate. The front of the place has been locked up and we pause long enough for Kellan to jump out to lock the gate behind us.

"Did everyone already leave?" I ask, a bit confused.

"Yeah, we usually all leave together at five but I told them we would stay behind since we got in late. You looked like you had your hands full anyway, so I didn't want to disturb you." He looks over at me, smiling like he absolutely did want to interrupt me but decided against it.

"Mhm," I respond before quizzing him about the radio situation. It doesn't make any sense to me that none of them wear headphones to listen to what they want instead of fighting over the one radio in the shop. We laugh about it on the way to my apartment, joking about how John secretly enjoys the pop hits that Tracy forces them to listen to but a sadness creeps in when I see my building come into view.

Work of any kind has never been fun, but looking out the window to see Kellan whenever I wanted has been wonderful. I'll admit to myself that I didn't really want the day to end; anything that happens for the rest of the day will be dull in comparison but I know I have things to take care of.

"I don't have a way to work tomorrow," I admit.

"I'll be here in the morning, Angel." His voice is reassuring, chasing away the embarrassment of not owning a vehicle.

"Bright and early?" I tease.

"Right on the money," he jokes back. I can tell he doesn't want me to go, but if I stay in this car with him I'm afraid that I will throw myself at him for the second time today. I slip my seatbelt over my shoulder while stuffing everything into my bag, feeling a surge of emotions when he comes around to open my door.

I'm not sure how to say bye to him and the longer I stand here, staring up at him, the more awkward I feel. Images of last night and this morning flash through my head until I feel flustered and can no longer look him in the eye. How does one go from naked porn star to doating boyfriend in the span of a day without there being some confusion on my end?

"Does your mind ever stop racing?" His voice interrupts my thoughts.

"I'll add mind-reader to your list of talents," I joke but it's strange how good he is at so many things.

He looks away, chuckling like I've said the most ridiculous thing he's ever heard. When he looks back at me, my insides do a flip and I catch myself leaning onto the car for support. Am I swooning right now? I want to slap myself, but I'm not sure it will do me any good.

"Can we take the bike in the morning?" I blur out, wanting to see him with that black helmet on again.

"Are you going to pack lightly?" He jokes as he takes my heavy bag from my hands. I was in a hurry this morning when I changed my clothes and didn't get a chance to do much to my hair so I brought half of my bathroom with me when I ran out the door earlier and wasn't going to sit around looking like I was well fucked the night before.

"As a matter of fact, I will."

"Then yes, we can. I'll bring a helmet in the morning for you." His smile would knock me to my knees if I wasn't already leaning against the side of his car but no amount of deep breathing could prepare me for the kiss he plants on my mouth. His lips are warm and inviting but gone too soon, pulling away from me before we go any further in this parking lot.

I sigh heavily and take my bag from him, smiling when I finally push myself away from the car without stumbling to walk up the stairs to go inside. Kellan's eyes sweep the parking spots all around before looking back at me, waiting patiently for me to go inside for the night. I happily spin around in circles once the door is locked behind me, feeling weightless from the unexpected turn of events that led me to where I am in this very moment.

I run through my nightly routine and settle into bed, scrolling on social media until my eyes are too heavy to focus on what's in front of me and eventually fall into a deep sleep.

My alarm came too soon, but I pulled myself out of bed and waited by the door with the smallest backpack I could find in my closet until I heard the familiar rumble pulling up. I feel bad for the people that are probably still sleeping when Kellan reeves his engine loudly to announce his arrival – as if it was needed.

I throw on my jacket and lock my door before throwing my keychain into my bag and skip down the stairs. Seeing Kellan in his gear again sends waves of lust through me, especially when he looks my way. The visor on his helmet is too dark to see his face, but I can feel those beautiful blue eyes of his roaming over my body.

He's dressed in all black except for the white star on the side of his boots that look heavier than the same cowboy style I've started to break in these last few days. Once I'm within arms length, he pulls a helmet from his arm and gently tugs it over my hair before working the strap to secure it on my head. Butterflies erupt inside me as thoughts of that first night together flood my mind.

I'm not sure what night I like most, the one at the shop or the one at his home, but I know I want to relive them both. I bite down on my lip, trying to hide the way my body is reacting to his gloved hands on my neck when reality sets in. I told him that first night that I wasn't on birth control and we still had unprotected sex... twice. What were either of us thinking?

He bumps his helmet to mine and holds his hand out for me to balance as I throw a leg over, but I'm not sure this is such a good idea anymore. Twice we've risked the unthinkable, what else could we do wrong so early on? I sit up, too afraid to touch him but unsure what to do now. I feel overwhelmed and anxiety builds in my chest until I'm on the verge of tears and close my visor to give myself some privacy. How could either of us be so stupid?

I feel Kellan reaching for my hands and hesitantly place them on the tank in front of him instead of holding on to his body then feel a soft glove slip onto my hand. Of course he would be considerate enough to try keeping me warm while we ride together. Guilt wrecks me, but the irony is not lost on me. Protect my head and hands, but everything else is unthinkable. I roll my eyes and pull away, holding out my hand impatiently to put the other glove on myself.

If he picks up on the change in my behavior, he doesn't show it. Instead, he circles us around the parking lot slowly before reaching for me again. I place my hands in front of him on the tank once more and lean forward, ready for the ride into work while anger builds inside of me.

Once we make it to the back lot, I hop off almost immediately and storm inside. I'm mostly mad at myself for letting myself get in this situation, but I'm angry at him too. I replayed that conversation over in my head the whole way here, wondering what changed from that night to now. How can he laugh at birth control and have a condom but the next time we are together completely forget?

I claw at the strap that's kept me safe and pull the helmet over my head, wanting to put it through the door of his bedroom but take a deep breath to calm myself instead. I stare at the door in disbelief, realizing I'm back to the exact spot of my first true orgasm and stop dead in my tracks. Kellan comes through the back door, stopping to stand behind me with his gear in his hand.

"You never take anyone to your house?" I ask him, but I know the answer. I turn to meet his gaze, seeing the panic before he looks down the hallway to see if anyone heard me.

"No," he responds in a hushed tone.

"Then why take me?" I press the situation, needing to know what made me different.

"Because I want to get to know you, Ava." His voice is still low but he doesn't bother to move our conversation anywhere else. His response bounces around in my head, until realization hits me.

"So, the other night, you didn't plan for us to?" I trip on the words, feeling embarrassed. *Just spit it out, Ava.* "You didn't expect us to have sex?"

Amusement flashes across his face before he clears his throat. "No, I didn't. But I don't regret it." He studies me, still unaware of my internal panic. I decide this is a conversation to be finished later and turn on my heels to get the day started. He follows me in silence into the office and sets down his phone on the desk before walking out. I watch him get to work, oblivious to what's been running through my mind and my heart sinks. He really has no idea why I could be so upset.

His phone immediately rings, pulling me out of my head and forcing me to focus on why I'm here. "Hello?" I answer and hear the phone disconnect before anyone responds. I toss the phone onto the desk, aiming for the kitchen to make some coffee when the shop phone rings. I answer the call and hear the click of someone hanging up on me for the second time. Irritation floods me in an instant and I scroll through the call log to see the number was blocked on both phones. I toss them both onto the desk and walk away, deciding that I need coffee more today than ever before.

Forty

Ava

The morning has passed by quickly once I woke up enough to deal with all the clutter that has been surrounding me for the last few days. So far, I've cleaned out the filing cabinet, found an entire box of manila envelopes that had never been opened and filed every scrap piece of paper in the office by date. When I finished that, I realized that it probably wasn't the best idea and decided to break those down even further. Then, I pulled out all the checkout forms for the vehicles that came and went, paired them up with the handwritten receipts that matched and stapled them together.

I feel pretty proud of myself once I stand back and look at the surfaces that peak from under the boxes of supplies and everything else now that all of the paper has been cleared away. By the time I had sorted through the filing cabinet again, I had a small stack of tickets with no indication of payment and groan in annoyance. No wonder this place is such a disaster and Kellan wanted me to step in.

I put them in a stack of their own beside the phone to ask Kellan about them later, then move on to organizing the desk drawers. I'm so consumed by the task that I never hear the loud squeak of the office door being pushed open or anyone coming inside. It isn't until someone pounds their fist down on the hardwood that I jump up, heart pounding in my chest as a giant bald man with a lit cigarette stands over me, looking every bit as menacing as possible.

I watch in terrified silence as he snatches the clipboard and scribbles across the top sheet. He tosses the pen onto the desk, followed by the crumpled half sheet of paper, a single key, then the clipboard. He grabs another key from the set of hooks on the wall before slamming the office door when he exits. Once he's gone, I let out a sigh of relief, gagging on the smell of his cigarette when I inhale. I quickly roll over to the clipboard and see that he has noted the checkout time for me and provided a full list of repairs he has done for the customer.

My eyebrows pull together. The guy still seems like a complete asshole, but he basically did my job for me, besides calling the owner. Am I supposed to be calling them? I push everything to the side, setting off to find Kellan. Before I make it out the door, my phone rings. Of course, I find it at the very bottom of my purse, under all the makeup and toiletries I threw on top of it.

"Hey, Mom," I answer.

"Ava, baby. Where are you?" She sounds worried.

"I'm at work. What's wrong?"

"Sebastian called and said he hasn't been able to get in touch with you, but he saw you in the back of a car with a man who looked like a giant. He's been worried, dear. Your dad thinks you were kidnapped." I roll my eyes at the situation while muffling a laugh when she describes Kellan from Sebastian's point of view. Anyone could stand next to Sebastian and make him feel small, especially the man that stands out on the floor right now with grease smeared on his tan, tattooed skin.

"No, I'm completely fine. Sebastian and Emily have something going on, so we're over. It's not a big deal, but I am busy, so I have to run. Don't worry about me, Mom."

"I hardly think that running away from the situation is good for either of you, Ava." Her tone becomes clipped. There's the person I know, temper shining through.

"Why would you think I ran away from the situation?"

"That's what your father and I have been told. Is it not true?"

"Not at all, and I would suggest that you consider the source. I simply turned my back on both of them. Regardless of what either of them have to say, I know the truth and I don't have to explain myself to anyone." I end the call, finished with their bullshit and release a deep breath to calm my nerves. They can all be miserable together and make up whatever stories they want about me, but I don't want to be dragged into their drama, even if I am the topic.

The office door swings open, squealing loudly on the hinges again. I turn to see Tracy staring angrily at the pegboard full of keys. "Did that mother fucker come in here and take the Ducati?" Her eyes pin me in place.

"I don't know." I answer, trying to stare back as menacingly as possible but she's intimidating as fuck.

"What do you mean you don't know?" Her nostrils flare with anger. Kellan's words echo in my mind. *Don't let them intimidate you.* I square my shoulders, ready to snap at her now that my mother has sent me into orbit.

"What part do you want me to clarify? I said, I don't know." Regret floods me as soon as the words are out of my mouth. She steps closer, and my stomach drops. As much as Sebastian has shoved me around, he's never actually hit me before. No one has ever hit me in my life, but I have a feeling she's the type to start and finish every fight that comes her way. I brace myself, trying to prepare for the hit, but it never comes. Instead, she picks up the clipboard while staring straight into my soul, only looking away to flip the page to find her answer.

"Tillman's ride is ready. I'm starting on the next Harley." She says as she scribbles on a sheet, pulling a piece of paper from her back pocket to clip under the rest of the loose pages. She turns on her heel, yanking a key from the hook on her way out the door and slams it shut behind her. I release my held breath, grateful to still have my face in one piece and sink down into my chair. I take a sip of my coffee, calming down now that I've survived two interactions that would have someone like Emily shaken up or crying.

My phone rings again but instead of answering it, I flip it face down to silence it completely. I'm not interested in talking to anyone but Kellan right now. I step out of the office door, noticing the shop is much cooler than the office, even with all but one of the roll-up doors closed to keep the heat inside. I wrap my arms around my chest to keep my hands warm and spot Kellan walking out of a side door to the parking lot with someone.

I walk to the door, swinging it open to watch the two men talk in front of a small red truck has the hood open while it idles loudly. The smell of exhaust and gas burns my nose the longer I stand downwind from the vehicle, and I wonder if this is something we will be working on soon. Kellan turns to see me in the doorway, smiling as he stares at me while listening to what the stranger is saying. "There she is now. Come here, Angel."

I step to his side, staring at the running engine, wondering what the hell he's working on. "Ava, this is Mike." He points to the man leaning out of the driver's door of the truck.

"Hi. How are you?" I ask. He nods his head, but I can't hear a word he says over the truck's loud idle.

"Mike wanted to sell both of these and owes me a favor, so he stopped by for me to take a look at them before anyone else. What do you think?"

I crinkle my nose, not understanding his question. "Both of what?"

"Both trucks," he smiles down at me but I still don't understand. I lean around the hood to see the other, surprised that it's the same model, but the colors are reversed. The truck Mike sits in has a black interior, complementing the bright red paint job beautifully, while the other is solid black with red seats.

"They match," I say. That's kind of cute.

Kellan chuckles. "Yeah, they match. One is his, the other is his wife's, but they need a family car now that they have the twins."

"They look nice, but what are you going to do with two trucks?" I look up to see him still staring and smiling at me and I wonder what he could be planning.

"Which one do you like?" He asks me with sincerity. I look between him, Mike, and the two trucks, then dash to the black one and hear Kellan laugh.

"I figured as much," he says to Mike. I open the door, running my hand over the buttery red leather seat and dashboard. The steering wheel is slick and shiny, matching the dramatically tall shifter that sticks straight up from the floor. I frown at the sight of it, remembering how I nearly killed us both when I drove Kellan's car. "Are they both the same?" I yell out the door.

"What?" Kellan yells back at me, barely holding back a laugh and Mike smiles from the driver seat of the other truck.

"I gotta shift both of them?" I can't remember what it's called.

They both chuckle to themselves, obviously laughing about my lack of skill when it comes to driving. "No, this '87 is automatic." I get out of the truck, shutting the door behind me before stalking up to the two of them. Mike sits in the driver's seat, twisting the key in his hand before tossing it to me and stepping out. I realize how big of a guy he is when he stands to his full height and see the bench seat is moved as far back as possible. The truck sits lower than any I've ever seen, even lower than the black one across the lot that it's meant to match. I like the way this one sits, like a cat crouched down to pounce on its prey.

I climb in, appreciating the simplistic setup and red details that outline all the black. Mike shuts the door behind me with a sad look in his eyes. I realize then, he's missing an arm. Shit. Did I upset him when I asked about how to drive it?

"You take good care of my baby," he grunts.

"She will," Kellan answers from behind him. We look at each other for a minute before he walks over to slam the hood closed. I sit in silence, trying to wrap my head around this situation. He's buying me a truck.

"She's old, but trust me. She runs better than anything else on the road. She wasn't intended for everyday, but she's reliable. If you don't want to put a lot of miles on it, you can drive her until you get something newer, won't hurt nothing if you park her for a few weeks. She fires up every time." I nod as Mike pats the hood before taking a step back to take one last look at his vehicle.

Forty-One

Kellan

I hand over an envelope of cash to Mike, accepting the two titles he has to offer before shaking his hand. He's a good man, someone I've considered a friend for nearly all my life and I'm happy that he's finally got the life he deserves.

Ava comes skipping into the office seconds later, smiling like she just won the lottery. "Mr. Mike, do you want your keychain?" Her voice is soft and innocent as usual, but there's an air around her now that wasn't before and I realize how upset she was this morning. There's obviously something I'm missing, but what could I have done?

Mike steps forward and shakes his head, "Just call me Mike, and no. The keychain stays with the truck. Brings good luck when you swing it just right." He winks at her like it's their own inside joke, but I know what he means.

The man may only have one arm, but he's been known to throw more than a punch when he has to; last time he was in a fight he busted a guy's temple with that metal ball. I don't think he has a set of keys that doesn't have one, and he doesn't even play billiards. For her sake, I hope he at least replaced it or cleaned it after that brawl, even if it was years ago.

I watch as her face turns pink from his gesture and an overwhelming sense of affection courses through me so strong I have to clear my throat. Does she not receive gifts from people very often? Her strong reaction pulls on me, telling me that I should have known this and changed it sooner.

"Alright, love birds. I've got to hit the road. See you later, Kelso, and remember what I said. If you ever want to sell either of those babies, I got first dips. Keep him in line, Ava."

"I will," she says as she smiles up at him.

"Will you?" I challenge her, wanting to see that blush deepen on her cheeks.

Her eyes roll to the ceiling, something that's growing on me, even if I do still want to take her over my knee when she does it but I wouldn't tolerate it from anyone else but her. I place a finger on that dark bruise I left on her throat earlier, feeling her blood pump under her delicate skin. She either doesn't know it's there, or she's showing it off on purpose.

"So, what kind of truck is that?" Her lips quirk up at the corners but now that Mike is gone, a little bit of her happiness is too. I've wracked my brain, wondering what I have done to cause her anything but happiness and come up short. Whatever is bothering her, she's keeping it quiet or doesn't want to tell me.

"A tank," I smirk, remembering she doesn't know anything about vehicles. "It's a C-10."

"That's what it's called?" She asks, comically.

"That's what it is, Angel. Are you hungry?" Her stomach growls, answering for her even when she shakes her head to say no. I take her hand to pull her from the office and grab the helmet she tossed to the side and push it over her head, laughing at the glare she gives me as I pull on my own.

"I said no, Kellan." Her voice is stern, warning me to back off. I freeze on the spot, not sure where the anger is coming from but this isn't a playful kind of tone.

"What did you eat for dinner?" I ask, point blank. Her silence is telling, but annoying. "What did you have this morning, besides the two cups of coffee in the kitchen?" Again, she remains silent and I narrow my eyes at her.

"Hands," I demand. She holds them in the air between us. "Smartass," I say before forcing gloves onto her fingers. She yanks her hands away, situating the gloves on the proper fingers before brushing her hair over her shoulders. I raise an eyebrow as that hickey is put on full display. She definitely doesn't know it's there. I shake the helmet on her head, making sure it's snug, before leading us out the back.

Lunch with Kellan was awkward, and I kept getting the feeling that he was trying to cheer me up but after Mike left, I still didn't have much to say anymore. The sinking feeling of not knowing if I could possibly be pregnant started to weigh on me again; and honestly the fact that Kellan doesn't seem bothered by it at all has also started to fester. We hardly know each other, raising a child together could be a big mistake.

I kept trying to tell myself to let it go; he was nice enough to give me a job and buy me a way to get to said job but the panic and uncertainty is weighing too heavy on me to forgive right now. I don't know how either of us could be so dumb in the moment, but I think what's bothering me most is how excited I was for it to happen. I wanted it to happen that way and I damn near begged him for it. What would he have done if I would have told him to keep going?

I chew on my nails, worrying about everything all at once but stop when he looks over at me for the millionth time. I half expect him to tell me to stop, but he never says a word about my bad habit, he just glances at me like he's trying to figure out the worlds hardest puzzle. I consider telling him what's bothering me so much, but I don't know where to start and I think we need somewhere more private than a chain restaurant or sitting in traffic where anyone could have their windows down. I definitely don't want anyone at the shop listening in on our conversation either.

Once we're on the way to the shop, I allow myself to feel some comfort from his body heat. The way he gently rubs my leg while navigating traffic is nice too, but I don't want to get caught up in him so quick again. The thoughts that plague my mind when he flexes the muscles in his stomach while leaning with the turns is exactly how I found myself in the situation I'm in. When will I learn from my mistakes?

After lunch, I show Kellan the unpaid tickets that I found earlier that morning. A few of them were from friends that he owed, so we trashed those. As for the others, he didn't want them to be trashed just yet, but he was skeptical that anyone would be willing to pay up, so he put me in charge of calling them. Surprisingly, someone wanted to pay over the phone. It took me a while to figure out how the card machine worked, but his payment went through. I wrote paid on the receipt and put it on the top tray for money coming in this week and went on with the rest of the list to call.

No one else answered the phone, so I spent the rest of the day looking up what the hell a C-10 is. Apparently, car guys go crazy for them. The older, the better. There are a couple of social media accounts that show the trucks being used for racing, and I roll my eyes. Of course, Kellan would want to own a couple and what could be better than his and hers? I count his vehicles on my hand, realizing he's probably doing better financially than anyone would give him credit for. Running his own business that seems to be drowning in work, owning a house, two motorcycles, and a car, now two trucks. I drum my fingers on the desk, wondering if there is more that he hasn't shown me.

Once the shop quiets down and the bay doors are closed, I see Kellan walking through the shop, mumbling to himself. His hands are covered in grease, and a black smudge glistens on his cheek as he kneels beside a motorcycle that I don't recognize. I flip through the clipboard, trying to remember the names of what we should be working on, but I can't find the bike's information.

A smile pulls up half of his mouth as he works, obviously lost in what he has going on. There's something mesmerizing about him as he tosses down a wrench to pick up something else; the way he moves is confident. He knows what he's doing; there's a lifetime of knowledge swirling in that head of his that I may never understand. I hover over the desk, watching him through the large window, half-hidden by the low wall but if he were to look up now, he would absolutely see me. He stands and lifts his shirt, wiping his face clean and my insides heat at the sight of him. His tattooed chest with a faint outline of abs below convinces me to let my anxiety and anger go. He isn't too lean or cut, but the muscles are there, begging for me to run my fingertips over them and take what I want.

The man is like my own personal thirst trap come true. What would he do if he caught me staring? As if reading my thoughts, he looks up, meeting my eyes as a wide smile takes over his face. My insides flutter. He doesn't take his eyes from me as he reaches up to start the bike, grinning when it starts. A loud rumble fills the shop, rattling the window as he revs the engine like a maniac. I feel the vibration course through me and hum my appreciation. I'm still slightly sore from the past day's events but, I find myself wanting him again.

I roll my eyes at myself, annoyed that I've been so angry but one lift of his shirt and I'm ready to go again like it's not a big deal. The office is suddenly too hot as I continue watching him; he's focused on his work again, but I swear he's putting on a show for me. Sitting on the cushioned leather seat and leaning every which way to look at, what's in front of him. What could he possibly be doing other than showing off? The loud rumble finally quiets as he kills the engine and I hurry to sit down, making myself seem busy. He comes barreling through the office door before picking up the clipboard and scribbling on the next page.

"Condoms." He blurts out.

"What?" I ask, completely horrified by his outburst.

"You're upset because of what happened. We messed around without condoms."

"Okay! Quick screaming about condoms. Yes, it's why I'm upset. Kellan, we hardly know each other. How are we going to raise a kid together?" My breath catches in my throat, I'm afraid that I may start crying if I keep talking but how do I get through to him that this can't happen again?

"Ava, it's going to be okay." He attempts to calm me down but his words piss me off all over again.

"How do you know that?" I scream at him, feeling like he isn't taking this serious at all.

He blows out a breath, ready to set the record straight but I can tell he doesn't want to say the words. "I'm thirty-six years old with no kids, Angel. I think I know when to reel myself back or when I've gone too far, not that I've ever made it a habit of sleeping around and risking it but you aren't pregnant."

"That's the stupidest thing I've ever heard. I bet there's millions of men that tell women the same thing all over the planet and next thing they know, she's knocked up and he's nowhere to be found."

"Do I look like I'm going anywhere?" Hurt flashes in his eyes, but I can't take his advice seriously. I don't care how much he's slept around; anything can still happen. "You're not pregnant, Ava. Not even close but give it a few weeks and we'll go buy every test from every store in this city and the next to confirm it. And if you are, then we will figure it out, but you aren't pregnant." He throws the clipboard down on the desk as if that's the end of the conversation and let's out a sigh. "You ready?"

"What for?" I ask.

"To go home." He answers.

I nod before standing and throw everything into my tiny backpack, wondering how he can be so casual now that we've just blown up at each other.

"Where are you going?" His words stop me as I reach for my helmet.

"What do you mean?" I ask, confused.

"Where do you want to go?" His eyes search mine, but I can't tell what he's hinting at.

"You said home." I stare back at him, patiently waiting for him to explain what he wants me to say.

"My home, or your home, Angel?"

"I guess that depends on where you want to go, Kellan." I fire back at him, earning one of those bright smiles that I love, but he isn't off the hook with me yet. Not for a few more weeks anyway. I try to pull my helmet over my head, but the truck keys fall from the opening to land at my feet. "Oh, I forgot. I'll drive."

I push past him, ready to hit the road but stop in my tracks when I realize I have no idea where to go. I could go home, or I could go with him and let him make everything up to me. Ugh, there I go again, ready to forgive and forget too soon. I shove the key into my backpack and walk over to the desk to grab the helmet and put it on. Maybe I will ride with him one more time.

I jog to keep up with his long strides through the parking lot but catch the smile he tries to hide by closing his visor when he turns to face me. I throw my leg over the seat and wrap my hands around his midsection, cocking an eyebrow when he flexes under my touch.

"What's with the backpack?" I ask him over the roar of the engine.

"I have to stop by a few places on the way," he responds dryly before we shoot out of the parking lot.

To my surprise, our first stop is a grocery store. He must visit here fairly often because the cashier doesn't bat an eye when Kellan strolls through the line while still wearing his gear. It made me feel too disrespectful to keep mine on, even with the visor open so people could see my face but once the doors open and the cold blasts against my eyes, I regret taking it off at all.

The next stop is a pharmacy, which I raise an eyebrow at but follow him inside anyway. I'm more than curious to see what kinds of things someone like Kellan could possibly be getting from here. I linger behind him as he walks up and down a few isles, wandering aimlessly before stopping to look at their selection of candies. I need something sour to snack on tonight when I lay in bed doom scrolling.

After making my selection I head to the counter, forgetting about my visor being closed and scare the hell out of myself when my reflection stares back at me at the front door and yank the plastic over my head. The poor lady behind the counter looks like she is seconds away from fainting too, obviously not used to seeing two people wandering around in the store like we are but calms down slightly when she sees my eyes. I feel awful for frightening her, but it was an honest mistake.

With shaking hands, she enters the price into the cash register but it cut off by Kellan tossing down a variety of boxes. I pick one up to see what he could be getting for himself and feel all of the blood rush to my face. Condoms.

He's buying all of the condoms they have.

"Do you need a bag, sweetheart?" The old lady asks with traces of humor in her voice.

"No, ma'am. She's going to carry everything for us," he spins me around to unzip my small bag before shoving all of the boxes and my candy into the pouch and pays the lady. I shut my visor, wishing I had kept it closed the whole time to hide from this horrifying experience.

I walk out the door before he's handed the receipt and wait on him outside. I'm going to have to get him back for doing this to me, if it's the last thing I do, I swear I'm going to pay him back. I would rather start my period on national television than go through that ever again in my life – well, maybe not on national television, but I would still rather anything else happen than to do that again. I fold my arms over my chest, watching vehicles come and go while he takes his time coming out the store.

"You jackass!" I yell across the parking lot to him. He stops to dramatically look around the parking lot, as if there is anyone else around that I could possibly be talking to. "You did that to me on purpose!"

He holds up his hands, signaling me to calm down. I point to the bike without saying another word but when he's within arms distance, he bumps our helmets together in a kiss of sorts and I melt. His charm is pretty cute, but this doesn't change the fact that I will have to pay him back for what he's just done to me. I can never come back to this place for as long as I live.

I stretch and yawn before pulling myself to sit up in the bed to wipe the sleep from my eyes. I regret staying up so late, but between the conversation and the movies we put on back-to-back, it was hard to resist. I don't know what time we finally passed out, but if I had to guess, it wasn't that long ago. It's too bad Kellan is used to rising so early because I could go back to sleep right now if he'd let me.

I peek into the bathroom, seeing his silhouette in the frosted glass of the shower and decide to get in with him. He didn't so much as make a move in my direction last night, something that surprised me but I figured he thought I was still mad at him. I wasn't, but maybe I should have told him that.

I reach up to touch his hair, scrubbing the suds around with my fingertips until he turns to peek at me. A wide smile spreads across his face, and I'm suddenly face-to-face with an entire frontal, naked view of him. I don't think I will ever get over the sight of so many tattoos on a person, or the way that he's built.

"I figured you would sleep a little longer," he says once the water has run out of his face.

"I tried," I tell him while watching him scrub himself with a body brush. I'm mesmerized by his every movement, too locked into him to see it coming until it's too late and I'm pressed against the shower wall. The water is hot as it rains down the side of my body, but not as hot as his body that's pressed against me. I gasp at the sudden movement, surprised that he moved us against the wall so quickly.

"You trying to be late for work this morning?" He jokes, but now I'm considering it.

"Maybe," I admit.

"Be careful, Angel. Just because I said I want to get to know you, doesn't mean I won't bend you over every surface of this house while I do it."

I swear if the shower wasn't already so hot, I would be as red as a beet at his words. He releases me and steps out the shower, letting me have it all to myself but I feel a little rejected. Why go through all the trouble yesterday to buy condoms and force me to carry them to not put them to use at least once? What's his play here?

I wash my hair and body, scrubbing myself with the harsh sponge until I feel like my skin will fall off before drying off. I wrap my hair up onto my head and stand in the doorway, suddenly hit with the fact that I have no clothes here. Shit.

I dash to the bathroom, rummaging through the hamper I just put everything in a few seconds ago and only find my leggings from last night. There's no way the man purposely took my panties and shirt to be washed that quick but left everything else in this basket. I slip my legs into the fabric and run to the closet for one of his shirts. Where the hell did he go so quick? I shove hangers left and right, trying to find something that doesn't look like it will fit me like a dress and give up. I grab one of the white graphic tee's and throw it on, not caring about the image plastered on the back but more focused on the way it hangs down above my knees. I do, in fact, have dresses shorter than this but I have no other choice right now.

I toss the towel into the hamper and dry my hair quickly before heading out, wondering where Kellan could have disappeared. I find him walking around aimlessly in the den, cell phone to his ear while someone continues to babble on the other end of the line. His eyebrows shoot up to his hairline when I come around the corner before giving me a thumbs up and a half grin. I roll my eyes at his reaction and walk away to find my bag, needing a hairbrush and some kind of makeup on my face before we leave for the day.

Eventually, we pull up to my apartment and I run like hell to put on a change of clothes. Once I pull off the t-shirt, I see the logo on the back and freeze. The design is beautiful, but obviously not meant for me. A pin-up style woman wearing nothing but a matching Santa Clause bra and panty set stares back at me, her large, perfectly round breasts spill out of the scrap material as she holds a candy cane to her mouth.

"I was wondering why you chose that one," Kellan's voice comes from behind me, making me squeal. I didn't hear him come in the front, much less down the hallway to my room. I scoff at him, as if I willingly chose to wear such a thing knowing what was on the back of it.

"Well, it wasn't like I had many choices. My clothes magically disappeared from your hamper." I screech at him before coving my naked body with the shirt. He nods as he sits on my bed, looking away to hide his amused expression. "Do you mind?"

"Not at all," he answers but makes no attempt to leave the room. I narrow my eyes at him before tossing the shirt onto his face and dashing to my closet. His laugh is infectious, but annoying and I can't help smiling to myself as I throw on a long-sleeved body suit and a pair of jeans. I walk from the closet, gaining another 'wow' from him.

"What? What's wrong with this?" I panic and rush to the mirror to see the horror that could possibly be on my body.

"Nothing, you just aren't going to make it easy on me."

"Easy on you? What are you talking about?" I question him while staring at the reflection, trying to figure out what's wrong with my clothes.

"Yeah, Angel. You aren't playing very fair, is all. Come on, we're going to be late." He tugs me away from the mirror, turning lights off as we pass through my apartment until we stand at the door in nearly complete darkness. I fumble around, pulling on my boots and coat while he waits patiently with his hand on the door's handle.

"Okay, let's go."

For the rest of the day, I catch him stealing glances at me through the office window but he never comes in to talk to me. Even during lunch, he keeps his distance, choosing to have something delivered for all of us rather than take me somewhere alone. We eat together in the kitchen, all together as one big awkward family. Tracy seems to be in high spirits, smiling around every bite of food even after being cursed out by John when she tells a disgusting joke. I eat with wide eyes, hearing the three of them socialize for the first time, surprised that John is always in a bad mood and it isn't just me that he hates.

Eventually, it's time to go and I'm excited. I decided earlier to drive my truck for the first time today, but I'm still unsure where I'll go once I leave the shop. I drum my fingers across my desk, wondering what Kellan will say when he comes into the office to announce that it's time to leave. I watch from the door, bag already on my shoulder and keys in hand as he closes and locks everything and waves bye to Tracy.

"So, hot stuff. Where you headed?" I ask when he comes swaggering down the hallway. His half grin catches me off guard, sending my heart fluttering in my chest before he ever utters a word.

He leans into the doorframe, towering over me in the best way. "Headed home, hottie. Where you headed?"

"Home, probably but I think I could be persuaded to go somewhere else," I joke but hope he takes the bait. I'm going a little crazy from watching him walk around in the shop all day, stealing glances here and there but never touching him. Even this morning in the shower he put some distance between us, which did nothing to put out the fire that's been building in me.

"Persuaded, huh? I think I could manage that." He bites his bottom lip, trying to sell a persona that isn't really his. I laugh before poking his chest, deflating him a little. He rubs his chest, feigning an injury but I won't admit that my finger hurts from the jab.

"Come on, Angel. Let's get out of here," he says as he grabs my hand to lead me down the hall. I follow behind him, giddy and excited to be driving on my own for the first time in my life.

Once I'm in the truck, I turn it over and listen as it roars to life. The powerful engine vibrates the seat under me, and I suddenly understand how this could feel exciting to the car guys. No wonder there's a whole community full of people who enjoy these vehicles. Kellan walks to my window, motioning for me to roll it down so he can talk to me. I look down and press the switch, watching as the glass slowly sinks into the door.

I smile playfully, feeling silly and prop my arm onto the door panel. "What can I do ya for, darlin'?" I add some extra twang to my voice, forcing a horrible country accent.

He chuckles, "Well, darlin'. I need you to follow me. How much gas do you have?" He answers in a much better country accent than I have. I'm surprised but turned the fuck on. "Earth to Ava."

I pick my jaw up from the floor. "What?"

"Gas, baby. How much gas do you have?" He smiles, knowing damn well that he just caused my brain to short-circuit.

"Half a tank." I state, gaining a nod of approval.

"Put on your seatbelt." He tells me before pulling his helmet over his face and walking away.

"You put on your seatbelt," I shout to him. He turns around, marching right up to the truck door to yank it open. His helmet is off in a flash before his mouth comes down hard onto mine. I wrap my arms around him, pulling him further into the truck to kiss him back before he breaks free.

"Your smart mouth is going to get you into trouble one day."

"I hope so," I tell him. My face flushes as I realize what he means. Even in the shower this morning, my ass burned from the smack he delivered on my bare skin days before. He studies me as if he can see my thoughts as they roll through my brain. His velvety laugh is muffled by him pulling the helmet down again. I don't hesitate to pull the seatbelt over my shoulder this time, making sure I hear the faint click and pull it tight across my lap before I put the truck in gear.

I swear I could watch him mount any bike and drool. His long legs sweep over in one quick motion before he stands it upright and launches in front of me. My insides clench when he turns around to see me still sitting in the back of the lot. Oh yeah, driving. I need to be driving.

The drive to his house is shorter than I remember, probably because I've been daydreaming through most of it, even though I should be paying attention to the road. For my first time driving alone, I think I did pretty good, no one even honked at me when I forgot to signal to change lanes. Kellan showed off once we were past the gate at the front of the neighborhood, popping his front tire off the ground several times and looking back at me every chance he got. I shook my head every time, afraid that he would fall and I'd run him over by accident.

Every time he turned around, my insides fluttered. Two and a half weeks ago, I was so depressed I could barely eat; this week, I'm silently suffering in pain from smiling too much. A seed of doubt plants itself inside me right then as I wonder if I'm falling in love with happiness or simply falling for a man who treats me better than the last. The thought is sobering. It can't be true, though. I've been happy before. Before Sebastian ruined everything, I was living with no care in the world, and I was free. I push all those thoughts aside, refusing to compare my past to the new person I am now. I wanted a fresh start, and now I have one.

I follow Kellan around the back of the house, parking where he signals before turning the truck off and sitting in silence for a moment, but my mind still wanders to the forbidden topic. There's no way I could be falling in love with someone that I hardly know. This could be just a temporary chapter of my life, but why does that hurt so bad to think of Kellan as temporary?

He waves at me through the windshield and does a thumbs-up. I nod, signaling back to him that I'm okay. For a fleeting second, I wonder what I would be doing right now if I had never run to him and nearly vomit at the thought of sharing a bed with Sebastian ever again.

I watch as Kellan rolls his motorcycle into the open garage door. He stands up tall, then flexes his arms like in a cartoon, casting a large shadow on the wall in front of us. I turn the truck lights off and whistle as I exit, screaming for an encore. He runs up to me, sweeping me off my feet before carrying me under the breezeway into the house. My heart thuds hard in my chest. I don't think it's the happiness that I'm falling for.

As Ava showers and washes away the memories of last night, I check my phone, reading through all the texts I received yesterday that she didn't open. I smirk, realizing she has my phone more than I do but still doesn't bother opening anything that doesn't have to do with the shop. I appreciate the boundary she's put in place, but I wish she would cross it. I need her to see that I don't have anything to hide, but I guess it will all come with time.

Thomas finally responded. It took him long enough, considering I helped patch up his neighbor's house. I don't give a shit how old he says she is; something was going on there between the two of them and I'm not sure how to feel about it. A blind man could have seen the chemistry they shared from a town over.

Maybe I'm reading too far into the situation, but I guarantee they will be together soon. I just hope like hell he's staying far away from her until she's legal. I forward Ava the list of shit the guy has text me. It's all toys and brands of things that I don't understand. What the fuck is a bubble guppy? Cartoons these days have gone downhill, but he ain't my responsibility so I really shouldn't care so much. I just really need someone to bring back Ren and Stimpy, or something equally fucked up so the new generation can know what real entertainment is.

There's one message that I can't bring myself to respond to, no matter how many times I read it:

Jackson is being released today.

I sit and stare at the words on the screen, not sure on how to process the news but I feel cheated in a way. Jackson may be older than me, but why do I feel like the one to clean up the family mess? I had to build up my reputation after my father tarnished our name with his bullshit, and my brother's decisions didn't help the situation either. I think back to all the money I've lost to the debt collectors over the past and grimace. There's no way I can go through that with Jackson, and we both know he is exactly like our father.

I don't hear Ava come down the stairs, but when she sits beside me, some of my anger fades. "I left my bag in the Chevelle a few days ago," her voice sings to me. I look down at what she's wearing, smiling at my sweats hanging from her hips. The ends are rolled several times to keep them from dragging on the floor but I don't recognize the maroon sweatshirt with a local college logo printed across the front.

She's so fucking beautiful, even in clothes too big for her and dressed for bed. My heart squeezes in my chest, and I realize this is the feeling that men went to war for centuries ago. I push my plate of food towards her, no longer interested in eating but I know she's hungry. I watch her dig into the omelet and bacon, happy to see her eating more than a kid's meal for once.

She stares back at me, searching my face. "What's wrong?"

"How do you know something is wrong?" I ask, surprised that she's able to read me. I thought I was hiding it better than that.

"Because you've got this going on," she places a finger between my eyebrows. "And this, too." Her fingers trace my cheek, poking at my clenched jaw.

A tight smile stretches across my face. I guess I'm not hiding it as well as I thought. "Jackson is getting released today."

"Who's Jackson?" She asks innocently as she finishes off the bacon.

"My brother." I tell her.

"And you're mad that he's coming home?" She questions.

"Duncan said he would be released in a couple of weeks. I feel like Jackson lied to our uncle about his release date. That's bothering me, but there's more to it. Some problems were never resolved before he went to prison. It's just not what I want to deal with right now."

She squeezes my hand, and I can't help but lace my fingers between hers. Our skin is so different; hers is soft, delicate silk, while mine has been hardened over the years. The grease has permanently stained my fingers, making the scars from years of busting my knuckles look worse than they truly are. "Let's go to work," she whispers.

Forty-Five
Ava
Two months later

Kellan drives us to the shop in my truck, beating most of the morning traffic as usual. I'm still not used to waking up this early, but apparently, this is the latest he tries to come in. Even running "late," we still beat John and Tracy by over an hour. I grab my bag from Kellan's car and go inside to change in his so-called bedroom. I feel like I'm going backwards, but I refuse to sit in sweatpants all day and not be on a couch or at least lounging around at home. Kellan is waiting for me in the office when I walk in, phone in hand, as he sits at the computer. I lean against the doorframe, watching as he struggles to type with one finger while holding his phone to his ear.

He pats his leg, pushing away from the desk to make room for me. "Hold on just a second," he says into the phone, then points for me to type. "A 2007 Harley, FXST. Yeah." I type quickly, filling out the information sheet as he repeats it to me. "Yeah, chain cam tensioner. Just bring it in today or tomorrow, so I can make sure, and we should have it out by Friday next week. Okay, see you, brother."

He ends the call and exhales before throwing the phone down on the desk. "This is for Mark Ellis."

"Mark Ellis. That sounds familiar. How do I know that name?"

"He's related to the Mayor."

"Oh, very nice. I didn't know anyone in that family rides." I try to picture the mayor riding a Harley through town. It's comical, really.

"Yeah, they don't really broadcast it, but our families have a long history," he looks at the screen, then back at me with surprise. "How'd you know that's a Softail?"

I shrug, "I've been studying some stuff, and we got one out there already."

He stares at me, confused. "Studying?"

"Yeah. If I'm going to be doing this, I need to know what everything is." I look at him over my shoulder, his face inches from mine. "Other than just doing the paperwork, I mean."

His half grin sends my heart racing, but I can't tell if he's amused or impressed. "Which one do you like the most?" He asks, staring at my lips.

"I think I like the Yamaha, the one that needs some kind of sensor replaced," I rack my brain to remember what it's called, but I can't think straight when he's putting me on the spot like this.

"The Mt-07?"

"Yes, that one." I say, the light bulb finally flickering to light in my mind. "I like the color of it too," I blush. The office door creaks open behind us as Tracy comes storming in, rolling her eyes at the sight of us sitting in the office chair together.

"Morning," Kellan says without looking in her direction.

"Hey, Kelso. Morning, Aves," she grabs a set of keys from the board and walks out without another word.

"She doesn't like me very much," I say.

"Tracy is as soft as an S.O.S. pad, but she likes you. She even said good morning; most of the time, she ignores me and John. I'd say she more than likes you."

"You say that, but I swear a few days ago she was a second away from punching me in the face." My eyes go wide. I shouldn't have said that to him; I don't want her to get into trouble.

He laughs, "Oh yeah? Well, physical violence is kind of her thing, I'd say she's your best friend now."

"If best friends punch each other, I have some catching up to do with Amber. If Tracy thinks we are friends, I should probably apologize to her for being a bitch." I look down at my thumbnail, eyeing that piece of skin that always grows out to bother me.

"From the way Tracy tells it, that was the highlight of her day. I think you should come out here and sit on the Mt-07. See how you feel on it since you like it so much," he says while his fingers creep up the back of my shirt. My skin reacts to his touch, sending a shiver down my spine. I can't see myself riding a motorcycle on my own, but I'd love to tease him with the vision.

The office door creaks open again. "Is this a bad time?" An unfamiliar voice questions us. Kellan's hand freezes on my back before he slowly turns us around. The man standing in the doorway is terrifying. Every bit as tall as Kellan, but somehow wider. His head is shaved, showing off tattoos on his scalp and more covering every inch of his body that I can see. He's wearing one of the shop's work shirts with the sleeves cut off, half tucked in the front of a pair of dark, ripped jeans. His black boots are unlaced and heavily worn.

"As a matter of fact, it is." Kellan's voice is low, taking on a dangerous tone that I've never heard before.

"This some kind of kinky business shit?" He looks me up and down, the sight of him drinking me in so disgustingly sends me into fight or flight mode. Kellan jumps to his feet, pushing me behind him before crossing the room in lightning speed to grab the guy and push him out the office door. I watch the two of them shove at each other as they walk out the bay door together. A sinking feeling in my gut has me feeling nauseous. I'm absolutely positive that's Jackson.

I chew on my nail as I finish the form Kellan was working on, finding the contact information from his call log, then hit print. Just as I add the form to the bottom of the board, Kellan comes walking back in with a bloody nose. I bolt out of the office, racing to him. Jackson is standing near the road, holding his side as he leans against the stop sign.

"Are you okay?"

He smiles at my question, waving me off as he walks down the hall.

"Just leave him be," Tracy's voice comes up behind me. I turn to face her, staring at the skinny, muscular woman with purple hair and facial piercings. She's really quite beautiful when she isn't scowling at me; for the first time, I look at her in a new light. "I'm just saying, when I fight with my sister like that, I wanna be left alone."

"Oh." I wouldn't know what it's like to have fights with my family that result in hurting each other physically. They are more the type to spin false stories and turn everyone against you.

"Know what I mean?" She asks, meeting my stare. I shake my head. "Alright, well. I'm done with the Ducati, here's my ticket, and I put the time on there. I'll go grab something else."

"Thanks," I take the slip from her hand, noticing the grease under her manicured nails. "You get your nails done?"

She glances at her hand, "Yeah, I don't have them done very often, but I did a photoshoot last weekend and wanted to look nice."

"What kind of photoshoot?" I wonder aloud.

She smirks at me before answering, "Not the kind you wanna see." I watch as she walks into the office before I go find Kellan.

Forty-Six

Kellan

I had to get Jackson out of here; it was stupid of him to show up anyway. I told Duncan weeks ago that I didn't want anything to do with him anymore, but they just won't listen. Nobody ever fucking listens. The bedroom door creaks open as Ava steps in and quietly closes it behind her. She looks every bit an angel in her white long-sleeved shirt and puffy vest, walking through my life and fixing everything that has ever been broken.

"I'm sorry," I tell her.

"What for?" Her eyebrows knit together in the center.

She inches closer before standing between my legs and wrapping her arms around my neck. I sink into her, accepting her affection as I bury my face into her jacket. She smells amazing, like florals and mint. "All of it," I say into her.

My life is a shit show. My brother has been in prison for running a meth lab, my father left this place to me with hundreds of thousands of dollars in debt. What do I have to offer her? All I've ever done is work hard my whole life to fix everyone's mistakes. I have nothing to show for any of it.

"You don't have anything to apologize for, Kellan." Her fingers lace through my hair, nails scratching across my scalp. That shit feels amazing. "Come on, we have work to do."

She tries to pull away, but I grab her thighs, pulling her into me. "Five more minutes."

After coaxing him from his cave, Kellan goes back to work, leaving me alone in the office to order parts from local part houses. Eventually, deliveries come in, filling the office with boxes and packages of every size imaginable. Tracy and John pick through everything, taking what they need before leaving; everything that's left has Kellan's name on it. I stand to look for him out the window, finding him in the corner mounting tires. I bang on the window to get his attention, holding up a plastic envelope. He nods, mouthing something that looks like 'open it'.

"There's a lot," I say to the glass. He nods, 'they're for you'. I look around the room, counting seven packages before tearing into them. I start with the biggest one, pulling out a heavy black drawstring bag. What the hell? Thankfully, the strings are loosely knotted and untie easily, revealing a black helmet with white wings painted on the side. I pull it over my head, surprised by how comfortable it is.

I rip through the other packages, finding some kind of cloth bag that is supposed to attach to the helmet to keep my hair from being tangled in the wind, a leather jacket, a pair of ankle boots, and several t-shirts from the same art company that he let me wear out of his house the other day. I look at the designs of the shirts, thankful that none of these have naked women on the back. I stack everything neatly on the desk before opening the other two. Kellan knocks on the window, surprising me. His mischievous grin has me hesitant to open the black and red package in my hand.

Something about the way he stands there, watching me with a glint in his eye warns me that something not so nice could be in this piece of mail. "What is this?" I ask through the glass.

He shrugs, "Open it and find out." I pull the tab and spill the contents onto the desk.

"It's just a black box," I flip it around, reading the cursive writing. My face heats. I definitely shouldn't open this here. My wide eyes find Kellan's. He's still standing at the window, still smiling as he watches with excitement before mouthing, "That's for me."

I shove the box under my stack of clothes, hiding it from the world before picking up the last package and shoving it inside the helmet. I can tell from the color of the plastic that it's from the same company, and I don't feel like answering questions from my co-workers if they were to see it.

I shake my head at him, but instead of shame, I feel confident. Whatever is in those packages, he bought intentionally and with me in mind. He laughs at my reaction before walking away, a little more pep in his step than earlier.

The rest of the day goes by in a blur. I'm starting to think Tracy and John are competing to see who can do the most work the fastest; when one comes in, the other isn't far behind them. I struggle to keep up with what they are working on and when. Now I see why the system they have works so well, even if it is old school.

I stack up their work, impressed by what they have done in a week's time, but I still have no idea what to do with any of it. I turn off the light to leave for the day, grab Kellan's phone from the desk, and set out to find him.

He comes around the corner, drying his hands. "What do you want for dinner?" I stop short to keep from bumping into his hard chest.

"Um, I don't know. What do you want for dinner?" I've never tried my hand at cooking, but some of the influencers I follow create some stuff that looks like it should be served in five-star restaurants, but that's not to experiment with tonight.

"Steak." He responds quickly.

I smile up at him, "If you already knew what you wanted, then why did you ask?"

"To see if what you wanted went well with steak." I roll my eyes at his answer.

"Steak sounds great." He grabs my hand, leading me to the truck.

"There was a new keychain in one of those packages. Did you get it?" He looks over at me as he starts my truck.

"No, but I have everything right here." I begin sifting through my new clothes, but I never saw a keychain. He hops out of the truck, quickly walking back into the shop while I keep sorting through everything. The black box peeks out at me from under the stack of shirts. I scan the parking lot, making sure no one is around, and open the end of the box.

Black tissue paper slips out, wrapped around pieces of silk and something hard. I pick up the silk, pulling it free and it slips free from itself. To my surprise, it's a very nice, if not provocative, nightgown. The lace trim is soft and delicate around the bottom and plunging neckline.

I hum in appreciation before folding it and setting it on top of everything on the floor. Picking up the metal pieces that have collected in my lap, I turn the pieces around in my hand. Two clasps connect to each other by a set of long, dainty chains, several more hanging down to give the set some weight.

"What the hell are these?" I mumble to myself.

The truck door is yanked open, startling me. I turn to see Kellan smiling at me sweetly before noticing what I'm holding. I try to set them down quickly, but I'm too late. His eyes darken as he watches me wrap them in the tissue paper and stuff them into my purse.

I clear my throat, embarrassed by whatever it was that I just held in my hands. Obviously, it's something for him, but my God. Why send something for pleasure to the shop for me to open in front of everyone? "Did you find it?" I ask, trying to change the subject.

"I did." He turns the truck off to take the key from the ignition and rips the package open, threading a small, silver ring to the one already on my single key.

I lean over, spinning the black leather strip around in my head to read it. "What's it say?"

"What's your favorite scary movie?" his low voice imitates the slasher film we both fell asleep to just a few nights ago. My face heats, remembering the time in the theatre. Oh dear Lord.

He pulls the strap through my fingers, starting the truck and pulling us into traffic with ease. As we sit at the stop sign, two women standing across the street stare straight at us, their clothes disheveled and their hair greasy. I stare back at them, wondering if they need help, until one of them points her finger at me, pretending to hold a gun as she pulls the imaginary trigger. I reach over to tap Kellan on the shoulder as he launches us around the corner.

"Did you see those people?" I ask him, turning to see if they are still there.

"No, what were they doing?" He looks in the mirror, confirming there is no one standing on the sidewalk.

"I don't know." I sit back, confused, and question if I'm seeing things. I swear I saw them. My phone vibrates from somewhere in my purse; to my surprise, it's Amber.

Miss you, bitch.
Wish you were here!

I react to her text before an image comes through. She's standing on a balcony with her brother, Tokyo in the background. I tug on Kellan's arm, "Will you take a picture with me?"

"Right now?" he asks while merging lanes.

I look up, seeing the next light change to red, and open my camera. "Yes, hurry!" Changing the settings to rapid burst, I lean over and smile. My phone takes a million photos in a matter of seconds before I click it again, taking several more. I lean up to kiss him on the cheek, pressing the camera icon again. He turns to kiss me when I take one more burst of photos, capturing his affection before the light changes to green and we shoot off again.

I sit back to look at them all, smiling at my screen when I see us staring back at me. Our eyes shine bright, cheeks slightly flushed from the heat filling the truck. I choose my favorite pictures and send them to Amber.

I miss you whore!

Oh my god
Is that the guy you've been seeing?

Yes

You didn't tell me he's hot

I laugh as one emoji after another comes rolling in. A fireball, a face with its tongue sticking out while pouring sweat, then several mouths. Yeah, my man is a walking sex idol and I'm not afraid to admit it.

"Amber says you're hot," I tell him.

"Tell her thanks, but I'm taken," he says, squeezing my leg as we turn into the grocery store's parking lot.

It's finally Friday, which means today I have to do payroll. Kellan has shown me how the system works and gave me a list of percentages that Tracy and John get from each repair they did the previous week. It didn't look very difficult before, but this is the first time I'm doing it alone. Once it's done, I look closely at the numbers and rework it again. The amounts come out the same both times, leaving me blinking in surprise. I run the monthly report just like he has shown me for the past several weeks, wondering how he could afford to pay them so well, then switch to the weekly total. I stare at the screen, amazed at the work and money they have made in such a small amount of time.

Kellan is definitely better off than I would have thought. Even if he put half of this money back into his business, he still takes home more than I thought he would. I hit sign, accept, and print on everyone's accounts, then seal them in the pink, tamper-proof envelopes, writing their names across the front.

Tracy storms through the door, all five feet, four inches of her looking every bit as terrifying as the day I met her. I can't help but smile at her now that I understand that violent rage is just who she is.

"Big plans this weekend?" She says as she stares at the envelope with her name on it. I didn't think the pink color would effect the way they accepted their money, but now that I see her reaction, I internally panic at the thought of John seeing it.

"No, I haven't thought that far ahead. What are you going to do?" I ask her.

"I'm going to sit around my apartment in my underwear playing video games and eating pizza rolls until I have to come back here."

"Well, that sounds fun." Besides the football videogame I often saw Amber's brother playing, I'm completely out of touch when it comes to gaming, but I feel like I should keep the conversation going. "What do you play?"

"Have you ever built a swimming pool, then spawned a bunch of people in it, and removed the ladder to watch them all drown until they die?" Her mouth crooks up on one corner as I stare in horror at her.

"No. I haven't." Is this a joke?

"What about working in a morgue and you have to do autopsies on bodies while a demon messes with your head?"

"Are you fucking with me right now?" I question the shit that's coming from her mouth right now. There's no way these are real games. Loud laughter explodes from her at my question.

"Bro, Kellan said you like horror movies, but you mean to tell me you've never played that?"

"No, I didn't know a game like that existed," I tell her, but my curiosity piqued now.

"I'm going to stream it for you tonight, then. Give me your phone," she demands.

I unlock it and hand it over. She scrunches her nose up at my new background, Kellan and I kissing in black and white. "Ew, gross," she playfully says before scrolling and typing her heart out. "I followed all my accounts on your socials. I usually start around nine. You better watch me play this shit, cause it absolutely scares the shit out of me, and I hate it."

"Then why play it?" I ask her, confused.

"Because weirdos online like to hear me scream, duh." She walks out, once again leaving me full of questions.

I unlock my phone, opening the last app to find her page. Scrolling through her uploads, she seems normal, until I see what type of photoshoot she hinted at before. Tracy stands there, smiling at me through my screen, completely topless. I gasp at the picture, then scroll to the next one. She straddles a black and pink toolbox, holding an enormous wrench across her bare chest to cover herself. I slide to the next post; a 5-second video auto-plays. Those pretty, pink nails from earlier this week come into the frame, slowly stroking that same wrench before it fades to black, replaced by a link to the rest of the video.

I exit the app, feeling guilty for seeing so much of her without her knowledge. "Holy shit." Is Tracy a porn star? Standing, I look out the window to see her walking towards the parking lot as a car with a silver spoiler pulls up to the bay door. She unfastens two metal latches at the front as Kellan gets out of the driver's seat, all smiles from the test drive. I can't tell what he is saying to her, but he points under the hood with a serious look on his face. She nods before waving him off.

For a second my heart begins to break, but she slowly turns and I can tell by her face she's annoyed with him. I watch the two of them argue, remembering the way he said that violence is her love language. But how would you differentiate affection from real arguments with her? Does Kellan know about the pictures she has online?

He turns to walk away from her, waving his hands to the side angrily, then spins around. They both yell over each other before he slams the hood and gets in the car to pull it forward. I sit down quickly as she comes storming back into the office.

"Ava, I've got a Nissan Skyline in bay one. I need you to call around and see if you can get parts. The chick's last name is Cranford. I got everything you need on here," she hands me a piece of paper before walking out, that hard mask falling back into place when John and Kellan turn the corner to face her.

Kellan outright ignores her as they keep walking, but I John has hearts in his eyes when they pass by one another. Longing and regret fill his face when she doesn't even so much as look at him. I can tell he has tuned Kellan out, looking over his shoulder to stare at Tracy's figure before grabbing a cart to follow Kellan. Does John know about her photos online?

If it's a secret, it isn't mine to tell, but I'd still like to know if Kellan has seen one of his employees naked, especially if we all have to work together.

Once it's time to leave, I've chewed my fingers raw; I've been so worried about so many things lately and my poor nails wont last much longer if I don't settle down soon. I've gone back to look at all of her social media accounts and am amazed by the number of followers she has across all her platforms. It will be a miracle if neither Kellam or John have seen her posts.

I zone out to a spot on the wall and let my mind race. I don't know how long I sit like that, but when Kellan's face comes into view, I startle. His eyebrows raise, questioning my reaction. "I'm sorry, I didn't hear you. What's going on?"

He chuckles, "I said, where do you want to stay tonight?"

"Oh. Um, it doesn't matter. I mean, I've stayed with you a lot week. If you want to stay here or go home alone, I understand." I ramble, my mind still wondering how much of Tracy he has seen.

He sits on the desk in front of me, "Yeah, I've been thinking about that, too. We've spent a lot of time at the house the past few weeks."

"I don't even remember what my apartment looks like anymore," I tease.

"Is that a bad thing?" He asks, fidgeting with my pens.

I pretend to think, "No, not really but I don't want you to get tired of me."

His eyes twinkle, "Where's your stuff?"

"What stuff?" I ask.

He leans in close, putting his weight on the arms of my chair, "Where's your new stuff?"

Blood rushes to my cheeks as I realize what he's asking me. I still haven't opened the other black box of mysterious treasure. "On your dresser at home."

He nods, "Home it is then." Butterflies flutter to life in my stomach, the idea of the unknown sending my heart racing. What could he have planned?

Forty-Nine

Ava

I follow behind Kellan through the neighborhood until his property comes into view. The overgrown trees welcome me with open arms as I turn my rumbling truck into the driveway. The setting sun in the distance gleams off the glossy black paint. I understand why Kellan's mother wouldn't want to live here, given the history, but there's something magical about the place that I love entirely.

I park and wait for Kellan to roll into the garage. The sounds of silence and an owl screeching echo around us now that we are away from the busy streets in town. I get out to stand in the driveway, listening to the sound of jingling approaching from around the truck. Spinning around, I don't see anyone, but something snags the leg of my jeans. I let out a squeal, expecting to look down to find some dismembered skeleton trying to pull me to the depths of hell.

Looking up at me are small, black eyes framed in the most adorable furry face. Oh. My. God. I sit, feeling the cold concrete bite into me through my jeans. "Where did you come from, cutie pie?" I croon, scratching the puppy behind both ears. Kellan comes around the corner, nearly stepping on both of us.

He jumps back, surprised. "Where'd you get a dog?" He asks, slowly kneeling down to look at it.

"I thought it was your dog," I look up at him, puzzled.

Shaking his head, he chuckles. "No, Angel. When would I have gotten the time to get a dog since we left this morning?" He spins the tiny collar around to read the tag. "There's a phone number on here."

My heart drops. Of course, puppies like this don't just appear from nowhere. I pick up the sweet baby, bringing it to my chest and melt as it snuggles into me. She whimpers and grunts as she tries to burrow into my jacket for warmth. Kellan pulls out his phone to dial the number and I hope like hell that no one answers. It rings once before a woman's voice picks up, sounding breathless. "Hello?"

"Hello, this is Kellan Smith. We just found a puppy down here off-" his words are cut off.

"They found her!" She screams at someone. "Oh goodness, thank you! Thank you so much! We've been looking for her for a couple of hours now. We live off Heritage Trail. Are you close by?"

Kellan's eyebrows furrow, "I'm about two miles west of Heritage Trail, but I can be there in a few minutes."

"Okay, we've got a white SUV parked off the street in front of the house. I'll meet you out front." The woman sounds relieved, but my heart is shattered. I stroke the soft, fluffy hair on the puppy's head as she softly snorts into the collar of my jacket. At least she is going home. We get in the truck together, making the short drive into the neighborhood quickly. A woman stands in the front yard of a large house, walking a large golden retriever on a leash while she waits for us. Kellan turns to me, "Alright, go give the mama bear her cub."

I shake my head. I don't want to let her go. "Do you need me to do it, Angel?" He asks me softly. I nod in response. The poor baby has been wandering around alone all this time and felt safe enough to fall into a deep sleep on me. I can't be the one to wake her. He leans over, gently lifting her off me. She lets out a grunt, complaining about being moved, and lets out the sweetest howl a puppy could make.

The mama dog comes running up to the truck as Kellan opens the door, aggressively sniffing the air in search of her baby. "Alright, alright." He says to the dog, pushing her off him before kneeling to let her smell him.

"Well, that's the last of seven to go," The woman says as she tugs the leash to reel the dog back in.

Kellan's head snaps up in shock. "There are seven more missing?"

The woman laughs, "No, seven more needing homes. This one sounds pretty content staying with you." I stare wide-eyed at Kellan.

"We aren't, I mean. I wasn't," he stammers before setting his jaw, looking down at the puppy he has held out for the owner to accept. "I don't know anything about dogs," he says to the woman while stuffing the puppy into his jacket to keep her warm.

"I'd say you need to learn quick, cause she doesn't want to give you up, but if you want, hand her here." She looks at Kellan's chest, watching as the jacket moves, then stills completely. I hold my breath, watching him struggle to accept what's happening. The lady picks up on his hesitation and starts to walk away, "I'll go get her papers."

Kellan looks at me through the windshield in disbelief. "I thought this is how the cat distribution system works. When did this start happening with dogs?" I shrug in response. I've never had a cat or a dog before.

The woman comes back, holding a folder and a small bag. "Okay, here's some food and a little toy she stole from my son. There's a blanket in here with Mama's scent on it to help her transition. Don't wash this for a while. And this is her information, you can read over it when you get back home, but you need to fill out the bottom half right here and mail it to this address to have her registered. Both mom and dad are registered. She's eleven weeks old tomorrow, so she's had good socialization, but if you want her to stay friendly, you need to take her around as many people as possible. Especially people you want her to be comfortable around, like your family and friends. We've started house training, but you're going to have to watch her cues. Vaccination records are in here, too. Look over those and take her in when she needs the next ones. Okay, sign here." She clicks a pen and hands it over to Kellan.

He reads over it quickly, "Five hundred dollars!" I cover my mouth, suppressing my laugh.

"That's with a discount, son. I won't dare break up a family. If you don't have it, just come by later this week. You can drop it in the mailbox if we aren't home." The woman points to a mailbox by the road.

With a heavy sigh, Kellan pulls out his wallet, handing over the money, but stops to look at me. "You found her, you come claim her," I scream, jumping out of the truck so quickly I forget to close my door.

I sign my name hurriedly, "Okay, give her to me."

Kellan turns his body away from me, "No. It's my turn to hold her."

The woman giggles at the two of us as she rips the receipt paper to keep her copy, handing me the folder. "What's her name?"

"Harley," Kellan responds.

"Nova," I correct him.

We stare at each other, eyes squinting to challenge the other. He gives in immediately, "Fine. We agree I've named her Nova."

"You can't steal her name from me, you ass," I tell him. The stranger shakes her head, walking off to go inside. "Thank you!" I yell after her.

"You're welcome! And good luck!" She yells back to me, waving over her head as she continues up the driveway.

I get in the truck, flipping through the dog's information to read her vaccination history and about the breed. "She's a Golden Retriever," I clap my hands excitedly. "Let's go to the pet store," I demand.

Kellan chuckles, "Pretty sure they will be closed by the time we make it there, Angel. We can go in the morning. I can't believe we just got swindled into adopting a dog." He backs away from the house with ease, even with a puppy silently sleeping inside his jacket. Our ride back is slower, and I feel the giggles building inside me. He must feel like we have precious cargo now because I feel like I could run faster than the speed he's going.

We pull up to the garage, parking in my truck's designated spot. As if on cue, little Nova wiggles, coming to life once we kill the engine and make our way inside.

"Where is she going to sleep?" I ask, looking around the kitchen that still impresses me.

"In the laundry room," Kellan says as she sets her down on the floor. She immediately sits to let out a long, sad howl.

I stare at him, blinking several times. "She said no."

He looks at me in disbelief. "She's been here for less than five minutes, and she's already making demands. This is unbelievable. Take your shirt off and give it to her; she fell asleep on you already."

"Are you using the dog to try to get me naked?" I ask him.

"Only if it works," he responds, trying to hide his smile.

"You take your shirt off and give it to her!" I tell him excitedly.

"Fine, I will!" He fires back at me, scooping the dog up and running upstairs to the bedroom while letting out a fake evil laugh. I've never fought with someone so playfully, but if this is my new normal, I will happily accept it. I chase after them through the house, laughing as I round each corner to find them still out of reach. By the time I catch up, Kellan is already in his walk-in closet, stretching out the puppy's blanket and his shirt across the floor. Nova looks up at him, not happy with her made-up bed.

"Okay, dog whisperer, what does she want?" He asks me as he stares down at her.

I peek around him, rolling my eyes as I inspect his work. "A bed," I say bluntly before reaching to grab a pillow from the shelf above him. "Who put these fucking shelves up here?" I grunt as I stand on my toes, still too short to reach.

His soft laugh from behind me is all the answer I need. His bare chest leans over my face as he stretches above me, easily grabbing the pillow. I look him up and down, appreciating his physique and the way his jeans hang from his hips, showing off that barely visible V-cut that disappears when he leans back onto his heels.

I try to lick my lips at the sight of him, but my mouth has gone dry. The man is walking sex. He stands back, holding the pillow out for me to take, but I don't move. Instead, I look him up and down, unashamed by openly checking him out. I've caught him staring at me plenty, doing double takes and stealing glances when he thought I wasn't looking. Now it's my turn.

His inked skin ripples as he leans down to grab his shirt, causing me to nearly dance with excitement as he flexes his biceps. I know he's putting on a show for me as he stuffs the pillow into the shirt, then drops it to the floor to curl his arms up above his head. He did the same moves a few days ago when we were outside, something he must think is funny or just purposely showing off his arms.

I laugh loudly when he turns to the side and grins, giving his best macho man pose. "Okay, muscle man. Are you done showing off?" I ask him, poking his chest to deflate it.

"Not if you're still enjoying it," he responds. His tattooed chest inches closer to me as he backs me up to the wall. I glance up, watching as he props his weight onto his arm to stare down at me.

Oh, he's a devil. A sexy, muscular devil that can make all my wicked dreams come true. I grab onto his sides, feeling his body shiver under my cold touch. My hands move over his stomach before traveling up his chest, appreciating every dip and curve. His breathing changes as my hands take on a mind of their own, slowly sinking lower until I'm prying at the button on his jeans. Once they hang loosely from his hips, I slip my hands into the waistband and grab his ass, smiling up at him as I squeeze.

His answering smile fuels me, but I doubt he will let me take charge for much longer. I remember how he paid me back for going down on him in the theatre when I decided to blow him while I had the chance and swallow. I liked the way his mouth moved between my legs in the front seat of his car that night, more carnal than the time at the shop. I think I want to feel that again.

I sink to my knees slowly, bringing his jeans to the floor with me until they wrap around his ankles and pause to let him think about what I'm about to do. He kicks off his jeans quickly before pushing them to the side, giving me the green light to do what I want. Nova hurries over to heap of denim, curling up and falling asleep in seconds. I sigh, glad that she's occupied so I can finally have what I want.

I lick my lips as I situate myself onto my knees, readying my mouth to give the best blowjob of my life. Or will it be Kellan's life?

A giggle escapes me as I consider the right word phrase. I let out a breath, remembering how messy this became last time I did it, but he didn't seem to mind. In fact, it looked like he enjoyed it more the filthier it was.

"Angel, if I didn't know any better, I'd feel like you were laughing at me." His voice is low and dangerous, sending a chill up my spine.

"I guess it's a good thing that you know better, then," I respond before pulling his boxers down in the front and taking him in my hands.

He pushes a breath through his clenched teeth before speaking again, "Do I?"

"You do," I tell him. My voice surprises me, I don't recognize the throaty tone I'm using.

I stroke him several times, watching as a drop of pre-cum gathers on his tip. I look up to meet his gaze and hold his eyes as I lean forward to lick his thick head, cleaning that small drop. His lips part to release a shaky breath and I take that moment in, loving the way I make this giant of a man so weak with a single swipe of my tongue.

The thought of him falling apart for me kicks me into gear. I stroke his length with my hand while pressing him further into my mouth and I groan as I taste him. My appreciation earns me praise as he mumbles and props his weight onto both of his elbows against the wall.

Holy shit. Why is that so attractive? I lean away, swirling my tongue around the end of him before stuffing my mouth as full as I can, then force my muscles to remain loose as I slowly push and pull him by the hips while setting a torturous pace for us both. When I can't take any more, I push him to my lips and take a deep breath to steady myself.

Before I can go any further, he leans down to grab my wrists and hauls me to my feet in an instant. I shuffle to keep from tripping as he steers me backwards to the bed in the center of the room. I knew he wouldn't let me be in control much longer but I have to try. To hold him off, I reach between us again to grab onto him. His cock slides through my hand easily, still slick with my spit.

A groan escapes him as I continue stroking and he faulters. The man in front of me isn't used to being disarmed, not used to the idea of someone else calling the shots; but it's my turn. I stand, adjusting my hand to keep holding onto him, but he shakes his head at me, staring with heavy lids. His shoulders sag as pleasure washes over him when I quicken my pace. He huffs out a breath before pushing me onto the bed, quickly pulling my boots from my feet and throwing them over his shoulder in different directions.

For a moment, I wonder if I should resist him. Should I make undressing me difficult to get under his skin and drag this out? I want to keep up the playful mood he has put me in but I'm not sure if he would appreciate it right now. Looking into his eyes sends a wave of longing through me; I won't be able to prolong this no matter how much I try. I crave his touch too much to make either of us wait much longer.

I unbutton my jeans and begin kicking them off as he rips my panties down my legs. In the blink of an eye, I'm completely naked from the waist down and panting as I watch him hover above me. He inhales sharply at the sight of me, then pushes my shirt up to see my black, shiny bra.

I look around, searching for my matching underwear. When I don't find them anywhere, I stare up at him in disbelief. Another pair gone just like that. Where is he putting them all? I grin, knowing what he's up to, but why did it take me this long to see it? I should start taking his boxers in return until both of us are out of things to wear.

I prop myself onto my elbows and watch as he sinks between my legs, his broad shoulders forcing them open as he positions himself between my thighs. My head tilts back as I accept the pleasure his mouth has to offer, reveling in the way his tongue swirls left to right.

My eyes roll as he claims me once again with his mouth, sucking gently while teasing me with kisses. Eventually, he dives in, eating me as if he's been starved, swirling his tongue before swiping up and down inside me until I buck from the overwhelming sensation.

He laps at my core, cleaning up the mess I've made before planting sloppy kisses on the inside of both of my thighs. I release a sigh, still on cloud nine from the orgasm that has wrapped around me but refuses to fully release. I feel the bed shift under me as I'm pulled towards the end of the mattress by my legs. A smug smile spreading across my face when I hear the familiar sound of a wrapper being ripped open.

Once my ass is nearly hanging off the bed, his thick cock slaps against my pussy's opening, pulling a gasp from me. The sound of him splattering against my wetness rings out around us, echoing off the walls of the room. I open my eyes too look at him, surprised by the hard expression on his face that transforms into pleasure as he slowly sinks inside of me.

My toes curl as I take his length and watch as his eyes close to soak in the feel of me. I try to keep quiet, huffing my breaths instead of moaning into the air to keep from waking Nova but once he bottoms out, I lose control. My groans and whimpers take over me until I cover my own mouth to muffle the sounds.

He looks up to the ceiling when he reaches the end of me, waiting until I've adjusted and accepted him before moving again. Barely, just barely his hips flex, promising to take me to where I want to be but keeping it from me just the same.

"You've teased me too much tonight, Angel." His voice is low, and gravely as he leans over while hiking up my leg. My mind swims in pleasure, too cloudy to understand what he is saying. When he slides out of me, I open my eyes, feeling too empty. Is he going to keep me from enjoying this?

He leans across the bed to guide my arms through the holes in my shirt, then brings the collar up to cover my eyes. He gently lifts my head to lay the long sleeves under my head before positioning me back into place. The sleeves are pulled tight on each side of my head, securing the fabric to prevent it from shifting out of place. I gasp at the sensation as my other senses try to make up for my sudden loss of vision.

His fingertips trail up my side, raising my skin as he lightly brushes across the spots that tickle the most until he reaches my bra. The fabric is pushed out of the way and suddenly, I'm revealing everything to him. He swipes across my nipples with his thumbs before squeezing and releasing me, letting me lay bare on the bed and offer my body to him. I swallow, imagining the look on his face as he touches me; imagining the way he watches as my tits bounce from being released from his hand so quickly.

I strain my ears, wondering where he's going to be next before his touch surprises me. I never heard him move away from me, but his strong fingers wrap around my ankles to yank them far apart. My God. If I thought I was exposed before, I can't imagine what he sees now.

I grab onto the sheet underneath me, balling it into my palms as the suspense fills me. I've never been on display like this for anyone, and while I want to close my legs to keep some of my privacy, another part of me wants to open them farther. I want to show him everything I have and tell him exactly what to do with me. I begin to pant again, longing for him until I'm nearly breathless.

I move my knees apart and arch my back, silently wishing he would take me hard and fast. In an instant, my wish is granted. His thick cock presses into me so suddenly, I see stars, but he doesn't stop. He doesn't give me time to adjust to his size like he did earlier. I whimper as he begins to pound into me, turning my head to bite the blanket that has bunched up around my head and finally release the moans that were building in my chest.

His hands grip my thighs harshly to hold onto me as I bounce off of him from the force of our bodies colliding, but I love it. I feel like there is a place inside of me that he has discovered and only he can reach it. Good God, the man can take me to places I've never been before. Places that border on too much yet not enough, and I don't mind. I want to be here with him in this moment as he thrusts into me so hard that my legs shake.

Eventually, he pulls the shirt from my eyes, and I blink up at him, suddenly blinded from the lights above us. I never heard him turn them on, and grimace when I realize he was watching everything. He wanted to see the way our bodies fit together with nothing holding us back. The shop was dark, the game room across the hall was dimly lit, every time we have been together the visibility had been too low for him to see. I wrap my arms around his neck, bringing him in to kiss me roughly, wishing that I could have seen the way I wrapped around him when he plunged into me. Our mouths collide and his motions slow when I slip my tongue into his mouth, tasting myself on him and groan.

"I didn't say to stop," I tell him once I break my mouth away. His eyes sparkle with something devilish before he picks me up from the bed. In an instant, I'm forced against the wall with my arms held high above my head. I knew Kellan was strong, but the sudden show of his true strength surprises me. The way he has pinned me against him so effortlessly fuels me on, threatening to take me to somewhere dark and sinister.

I wrap my legs around his waist, urging him to move. I didn't know that I liked rough sex so much until I got a little taste of it, but now I want more. His mouth comes down on mine, and I nearly explode. I'm so close to that finish line but still feel so far away. I bite down on his lip, moaning when he warns me by thrusting deeper into me.

My hips take on a mind of their own, grinding into each of his harsh thrusts until he releases my hands to hold me still. Now that my arms are free, I can't decide what to hold onto. His arm and shoulder muscles flex as he rocks me into the wall, holding my weight up each time he pulls away. My eyes roll to the back of my head as he burrows into me over and over again until I fear the wall will cave in.

I wrap my arms around his neck, feeling his heartbeat beneath his skin. My orgasm surfaces, threatening to spin out of me but there's just something keeping me from it. Something keeping me from that sweet release that I crave. I bring my hands down to his throat, squeezing from both sides until a slap to my bare ass startles me. I feel the slap in my core, vibrating down to my bones before fading completely.

"That's it," I say out loud. "Fuck, that's it." That's what I need. I wrap my hands around his neck and throat again, feeling him swallow as I begin to squeeze. He slaps my ass again, pulling a deep, animalistic groan from me. Another slap bites into me from the other side, stinging my skin while inching me closer to erupting. I squeeze harder, silently begging my body to quit holding back. He slaps my cheek again, never losing his rhythm as he pounds me into the wall. His throat bobs under the palm of my hand when I dig my nails into his skin, but I can't stop. I need us to finish, and I need the pain to get me there.

"Come on, Angel." He says through gritted teeth. His voice barely a whisper from being choked. His fingers dig into my hips so hard I know I will have bruises tomorrow but I need the pain and pleasure to mix into me until I'm thrown over the edge. He slaps the bare skin of my ass one last time, so much closer to where we're joined together; the quick sensation pulses through me until I feel it in my bones.

My head tilts back and I scream as my orgasm rips through me. I finally finish, feeling like my soul has left my body, but God, does it feel good. He slips in and out of me more easily now, slower so I can ride out my high and feel him empty himself into the thin condom he wears. He pulls out completely, letting my legs fall but continues to hold me up to keep from falling over. His thick cock presses against me, painting my stomach as it pulses and throbs against me until all that's left is us panting onto each other's shoulders.

"You always surprise me, Ava." He mumbles as he presses a kiss into my neck and moves us to the bed. I close my eyes as he lays me down on the pillow, suddenly exhausted. A soft towel swipes across my skin, cleaning up the mess we've made and I let out a sigh.

"Speaking of surprises, Tracy is into some weird shit." I tell him, wondering if he already knows.

"Tracy is a very strange person, I wouldn't put it past her to have weird hobbies and shit."

I prop myself up, more questions flooding me. "You know her, then?"

"Not really. I went to a car show and she was driving someone car and screaming at them that it was a piece of shit. The guy was pissed and threatening to fight her but she looked like she was willing to go toe-to-toe with him. She got in his face and was telling him what was wrong with it and I realizes she knew her way around an engine." He lays down beside me, obviously uncomfortable talking about her while we're laying here naked.

"And you hired her on the spot?" I ask him, wanting to know the rest of the story.

"Kind of. I was at the car show with Mike, the guy that sold me the C-10's. That's his world, always has been. He had been begging me for years to start expanding into the car world, instead of just working on bikes but I hate it. Smaller engines speak to me in a way that car's don't. I can work on them all day just like everything else but I don't want to. The drive isn't there," he shrugs.

"So, Mike told you to hire Tracy?"

"No, Mike hired Tracy that night on my behalf." He laughs and shakes his head but I stare in disbelief.

"I didn't know anything about it until the next week when she showed up asking for him and where she could drop her box. We got into it and she laid out some rules about don't talk to her, had no idea who I was and didn't care. It was a shit show but Mike laughed his ass off when I called him, now I see the numbers the cars bring in and wonder why I didn't do it sooner, but I won't ever tell him that."

"That's pretty funny," I admit as I roll off the bed, taking the sheet with me.

"It's funny now, we all look back and laugh at it. Where are you going?"

"Tracy is streaming tonight and I told her I would watch. She said it's a stream just for me but I've never seen anyone play this game before. It sounds interesting." My words trail off as he stands from the bed, completely naked with no shame and walks to the long dresser across the room. I blink several times to make sure I'm not imagining this and watch as his tattooed back and legs flex while putting on some loose-fitting black sweatpants.

He turns to face me, offering another pair that's identical to his own but I shake my head and go to his closet for one of his shirts instead. I'm too hot to wear pants right now, but when I catch him staring at my bare legs I regret my decision. I quickly run out of the room before he can grab onto me again and flop down on the green sofa in his private man cave.

"So, it's like that now?" His voice booms from down the hall.

"What do you mean?" I yell back at him, startling when he leans over me. He's much too big to be that quick and silent.

"Trading me in for a girl's night after using me for sex."

"Yes," I lie to get his reaction and regret it immediately. He reaches down to grab onto my side, sending me into a fit of giggles as I throw myself around to break his hold on me. "Stop!" I scream, surprised that he listens so well. "I'm a grown woman. What is your obsession with tickling me?"

"Yeah, you're right. You are grown," he says before pinching my nipple. My body rolls into his hand as pleasure washes through me, but there's no way I'm going to give in to his devilish ways right now, I promised Tracy I would watch her.

"Ugh, you're impossible. Turn on your stupid oversized projector so I can watch it."

He smirks at me before pulling away, grabbing a collection of controllers before handing me one to the console. "You're going to have to put in her tag, I don't know all that shit she does."

Relief washes through me as he answers the question I was too afraid to ask. If he doesn't know her name, then he doesn't know what else she has posted. He flops down on the end of the couch, pulling my feet into his lap while watching me type away. Her name comes up immediately and I'm terrified of what we may see.

I select her profile quickly, going to the live countdown before he can see any of the other videos that fill up the screen. My heart pounds in my chest when the page begins to fill up recommended videos of her channel. She's topless in nearly every thumbnail with emojis covering her nipples. I look at Kellan with wide eyes, thankful that he hasn't taken his eyes from me. This was definitely meant to be for me only.

Tracy's voice cuts through the silence, filling the room as she introduces herself and the game. I look up, seeing her wearing clothes but there's obviously images on the wall behind her that are X-rated. The camera is focused on her face, blurring the photos but it's still very obvious what they are.

I consider turning it off, coming up with a lie to tell her tomorrow when the screen suddenly fills with a game menu and she shrinks to the top corner. I let out a sigh of relief and settle into the pillows behind me, ready to see what the hell she's gotten me into.

I woke up to the sound of whining and crying a few times last night and got up with Nova. Every time she would howl, I would take her outside to potty, but she hardly ever did anything. I woke Kellan from the couch and told him to come to bed with me, too afraid to go alone after being jump scared too many times last night.

I got up a few more times to take Nova out and at some point, I stopped putting her on the homemade bed in the closet and sat her in the bed with us instead. My brain short-circuited in the middle of the night, but it seemed to help because she didn't make another peep. Her soft, fluffy self curled up in the crook of my neck and fell quickly asleep, and I did shortly after.

It was well into the morning when Kellan's sudden scream woke me up. I sat upright, wondering what the hell was happening and images from last night flash through my mind. I immediately pull the blankets back, expecting to see a demon attacking him but nothing is there. Once he calmed down enough to realize it was Nova licking his armpit under the sheets he started laughing uncontrollably.

"What the hell is going on!" I scream at him, still groggy from lack of sleep.

"Jesus Christ, I didn't know what that was. All I felt was hair and a warm tongue going to town in there. Scared the hell out of me!"

I kill over with laughter, both at his description and his reaction to finding her in the bed. "She woke me up a million times last night. I didn't realize I put her in the bed until it was too late," I explain.

He rolls over, grabbing her head to give her a little shake. She answers back with a little growl that is hardly intimidating, but he releases her anyway, boosting her confidence enough for her to sit and let out a bark. We both dote over her, watching her tail wag in return.

"Alright, breakfast, then a trip to the pet store for a bed and other shit she needs. What else do you want to do today?" He asks, tapping her nose to rile her up more.

"I don't know, I haven't thought that far ahead. Do you think we should get her a bed for the shop too?"

"What for?" He asks, letting her chew his fingers.

"Because that lady said she needs to see people to be comfortable around them. We're always around Tracy and John; she needs to know them, too."

His fingers drum across the mattress, letting Nova chase them. "Sounds like a plan," he agrees, then flings the sheets off his body. I stare as his bare naked ass crosses the room and into the bathroom. He leaves the door open behind him, an open invitation if I had to guess.

I take Nova outside, giving her pieces of kibble as a treat when she squats to do her business in the grass before taking her back inside to get my day started. I set her down in the living room, expecting her to wander around to explore but she follows me up the stairs instead.

She slowly hops and stretches up the flight of stairs, taking her time and only struggling once when she reaches the top and falls back down several steps. The poor baby doesn't stop trying to climb up to follow me, and I wonder if this is going to cause problems in the future, but also feel like I should let her do it herself. If I carry her up the stairs once, she may expect me to do it every time. I don't want her to be full-grown and think I should carry her up.

I put my hands on my hips, wondering why I'm suddenly fantasizing that I will be here with Kellan when Nova is older. Maybe I didn't think the dog thing through well enough, or the biker boyfriend situation either. We're only fooling around right now, but how could I ever bring him home to meet my parents after being with their precious Sebastian? I let out a frustrated groan, realizing that I have more to worry about than I thought.

In the bathroom, I strip my clothes off and wash quickly, scrubbing my skin raw with the rough half-net, half-cloth thing that Kellan said he bought for me before getting out and dressing in a hurry. Nova confuses my hurried movements as playfulness and bites at my feet as I push them through a pair of jeans. She's too cute to ignore, so I pull my pants back down my legs and slowly throw my legs around to get her to attack again.

Kellan's large body leans in the door frame of his bedroom, watching as I stand, half-dressed, to play with the golden ball of fluff on the floor. Nova grabs onto the leg of my pants with her teeth, violently shaking it while growling. I laugh as I gently tug the jeans from her, but pull to hard and send her tumbling around while she's still attached. In an attempt to save the fabric from ripping, I shimmy out of them and let her take off running. She hurries past Kellan to trot down the hallway, happy to win a fight against an imaginary monster in the denim.

"I think I was just mugged by a dog," I tell him. He smirks as he walks across the room and plops down on the bed, energy crackling between us as I watch him admire me.

"I'll have to give her a treat for doing that," he responds. His eyes travel up my legs, and I blush, feeling his stare when he sees the panties I'm wearing. The dark blue thong suddenly feels too revealing. I tear my gaze from him, looking around the room for anything else to wear to hide my curves that I have become all too aware of in the past few months since I quit going to the gym.

I look at the bed, sure that I had put my bag there earlier, and see the growing bulge that has formed in Kellan's jeans. My insecurities fly out of the window at the sight of him adjusting himself, but my God. How is he ready to have sex again already? I press my thighs together, aware of my body's reaction to seeing his visible attraction to me and suck in a breath. I'm sore from last night, even the way I shift now to hide my arousal reminds me of the rough way we took each other, but I can't deny that a slow craving is building inside me again.

I tell myself that no matter how good he looks, I couldn't possibly do that again so soon, but my legs disagree. Before I know it, I'm walking across the room to straddle him where he has laid on the bed.

I throw my leg onto the edge of the bed and crawl over him before finding a spot to sit. His dick presses against the soreness between my legs, bringing me to sigh and adjust myself on his lap. I know what I would see if I were to look down between us right now, so I keep my eyes on his face, too embarrassed at the thought of my own damp panties.

He runs his hands up my bare thighs appreciatively. "You're beautiful, Angel." His words dance in my mind, filling me with happiness that I've never felt before. I lean down to kiss him, melting completely as he reaches up to brush my cheek with his hand. He grabs onto my hair, lacing his fingers into the damp strands to deepen the kiss, and I lose myself. My tongue parts his lips to slip into his mouth, rolling and tangling with his until his short stubble has rubbed my face raw.

I break away to sit up, very aware that my seat has done nothing but harden beneath me. I look at the fabric of his shirt as it stretches tight across his chest, wondering how long either of us will last after what we accomplished last night. My fingers work quickly and before I think too much about it, I've unbuttoned his jeans and reached inside.

"Ah, fuck." He groans as I stroke him awkwardly, the fabric of his jeans keeping me from going any further. He pushes his pants down to his knees, easily slipping them from under me before settling back into place. His cock springs free, standing to attention for me. I take him in my hands again, pumping him until a bead a pre-cum leaks from his tip before positioning myself.

Before I go any further, he stops me and reaches down to the jeans that have fallen past his knees. He opens his wallet and pulls out a condom, rolling it on quickly before smirking at me and leaning back to let me continue on with my mission.

I stand on my knees, angling the both of us while pushing my panties to the side. I don't want to bother taking them off, and I don't want to waste any more time; I want him just like this. Slowly, I ease my weight onto him, easing him out before going down again. I feel his head spread me open and sink inside, the sensation sending a shiver down my spine. He grabs onto my hips, squeezing me as I continue to lower myself. Once I've sat down on him fully, I begin to move. Grinding into his lap to feel just how deep he truly is and pull back, unable to take him fully from being too sore.

"God, damn. Angel, that feels so fucking good." He mutters as his eyes close. I already feel myself building up an orgasm and fight through to keep going. I clench around him, feeling myself beginning to ache. He's right, this does feel good; but I'm not going to be able to keep going for much longer. I sit up onto my knees before slowly working my way back down again, using him to pleasure myself until I feel nearly crazed.

One of his hands snakes up my shirt and bra, pushing it out of the way to find my nipple. He rolls it between his knuckles as he holds onto the weight of my breast, bouncing it in his hand before massaging it. I buck as the pleasure floods me, then I stop. What was that? I buck again, feeling the pressure on my clit as I move. I moan, as I move again and again, fucking him until my hips hurt, but I don't stop. I twist my hands into his shirt and bear down again, bucking my hips and forcing him deep at the same time.

I try to keep working myself past the tender spots inside of me, but it's too much and I have to pull back. He picks up on my unease and laces his other hand between us to put pressure on my clit. A few swipes of his thumb while his other hand teases and squeezes my nipple sets me off. I rock forward, one last time onto him and come under.

I finally find my release, soaking my panties as everything spills from me and topple over, landing on his chest and shoulder in a dazed but satisfied state. Kellan grabs onto my hips and thrusts into me relentlessly. I let him take me, reveling in the harsh beating until he yanks me down onto him. I scream out when he hits the end of me and begins filling up the condom. I feel every pulse and spirt in my core until he's done and gently lifts me until he slips out.

He sets me back down onto his lap where I stay lying half on top of him, not daring to move to make a bigger mess than I already have. Once our breathing has returned to normal, he gently moves my leg to the side so he can move, planting a kiss on my shoulder before walking away.

I stay on my knees, ass in the air, while he removes his shirt and cleans me. A soft moan leaves me as he reaches between my legs with the soft cotton, gently swiping until there's nothing left and plants a wet kiss on my ass before squeezing both of my cheeks. I inhale sharply as he pulls my thong down my thighs.

"Kellan," I groan his name, too raw even to consider doing anything more.

"I just want to see that pretty pussy before you get dressed, Angel." His words leave me speechless; I'm certain that he has seen more of me than anyone else ever has. I grin over at him, snaking my hand between my legs and see his eyes go wide. He watches as I take my two fingers and slide them over my labia, opening it wide before lightly slapping it several times. I flinch, realizing just how raw I really am.

I may be playing with fire, and the soreness that has taken over may take a few days to begin to ease up, but I can't let him get away with saying things like that and doing nothing about it. Two can play this game. I spread myself wide again and watch as he licks his lips.

"Do you want to be spanked?" His voice is low as he stares down at me on the bed.

I lift a shoulder to shrug, "You started it."

"I think you want my balls to shrivel up and fall off," he tells me before ripping the fabric from my legs, knocking me onto the bed as he steals my underwear and stuffs them into his front pocket. "You know I can finish it too, Ava."

"Give me those," I argue with him, ignoring the warning in his tone.

"No," his voice is confident, refusing to give in to me. I blink up at him, considering asking again but something tells me to accept his answer and move on. I huff out my annoyance and fish around in my bag until I find another pair of panties. Glancing over my shoulder, I see his eyes darken and move quickly to find the rest of my clothes. Nova comes waddling into the room, barking and howling at me as I try for the second time today to get dressed. I ignore her completely, feeling my bare ass heat under his stare. Would he really spank me into obeying him?

Fifty-Three
Kellan

Ever since we got to the pet store, I've had the feeling that someone is watching us. I've looked over my shoulder a dozen times to see no one around, but the feeling lingers. I watch the mirrors as we drive across town, never seeing anyone trailing too closely, but I know someone is back there.

We make it to the third pet store of the morning, walking a proud Nova on a brand-new leash and collar, directly to the toys for her to choose from. Ava kneels down, holding different plushies up for the pup to smell, talking to her like she understands words. I stand still, watching the ends of the aisles like a hawk until I see her.

Crazy Fucking Bethany.

She looks thin and frail, like she hasn't eaten in weeks. Her hair is a disaster, stuck to her head in some places while matted into knots at the back. She keeps walking, passing us by before coming down the next isle to stand at the end of ours. I hear her talking on the phone, telling someone exactly where she is, but I know what she's doing. Whoever is on the other end of the line is on their way here, and she's telling them where we are.

I kneel down beside Ava, petting Nova on the head to keep from startling them. I always called Bethany crazy for a reason, but stalking is a new one for me. Usually, she would do things like trash the shop or accuse me of trying to have her locked up. Rage fills me when I remember the time she pulled a knife on me after I closed the shop late one night; if it weren't for John coming around the corner right then, she probably would have tried to push that knife into my throat.

And now Ava is with me. If Bethany was stupid enough to pull a knife on me, as big as I am, what the fuck would she do to Ava? I look over my shoulder to see her walking away and whisper to Ava, "We have to go, Angel." She looks up at me, ready to argue but I shake my head. I really need her to cooperate with me right now.

It doesn't take long for Bethany to walk by again, but now she's pacing the outside wall, trying to get a look at Ava. Bethany locks eyes with me, smiling with ugly, rotten teeth. What the fuck happened to her? I stand, ready to tell her off, but the way her face morphs into something demonic pins me in place.

She looks down at the dog by my feet and her expression falls, changing to something of longing and then pure fear. What the absolute fuck is wrong with her?

It's as if she's suddenly terrified of me and what I may do to her, but I've not moved at all. Ava stands next to me, completely unaware of the situation we're in and laces her fingers through mine. I squeeze her hand, refusing to let her go, the gesture must set her off because her gaze follows mine.

I hear Ava's breath catch in her throat as she stares at Bethany. None of us move for what feels like an eternity until Bethany's eyes travel down to Ava's hand in mine. The sad, scared expression that held her face is quickly replaced by nothing but anger.

"Get to the truck," I tell her quietly. She turns to leave, stopping before ever releasing my grip. I turn to look over my shoulder, seeing a blonde that I don't recognize, but Ava does. She leans down to grab the dog before squaring her shoulders, curling Nova into her chest.

"What do you want, Emily?" She asks. Her voice is so cold I barely recognize it. I glance over at her, surprised that my Angel has some fire in her.

"Your family is threatening mine, so now I'm here to return the favor." The short blonde spews. Her voice is nasally, like she has been crying or possibly sick.

"Whatever my family is doing to yours, I have no part in." Ava snaps back, her face reddening with anger. Women may be a bit of a mystery to me, but I'm too aware of the fact that I stand between three of them right now with tension building at every angle. Whatever is about to happen, won't end well.

"Oh, quite the opposite, you stupid little bitch. Everything is falling apart because of you." She inches closer, but Ava doesn't move. She plants her feet and releases my hand to shuffle Nova into a one-armed hold. I shift my body to put my back to hers, keeping an eye on Bethany as she stares at us with rage. Her eyes aren't exactly focused on me, just looking down the isle like she's awake but sucked deep into her mind. I know this look on her, it's how she would be right before she would snap and fall into a violent rage.

"I don't know what you're talking about." Ava's voice lowers, and I can tell the blonde is closer to her now.

Fuck.

"Yes, you do, Ava." I feel Ava's head shake against my back as the girl continues. "You left Sebastian and told Amber what you think you saw at that party. Guess who she ran to tell? Your precious mommy and daddy."

"So what?" Ava spits back at her.

"Now everyone thinks it's my fault, Ava. I've had to give up my whole life so my parents could pay your family back. Everyone thinks that I betrayed you. Now everyone has cut ties with us, with me. I have nothing because of you, and now you owe me!" I turn my head to see Emily lunge for Ava, but I knew it was coming long before she did. Never in my life have I hit a woman, and I don't plan on starting today, but this bitch is going to be the death of herself.

I step to the side quickly, pressing Ava into the shelf to give Emily enough room to get by. At the last second, I throw my arm out, letting her throat catch on my forearm. She falls to the floor, withering in pain and gasping for air as she clutches her neck. I grab Ava's elbow, hurriedly leading her down the aisle, refusing to release her until the truck is in sight.

"Are you alright?" I ask her.

"Yes," her voice is clipped. For the very first time, I see the angry side of her. Her steely gaze pins me in place, "Who was that, Kellan?"

I shake my head, regret filling my chest. This is why I wanted to be so open with her, but no matter how many times I tried to bring it up, there was never a good time. I fucked up, but I hoped that Bethany would stay away and it would never come to anything like this.

"Don't you dare. You asked me about Sebastian and I told you everything from day one. Don't sit there and keep something like this from me after I opened up to you." Her words cut deep, but they are true.

I think back to our conversations and how I pushed her to talk about something that she could hardly finish saying, and by the time she let it all out, we were both angry by the way she had been treated. I realize that there was never a good time to talk about my past because Bethany was something I never wanted to discuss with her. There were more than enough chances for me to mention it, but I never did.

I felt like time was passing by and it didn't matter anymore, Bethany was keeping her distance and I was fine with her no longer existing. If she didn't come around anymore, I didn't have to talk about it. But I should have. I guess I didn't want to because I was holding onto resentment for the way I had been used, but mostly because I'm fucking embarrassed by her.

"She was a mistake I made a long time ago, Ava. She doesn't matter now, and she never mattered before. I haven't seen or heard anything from her in months. I thought she was in jail."

"Well, she's not in jail, Kellan! That's the same woman who was standing outside the shop earlier this week, and I saw her last week too. She's been walking around all this time watching us together, I thought she was a homeless person." Her eyes fill with tears on that last word, tearing my heart open to see that she has compassion for a crazy woman that has us in her sights.

"I'm sorry. I don't know what happened to her; she's never been a very stable person, and it looks like she's finally lost her grip on reality. But I haven't seen her since some time last year, and I didn't care enough to ask around because I wanted her to leave me alone a long time ago and I thought she did." I try to explain, but she doesn't understand the situation.

"Just take me home," she says as she shuts down, turning away from me to pull out of my grip and sits as close to the door as possible. I stare at her, watching as she wipes the last of her tears from her cheeks, a hard mask replacing every emotion on her face until my Ava is gone, leaving behind a shell of herself sitting silently in the truck with me. I know there is nothing I can say right now to fix this, and that thought alone nearly breaks me. With nothing else to do, no other solution in sight, I start the truck.

I know we've been spending a lot of time together, burning bright right out of the gate for nearly three months now, but there's a part of me that refuses to believe that this is what breaks us. I've let her into my life more than anyone else, more than anyone that I've dated before her. I don't know why I chose her, but I don't want this to break us.

For a moment, I question everything that's been happening and ask myself what happened the night we met. I sat in my car and thought it through until the sun rose. I told myself she was out of my league and I didn't know how to do this. But I swore I'd make it work because I wanted her. What made me do this? Why did I choose her?

A New Year's Ride

My eyes roll through the parking lot, watching as cars pass by and I play that night over in my mind. Maybe it was the way that she showed me how fearless she was on that first night that drew me to her. Maybe it when I looked into those big eyes of hers and saw how innocent and sweet she really was that I decided that she was the one I'd give up everything for. Regardless of the why or reason, I wanted her a part of my life. And now Bethany has ruined something else for me.

"Take me home, Kellan." Her words cut through me worse than the first time she said them.

I hear the hurt in her tone and let out a sigh; if my mama was here right now I know what she would say that we both need our space. 'No good decision comes from an angry mind. Calm down and think it all through before you act.'

I know what Ava means by home, even though every muscle in my body screams at me to put the fucking vehicle into park, I can't keep her from what she wants. So, I keep going. Deep down, a part of me knows that she needs time to herself, and maybe I do too. Maybe I need to figure out what it is that Bethany and Emily really want and lay those skeletons to rest.

I look at Ava in the passenger seat, watching as she fights to keep that emotionless mask in place so she can't be hurt anymore than what she already is and nod to myself. Yeah, she needs time to settle down and think it all over, even if that means time away from me. I pull into her apartment's designated spot and wait for her to tell me what to do, but she never speaks. We sit together in silence until Nova wakes and begins to whine.

Without saying a word, Ava gathers the bags and gets out of the truck, pulling Nova along with her down the sidewalk. My heart thuds in my chest as I watch her walk away, pain tearing itself through me with each step she takes.

I turn the truck off and jump out, chasing after her as she takes the stairs with sagging shoulders. Once she begins to fumble with her small purse I grab the bags, freeing up her shaking hands while silently praying that she speaks to me. If she yells, I'll take it. Scream at me, cry, hit me. I don't care; anything is better than this silence.

We approach a white door with a thin string of tiny lights tacked to the frame. I realize now that these are the same lights that were hanging around her door for New Year's and I feel guilty for keeping her away for so long, sure she's been coming back and forth but the bulk of her time has been with me. Ava had a life before me and I've kept her from doing even the smallest things, like taking down some fucking holiday lights.

I think back to my life before her and admit to myself that I don't want to be who I was before Ava. Maybe it's too soon to be admitting those things out loud, but it's true. The door swings open, and I let out a sigh of relief as she walks through and leaves it open for me to follow.

It's the same from the last time I was here, everything inside is bright, with splashes of dark grey breaking up the white walls and cabinets. Pictures of her and her friends hang in random clusters everywhere, some in frames, others taped on the edges. I look at her face in every photo, noticing how the smile she wears never quite meets her eyes and how she always stands on the outside, like she never really feels like she belongs.

In one picture, she hugs an older man and presses her cheek to his. This must be her father; the resemblance is there, but she bears a striking resemblance to the woman sitting stone-faced beside them. Despite the cold and distant stare from who I assume to be her mother; this is the photo in which Ava looks the happiest. Even her father seems to be having a wonderful time, showing all his teeth as he smiles and hugs my girl.

My heart throbs in my chest. I don't want to leave her here broken and alone. I need her to know that I want to worship her, and I will do anything she wants me to do to keep her happy but I know that's not what she needs to hear right now. As much as it's going to kill me, I'll give her all the space she needs to think things through.

"Are you ready to tell me who was with Emily?" Her voice is strong, punching me in the gut when I realize that she's using that same tone from the day that she told off her bitch of an ex-boyfriend.

I'm proud of her, though, even if I'm on the receiving end of her temper, I'm proud. She isn't the same scared girl running from a crowd of people at a party anymore. She has found her voice, and I'm happy for her, but fuck. Why does it have to be me that she releases her all wrath upon?

I sit, waiting for Kellan to explain why we were just cornered in the pet store by someone who looks like she drowns kittens for fun while Emily threatened me. Obviously, it's someone he knows because I have never seen that woman in my life and I don't ever want to see her again. The look in her eyes flash in my mind again, sending a shiver down my spine.

His throat bobs, fear shining in his eyes for the first time since I've known him. I refuse to comfort him; instead, I opt to be busy by giving Nova a bowl of water and food to keep her occupied. When he still has no answers, I huff out a breath and start looking for a pair of scissors to cut the tags from all the toys.

"She's just someone who used to come around the shop. We never dated." His words are slow to come out, letting me know that there is more to the story.

"So, you used to fuck her." I spit the words out, disgusted at the thought of them together. He flinches as I stop what I'm doing and fix my gaze on him.

"I did not," his voice is low and ashamed.

"Don't dare stand there and lie to me," I tell him. Watching as the muscle in his jaw tenses and releases several times.

"It was once, and it was a mistake. We both knew that, and it never happened again. For as long as she came around, it was only once. I started paying her to leave. She would show up, get money, and disappear for a few days, sometimes weeks. I hardly spoke to her after it happened unless it was to tell her to leave and stay gone." He looks up at the ceiling before sighing. "I swear to you, Ava. It was only once, and I regretted it. You can ask Tracy, ask John. I never wanted her coming around to begin with. I don't even know where she came from. She showed up and never left no matter how many times we all told her she wasn't wanted there."

My eyes prickle as I stay silent to let his words sink in. I won't ask Tracy and John about this. Tracy may be honest about it, but at the end of the day, they are both his friends, and they work for him. They would lie to me if they saw it was for the best for everyone involved. I gather everything from the counter and head to my living room, moving the couch away from the wall and set Nova's bed down, surrounding it with all the toys. Kellan stares at the couch with a solemn expression, not sure what to do or where to go from here.

I push past him, feeling like the walls are closing in on us and it's too small a space for him. This is the first time he has ever been here and actually stayed long enough to see my place, and I fear it may be the last. I see his hand come up to grab me, but he stops himself, awkwardly holding his hand up like he wants to hold me but keeps his distance.

I go back into the kitchen, feeling stable now that the counter is between us and I prop my elbows onto the cool surface, leaning down to breathe deeply to clear my head. I stare at the floor, wondering where to go from here. I've stayed with Sebastian through all of his cheating, lying, bullshit, but why can't I accept this from Kellan?

Is it because I finally know what my boundaries are and how to keep them? Or is it something deeper than that? Maybe I'm afraid of what people will think when they see us together and tell everyone in my life who and what I'm been doing these past few months. I step back to consider why this has hurt me so badly and realize that in the short time we have spent together, I've developed feelings for him.

I sigh, realizing that this could only go one of two ways, and I'm not prepared for either of them. There's more of my life that I want to live before settling down with someone, but there's also the possibility that I could never be happy with anyone else. I think back to all of my past relationships; there aren't many, but the people that I have dated could never hold a light to Kellan.

I think back to how I've felt with all of them, always feeling like something was missing, until I'd realize there was no chemistry there and I'd leave or let them go. But why has it taken this man in particular to show me what I deserve in life?

This man. The words echo in my mind before bringing me to a standstill. It's because he's a man in every way there is and he's what I've needed. Because of him, I've learned how I should be treated and what to expect from people. I've learned who I am and how to be heard and how to get what I want. I didn't necessarily need him to know all of these things. I had the power to find it all myself, but he woke something inside of me and made me actually harness it. But at the end of the day, I chose to become this version of myself. I chose to get on the back of that motorcycle and I chose to peruse this.

Everyone I've dated, I did it because I felt like it was expected of me or that I was choosing to be with someone that everyone else approved of. Kellan is the first person that I chose for myself, and I couldn't be happier, but does that mean I will be happy if I choose someone else? Or will I be looking for him in everyone that comes after? "Fuck's sake."

I stand up, looking at him one last time with heartbreak in his eyes. He stands there, still staring at the ugly white couch that my mother insisted on buying for me. "What is the obsession with the couch, Kellan?" My voice comes out sharper than I intend, but seriously. What the fuck?

When he looks at me, I can tell that he has mentally prepared himself for the worst possible outcome. Trying like hell to build walls up quickly before I can damage him with what I may say. It's clear to me in that moment that he's been through bullshit before, just like I have. Maybe not the same situations, but he knows how this feels.

Maybe he was the one standing here asking questions with no answers, or maybe he is in the same position all over again. And in that moment, the idea of him being with anyone else pisses me off. Before me, or after me, doesn't matter. No one else can hurt him but me.

I stalk across the room, closing the distance between us before grabbing him by the back of his neck and bringing his lips to mine. There won't be anyone after me. That crazy bitch and Emily can go straight to hell.

Fifty-Five

Ava

It's been two weeks since anyone has seen or heard from Emily; two weeks since she threatened me in that pet store across town and vanished from the face of the earth. I've called a lot of people trying to track her down, but she's just gone. Kellan went to file a restraining order against the crazy woman who helped corner us, but not a day goes by that I don't look over my shoulder.

Even now, as I pull into the shop's lot, I can't help but glance around. The sun is coming up, and I still feel the need to keep an eye out for anyone who may be lurking around in the shadows. They approached us during the day the first time; I do not doubt for a second that they would do it again if given the chance.

Once I've checked every direction and see no movement from any hiding places, I open my door and quickly walk to the back of the shop. Nova keeps her eyes on my face, just like we've practiced at home a million times. She's a quick learner, always eager to learn something new for a few pieces of jerky. I know I shouldn't be giving her human food or snacks, but the girl will do anything I tell her to for some cured meat.

I yank open the heavy metal door, feeling safer as I walk into the empty hallway. Nova slips in behind me, her nails tapping on the ugly concrete floor as we head into the office. I toss our bags into the corner and give her a small treat before starting up my coffee machine. It springs to life when I turn it on, but once I open the lid, I stare in confusion. I could have sworn I threw away the pod Friday when I left, but there's one in the top already. I crinkle my nose in disgust. I hate leaving used coffee sitting in this thing. It always gives off such a bad odor when it sits longer than a day.

I pinch the edges of the plastic pod and pull it out to drop it in the bin, surprised that it still smells fresh. Glancing around, my mug is nowhere in sight. I let out a heavy, annoyed sigh. I guess I washed it out in the kitchen and never brought it back in here. Maybe I was a little out of sorts on Friday, but I didn't think my routine was thrown off that badly.

My mug sits on the kitchen counter, water pooled in the bottom, as if it were recently washed. I stare at it, trying to remember where I placed it when I closed up last week. No, I clearly remember washing this and taking it back to my office before I left. Dumping out the water, I rewash it before continuing on with my morning.

At the end of the day, I go to wash my mug and make a mental note of putting it under the coffee maker that I bought for myself to keep in my office. I stare at it, wondering who the hell used it and why they didn't drink the coffee from the kitchen then turn out the lights and leave.

The days go by quickly, and every morning I find my mug in the kitchen, washed and dried but never in the spot I leave it in every evening. Today, it annoys me than usual; this has gone on long enough, and everyone should be drinking from their own mug. I feel the rage build inside me and check the calendar, realizing I'm another day closer to my cycle starting, and I'm one more minor inconvenience from being on an episode of that snap murder show.

With a sigh, I rinse the suds from my cup and head back to continue making my own cup of heaven but when I pull out the creamer from my mini fridge, it's nearly gone. Red hot anger swirls inside me. Not only has someone been drinking my coffee and using my mug, but now my creamer is gone, too. Tracy and John come through the door in a shouting match, screaming over each other so loudly that I can hardly think.

"Hey!" I scream at them, putting their argument to a stop in an instant. Their eyes snap to me, surprised that I've raised my voice at all. "Have one of you been using my creamer?" I ask, my annoyance loud and clear.

They both shake their heads to respond. If neither of them has used it, that means it's Kellan. I stomp out of the office, aiming to find him and get to the bottom of this. When I find him, he's covered head to toe in black sludge like he's just went swimming in a pool of oil. His bright smile puts out some of the fire in me, but I'm still running on fumes.

"Hey! You owe me coffee and creamer." I cross my arms as I yell at him. He looks puzzled, unsure where my annoyance is coming from.

"Okay, Angel. Just use my card." He cuts his eyes to the coffee maker across the room, seeing the pot still on from this morning. I look at it too, confused why he would be making more so soon already.

"If you wanted some creamer, you should have just told me," I tell him over my shoulder.

"I have creamer. You can use it if you want."

"If you have some, then why are you using mine?" I stare at him, wondering what the hell he's up to.

"I haven't used yours," he admits. "It must be one of the other two stooges."

"They said they haven't." I snap at him, feeling guilty as soon as the words leave my mouth.

"Well, Angel. I have no idea, but I know that I haven't used your machine. I don't even know how to turn that damn robot on." His smile grows, but so does my agitation. Why would Tracy or John be using my shit? It can't be John, he comes in every morning with a cup from that shop downtown that he likes so much. I narrow my eyes and go to Tracy's toolbox.

There's nothing but energy drink cans cluttering her area, empty candy wrappers stuffed into a plastic bag hanging on the side, with an iced cold water sitting on top of it. What the hell? I throw my hands in the air, giving up on the mystery that has sent me into a coffee-feigned manic episode.

I grab my keys and drive straight to the small grocery store a few blocks over, grabbing two different creamers and four boxes of coffee pods. I take my time sorting through their small selection of mugs until I find the perfect one. A little provocative, but it's how I'm feeling currently.

I race back to the shop, happy with my mini shopping spree and set out on a mission to make my coffee again. Kellan walks in, cleaner than earlier but smelling like a used oil pan.

He picks up my new mug and reads it to me, "Fuck off, I haven't had my coffee. What's this about, potty mouth?"

"I think it's fitting considering my usual mug has been coming up missing every morning. Maybe no one will steal this one." I roll my eyes and take the cup from his hands, careful not to spill my life source.

He smirks down at me, as I sip my delicious caramel-flavored morning drink before taking it from my hand to taste it for himself. He nods in approval. "I can see why someone would be drinking this," he says before finishing the rest in one swallow.

I squint my eyes at him, knowing that he or someone else has been dipping into my stash, and I will find out who it is. The creamer I have been mildly addicted to for several years now is not something I will tolerate being taken from me. They can pry the vanilla and caramel swirl from my cold, dead hands, but while I'm on this planet, I will fight anyone who dares to take it from me.

"What did you come in here for? Shouldn't you be working?" I ask him, still annoyed. His smile grows as he sets my empty mug down to lean his weight onto the arms of my chair.

"Just wanted to come see your beautiful face. You were mad at me earlier, and I wanted to make sure that was taken care of." His eyes darken as they search my face before landing on my lips. A slow fire begins to build in my lower belly as his eyes darken.

"I just needed my coffee, Kellan," I tell him, not wanting to give away how flustered he's making me feel. Honestly, I feel like I'm on the edge for so many more reasons, but being sexually frustrated is first on my list.

We've been staying away from each other to keep a low profile in case Emily or Bethany shows up, but I'm going to lose my mind soon if I don't have my way with him. The looks he's been giving me mirror my own, and I'm beginning to think that I may break before he does.

With all the extra time on my hands, I've taken it upon myself to order new panties that I know he will undoubtedly steal, but that's become my new favorite game with him. I still haven't found out where he has been collecting them, but since we've been apart, I now have an abundance.

Maybe I should up the stakes and drive him a little crazy. I want to see how long is too long to tease him before he caves in. I swallow, fighting back my racing thoughts of us sneaking away to the back bedroom for a quickie. My thoughts must be written on my face because he looks me up and down, a devilish grin growing before he kisses me softly.

Game. Fucking. On.

A New Year's Ride

If I didn't know any better, I'd say my girl is starting to get a little cranky by the distance we've put between us. We both agreed that it was for the best to slow down. While I've been undoubtedly regretting the decision, and I can tell she's having second thoughts too. Yesterday, I saw that she was looking at panties on the work computer and had already added several to her cart. It's fine, I can understand the need for new things when I have about a dozen pairs stuffed away at home, but damn, why did I have to see the new ones?

I've also noticed the pair that now hangs from her own rearview mirror, like she's begging for me to bend her over that driver's seat and give her a reason to have them there. If I'm being honest, I've been thinking about what she has under those painted-on jeans since day one of our agreement. The way her ass fills out every pair of jeans she owns kills me a little more every day that I don't get to peel her out of them.

I suck in a deep breath, then blow it out quickly as she walks through the parking lot, looking over her shoulder as Nova watches her like a hawk. The sight of them together brings a smile to my face.

If anyone had told me last year that they would be in my life today, I would have called them a liar. I follow Ava's gaze to the dark blue van that has been parked next door, wondering what she is looking for. People dump cars there all the time, and the city tows them away eventually, but this one has been parked for a few days now.

It's good that Ava is more observant now, but I hate the reason behind it. I pull out my phone and snap a picture of the van, sending it to John and asking him to check it out. I wouldn't be worried about it at all, but the fact that no one has come to tow it already is suspicious.

John has his way of figuring out who owns all kinds of shit; some of the things he has taught me, but it still blows my mind that you can find out so much about someone by looking through public information online. I never asked how he figured that out, but it's helped me with some shit a couple of times in the last few years.

I watch from the back of our lot as John walks his big ass over to the vehicle and take pictures of it up close, even getting the license plate and VIN before strolling back inside like he was never there. He holds his hand above his head, signaling that we're good to. I turn around and walk into the shop, finding him leaning into the opening of his toolbox, scrolling on his tablet.

"We got a problem, Kelso." His voice puts me on edge. John is usually a serious person; that's just who he is, but I don't like his tone. He steps to the side, showing me my brother's mug shot from years ago. I walk outside to look at the van again and my blood begins boiling with rage. I told him too many times not to show up here, and the fight that broke out between us a while ago was over too quick for me to gain any satisfaction from it. I kick the door out of my way, temporarily blinded by the bright sunlight. My eyes eventually adjust, and I blink in surprise.

The van is already gone.

Fuck.

I hum to myself as I scroll through the program to calculate repair times for all the different motorcycles that we have in the shop, mindlessly looking at all the names and years to give myself something to do. The little vibrator that I bought a few days ago was waiting for me when I got home yesterday, and boy, did it work wonders. I let out a sigh, wondering what I could do to get Kellan's attention.

As my fingers drum across the desk, an idea comes to mind. Something that may or may not work, but it's worth a shot if it does. I dump out the contents of my purse, looking for the red lipstick that I keep on hand but rarely wear, and head to his bedroom.

I slip inside, sneaking to the dresser that has a mirror propped up behind the TV, and notice the strange smell that's no longer Kellan but not quite the oil either. I look around the room, looking for anything misplaced or strange, but see nothing unusual; it's just an oddly clean room. Granted, there wasn't a whole lot here to start with other than the bed, dresser, and television, but still, something is off.

I pull the heavy mirror out, lean it against the wall where it can be seen easily when he walks through the door, and squat down in front of it to write my message in lipstick, then apply it and kiss the mirror in a few spots. I stand back to look at my work, feeling like something is missing, and look down at myself. I smirk before kicking off my shoes and wiggling free from my jeans.

I didn't really prepare for this, but I think I can manage a few hours with no panties. I take the fabric and balance it on one corner of the mirror before getting dressed and quickly leaving. Now I just have to wait for him to see what I've done.

For a second, I stop and consider the odds of someone else finding my handiwork, but let it go. John doesn't usually walk any further down the hall past the office, but I will be mortified if he's the one who finds that message. There's no reason for anyone to be there but Kellan; the descriptive love letter that I left behind will be our little secret.

I sit down at my desk, feeling the stiff fabric of my jeans rub me in places that it shouldn't, causing me to crinkle my nose. The vibrator took the edge off, but it doesn't compare to the real thing at all, which I'm reminded of how long it's been now that the crease in my jeans begins to apply some pressure. I huff out a breath and stand, deciding that I'd rather have sore feet than a raw vagina by the end of the day.

Kellan walks by the large window, zoned out with an angry expression on his face. I can't tell where he's going, but John falls in step beside him. They stop and talk for a few minutes before Kellan swipes his hand down his face, obviously stressed about something. Whatever is happening must be serious to have them both this worked up. They nod to one another before going their separate ways; Kellan heading deeper into the shop while John disappears around the corner. I can hear the back door slam closed, followed by the sound of a motorcycle leaving the lot.

Whatever they have going on really isn't my business, but that was very strange. I sit back down, wondering what they could be planning, when Nova comes over to whine, signaling she needs to go for a walk to relieve herself. I snap the leash to her collar and take her out back, eyeing that blue van that keeps coming back to park on the property line towards the back of our lot.

I steer Nova towards the truck, trying my best to lead her to the back of our fence line, where grass has started to grow and I can keep the show in my line of sight at all times. I don't like being out here alone, but at least it's fenced in with only one way in or out.

Fifty-Eight

Ava

Time crawls by as I wait for Kellan to confront me about the message I left behind for him, but he's still caught up on the floor. Eventually, my screen reads four o'clock, and I throw my hands in the air. I don't know if I should go track him down and spoil the surprise or keep waiting, but I'm growing impatient. I thought he would have gone back there by now.

I let out a frustrated groan, catching Nova's attention. She's been awake more lately than she has before, so I assume she's growing and doesn't need to sleep as often as she used to. While I love that she is awake more now, she's also harder to keep occupied. All the rawhide bones and antlers in the world can't keep her attention anymore and I worry that she's getting bored. Kellan usually plays rough with her in the evenings to help her burn some energy, but I can't do that with her during the day or let her run wild at my apartment like we do at his place.

With a sigh, I walk out the door, telling Nova to follow behind me to look for Kellan. I find him in the corner, mounting a set of tires onto some brand-new rims. I prop up against the stack of used ones to watch the show he doesn't realize he's putting on. I could never get tired of seeing those muscles put to work, but I realize my mistake much too late. My core clenches as he grunts to pull a lever down before picking the tire up to remove it from the machine.

I pop my mouth open when he turns to face me with dirty hands and sweat streaming down his arms from the heat in the shop. He's filthy, but dear Lord, he's fine. Tattoos peek out from the collar of his button-up shirt, sending a bolt of need through me. My mouth goes dry from his halfcocked grin, all traces of his annoyance earlier leaving when our eyes meet.

"You trying to catch flies with your mouth open like that?" He asks with a grin. His joke isn't nearly as funny as he thinks it is, but since he wants to call me out, I think it's only fair for me to shut him up.

"No, trying to catch something else in it instead." I mentally pat myself on the back, proud of how straightforward I am, for once. The tire drops from his hands before he rolls it out of the way with his foot and wipes his hands on a rag. His eyes never leave mine as he takes his time cleaning between each of his fingers. I can't help but feel like I've just poked a bear.

He stalks up to me, pressing my back into the tires as he leans over to look down at me. The smell of grease invades my senses, mixing with the faded scent of his laundry detergent; the combination is lethal, scrambling my brain and chasing away all of my logic at once. I feel giddy as he traps me here, hoping that he takes advantage of the little privacy that the wall of rubber provides.

He leans down, inches away from me to whisper, "If you're so wound up too tight, all you gotta do is ask, Angel."

My heart thuds in my chest, threatening to climb out of my throat at his words. I didn't think I was asking, I'm telling him what I want. But since he wants to play a hard game, I can too.

"What do you want me to ask, Kellan?" I look up at him through my lashes, playing the part of the angel he wants me to be. His throat bobs at my question, but I still want to press him further. I lick my lips before reaching up to play with a button on his shirt, teasing him by barely touching his chest with my fingers.

He backs away, picking up another wheel to mount it on the rim at his feet before turning around to face me again. "I think you left something behind earlier," his eyes darken as he looks my body up and down.

"I don't know what you mean," I lie.

"Are you telling me that you didn't write 'make me sore again,' on the wall in my bedroom?" He narrows his eyes, calling me out on my bullshit.

"Hm. Seems I remember writing something similar on a mirror lately," I grin up at him. He's amused, but there's still an edge there. Something must be bothering him.

"You keep talking like that and you won't be able to sit right for the rest of the week," his words bring me to attention, but I stay silent. If he's worried about something, then I should be too. Nova sniffs around on the floor at our feet, pawing at one of the old tires before chewing on it. I try to walk away, taking Kellan's words as a playful warning, but he stands in the way. I look up at him, waiting for him to tell me what's weighing on his mind but he doesn't say another word, just stands there looking at me with amusement and lust on his mind.

In the blink of an eye, he slips his hand into the back of my jeans. I gasp at the sudden intrusion as his hand cups my bare ass, pulling the material of my jeans tights between my legs. The inside seam presses harshly against my clit, and I nearly faint when his fingers move lower.

"Jesus Christ, Ava." He lets out a breath when he touches my bare skin, feeling how wet I am. I close my eyes as he slowly pulls out of my pants, trying hard to keep from moaning. I miss his rough hands on me. My eyes pop open when he reaches between us, situating the front of his jeans as his growing erection becomes more visible by the second.

"All you gotta do is ask, honey," I tell him before lightly patting the front of his zipper. I duck under his arm quickly, running out of his grasp before he can reach for me and call for Nova to follow. Kellan looks around the corner but steps back into the hole.

"Hey, Tracy," I greet her while spinning to walk backwards, holding her stare. I wave at him as I continue to put distance between us, making sure to add a little sass when I turn my back to him again.

Checkmate.

A New Year's Ride

The clock hits five, and I hurry to shut down my computer, grabbing my bag to throw it over my shoulder to make a quick getaway from these four walls that have been shrinking all week. The office door swings open with a bang as the lights in the entire office shut off at once.

Nova barks loudly as Kellan stands in the doorway, looking more devilish than I've ever seen him. He leans onto the frame, looking at his hands for any grease that he may have missed when he was cleaning up for the day. I lick my lips before swallowing; he's never looked like that before. He pushes off the wall, coming into the quiet office with determination set on his face.

"What's that?" I ask, pointing to the object in his hand.

"A toy for Nova," he says as he drops the rubber tire in front of her.

"No, what is that?" I point to his other hand, watching the silver glisten as he walks towards me.

"Something we never got to use that was forgotten about until you wanted to play dirty." His voice drops low, sending a shiver down my spine. A light glows from somewhere in the shop, barely illuminating his features, but I can tell he's changed clothes recently.

"Did you go home?" I ask as he marches up to me, taking my purse from my shoulder to set it gently on the floor. "Kellan, I-" My words are cut off by his mouth on mine.

His lips are demanding at first, but soften when I kiss him back, drinking him in until I can hardly breathe. God, I've missed him. I fight to pull in air through my nose, refusing to break away for even a second. I grab onto his shirt, pulling him against me until our bodies collide. He definitely went home to change clothes. I can smell the cedar and pine scents lingering on him from the house.

A soft moan escapes me as he begins to explore my body, grabbing onto every curve I have and caressing it before moving to the next. When his hands slip between my legs, I finally break our kiss to pull in a ragged breath. Even through my jeans, he knows all of the right places to touch. I suck in a breath as he rubs me, finding my clit to apply just the right amount of pleasure before moving to take my shirt off.

My bra quickly follows, falling to the floor beside us. His hot breath blows across my bare chest when he leans forward, taking one of my nipples into his mouth. I lace my fingers into his hair, arching my back to give him better access to me.

His tongue rolls across my skin, licking and sucking before giving just as much attention to the other side. I let out a cry when both of my hardened nipples are suddenly pinched. A lightning bolt of pleasure travels through me, ricocheting throughout my entire body. I feel my heart beating between my legs, causing me to sag forward and rest my head on Kellan's hard chest as I heave in another deep breath.

I look down at my chest and gasp at the sight. Several dainty chains hang in various lengths down my torso, attaching to my nipples to create one full body piece. I stare at the clamps in disbelief. God, this feels good. Kellan's hands slowly slip down my sides, leaving behind a path of fire that travels deep to my core. His fingers make quick work of the button on my jeans, pulling them down my hips to show him how bare I have been for most of the day.

I fist his shirt with both hands when I feel the cold air on my ass, fighting back a moan when he smacks each of my ass cheeks before softly rubbing circles to ease the sting. I feel every beat of my heart with hyper awareness where the clamps are attached to me, and fear that I may get off from the feeling alone.

His hand reaches between us, slowly traveling down my stomach as low as he can go. My mouth hangs open as I stare down at his hand, watching it slip between my legs. His strong fingers glide through me, spreading around the wetness I've created until he's able to press a single finger inside me. I try to breathe evenly as he curls it around inside me, slowly fucking me with his digit until he adds another.

A low groan leaves me, filling the silence around us. His other hand comes up to gently tug on one of the small chains, and my knees buckle. I fall into him, holding my weight up by his shirt.

"Shh," he whispers to me before kissing the top of my head. He pulls his fingers from me, swiping my clit quickly before pushing me back onto my feet. I buck from the quick touch, ready to explode on his command.

"Kellan. I can't. I can't, please." I begin to beg as he sits me on the desk; I need him to finish me quickly. It's been too long since I've felt him, and I'm turning into a mess. The chains sway against my stomach, sending waves of pressure through me in a torturous rhythm. He fights to remove my boots and jeans, pulling and yanking until I'm nearly falling off the edge of the wooden desk.

By the time my clothes are piled on the floor, I've turned the surface under me into a slip and slide and open my legs as he steps up to me, ready to take all of him. I swallow my pleas, focusing on taking in air to quiet my shallow panting and watch as he unfastens his belt. His pants fall loudly to the floor, allowing his cock to spring free.

I lick my lips at the sight of it, remembering the last time I tasted him. It's been weeks and I can't take it any longer. I open my legs as wide as they can go, sliding myself closer to the edge of the surface, then grab ahold of him. I pump his length twice before he steps between my legs to swipe the tip of his cock through me. I look down between us, watching as he coats himself before pressing any deeper.

I feel him throbbing and pulsing as he slowly eases into me. The sensation causing us to both gasp as we watch and feel every inch. Once he's buried completely, he backs away to dive back in. I let out a cry as his thick head spreads me open and his shaft fills me.

"How's that, Angel?" He asks through gritted teeth. Words fail me as he continues to slip in and out repeatedly, causing me to spill onto the desk under me. My orgasm builds quickly, but once he presses a thumb to my clit it's over. My legs shake as I clench around him, moaning to the ceiling as I lie back to let it consume me. My nipples are freed from the clamps, sending blood rushing to the spots that are no longer being pinched.

I grab onto the ledge as my back bows from the surface under me, screaming out into the night. It feels like a live wire has been attached to my chest, traveling deep inside me to heighten my orgasm by leaps and bounds.

My hands hurt from the edge biting into my palms and fingers, but I can't let go. Kellan continues to fuck me, his rhythm never changing as I release my entire soul onto him. His fingers stroke and tease my clit until my toes curl from the pleasure that has me in a chokehold.

I grab onto my breasts, holding them to keep that deep, pleasurable sensation going, and roll my hips up to him, forcing him to go deeper until his balls press against my ass.

"Holy shit," I exclaim as he picks up his pace. Our skin slaps together loudly, the sound filling the quiet room and echoing off the walls.

His grunts and groans are like music to my ears, sending a fire up my spine that consumes me entirely.

"Fuck. Ava, come on." He grunts as he grabs onto my hips to pound into me. The desk rocks against the wall, banging against it until the computer screen clatters to the floor. I push everything off the surface, sending all my pens and receipts out of the way. I meet him thrust for thrust, impaling myself onto him as he forces himself as deep as he can go until we are both sprawled out onto the desk. He starts to hit that one spot inside me, driving me insane with each stroke until I can hardly breathe.

I wrap my arms around his shoulders, pulling him closer to me and holding on tightly. "Please, don't stop," I beg him. I'm so close to that finish line, just one more time. Just once more, and I'll be done. His heavy hand comes up to squeeze between us to squeeze my breast tightly, sending a bolt of pain through me that mixes with the pleasure until I dive over the edge, exploding around him until we are both slick.

He glides through me effortlessly, fucking me through my second orgasm until I see stars and his thrusts become erratic. I finally come down from my high as he yanks out of me, spurting onto my already soaked pussy until we both leak onto the floor. He collapses on top of me, breathing heavy as he kisses up and down my neck.

"I miss you, Angel." He mumbles into my ear.

I hum in response, too afraid to speak or risk saying something I'm not ready to admit yet. He stands upright to pull his shirt over his head, cleaning me off before moving on to himself, then tosses it into the trash can under the desk. I slowly sit up to look at the computer lying on the floor; I'll be surprised if the screen isn't cracked. With a sigh, I stand on my shaky legs and fill around on the floor to find my clothes.

Kellan's strong hands grab onto my arm before taking my hand. I squeeze his hand in return, accepting my bra from him. Once I have it clasped, he pushes my shirt over my head. I push my arms through, smiling in the darkness; I've never had someone help me get dressed after sex before, but this is a welcome change. He holds onto my hips as I step into my jeans, giving me the stability I need to pull them up my legs before releasing me to find my boots.

"Can we go home now?" His soft voice comes from across the room as he opens my small fridge for a bottle of water. The dim light fills the room, showing off his tattooed skin as he leans down to sort through my personal stash of snacks. "I thought you had more shit in here," he says over his shoulder.

"I did, it's all still coming up missing," I tell him as I sling my purse over my shoulder.

He takes my last bottle of water from the fridge and downs half of it, offering me the rest before standing to shut the door with his foot. The look on his face worries me before the darkness of the room swallows us.

I drink the water as he pulls me towards the door, stopping to lace our fingers together. "You never answered me, Angel."

"I'd love to, Kellan," I tell him as emotions swell in my chest.

Nova wakes from her bed in the corner and trots behind us, her nails clacking on the floor as we make our way down the hallway. I don't see how Kellan can see where we are going, but he opens the door to his apartment to flood the hallway with bright light.

He lets go of my hand to grab a shirt, pulling it over his head before walking back to me. Nova sniffs around on the rug, growling softly until she gets too scared and runs towards me. I reach down to scratch behind her ear, letting her know she's okay while looking up at Kellan for answers. I've never heard her growl like that before.

Kellan attaches the leash to Nova's collar before we open the back door to leave, fearing she may run off if she's startled by anything in the parking lot. I agree with him and slip the open end of her leash onto my arm in case she tries to pull it from my hand. Kellan locks the door behind us, making sure no one can get inside the building over the weekend. He grabs my hand again, looking left and right to check that no one is lingering where they shouldn't be before we start walking through the dark parking lot.

Halfway through the lot, I come to a dead stop when footsteps approach us from behind, spinning quickly on my heel to see Bethany coming towards us. Kellan's hand slips from mine as I pivot to face her head-on. It takes him half a second to step in front of me, blocking her from me completely. I step to the side, wanting to see what she will try to do to either of us before it happens.

The twisted smile that takes over her face when she sees him fills me with blinding rage. She's a few inches taller than me, skinnier too, but I don't give a shit. I pull Nova along with me, passing Kellan as he stands, waiting for her to close the gap between them.

I move in fast, my feet carrying me before I can fully understand what I'm doing, and ball up my fist. I pull my thumb across the front of my fingers and pull my arm as far back as I can before throwing my entire body into a full swing.

Pain surges through my hand as it connects with her face, causing blood to splatter on the ground as she topples over and smacks the concrete. I let out a scream when I land on top of her and swing again, spraying more blood onto the ground. She kicks and squirms away from me, cutting her legs up on the loose gravel as she crawls.

"You fucking bitch!" She spits at me. I see red as I look over at her, lying there bleeding but still having the audacity to look at Kellan for help. I slip the leash from my hand, followed by my purse, and toss it all to the side.

"Ava, no." He warns me, grabbing my arm to keep me from going any further. I look into his eyes, seeing the worry and stress creep into his features. His expression douses the fire in me, forcing me to face the reality of what I've just done. My shoulders sag as my anger dies down.

Kellan pulls his phone from his pocket as Bethany lets out a gurgled laugh from behind me. "I'm glad you got both bitches on a leash now, honey."

I turn to look at her again, watching as she sits up and pulls the ugly skirt down to her scraped knees. She tries to stand, but just as she finds her footing, I shove her down to the ground again. My open palm connects with her cheek, causing a loud smack to ring out into the night.

Her head snaps to the side, matted hair covering her blood-smeared face, but I see the sick smile she tries to hide. Kellan sputters into the phone behind me, giving the shop's address before stepping up to grab my shoulder.

"Come on, Ava, let's go. Let the police take her for the night, just like we talked about." He tugs me to the car, puts me in the passenger seat, and closes the door to lock me in. My eyes never leave Bethany's as she sits in the parking lot, a dangerous smile tugging at her lips before she reaches into her purse. Kellan walks around the front of the car, still holding the phone to his ear as he talks to the dispatcher on the other end.

I see the glint of the gun as she pulls it out, aiming it in our direction. A blood-curdling scream bursts from my throat, followed by several pops as the gun fires. Glass explodes around me as the windows of the Chevelle shatter as she continues to pull the trigger.

I continue to scream until my voice is gone. I sit completely still when my door is yanked open, fearing that she has come to finish me off and begin praying to any God that is listening. A face comes into view, one that I recognize, but I don't recall from where. His eyes match Kellan's, but it isn't the man I know and love. He yanks the seatbelt off my chest and pulls me from the car, putting me in the driver's seat of my truck and pushing me over until I lie on my side. Nova jumps in behind me, crying and whimpering as she licks blood from my face.

A bald, tattooed head quickly disappears from my sight, leaving me alone to lie here as silent tears stream down my face. Eventually, sirens and lights flash all around me, but I'm too numb to react.

My body trembles as I stay curled in on myself while Nova barks at the shadow that approaches the truck. I try to shush her to keep her from letting them know where we are, fearing that it may be Bethany. Voices surround us, and my door is slowly opened. The sound of glass crunching under their feet fills my ears, causing my body to shake violently with fear. I realize then that I may be injured and my body is in shock.

"Miss, are you alright?" A blinding light shines on me as someone asks the question. I ask myself the same and begin taking my time to explore all of the places I feel pain. My hand aches from the punch I threw earlier, and my face stings from the tiny cuts the glass has caused, but other than that, I feel nothing. My body continues to shake, even after a warm blanket is draped over me and the door is closed again.

Where is Kellan? Did she shoot him? My mind races, trying to play back the scene in my head, but I can't. I try and try, but all I remember are those dark, dead eyes and the gun. A sob breaks free from my lips, and hot tears burn the cuts on my face as they fall from my eyes. What if Kellan has been shot? The words echo in my head, causing my stomach to roll. I need to find him.

I slowly sit up and take in the scene. At least twenty police cruisers are in the parking lot, surrounding the building, and cars are parked all around as officers walk the perimeter. Yellow tape has already been put up around the gate, trapping us all inside the tall chain-link fence. A white sheet covers the spot where I last saw Bethany, blood soaking through in several places. I turn to the officer who stands on guard at my door and see his face for the first time. We lock eyes for a moment before I lean over to push the door open, vomiting at his feet.

The image of her body flashes into my mind, burning into my brain. I continue puking until my stomach is empty, and dry heaves take over. I spit, trying to get the taste of bile out of my mouth to no avail but it never fades. I rest my head between my knees, feeling like I may pass out and my vision begins to go black around the edges. The only thing that brings me back to the present is the sight of her replaying in my mind.

"Who killed her?" My voice cracks as I shout the words, heaving again at the thought of her being dead.

"Just relax for now, ma'am. We'll figure it out, alright?" His voice is not soothing at all; there's no compassion there as he takes a step back to get out of the pool of half-digested food. I look up to meet his gaze, feeling his judgmental stare on me.

Where's Kellan? I tear my eyes from the officer's face and look across the parking lot, not daring to look in the direction of Bethany again. The suspicious-looking van that has been parked on the other side of the fence for the last two weeks is gone, replaced by several police cars and an ambulance. Kellan sits in the back of it, bleeding from his head.

I let out a scream when I see him, startling the man who stands outside my vehicle. I jump out of the truck and run through the parking lot to get to Kellan. He jumps up at the sight of me and walks toward the fence, grabbing it to open the gate that should be locked. Several officers step forward to stop him from entering and shove him towards the opened ambulance.

I'm suddenly yanked backwards by my midsection, causing me to fall to the ground and scrape my hands on the loose gravel that has eroded from the asphalt over time. Two officers pull me to my feet and walk me backwards before opening a door and setting me in the backseat. I begin to hyperventilate as I'm closed and locked away in the night. An officer sitting in the front seat startles me when she finally moves to exit the vehicle. She opens my door, telling me to swing my legs out and lean forward to take a deep breath.

I do as she says, hugging my knees and swallowing back tears as I try to breathe. An ambulance pulls up beside us, and I'm loaded into the back of it. Someone sits in front of me, wrapping my arm to take my blood pressure and wiping an ointment on the cuts on my face, but all I can do is think of Kellan. The large gash on the front of his head was brutal. Blood had coated the side of his face and neck, soaking into the fabric of his shirt.

Another warm blanket is wrapped around me, but I continue to shake. Eventually, the officer gets into the truck with me again, offering a small smile to me before flipping open a clipboard.

"Ava, I'm Officer Thomas. I know what you just went through has shaken you up quite a bit, but if you can, I need you to tell me what happened here. Okay?" Her eyes search my face, searching for answers that I don't have.

I nod in response and try to speak, but no sound will come from my mouth. I try to clear my throat, but I end up coughing. She hands me a tiny bottle of water, which I gulp down immediately. My stomach gurgles as the liquid sloshes inside me.

Maybe water wasn't such a great idea. Bile builds up in my throat, but I swallow it down, trying to find some sort of strength to tell this woman what I know just happened.

I clear my throat again, surprised that my voice is only a whisper when I speak. I tell her what happened, starting from us leaving together and Nova acting strange before we ever made it outside. She nods along, writing quickly as I tell my side of the story.

My voice eventually fades while I'm still talking, and she hands me another water. I sip it slowly, wondering if I shouldn't have admitted to striking Bethany.

"Do you have any weapons on you, Ava?" She looks at me with pity in her eyes.

I shake my head. "No, but I have some wasp spray in my purse."

"Wasp spray?" She asks.

"Pepper spray expires, and wasp spray has range," I explain to her. She nods and scribbles on the metal clipboard again.

"Can you tell me anything about Bethany? How long you've known her and about her drug use?"

I shake my head again. "I didn't know her at all. I met Kellan in January, and we started dating. She cornered us at a pet store a few weeks ago, and we filed a restraining order against her. This is the second time she's shown up here and confronted us." I sip the water again, wetting my mouth to keep talking, but she closes the clipboard.

"Alright, Ava. Here's what's going to happen. You aren't under arrest, but the state requires me to cuff you if you ride in the back of my car. Okay?"

I nod, understanding what she's saying but not fully. "Wait. I'm being arrested?"

"No, Ava. You are not under arrest. The handcuffs are for my protection while I drive and you sit behind me."

"Oh. Okay. What about Nova?"

"She's going too, she's just going to be in a different car, and we will have a vet make sure she isn't banged up." Her voice softens as she explains the situation. Nova could have cuts on her, too.

The officer looks to the EMT sitting in the front seat, letting them know we are ready to get out. Someone opens the door from outside, helping me step down, then guides me towards the blacked-out SUV. Officer Thomas comes up beside me, patting me down quickly before pulling a pair of metal handcuffs from a pouch on the front of her vest.

A New Year's Ride

Tears spill from my eyes as she explains once again that this is a mandatory step she has to take to transport me anywhere with her, and I'm not under arrest, but her words fall flat. I feel like I am being arrested and that I should call my parents to explain to them what's happening.

The cold metal bites into my wrists harshly, falling down and scraping my skin when she releases them. She gently turns me to the side, instructing me how to get into the back of her vehicle comfortably without hitting my head, and buckles the seatbelt across my chest.

Once the door is closed, a sob escapes me. I can't believe this is my life now.

I watch as Kellan's number shows on my screen again for the millionth time today and flip my phone over to ignore the call. It's been nearly two months since I last spoke to him, but everyone keeps telling me it's for the best.

I've locked myself away from the world, grieving in my own kind of way over the situation that I was put through. Apparently, Kellan's brother, Jackson, had been staying at the shop without anyone knowing, and saw the whole thing unfold from next door. He was sitting outside, waiting for us to leave so he could break into the shop to sleep for the night. He ended up shooting Bethany six times in total, something that seems insane to me.

My body shivers as I remember his eyes looking at me. He killed a woman in the middle of the night and stared into my eyes, holding his face inches away from mine before running off to hide.

I don't understand why he didn't kill me, too. Instead, he loaded me into my truck and hid me from whatever else he had done. The police eventually searched the shop for him and watched everything unfold from the cameras, clearing Kellan and me the next day, but I will never forget the feel of those handcuffs locking around my wrists. I absentmindedly rub them, still feeling the cold metal biting into my skin.

I shake my head, turning my phone to silent to keep it from disturbing me again and stare at the wall. I know Kellan is going to be okay, despite his brother being on the run for the rest of their lives, but there's no way that this experience won't weigh on both of us forever.

Jackson hit him pretty hard, Kellan believes he knocked him unconscious so he wouldn't be an accessory to murder, but I have my doubts. Still, it must be difficult to know that you can never see your brother again after something like that happened. It's heartbreaking to know that Jackson can never come back here; he can never see their mother or Kellan for the rest of his life.

He may already be in prison for all I know. I shrug to myself and roll over, wrapping Nova into a tight hug. She's gotten so big so quickly, but still doesn't take up the room Kellan did when he slept in the bed with me.

A New Year's Ride

My heart squeezes in my chest as I envision him lying next to me instead. He puts off more body heat than she does, and snores louder, too but she's much softer than he ever was. Soft knocks come from my front door, and I know it's Amber. She's been coming by every night to make sure I'm eating and taking care of myself but I wish she would stop. I can take care of myself, I just need a little more time to figure out what to do now.

Kellan keeps paying me even though I haven't been to the shop all this time, and I'm thankful, but I don't want him to keep this up for long. I don't need the constant reminder that I was at that place.

Two weeks ago, Amber told me that Emily disappeared off the face of the planet again, which is strange considering who her parents are. She believes they are hiding her to keep her from getting into trouble for stalking me and they linked her to Bethany, which means that she could be arrested since Bethany did try to shoot Kellan and I.

Amber agreed it was strange that Emily ever cornered me the way she did, but she also dropped a bombshell that I never saw coming. Spiraling rumors say Sebastian and Emily may be secretly married now. Amber has been trying to snoop through their business, but neither of them will return her calls, and eventually Emily's number was disconnected. So, we are patiently waiting for the news to be confirmed before we put that story to rest.

She continues to knock at the door, even though I'm slow to get out of bed to answer. Nova lets out a huff as I slip out of bed and creep down the hallway to unlock the door. She's used to Amber coming and going now, but I'm beginning to regret letting her come over so late each night.

Even though I sleep most of the day, my body still wants to be still once the sun goes down. Sometimes I lie there in bed, staring at my white ceiling, seeing blood spots that match the stains on the sheet that covered Bethany's body, and then I spend hours trying to get the image out of my head. It's a vicious cycle that I don't know how to break but the visions are slowly fading.

I finally open the door for my best friend and she immediately holds up a white paper sack filled with food as she texts with the other hand. I take the bag from her, seeing cheesecake in a clear container, my favorite dessert. She smacks her gum as she walks past me and flops down on the couch.

"Let's watch one of those horror movies you like so much," she says as she kicks off her shoes to fold her legs under her body, still texting away and not looking in my direction at all.

"Since when do you want to watch something like that?" I raise my eyebrow, questioning her.

"Fine, put on that show that we've been watching. The whatever wives." She waves her hand at the TV, still deep into the phone in her hand. I don't really feel like watching anything tonight, but I guess I can deal with the background noise while she types away on the screen in her hand for the next few hours.

I set the bag of food down in front of her and grab the remote to select the same show we have been ignoring for the past several days. Nova comes down the hallway, letting out an irritated groan when she sees Amber sitting in her spot on the couch. I smile at her and pat the middle cushion, letting her know she is welcome to snuggle with me. Instead, she plops down where she stands and stares at Amber with sadness in her eyes.

"Why does she always do that?" Amber says, looking at Nova.

"She always sits there. That's her spot," I explain.

"She wants to sit on the spot that has black stains and a tear in the cushion rather than sitting in your lap? Your dog has problems, Ava."

I sigh when I realize why that spot means anything to her. That's where Kellan would sit to play with her after work sometimes. It lines up perfectly with the hallway, giving them the room to play fetch while he relaxed. The tear came from their roughhousing when his key punctured the fabric as he rolled around to take a toy from her.

I turn the volume up on the TV, trying to drown out any thoughts of him, but it doesn't help. I sit on the couch, unmoving, as silent tears fall from my eyes. Amber hardly says anything when she puts her phone on the table and sits with me, handing me tissues to dry my face for the next several hours until I fall asleep.

A New Year's Ride

I watch as my mom scratches Nova behind her ear before tossing the tennis ball for her for the millionth time. She seems more carefree and happier lately, and while I have my suspicions, I don't want to pry into my parents' relationship. I'm just going to assume that my father has finally agreed to retire and spend more time at home like he has promised so many times over the years.

"Is dad really allergic to dogs, or is that something he said to make me shut up when I was a kid?" I ask her as I lay back to soak in the sun.

Mom laughs, the sound a welcome change from her usual agitated tone. "No, he isn't allergic, but we didn't want to put that kind of responsibility on you."

"How come you don't have a dog, then?" I question her. Sometimes I think she invites us over just to see Nova, rather than her only daughter. The idea makes me smile; at least someone finally makes her happy.

"Good girl, that's my good girl," her voice is loving as she leans down to kiss my dog on the head, but she changes when she speaks to me. "When I was a kid, I had a dog. She was a dalmatian I named Dottie." Her voice fades, taking on a sad tone. I let her drop the subject and stare into space. After a while, she turns to me, "Why did you name her Nova?"

I stare at the diving board stretching over the pool in my parents' backyard, ignoring the way my eyes sting with unshed tears as I remember the night Kellan and I found her. I'm grateful for the sunglasses I wore today to keep the late August sun out of my eyes. "I named her after the car," I whisper.

"A Chevy Nova?" Her response surprises me.

"Yeah. You know what I'm talking about?" I've never in my life seen my mom interested in vehicles.

"We have one," she says casually, causing me to spit my drink out. "Jesus, Ava. Are you okay?"

I cough the rest of my lemonade up before pulling in a ragged breath. "I'm fine. I'm fine. It's just, what did you just say? What? Where do we have a Nova?" I sputter, wiping my face off as my dog tries to lick my chin.

"Your father has a whole fleet of cars uptown, honey. We used to drive down to the beach in one every year, don't you remember? He used to let you run through the garage and let you choose which one we took that year."

A faint memory of me running through a concrete jungle comes to mind, but I can't remember any vehicles other than our large family SUV. "Can we go see them?" I ask, feeling a surge of happiness for the first time in weeks.

She shrugs her shoulders, "I guess."

I jump to my feet, startling Nova as she chews on a twig.

"Where are you going?" Mom calls after me.

"To put on some clothes!" I yell to her over my shoulder. "Come on, let's go." I run through the house, taking the steps as quickly as I can to the bathroom where I've left my clothes. I yank my swimsuit off, throwing it in the sink before fighting my jeans onto my damp legs.

If my dad has a garage full of old cars, I want to see them. I don't care how much it hurts to think of Kellan anymore. I don't care that he would have loved to see these cars just as much as I would. I stop for a moment, no. He would probably love this even more. I clasp my bra behind my back, trying to ignore the stinging in my eyes when I imagine his eyes sparkling while driving the Chevelle. I shake my head; I don't care that he is the reason I ever looked into cars in the first place.

The pain in my chest is something I've learned to live with, something I've accepted that will always be a part of me now, but he made me realize I can't let people treat me however they want just because it benefits them—even him. The truth is, I feel betrayed. I opened myself up to him and let him see the most vulnerable parts of me, only for him to hide pieces of his past from me, and it nearly cost me my life.

I spent the last several weeks locked in my apartment, hiding my broken self from the world until my mother put her foot down and said enough is enough. I admit, I hated coming back to this house, but now I can see the life that it has breathed back into me, and I can see how my mother has changed, too.

She's so much different than when I was younger, and it pains me to think that I was one of the issues in her life. But she's also not the same as she was just last year, either, and I wonder what's been going on with her that she hasn't told me.

As we ride to the garage, I tune out my mother's rambling, too excited to attempt conversation. We eventually pull up to a tall, concrete building and I watch as my mom leans out the window to enter a code into the metal box before the gate slowly rolls away to allow us to drive forward. I scoot to the edge of my seat, looking out the windshield as we climb higher and higher into the building. Once we hit level five, she exits the ramp and pulls onto the main floor. I hold my breath as overhead lights come to life, revealing row after row of cars, a few stacked two high to maximize the space.

"Holy shit," I blurt out.

"Ava!" My mom shrieks, giving me a dramatic expression before getting out of the SUV. I stare at the sea of vehicles, memories flooding me as I suddenly remember coming here year after year as a child until we eventually stopped. I swallow the emotions building inside me, missing my father more than I want to admit.

"Are all of these dads?" I ask as I slowly walk down the aisle.

"Good God, no." She answers.

When I grow up, I wanna have that one, daddy.

I close my eyes, picturing the bright yellow car in front of me with the metal horse set into the grill, and take a shaky step forward. Eventually spotting the familiar color peeking up at me from the very end of the row. Looking back at my mom, I see her digging through her purse, ignoring me completely, as if this isn't one of the best moments of my life.

I stand still, taking in the sight of the car I cherished as a child, feeling three feet tall again. I remember my dad laughing as he opened the door for me that day, letting me climb into the driver's seat to pretend to drive it.

If that's the one you want, sugar, you can have it.

I wipe a tear from my eye, thinking of how my hand fit into my dad's when we would walk up and down this garage until I would make my decision. I always hated it when he took trips without us, but I never let him know. I never wanted him to feel sad or guilty when he left us. I feel my mom walk up to stand quietly beside me, comfort washing through me as we stand shoulder to shoulder, both reliving memories from long ago.

"Your father always said this one was going to be yours," she whispers. I can hear her fighting back tears as she slips her hand into mine, pressing two keys into my hand. I look down, staring at the black plastic dipped metal set in disbelief. I spin around, throwing my arms around her, and begin to cry.

I let my tears fall freely, every bit of hurt that Sebastian has caused me, all of the pain that is still fresh from Kellan breaking my heart, the loneliness I carried when my dad would go out of town, and lastly, the angst and resentment I held towards this woman who would always be my rock through my life, no matter how often we fought.

I cry until my body finally stops shaking and my mother stands me up straight to move my hair from my shoulders. "I thought we were going for a ride?"

I wipe my face before pulling in a ragged breath to clear my head, feeling like a new person. "We are. Let's get Nova out first." I turn on my heel to go back to the SUV, noticing there is an empty spot in the center of the lot. "What happened to this one?"

My mom looks to where I point, "Oh, your father sold that a long time ago. I think it was a blue car, but I don't remember what it was."

My heart skips a beat in my chest as I remember the last time I was here, over twenty years ago. The shiny blue paint was driving away as my dad held my hand to go back home. "No way. No fucking way."

"Ava Marie! What has gotten into you!" My mother storms up to me, looking me in my face with her hands on her hips. I stare into her eyes, smiling as I see myself in her.

"Who bought the car?" I ask her.

She blinks rapidly, as if I haven't just offended her and moved the conversation forward like her anger was nothing to me. "I don't know the man's name, Ava. Your father always called him Smitty. He was some construction guy. Why?"

Deep down, I know who she's talking about and I know it wasn't construction. He was an architect who had a subcontracting business on the side, taking money from one pocket to fill the others.

"We gotta go," I run to let Nova out of the backseat, then dash to the Mustang, leaning the seat forward for her to get in first. My mom gets in the passenger seat, still huffing about having a potty mouth. I start the car, feeling the rumble of the engine for the first time in my life, and fight back more tears as I put it in drive.

My mother's voice brings me out of my deep thoughts, stopping me immediately. "Ava. I think it's time you told me what has been going on." She looks at me before leaning over to look at my feet, then pulls the emergency brake up. "I didn't want to pry too hard, but it's been difficult watching you go through this and feeling like I had left you to sort through something on your own. I've been here for you, but you still haven't told me anything. Some things need to be said, and I'm ready to listen."

I take a deep breath, grabbing onto the steering wheel tightly as I start from the very beginning. I tell her everything, even the parts I skipped over when I opened up to Amber and Kellan about the things Sebastian said and did to me. I told her how I met him and how I felt like myself for the first time in my life, and how I worked at the shop for a while. I open up about how I felt at peace there, even on days when it was so loud you could hardly think.

Then the time comes for me to tell her why I left, what Emily said to me, and the woman who was with her. I slow down, choosing my words very carefully when I explain the night Bethany died, omitting the way she shot at me. Instead, I circle back to the day at the pet store, telling her how I felt lied to and felt there was more that Kellan could keep from me if he would so easily hide someone like that from his past but I set it aside and stayed anyway. I admitted that I never regretted my decision to stay, but I hated how I never felt safe after that.

For the first time in my life, my mother sits quietly and listens to everything I have to say. She waits patiently for me to be done, and long after I had finished, she still sits silently to process everything. "Darling, I don't think you gave him time to explain anything to you."

I fix my eyes on her, annoyed that she could take his side. She holds her hand up, silencing me.

"It sounds to me like he had a skeleton in his closet that he wanted to bury, but he was too wound up in falling for you, he simply couldn't be bothered with anything else.

"We all have things from our past that haunt us. Some people will go through hell trying to cover them up. His demons just confronted you when you were both out together. I think there is a reason he lets even his closest friends believe he still lives in his childhood home. The man wants peace. I doubt he wanted to admit to you that this girl he knew became a junkie and they had a relationship."

I wince at the word, hating how she just labeled Bethany. She was someone's daughter, just like I am. Bethany had a life before she died, even if it wasn't one that I understand. She could be a sister for all I know, or have someone who misses her.

"Mom, don't say things like that about people," I sigh. Maybe she's right about Kellan's past and his reasons for wanting to keep his secrets from me, but there's only one way to find out. I suck in a deep breath before blowing it out quickly, then lower the parking brake.

I maneuver easily from the spot, enjoying the way the tires glide smoothly over the concrete and enter the exit ramp. I never accelerate the car, letting gravity and weight glide us down, only breaking around the turns to keep my mother from screaming. Once we're at the security gate, I stop to enter the code, pressing the numbered buttons as my mother says them out loud.

The gates open slowly, burning through every bit of patience I have. I look over at my mom, a broad smile taking over my face. "Put on your seatbelt." The familiar words echo through me and I buckle my own, missing the way Kellan would remind me every time I got in a vehicle.

I wait until I hear the click, then catapult us onto the street. Her head snaps backward and stays there until I let off the gas to shift, just like he taught me. Luckily, it's the middle of the day and traffic is light, giving us a nearly empty road. The few cars that pull out in front of us, I easily avoid. I race past them, not slowing down until we reach the single-lane roads downtown.

As we sit at a light, the car idles loudly, easing my racing thoughts. I drum my thumbs on the leather steering wheel, waiting for the light to change to green. When it finally goes, I feather the gas pedal, easing around the corner — my heart pounds in my chest when the shop comes into view and I see my beautiful truck sitting in the front lot. I look over at my mom, hoping like hell she understands what I'm about to do. I pull into the rear parking lot, spotting the Chevelle immediately and circle around it.

"Is that it?" I ask her, suddenly unsure of the whole situation. The windows in it have been replaced, but they are darker than I remember.

She does a double-take, her mouth popping open in surprise. "Yes, I think so. I don't remember it being that sparkly, though."

"It was repainted a few years ago, but that's as close to the original color that he could get," I tell her when she turns to search my face for answers. I circle the parking lot, pulling into a bay door as far as I can before putting the car in park.

Tracy comes around the corner first, looking pissed that I've invaded her space until our eyes meet, and that hard mask she puts on for the world melts away. Her smile shines bright, seeing me for the first time in person in what feels like years, even though she has seen me join her stream to watch her play every week I've been away. John comes to stand in front of her, angrily walking towards the car until he realizes it's me, then stops short.

"Lord, have mercy. That man is menacing," My mom murmurs, looking him up and down before fanning herself.

"Mom!" I shriek at her, embarrassed by what she means, and of John, of all people.

Tracy comes bouncing up to the car, opening my door to lean inside. "Is our sweet little angel back for good now?" She jokes, using my nickname they have all picked up from Kellan but from her, it's always funny. She glances over at my mom, looking her up and down before whistling her attraction. "Hey, lady."

I snort at the casual way she greets my mom. No one but Tracy would dare do such a thing. "Tracy, this is my mom. Mom, Tracy."

"Hello, dear." My mom stretches out her hand, taking Tracy's in the most feminine handshake I have ever seen. "And who is the big hulk back there?"

"That's John," Tracy says to my mom before looking at me, "We're kind of a thing now."

I crinkle my nose, "Gross. But, it's about time."

"Let's not talk about time right now, I think we can all agree that you've been gone long enough. Kellan has been," she pauses, noticing Nova for the first time. "What's that? You trade your man in for a dog?" My mom laughs at Tracy's joke, but I feel guilty for keeping her from him. "And a swank ass pony. Damn girl, savage. I love it," She glances around the car, checking out the interior of what I drove here. "But, like I said. He's been difficult."

"She is Nova, and yeah. I know he has been, he stopped calling," I tell her. Nova's head pops up at her name, whining when she notices where we are.

"The best girl in the whole world," my mom says, earning a tail wag. "Go get your man, dear. We'll wait right here," she says to me. My heart squeezes in my chest at her words. I never thought she would be in my corner, but I'm so glad she is.

Tracy backs up, giving me room to get out of the car but I stay seated, looking past her into the office window as Kellan pushes away from the computer to stand. His gaze lingers on mine, the tension between us so electric I feel like I'm standing on a live wire. Tracy grabs my hand, slowly pulling me further into the shop before letting me go. I stay still, too afraid of what he will say if I go to him, and wonder if he will meet me halfway.

For a moment, I'm afraid he won't, but he eventually walks out of sight. I hold my breath as the office door creaks and slams shut, sending my heart in a freefall. He could walk out the back right now and leave me standing here. He could run just as I had months ago. The possibilities play through my head quickly until I see his face come around the corner.

I blow out my held breath before pulling in another, all too aware of the audience we have that pretends not to watch. He takes his time approaching me, but I accept that. I deserve it after ignoring him until he eventually quit calling altogether. My throat burns as memories of us flood me, wondering if there will be more to come. I've missed him more than I was willing to admit to myself, but I thought it was for the best.

We stand toe to toe, neither of us speaking or looking at the other. Too afraid to make a move or risk saying the wrong thing.

"Do I need to force Mom and Dad to kiss, or what?" John's voice booms from the corner where he's standing, cleaning his hands on a rag. Tracy leans against her toolbox, smirking as she pretends to occupy herself with a bag of Skittles before pouring some into John's hand. I smile up at Kellan, hope blooming in my chest as his eyes soften.

"I'm sorry," I whisper.

His mouth comes down hard on mine as he snakes his arms around me to pull us together. I can't stop my hands as they wrap around his neck, pulling him closer to me until I feel like we will meld together into one person. He kisses me until we are both out of breath, and my lips are sore from his unkempt facial hair.

I hear Nova's nails running across the concrete floor seconds before she puts both of her paws on my back, pinning me against Kellan's chest. He reaches around me, scratching her chin and chest before kneeling to see her.

"They got a dog," Tracy says to John.

"I see that, Catherine Obvious," he says to her.

"It's Captain Obvious; you dick bag. And I told you because I knew you were going to ask where the hell the dog came from." She elbows him in the side, gaining a side eye as he rubs the sore spot.

"I know the saying, cunt for tits. I was copying something my niece says because it's fucking cute." He spews back at her. I roll my eyes as they begin to argue, leaning down to pet Nova.

"She's gotten big," Kellan says as he shakes her head like they haven't missed a day apart.

"Yeah, but she's still a puppy. Last week, I had to buy shoes from a thrift store to keep her from chewing up any more of mine."

He pets her head, smiling down at her with so much love in his eyes that my heart squeezes. "There's someone I want you to meet," I tell him.

We make our way to the car, my mom getting out to stand with a leash in her hand. "I'm sorry, dear. I tried to catch her, but I wasn't fast enough." She smiles sweetly, but I know she's lying.

"Kellan, this is my mom, Avery. Mom," I take a deep breath. "This is Kellan."

He stretches out his hand to shake hers, but she hugs him instead, something I have never seen her do to anyone, even my own father. I raise an eyebrow at her sudden warmth, but decide it's best to let it go, or else I risk snapping her out of her good mood today.

"I've heard a lot about you, young man." She says to him.

"I hope it was all good, ma'am," he responds before stepping away from her.

She studies his face curiously, "You're much too young to be Smitty's son, but I swear you look just like him."

"That was my grandfather," he explains.

"My husband, Ava's father, knew him well."

"I didn't know him at all, but I hear he was a good man," he says as his jaw tightens. I wince, remembering the conversation we had several months ago about the man. I know how exhausting it is to be associated with people you would rather forget; I wish there was something I could do to help him cut ties with his grandfather, but unfortunately, his legacy will live on.

Thankfully, my mother sees his unease and drops the subject. "Ava, I need a ride back to my car. Kellan, I expect you to be at dinner tonight." My mother adopts the matter-of-fact tone I have known my whole life, leaving Kellan speechless. His face fills with understanding when I look up at him, realizing those late-night conversations we've had in the past were anything but fabricated when it comes to how my mother works.

"Yes, ma'am," he says, looking down at her. My heart flutters at his respectful attitude towards both of us. I've known he would do anything to anyone for disrespecting me, but seeing it so obvious in this moment has too many emotions swirling in my chest. We may have more to talk about, but for the first time in a long time, I feel like I will be okay, like we will be okay.

"I won't accept you being late, young man. And," she pauses, staring into his blue eyes that captivate me just the same, "bring your mother as well. Tell her to bring pie; she will know what I mean."

Sixty-Four
Kellan

I watch as Ava pulls away, Nova barking in the backseat as she stares at me through the window. I'd completely given up hope of ever seeing either of them these last few weeks, and now here they both are again. I feel like I have a second chance, but I don't know how to accept it. Tracy comes up to me, all smiles for once, which puts me on edge.

"I think I prefer you walking around angry at the world," I admit to her.

"You've been angry enough for both of us, Kelso." She fires back at me, some of her usual annoyances thankfully coming through. "And to think I was coming over here to tell you to leave for the day to go chase after women." She glares at me before walking away, closing my box as I stand in stunned silence for what feels like the millionth time today.

I look over at John, wondering what the fuck is going on with everyone. He shrugs before turning around to walk away. That's not like him, either.

"Hey," I yell loud enough for both of them to hear me. "What's going on between the two of you?"

They look at me like I've grown two heads, and it dawns on me. All the fighting between them has died down; considering how it used to be, it's nearly non-existent. Sure, they bicker and argue, but they have both been flying under the radar for the last week or two. I thought they were just tiptoeing around me to keep me from derailing, but I see it now. All those times they've passed by each other and brushed shoulders, the lunch breaks together, and funny looks when I'd be talking to one of them about some dumb shit they had done.

"Un-fucking-believable." I walk off, leaving them to close the shop together since Tracy was so willing to do it earlier.

I drive straight to my mom's apartment in silence, my mind reeling as I think about tonight. What the fuck kind of pie is she going to make on such short notice? I replay Avery's words in my head and can't find the puzzle piece that I'm missing there. But Ava's father knew my grandfather, which means he could have known the man that was my father, as well. Grand-dad was in his eighties when he died, though, so why would he know Ava's parents? I shake my head, no longer caring about the strange ways small towns tend to link people together.

A New Year's Ride

I take the old stairs two at a time, trying my best to hurry so my mother will have time to bake. I don't want my mom to rush to make something, but I think we're past that. I beat on the door, waiting as my heart pounds in my chest with growing anxiety. She opens the door, annoyed until she sees it's me.

"Good lord, son. What's gotten into you?" Her voice echoes in the hallway as she scolds me, but I brush it off.

"We don't have a whole lot of time, and I can explain on the way," I push past her, heading straight to the kitchen to look for her mixer and bowls. She looks at me like I'm crazy. "Come on, Mama, we have to have two of them."

"Two of what, Kelly?" She asks, stepping forward unhurriedly.

"Two pies!" I frantically yell. "We have to bring two pies to dinner." Her face crumples in confusion before she laughs and leans across the kitchen counter. "Is this about that girl you've been seeing?"

"Yes, we have to go," I tell her as I fill a whole bowl full of flour. I don't know shit about baking, but I think starting with a crust is the best option. Crust is made of mainly flour, right? I pull my hair; all I know how to make is fucking steaks and burgers. "Where's your butter?" I yank open the fridge, pulling out a grey container.

"What's her name again?"

"Ava," I say flatly as I hurry to pry the lid from the tub. Why is she not helping me?

"What's her mother's name?"

"Avery," I respond, throwing the whole tub into the microwave. I think this shit is supposed to be melted before I mix it. She places a hand on my arm, stopping me from turning on the appliance, and removes the butter.

"I'll go get dressed."

"But Mama. She said bring two-"

"I heard you, Kelly. I've got her pies. You go shower, you stink like you worked in the shop all day."

"I did work in the shop all day," I respond under my breath.

I sit at the island in the middle of my parents' kitchen, peeling potatoes with my mother. We sit in silence; both left alone with our own thoughts, but in a far happier place than we were this morning. We even had a video chat with my dad, who couldn't believe I had forgotten so much of my childhood. He was elated that I had found and driven the mustang for the first time.

To my absolute shock, he had already prepared the title for me to own the car; all I have to do is sign it, and it's mine. He was also happy to hear that I was interested in the Nova and had found the Chevelle. Mom and I both left out the part that it belongs to Kellan, opting to tell him about that part of the story in person, but I suspect she will tell him once he's back home.

His business trip is going great, and by the time he gets here, he will have yet another company to his name. Mom just rolls her eyes, shutting down all business talk as she prepares a dinner for 'friends,' she tells him. I hand her a peeled potato, watching as she begins to slice it and arrange it on the bottom of a baking dish, then pick up another to keep my hands busy.

My dad also got to see Nova while we were on the call. She didn't understand who or what she was looking at, and howled in confusion every time my mom showed her the screen so my dad could speak to her. I could tell my dad wanted to complain about a dog being in the house, but he thought better of it when he saw how happy my mom was having her over. There's no doubt in my mind that he is saving that battle for another day, and by the way my mom looks at Nova, I have a feeling she has a battle of her own planned and ready to go when he gets home.

I watch my mom twirl through her oversized kitchen, pulling things from shelf after shelf until she has prepared four small chickens. I crinkle my nose when she skewers them on metal rods and sets them into the oven on the preinstalled rotisserie gears. She pulls out a bag of Brussels sprouts and a bundle of asparagus, and I groan.

"Quit your grumbling and chop these so I can roast them," she pushes the bag of nasty greens my direction before pulling out cream cheese and strawberries, setting up the next side dishes to be assembled.

"What are those for?" I ask her as I eye the fruit.

"Dessert," she deadpans.

"I thought you said-" She cuts me off before I finish my sentence.

"Yes, yes. I know what I said, but that's different." She turns away from me to hide a smile. What has gotten into her? I pull out my phone and text Kellan to warn him that something strange is going on. To my surprise, he has already texted me.

> *I don't think pie means edible dessert kind of pie*

> *I was thinking the same thing.*

> *Old people are weird*

> *Thats your mother you're talking about*

> *I just call em how i see em*
> *Do you want me to bring anything else?*

I drum my fingers on the counter, still daydreaming and holding out hope that this dinner will bring us back together, when an idea snaps into me. "I don't hear chopping," my mother calls out to me. I quickly text Kellan before sliding my phone across the counter and chopping the rest of the brussels sprouts for her.

Once all the food is ready, my mother organizes it all on the table, shooing me away as if she's afraid I will mess up her perfect placement. It seems like she has used me for the prep side of dinner, and by the way she has left the kitchen, she will also use me for the cleanup crew. I wander into the kitchen, picking up trash and pieces of raw vegetables before dumping them all in the bin. I'm halfway through putting all the dirty dishes into the sink when the doorbell rings throughout the house.

My heart stops beating as panic sets in. I realize too late that this is the first time I will meet Kellan's mother, and look down at what I'm wearing before bolting up the stairs. I think I can find something in my closet to wear, but it will be slim pickings considering I haven't lived here in a while. Everything I've left behind is old or doesn't fit anymore.

Halfway up the stairs, I hear my mother yell for me to get the door, but I keep going, ignoring her completely. I dash to my bedroom, ignoring all the boxes of memories that I packed away so many years ago and never took with me. Flinging open my closet doors, I look for anything that may still fit me.

All I find is an old ripped t-shirt and jeans that were too tight against my legs, even for the style so long ago. I groan at the sight of them; there's no way I would be caught dead wearing something that requires permanent hair removal before going out in them. I hold them up to my body, shuddering at the faux button's low placement, then throw them into the trash where they belong.

I sift through the hangers before finding a horribly faded Paramore shirt and throw it on. The logo is barely visible, but anything is better than being covered in dried potato peelings and chicken juices. I hurry to the dresser, praying to any God that is listening that I find something in the drawers. I open the very last one, and by a miracle, pull out a pair of light grey denim jeans. I remember buying these so long ago and hating the way they fell off my hips; I had intentionally cut the knees with a straight razor to keep me from having to wear them around my family, but they will have to do for today.

I think back to all the times Kellan dressed in front of me, even the clothes he had that weren't covered in oil stains had rips and tears on them, and he still looked dressed to impress. But then again, the man could wear scraps of fabric and I'd think he was perfectly presentable.

I slip my feet into my black leather and cork sandals and try my best not to throw myself down the stairs as I navigate them as quickly as possible. Once at the landing, I stand still to listen to the conversation coming from the living room.

"Damn, Avery. This place is enormous. You stay here alone when J.P. is gone?" A woman's voice echoes down the hallway to me, but I strain to hear my mother's response at the confusing question. It dawns on me then that J.P. is the nickname my dad answers to when people visit for anything other than business, which is rare.

"There you are," a gravely voice says from behind me. I let out a scream as I spin around with an open hand, slapping whoever dared to scare the life from me. Too late, I realize it's Kellan, and the loud slap as my hand connects with his cheek is heard around the world.

"Oh my God. Oh geez. Oh no, I'm so sorry. Are you alright? Please tell me you're alright," I pull on his face to see the red mark I've left behind. He reaches up to touch his cheek before staring down at me in disbelief. "I'm sorry," I say to him again.

"Well, that's surprising." His voice is low, traveling down my spine to places it shouldn't be.

"Where did you come from?" I hiss at him, confused why he isn't in the front room with our parents.

"Well, the 'pies' had to go in the freezer." He answers as he rubs his jaw. "You've got one hell of a swing, Angel."

"So you found out what they are talking about?" I question, ignoring his comment on being slapped. I can make that up to him another time. I need to find out what the hell my mother has been scheming first.

"Let's just say that I may be leaving my mother here with yours tonight because she isn't getting in my car." We both look down the hallway, hearing them burst into a fit of giggles.

"What the hell is that?" I've never heard my mother giggle like a schoolgirl in all of my life. We walk slowly towards the living room, watching in silence as the two women whisper to each other. I grab Kellan's arm to pull him around the corner quickly, trying to stay out of their sight. Opening the freezer, I see eight bottles of alcohol.

"Cinnamon whiskey and vanilla vodka? That's their pies?" I look at Kellan, exasperated, but he shrugs, a slight redness to his face and neck. My mother never drinks. I can only imagine how well this will go over. Our parents come around the corner, smiling ear to ear as if one of them just said the funniest thing in the world. I let the freezer door close.

My mother is the first to fix her face, "Sharon, you remember my baby, Ava."

Sharon looks at me, her smile growing as she pulls me in for a hug. "I remember a baby, but not a beautiful woman. How are you, sweety?"

"I'm fine, Miss Sharon. How are you? I hug her back, but I've never met this woman a day in my life.

She turns to my mom, giggling. "Miss Sharon. That makes me feel older than daylight. Did you hear her, Avery?"

My mom elbows her friend in the side, "We are getting older than daylight. Look at our kids, standing here scolding us. I think they've found the pies." They erupt into laughter together, throwing their hands up in unison to slap each other's hands.

"What kind of pie calls for whiskey?" I ask them, dumbfounded. My question sparks another round of laughter between the two of them, until they grab their midsections to try to catch their breath. I look up at Kellan, watching as his whole face turns red with embarrassment. Am I not in on the joke?

"Avery, I have to tell you what Kelly did," Sharon takes a deep breath in through her nose before letting it out from her mouth, trying to calm herself down enough to speak.

"I think I'm starving, and we should all sit down to eat," he says to cut her off. It's my turn to smile, realizing he isn't embarrassed by them, but more himself. Oh, this has got to be good.

"Why don't we do both?" I propose, gaining me a strong head shake from the gorgeous man beside me. I wait as my mother steps forward, leading us into the dining room. I look down at the placemats, seeing handwritten name cards leaning against the water glasses. Glancing over, I see her name on the place beside mine. I grab them both and fling them under the table, pulling Kellan into a chair quickly before she has time to say anything.

"I saw that, Ava Marie," she calls me out. I smile up at her, feigning innocence. What is the point in having them over for dinner if I can't sit beside the man?

"Okay, Miss Sharon. What were you saying Kellon did today?" I turn my attention to her, ignoring my mother's temper. Kellan kicks my leg under the table. "Ow." I cut my eyes at him.

The woman covers her mouth, trying to hide her smile before speaking. "Well, I was sitting at home reading when I heard this beating and banging on my door. It was so loud, I thought there was some kind of emergency from a neighbor or someone. I open the door to see Kelly standing there, and he bursts inside, telling me to hurry, we have to go. Lord, I was so worried there for a second that we were about to run for our lives," she stops to take a deep breath, trying to hold herself together before continuing.

"And then we got in the car and came here," Kellan finishes for her. I squint my eyes between the two of them, knowing there is more to the story. She starts laughing at his summary.

"Not exactly, honey. So I am trying to gather my thoughts when he runs to the kitchen and pours out an entire bag of flour into a bowl and starts yelling about needing pies!" She slaps the table a couple of times, laughing, but there is no sound coming out of her. My mother joins in, her loud laugh echoing through the house. I smile up at him, my heart fluttering at his boyish innocence. My mother did say to bring pies, and neither of us knew what she meant; we still don't. His neck and ears turn red as I look at him; he's obviously embarrassed, so I grab his hand under the table, trying to provide some comfort.

Sharon finally calms down enough to speak, "My poor baby was trying his best, but I don't think he's made a real pie a day in his life. Have you, sweetheart? Then he asked where the butter was and threw the whole tub into the microwave! Oh, I about died on the way over here thinking about it. And you should have seen the look on his face when I asked him to stop by Liquor Cove."

I lean into him, "Do you wanna go get burgers?" His eyes meet mine, silently pleading to save him from further embarrassment.

"No, no, no." Sharon says, "You two aren't going anywhere. Avery, look at them, acting like they know more than we do. Children age, but I tell you they never stop believing that they know better than we do." My mother nods in agreement, staring into me.

"I tell you what, though. I think it's just downright sweet. Even with their five-year age gap, they still have more in common than most other couples I know."

"Oh, I can't believe I forgot about that. You know, five years seems like a lifetime when you're younger, but somehow, they still found each other." My mother speaks, but she keeps her hands busy with the serving spoons. I can't tell if she's still upset by me leaving Sebastian or if there's something else weighing on her.

I stare up at Kellan, tuning out their conversation as I try to take in every detail of his face. His thumb slowly rubs circles on the side of my hand. "I've missed you," I say, lowering my voice so only he can hear. He releases my hand, and my heart sinks. All eyes turn to us as he grabs my chair and pulls it close to his, the legs scraping loudly against my mother's precious floor. I cover my mouth, stifling my laugh at her horrified expression, before she goes back to filling Sharron's plate.

"Are you laughing at me, too, Angel?" He whispers, dangerously close to my ear. I shake my head. "I think you are." He grabs onto my leg, squeezing right above my knee to tickle me. I push his hand off my leg, laughing loudly as I try to fight him off to no avail. That's not where I want his hands, but it's a start.

"Alright, you two, that's enough of that. It's dinner time." My mother's stern voice comes down on us, scolding us like we are toddlers, but Kellan doesn't stop. Instead, he moves to my side and tickles me until I threaten to pee on him. He finally releases me and turns his attention to filling his plate with food.

"Let them have their fun, Avery. Don't you remember what it's like to be in love?" Sharon's voice softly prods at my mother, but I can tell she means no harm. I, on the other hand, clam up at the mention of the "L" word, and so does Kellan. He freezes beside me, water class halfway to his mouth like his brain is processing what he just heard come from Sharon's mouth.

"Mom, what did you do with those strawberries?" I try to change the subject.

"They are in the fridge, dear. I made a cake with cream cheese icing that you like." She continues talking to Sharon like I was a minor blip in her existence, which I'm grateful for. I excuse myself before pushing away from the table, ignoring them as they begin planning a party for next weekend.

It's one thing for me to think months ago that I could be falling in love with Kellan so soon after meeting him, but for other people to point it out now is unsettling—especially his own mother. I take a deep breath, trying to settle my racing thoughts, but her words play back to me on repeat. I grab the cake from the fridge and take it back to the table, where everyone is silently eating. I sit down to join them, wondering what I missed out on. I look up at Kellan, seeing his jaw tense while the two women across from me seem embarrassed but still amused.

After dinner, my mother volunteers me to clean up, just as I thought she would. What I wasn't expecting was for her and Sharon to make Apple Pie Cocktails for themselves and sit poolside, taking pictures together like middle school girls.

"I still don't understand the pie reference," I say to Kellan as he leans against the counter, stuffing cake into his mouth.

"Apparently, my mom showed up to your parents' wedding and threw up on my dad. When your mom asked what she had eaten to make her sick, she screamed 'pies' and passed out. Nobody realized how drunk she was when she showed up, and when Avery asked her about it a few weeks later, she said it was Apple Pie Cocktails, and that's what they always drank after that." He shrugs.

"That's pretty fun," I admit. The inside joke makes me miss Amber, even though I've talked to her on and off for the last few weeks, and she's tried her best to get me out of my apartment. If she knew what I had done, going back to see Kellan and taking my mother with me, she'd probably kill over. These last several weeks we have gotten into many arguments over Kellan. I know she despises him for breaking my heart, but there was something already there between them that never sat right. Maybe it was the way I ran off with him on that first night, but even earlier that night she was afraid of John – we both were.

I dry my hands on a towel, watching my mom lean close to Sharon. "Why do you think they didn't tell us they knew each other?" I ask.

"They probably didn't know until you drove up to the shop today," he explains.

"I feel like that could have made life a lot easier a long time ago," I admit.

"I don't think it's ever going to be easy, Ava." His voice drops.

"Why?" I ask him, my heart sinking.

He stares out the window for a while before turning back to me with a smile. "I thought you said we were going swimming?"

"But it's dark now." I protest.

"So?" He stares at me, unwavering.

"Fine." I head upstairs to put on my swimsuit, sighing when I see it still wet in the sink. I squeeze out the excess water, then turn the faucet on as hot as it will go to warm the fabric, and ring it out again before tying it onto my body. The warmth helped, but now I feel self-conscious showing this much skin in front of our parents. At least earlier, it was just my mother.

I wrap a towel around me, covering most of my body, but as I step outside, I'm still uncomfortable. I look around, finding Kellan already in the water, our parents laughing to themselves again, and pouring more drinks. I can tell my mother is drunk already, nearly falling out of her chair as she reaches over to hug Sharon for the millionth time. Who knew she was so affectionate?

As I sit on the edge of the pool, Kellan's words play back to me; It's always going to be difficult. What does that mean? I watch as he dives to the bottom of the pool, his tanned, tattooed skin cutting quickly through the water like he was born for it. The man is good at damn near everything already. Why not add swimming to the list, too? The lights of the pool illuminate the water from underneath, making him seem more fictional than real as he rises from the depths, running his fingers through his hair to keep the water from entering his eyes.

I stare at him, appreciating the way the thick cords of muscles on his upper body move as he treads water. A wide smile takes over my face, someone carve the man in stone already. He leans back, entirely at ease as he floats over to me. This version of him is so much more relaxed than the version I get to see in the shop, when he runs around, mumbling to himself about everything that needs to be done. Or throwing tools around when he is looking for something that someone shouldn't have moved.

The longer I stare at him, the more I realize this is a different side of him that I see when he's home, too; he's more open now, like he isn't hiding from anyone in the middle of the woods anymore.

"Now it's my turn to ask questions," he says breathlessly.

"What's your questions?" I poke him with my toes, testing how buoyant he is.

"Why would you ever want to leave this place?" His question surprises me; that isn't where I thought he would take the conversation.

"Because, if you look over there, to the woman who is lacing her toes together with your mother's, you will see a carefree person. But on the inside, she's so anal about everything that you could breathe around her, and she would tell you that you are doing it wrong."

He briefly bobs under water, nearly sinking. He comes back up, laughing while spitting out water.

"You said she's so, what? Wait." He turns to look at our parents, surprised at what they are doing. "What the hell?" He says at the sight of them with their feet in the air, holding on to each other with outstretched toes as they nearly fall from their sun chairs.

"Part of me is happy that she is letting loose and having a good time, but I'm mostly concerned. I've never seen her act like this before," I admit.

"Well, at least you didn't hear them start talking about their sex lives earlier," he responds with a shiver rolling through his body.

"Is that what the silence was for when I came back?" I had thought they were quiet because I was the topic. Past experiences had me believing that once a room went silent when you walked in, it was because you were being discussed. I shake my head, glad I had left the room before I heard about my mother and father sleeping together.

"Hell yes. I don't want to hear about her going on a date with some guy she met through my uncle Duncan, or what happened afterwards." He twists his face up in disgust.

"I didn't know you were such a mama's boy," I tease.

"Look, I want my mom to be happy, but I can do without the picture she was painting." He says as he paddles over to me, grabbing my leg to pull himself closer. I lean down to him, clutching my towel to keep from losing it in the pool, but my efforts are wasted when he pulls me in.

I hold my breath a second before hitting the water, going under before bobbing up quickly, hair plastering to my face, spinning around to find my towel drifting away. Kellan comes up from the bottom, spraying water around us, grinning unapologetically.

"You're insufferable," I say as I splash him.

"I'm adorable," he says, batting his eyelashes at me. This version of him is undeniably pulling on my heartstrings, and I know there are things we really need to get out of the way before we get too carried away with the night.

"My turn to ask questions," I tell him before taking a deep breath. "Why'd you say it's always going to be difficult between us?"

He pulls me through the water by my elbow, placing my hands on his shoulders as he slowly brings us to the shallow end of the pool; his silence worries me. "Kellan?"

He stops swimming to look me in the eyes. "Because I love you, Ava." His shoulders are tense as the weight of his words presses down on us. "But I don't think I'm ever going to be good enough for you, and that's fucking with my head."

"You're always going to be enough for me." My chest heats as emotions surge inside me. He stares into my eyes, searching for something, but I don't know what it is.

"Don't pull away from me because of something you've created in your own mind. And don't you dare sit here and tell me what isn't good enough for me." For a moment, the world narrows to the gentle current around us, his eyes reflecting both hope and hesitation, and I know we are on the fence. This is where either of us could choose to walk away and live the way we were before we met.

I close the distance between us, letting my forehead rest lightly against his and let my heart tell me what to do. I prepare myself to say something that I've never said to another person before, and fear grips me tightly. The words fill my head and threaten to pull me to the bottom of this pool if I don't get them out quickly. It's either I tell him now, or I keep it a secret forever and never tell anyone else for the rest of my life. "I love you," I whisper.

He wraps his arms around me, letting my words sink into both of us. Kellan's hands linger at my waist, anchoring us in the shallows as he battles with his own mind.

"Will you move in with me?" His question catches me off guard, leaving me speechless until he bursts into laughter. All the months we were not together seem to disappear as I imagine us swirling around in the massive kitchen together again, but what a way to ask something so sensitive. I smile back at him before shaking my head at his inability to pace the conversation.

I brush a strand of wet hair from his forehead, letting my fingers linger on his temple before I answer, "Yes."

I hold onto him, hoping he feels everything I struggle to put into words. "Maybe we both mess up, sometimes, but that doesn't mean it has to be difficult," I say softly.

He lets out a breathless laugh, tension releasing from his body. "Can we go home?"

"That sounds amazing, actually," I admit. We drift in silence for a moment, water swirling gently around us, before we walk out of the water, hand in hand.

"Nova!" I yell for her, waiting patiently as she climbs out of a chair to stretch before trotting to me. The poor baby is struggling to stay awake; she knows it's past our bedtime. We yawn in unison as we walk to the house, Kellan and I leaving wet footprints along the way. I look back to where our parents were sitting not long ago, finding empty chairs and drinks left behind.

I hand Kellan a towel from the stack I set out earlier in the day, watching as he dries his body. "Did it hurt when you got your tattoos?"

"Some of them hurt more than others," he says. "This one hurt the most," he points to the roaring bear on his side. I look it over, appreciating the fine details.

"Which one hurt the least?" I question.

"Just depends on the area. Some of the pieces hurt in a spot, but an inch above or below it, it won't hurt as badly," he explains. I nod along, contemplating the idea of getting a tattoo of my own.

He studies me, reaching out to turn me around before lightly drawing circles on my shoulders. "If you're thinking about it, start here. Shoulder blades won't hurt as bad. Stay away from your hands and feet." I soak in the heat from his hands as he trails across my midsection before spreading his fingers across my sides. "And stay away from here." His voice drops, and I know if I turn around to face him, his eyes will be lingering on places that would make both of our mothers scream if they saw him.

His fingertips leave behind trails of fire, leaving me wanting more when he pulls away. I nod again, trying to push the longing feeling away that has resurfaced. I still feel like we are at a fragile point in our relationship, and I know it's by my own doing; we've both hurt one another, and it will take time for us to heal. Asking him to rip this swimsuit from my body probably isn't in our best interest.

A New Year's Ride

I finally fell asleep just to wake up again an hour later. Every time I think I will drift back, I'm pulled awake all over again. Mostly, I feel restless because I promised myself to slow down with Ava, and I still think that's something we need. But her body is right there, calling to me in the darkness of our bedroom like a siren in the night.

Our bedroom, I smirk. The last time I shared anything in a house was with my brother when we were kids. This is really going to take some time to get used to. I roll to my side, grabbing onto her waist to pull her closer to me. I've missed having her in my bed; the short time we spent together before had given me a taste of something that I've craved ever since.

I haven't been able to sleep peacefully without her touch since she left, and I don't think I will be able to sleep without her by my side ever again after this. Her body curls around mine, twisting her legs with mine until I can't tell where I end and she begins. I breathe in the smell of her hair, sighing into it as her shampoo washes away the stress that has built up in my body over the last few months.

I've been in hell without her. I knew I should have done something about Bethany a long time ago, but I never imagined she would turn to drugs and go off the deep end the way she did. But for all I know, she had been using for as long as I knew her; I was just too stupid to see it. That would explain a lot of her issues, but I will never forgive her for taking Ava away from me.

I don't know how long I lie there thinking about everything I could have or should have done, but eventually, Ava stirs. She turns around, wiggling against me, sending all of my blood rushing to my dick as her soft ass and thick thighs brush against me before trying to get comfortable again.

"It's too hot in here," she grumbles. I grab my phone, adjusting the temperature via the app for my system for her. The air begins circulating, but she can't wait any longer; she sits up straight, pulls her t-shirt over her head and throws it on the floor. I can hardly see her in the dim light from the lamp left on in the next room, but I know what parts of her are pressing against me – I can *feel* it all.

"You're killing me," I whisper against her hair.

"Not yet," she yawns. I smile in the dark as my chest fills with emotion. I've fucking missed her. We quiet down, lying so still, I believe she is asleep again until her hand reaches up to my chest, lightly drawing random patterns across my skin.

She moves lower at an agonizingly slow pace until I feel like I might explode if she were to take me in her hand. What kind of game is she trying to play with me? I grab her hand before she slips under the waistband of my sweats.

"Ava."

"Hm?" She responds sleepily. Her fingers flex, wiggling in my tight grasp until she reaches her target anyway. I loosen my grip, feeling the way her hand wraps around me, a groan building in my throat. All thoughts of waiting escape me as she tightens her hand, tormenting me as she takes her time – I can't believe I'm giving in so easily but her touch feels too good, too soft.

I squeeze her hand before trying to use it for my own pleasure, picking up the pace before she slaps me away. She wraps those delicate fingers on my cock as much as she can, struggling to close her fist completely. I bite down on my lip, forcing my head back into the pillow but nothing stops the low groan that comes from me.

"That feels good, Angel."

She turns her head to whisper in my ear, "I know something that would feel better."

That's it, I can't take it anymore. I sit up abruptly, throwing the sheets from our bodies before yanking her down the bed to pin her under me. I grind my dick against her, warning of what's to come, but she doesn't back down. She grinds onto me, moaning softly as she pleases herself. I feel like Ava never stops surprising me; her directness stops me in my tracks, leaving me to sit and stare as she squirms. No matter how hard I try to hold her still, she finds a way to wiggle against me for her own pleasure.

I realize suddenly, my angel has been starved just as much as I have been; she must have been lying there all that time, letting a war wage in her mind before she knew how to get what she needs, what we both need. I lift my hips, keeping her from going any further, attempting to gain control of the situation.

I lean close to her ear, aware of the pressure I'm applying to both of us when I slip easily between her legs, "You want to tease me, but this is a game that I love to play, Ava. And I think we both know that."

Without hesitation, I press my mouth onto hers and force her tongue to intertwine with my own until she can hardly breathe. She has no idea what she has started but I intend to take it as far as I can. I make my way down her neck, sucking and licking until I've marked her soft skin with faint bruises before moving to her chest.

She heaves in shallow, quick breaths as I take my time, working one nipple at a time before going back to the other. I dance my fingers along her body, opening her legs to tease for a second only to move up her body again. I squeeze her neck just to release it before slowly dragging my fingertips down her side, letting her squirm under such a light touch until I've traveled between her legs again.

The longer I drag this out, the wetter she becomes, surprising me every time I dip into her until I can't take it anymore. I need to taste her. I slide down the bed, gently biting her sensitive skin until positioned between her legs, then work on her thighs. Her soft moans fill the room as I bite into her, kissing my way from her hip to her knee, traveling back up to her center and over to her other leg, mirroring what I've done to the other.

With each bite and lick, I softly blow, watching her skin react before sliding my thumb into her. I work her over until she drips onto my hand, loving the way her body responds. I remove my thumb, letting my mouth hover above her until she tries to lift her hips, but I want her to wallow in hesitation. I kiss her pussy once, licking her quickly before pulling away.

"You still want to tease me, Angel?"

Her gurgled response makes me smile, knowing she's nothing but a puddle of desperation beneath me. I dip low, ready to give her what she wants now that I have her where she needs to be.

Sixty-Eight

Ava

My body feels alive for the first time in months, burning with pure bliss and need as his mouth roams my body. My God, I've missed this man. I could get off just from his one finger being inside of me. I bite down hard enough to keep myself at bay, but I don't know how long I can hold myself back; I know I've already made a mess out of these sheets.

I can feel his mouth hovering above me, but I don't know what he's waiting for. Is there a fucking password? I lift my hips, bringing myself to his mouth, only for him to tease me further by softly blowing across my skin and continuing to kiss my inner thighs. Finally, his lips press into me, caressing my clit like he's fallen in love with that one part of my body more than any other. I groan. That's exactly what I want, what I need.

His slow torturous mouth caresses me over and over again, sending waves of pleasure through me until I fear that I will melt into nothing. He pulls away suddenly, leaving me dazed while on the brink of finding the sweetest release I could imagine.

"You fucking asshole!" I scream as the tension builds inside me. What kind of monster is he? Why keep stopping like this over and over again? This will bring me to madness.

Immediately, I'm spread open and filled with him. He thrusts into me so quickly that my body convulses and bucks at the intrusion. He's too big and hard for me to take all at once, but there's no pain as I explode around him suddenly. The shock wave of my orgasm lifts me from the bed, causing my back to arch until I'm afraid I will break in half while his rough hand covers my mouth to muffle my loud screams of pleasure and obscenities. He stills, letting me ride out the waves of pleasure until I'm finished and covered in sweat.

Once I lay still, he begins to move at a slow pace. My breath catches as he gently rocks in and out of me, kissing every inch of my chest and neck that he can cover. I wrap my arms around his neck, pulling him closer to me until we are a tangled form of limbs that cling onto anything we can grasp. I feel whole, like our bodies were made for one another as we begin to move.

I open my legs for him as wide as I can, wanting him to take me however he pleases, but he continues to move slowly, unwilling to give into the rough pleasure like we have so many times before. I grab his arms, feeling the way his muscles flex with each thrust as his weight shifts while holding onto me before grinding into him harder until he picks up the pace. The way his growls fill the room as he finally gives in makes me feral; I need this more than I need air in my lungs.

He holds me at my waist in a death grip, taking over my movements to match his own, causing my eyes to roll with pleasure. Reaching up, I grab onto his neck, feeling the muscles there constrict as he takes us higher once again. I feel his heartbeat pounding against the palm of my hand before I lace my fingers into his hair, tugging hard enough to pull his head back.

"Ah, fuck. That's a good girl," his voice echoes in the room as he praises me before he closing that small gap between us, propping himself up on an elbow to grind into me as deep as he can go. I wrap my leg around his waist to force more of him inside and pray he keeps going at this pace. I feel him reach the end of me, my body bucking under him at the sensation until I see stars.

"That's it, please don't stop," I beg him.

Whatever place he has found inside me makes my toes curl. It's a place I didn't even know existed, a place only he can reach.

"Please, please, please, please, don't stop." I scream, feeling something inside me build until I fucking jump. I jump off the cliff into a sea of nothing but pleasure and bliss, letting myself free-fall.

I'm not sure if my vision goes dark or if I have my eyes closed completely as this orgasm washes over me. Every muscle in my body tenses and releases all at once before leaving me trembling. For a second, my body floats in space before every pore on my body is electrocuted. I grab onto him, my nails digging into his back as I fight to pull my soul back into my body.

"Ava. Ava, stop clenching so hard, baby. Please," I hear him, but I can't stop it.

I can't control my body anymore. He pumps into me further before I can't take any more of him. I'm too sensitive. Too raw. My body relaxes, releasing him a second before he pulls out of me harshly.

I feel the warmth on my skin as his release drips between my legs. I feel it as it slowly makes its way down and pools under me on the sheets. I'm somewhere on cloud nine when he takes my face in both of his hands, kissing me deeply and passionately before finishing with a soft and final peck.

"I love you," he whispers against my lips.

With a shaky hand, I pull his face down to mine, kissing him once more. "I love you, Kellan."

He leans his forehead against mine, breathing heavy. After a while, our breaths finally return to normal and he chuckles.

"What's so funny?" I ask, sleepily.

"I almost didn't make it."

"Hm?" I barely have the energy to ask what he means.

"I mean, I've never felt you like that before. I almost couldn't pull out," he explains. My mouth forms an *oh,* but I can't find my voice anymore.

"Stay right here, Angel." He says as he climbs from the bed.

He returns minutes later with a bottle of water and begins cleaning me with a towel. My nose wrinkles as he spreads the evidence of what we have done around on my skin. When he finishes, he opens the water and hands it to me. "Here, drink this."

I sit up, still feeling shaky and exhausted, but drink the water. It travels down my throat like a much-needed rain over a desert and I hand it back to him. He drinks the rest of it and falls on top of me, leaving a trail of kisses on my neck before covering me with the soft sheet and I fall into the deepest sleep of my life, dreaming of feeling the wind on my skin as we ride across the levee, fireworks exploding all around us.

I pull Ava close to me as we watch the fireworks shoot into the sky, admiring the way the colors light up her skin. Nova paces inside at the door, howling as the fireworks whistle all around us when John comes jogging up the driveway, holding a case of beer and a giant brown paper sack.

"Jesus, John. How much did you spend on all of this?" Ava teases.

"I don't know, I think she said it was like four hundred, but I wasn't listening," he shrugs as he pours the sack out on the ground, picking up some sparklers as he cracks open a can.

"Okay, so my plan is to start with these little shit's and work our way up to this." He turns around, grabbing a three-foot-long box.

I turn my head to the side and read the description. "You bought eight cannon balls?"

He laughs, "Hell yeah, brother. Happy fucking new year!"

Tracy comes walking up to the house, her smile wide as she vibrates with excitement. "I love this!" She screams before throwing herself onto John's back, kissing the back of his bald head.

"Hey, look what we did," she says as she lifts her shirt up, revealing a new tattoo on her side. "Hey, jackass. Show them your ink," she nudges John with her boot.

"What? Oh, yeah." He drops his pants and turns around to show his bare ass.

"Hey! Whoa!" I yell at him before putting my boot on his ass and pushing him forward onto the grass. Ava burst into a fit of giggles in front of me, covering her mouth with the sleeves of my jacket that hang past her hands. She's been stealing all of my clothes, even though they are all too big for her.

"Your tattoos match?" She asks Tracy.

"Yeah, they do. Ain't that some shit. We thought this would be more romantic than getting married and shit," she turns around to John, watching as he stuffs himself back into his jeans.

"Damn it, Kelso. You spilled my beer!" He says as he stomps up to us again.

"There's a whole bar inside, man. Get what you want from in there." I tell him.

Headlights shine across the yard as an old car pulls in, sounding damn good, but I don't recognize it.

I look down at Ava, "Did you invite someone else?"

She smiles up at me, "Mom, Dad, and a few others." I smile back at her, curious to see who else could be coming. The car comes into view, and she takes my hand to lead me down the breezeway to see it up close.

"Is this a Plymouth Barracuda?" I stare at the vehicle in disbelief.

"It is," says her dad as he gets out of the driver's seat. He walks around, holding his hand out. "Just bought it today, as a matter of fact." His grip is firm in mine before he slaps my shoulder with acceptance.

Ava is quick to run to her mother, wrapping her arms around her before they start whispering. They both break out into laughter before she pulls away and runs to cling to the man standing quietly to the side as he stares at the car.

"Dad, remember last time you were home, and I said I had something to show you next time you came in? Well, Kellan has it in the shop."

She bounces up to me, snagging my keys from my hip before slipping her arm into his. Avery and I follow behind, already knowing what she wants to show him. As she unlocks the side door and steps through, the lights flicker to life, her father's throaty laugh echoes through the shop when the Chevelle sparkles into view. He holds his arms out wide in disbelief as he takes in the sight of the perfectly restored machine.

"Hot damn, look at that!" He grins like a kid in a candy store before leaning down to look inside the window. Realization dawns on him seconds later, before he looks back at me, lifting a finger to point at my chest. Sadness covers his face as he shakes his extended finger towards me.

"You look just like him, son. At first, I didn't know. But now," he sighs. "Smitty was a good man. I want you to know that."

"So I've heard," I tell him, but the subject is still sore for me.

"We all make mistakes, and he made a big one that cost him everything, but there wasn't a day that passed that he didn't talk about his daughters. And he loved your grandmother dearly. I know that to be true.

I'm sorry about what happened to both of them." He stands back, looking at the car, appreciating it the same way I do every time I see it.

"Alright, my love. We didn't come here to stand around gawking at machines," Avery links her arm into her husband's and attempts to drag him away, but he doesn't move.

"Maybe you didn't, but my son and I beg to differ. Don't we, Kellan?" He stands up tall, looking proud to be giving his wife a hard time.

I grab Ava's hand, lacing my fingers with hers, a sign of disagreeing with him. I'd do anything to make my angel happy; he should do the same. He stares at our conjoined hands briefly before deflating and makes his way towards the door.

"I think tomorrow you should take Kellan to the storage. Let him see the rest of your collection," Ava says to break the tension building in the room.

"You're right, sweetheart. That's the best damn idea I've heard all night." He says, holding out his hand for us to walk out of the garage first. I let Ava tug me along, happy to go wherever she wants me to go.

Another set of headlights comes down the driveway, followed by another, until I hear a familiar rumble down the street.

"You invited Uncle Duncan?" I ask her.

"I did," she says over her shoulder.

I see my mother's car pull around first; it's barely parked before she jumps out and runs through the yard, arms held open wide to greet Avery.

"Baby, you're never going to believe what I have for us," she says to her friend as they collide into an embrace.

"Sharon, you better not have that damn liquor," Ava's dad starts to complain before her mom slaps his chest to silence him.

"I brought pies!" My mother screams out into the night, pulling a laugh from everyone, but there's one in particular that I tune into. I watch Ava as she lets out a snort, covering her mouth and red nose as she loses control at the joke that she now understands.

The sound wraps around me, filling my chest with pride. What did I ever do to have her in my life? She sees me staring at her, awarding me with a quick kiss before crossing the yard to greet whoever is in the other car.

I wait for her to come back, giving my mom a hug in the meantime, when a tall figure comes up behind her.

"Kelly, I want you to meet someone," she says quietly.

The old man steps up to me, stretching his arm out to introduce himself. I size him up, noticing the faded ink on his hands. His white hair blends in with his white mustache and beard; the man looks like he could play Santa Claus year-round.

"Clay Jameson," he says as we shake hands.

"Kellan Smith," I respond.

He chuckles, "Yeah, you and your guys work on my Fat Boy from time to time. You got my Softail right now." A light flickers on in my head. This is who Ava spends hours every week talking to on the phone. The guy could talk paint off a fucking wall. I can see how my mother would be smitten with him.

"Come on, honey. Help me carry in the pies," my mother steers him back to the car.

The sound of kids arguing grabs my attention, and for a second, I think I imagine it until I hear Thomas telling them to knock it off. I round the corner to meet him, bringing him in to slap him on the back.

"You brought a whole crew with you this time, man."

"Yeah, got the whole gang. We got some small poppers too, keep 'em occupied so they don't make too much of a mess."

I open the door to let them inside, grabbing Nova by the collar to keep her from running out while people park up and down the drive. She wags her whole body once she sees the kids, licking them in the face until they are laughing and hugging her.

I look up to see Ava gushing to Tracy and a young woman about some show that's streaming. The three of them wave their hands around frantically as they talk.

"Tom, is that the neighbor girl we fixed the trailer for a while back?"

He comes up behind me, sighing like he's been hit in his gut. "Yeah, man. It is. She came over a couple of weeks ago to hang out, and it's all been good from there."

I stare at him in disbelief. "I thought she was underage."

"She's not, man. I'm not like that; you should know me better than that. I'm not some fucking weirdo. I hardly talked to her after that weekend we patched everything up. She would come over to ask for simple shit like the toilet kept running, but I'd fix it and be on my way. Never laid a hand on her, I swear."

"You said she was a kid back then," I tell him, anger flaring inside me.

I've gotten to know Thomas, but this is some shit that I never thought he would do. I know he's younger than me, but the shit still doesn't sit right.

"She just turned nineteen on Christmas Day. Look, man, there are five years between you and your lady. Only five years between me and her, too. Only difference is y'all are older."

I shake my head at his explanation. The shit still feels wrong. Nineteen years old is still a kid in my book.

"If it makes you feel any better, she came over and told me how she felt about me and I told her that I didn't want to push her into doing anything she didn't feel comfortable doing and I still mean that. Hell, sometimes I go over just to give her a break from taking care of the boys. I swear to you, brother, I haven't crossed the line with her at all. Not even a kiss."

"No, man. It doesn't make me feel better at all. Don't steal that girl's life from her just so you can settle down." I let out a breath and move on from the subject before I get carried away. The last thing I want to do is lay into this guy in the middle of Ava's party, but he'd better watch out for me because I will be checking in soon. "Still can't find her mom?"

His voice drops to a whisper, looking over his shoulder to make sure the kids aren't close enough to hear. "No. I've called every police station in four more counties just in the past couple of weeks. She just gone man. I know that's got to be eating at her, and them, but she don't ever want to talk about it so I let it go."

I sigh, "Text me her name, age, and a description. I got some people who may be able to look for her."

"I can do better than that. I got her whole profile pulled up all the time. Sometimes I catch myself staring at people on the street, wondering if she's walking by. She's been gone long enough that I think we should do some type of funeral, but I don't think it's my place to bring it up."

He rubs his face, defeated. I know how he feels; I did the same thing when no one could find my dad. I just hope this situation isn't the same as mine; finding out the man had been murdered was tough, and I wasn't really that close to him.

John walks up to the door, waving sparklers in the air to get the boy's attention. They run towards us, screaming about booms before opening the door so hard I fear it may come off the hinges and cringe. I look at Thomas, understanding why their house needed so much work done before following the kids outside.

Duncan finally comes around the side of the house, saying he had found a straggler who got lost in the neighborhood, when Ava screams. She takes off running through the yard, throwing her arms and legs around a short brunette. They fall to the ground, laughing before standing up and cleaning the dead leaves from one another.

I recognize her from the pictures Ava has shown me. Even though I've talked to her on the phone several times, I've never seen her in person, which has always puzzled me since she lives so close. I make my way across the yard, leaning in to give Amber a small hug, letting her know I'm glad she could make it and back away quickly. There's still some tension between us, even after all this time but I've let it go. Whatever she has against me is obviously one-sided.

I wrap my arms around Ava and look out at everyone gathered in our yard. I never in a million years would have thought I'd let anyone in on my slice of heaven, but now I see them all standing around, and I wouldn't have it any other way. I feel like this would have never happened if it weren't for the woman by my side.

For the first time in a long time, I feel like I'm complete. Like this was what my life had been missing all along. Ava turns to face me, standing on her toes to whisper in my ear. I smile down at her, nodding in agreement, and we walk to the front door together before facing our family.

"Hey, everybody!" Her voice rings out into the night.

My insides drop to my ass as they all look at us. So many faces spread across the yard, all looking between the two of us for answers, but I have no words.

"We just want to say that we love you all, and we are glad that you're all here to bring in the New Year with us."

Our eyes meet, and for a fleeting moment, I feel like I'll die if I don't get it off my chest.

"We're engaged!" Ava shouts the words, thrilled to be sharing the secret.

Our friends cheer around us, rushing up as I put the ring back on her finger. Once they're all standing closer to us, I do my best to clear the swell of emotions in my throat, but it doesn't help. I try again, coughing a few times before taking John's beer from his hand, downing it in one pull before handing him the empty can.

"What the fuck, man?" He burps at me, already half drunk.

"That's not all, folks." I can't say more or else I'll fucking cry in front of everyone.

Their eyes go wide, impatiently waiting for me to finish what I have to say.

"I'm not pregnant. Everyone, calm down." Ava's words are drowned out by whispers as they begin speaking to each other all at once, confused about why else we would have them all here.

It's not just about bringing in the new year together; this is an engagement party, but it's more than that to us. I rub my chest, feeling too much at once as our families gather around her to pepper her with questions.

"I've been going to college for the last few months," her voice shakes as she speaks, looking at her dad with a broad smile on her face.

He winks at her, approval written on his face before looking up at me. I know he thinks this is my doing, but Ava opened up about it a while back, and I told her how I feel about it. I want to support her in any way possible. She is her own person, and I want what's best for her, even if I will have to start managing the shop on my own again when she is ready to spread her wings.

"I've got a few semesters left before I start my majors, but I'm going to have to take a break for a little while." Her voice is strong as she admits to everyone what our plans are, but this little bit is going to be hard to say out loud.

Silence rings out into the night as they all stand, waiting for us to tell them what else could possibly be happening.

"Because I'm pregnant," I admit to the crowd.

Everyone erupts into laughter and I realize what I've said. Ava grabs onto my arm, supporting me as I try to take the weight off her shoulders with my accidental remark.

"Okay, yeah. I'm pregnant." She admits to our families.

Everyone loses their minds at once, and questions are rapid-fired at us, but I can't understand so many people talking at once. John comes up behind me, handing me a beer as he chugs his.

"Congratulations, brother."

I try to say thank you, but the words won't come out. Instead, I nod my head, watching my angel as she glows and brightens my world while answering everyone as fast as she can.

I follow the huge biker through the neighborhood, my anxiety skyrocketing when we pass the last possible street to turn onto. I scrape my nail across the stitching in my steering wheel, hoping like hell this guy knows the house I'm looking for. I was in a panic when I realized my calls to Ava wouldn't go through, even though I had a full signal.

I flagged the guy down because I saw the motorcycle and just assumed it would be one of her new so-called friends, but now I have my doubts. The guy rides a bike big enough to hold up to his weight and height, but I'm not going to lie. He's fucking terrifying.

The road stretches on long enough that I'm starting to think I should turn around now and go back home, especially when the guy starts to weave from one edge of the pavement to the other in front of me. Eventually, we slow down and turn onto a roughly paved driveway that I would never have found by myself. I let him pull in ahead of me, hesitant to follow behind the giant.

Trees hang over the driveway, barely allowing a peek of light from the house to come through from the road. There's hardly any sign of life until a few fireworks shoot up to the sky from somewhere close by. Taking a deep breath, I take the turn and say a silent prayer, hoping this guy hasn't led me to a shack that I will die in.

Once I pull through the tree's canopy, I'm greeted by what looks like an old Tudor-style house that borders on the size of a small mansion. I balk at the view; there's no way I have the right address. I thought Ava said this guy was a mechanic.

I ease my car forward, pulling up to park behind a vehicle that looks like it shouldn't even be on the road anymore. The loud rumble of the motorcycle shuts down, allowing voices to be heard from around the corner, and I let out a sigh of relief.

I half jog to catch up to the large man who struggles to walk down the driveway. He hobbles back and forth, favoring one leg more than the other, while a long chain slaps against his jeans noisily. I try to tune into the voices, wondering if Ava's mother is here or if I'm losing my mind.

He rounds the corner, announcing my presence before I can see who he is talking to, causing me to panic.

"Found a straggler," he chuckles.

I try to shake my nerves and tell myself that he isn't a bad person, but it goes against everything I've been forced to believe. Even though he stopped for me when I waved at him earlier and was nice enough to guide me here, there's just that fear that I can't shake.

Fear that has been fed to me my whole life about bikers and their reputations. I'm not comfortable being around the guy by myself, and I'm sure there are more here that I haven't laid eyes on yet. The thought terrifies me. I've tried my best to talk Ava out of being around these people, but she's honestly changed in the last year more than any other person I know. It's like she has suddenly realized that she can make up her own mind and never be persuaded by anyone, even when they want the best for her.

The man continues walking through the yard, and Ava turns to look at me. Her smile is contagious, erasing all the fear and anxiety that has built up inside me since I left the house. I run to her, catching her as she wraps her legs around me and takes us to the ground. We laugh together, rolling on the plush grass before she helps pull me up.

"You bitch, you ruined my hair," I tell her as she dusts off the dead leaves from my sweater.

"Shut up, cunt. It looks fine," she bites back at me.

I swat the leaves from her rear end before straightening myself and smiling at her. I've missed her more than she knows. Even though we talk on the phone nearly every day, there's still that void between us. I know it's partially my fault, but I think I've overcome a lot by coming here tonight.

I've hurt my best friend by pulling away because of who she associates with now, and that's wrong. I knew it was wrong when I did it, but at the time, I felt like I didn't have a choice. I was uncomfortable, but I think I can do this for both of us.

Seeing her now, smiling and happy, I see how wrong I was to judge these people so harshly. She doesn't look hurt or injured in any kind of way; she's almost glowing. I let some of my walls down, accepting that this is the happiest I've ever seen her.

If she's comfortable here, then so am I. We hug again, and a miniature Hulk comes walking up behind her, snaking his arm around her hips to bring a laugh from her before he leans in to hug my shoulders lightly. I know this is Kellan because of the pictures Ava and I send to one another but seeing him in person is a whole other story. I hug him back with one arm, feeling somewhat dwarfed as his lower chest presses onto my face. The man is a muscular wall covered in graffiti, but I can see the appeal more than ever now. He's easier on the eyes in person than the pictures do justice.

"Glad you could make it, Amber." He says to me.

I smile between the two of them when he pulls away to hold onto her, and the rest of my walls begin to fall away. They look perfect for one another. Her soft features are the complete opposite of his huge, bulging, tattooed self, but it works for them.

I can see how Sebastian would have been afraid of Kellan now that I see him with my own eyes, especially if he was scowling. This man makes Sebastian seem like a runt.

A loud burst of laughter catches my attention across the yard. I stare in horrified confusion when I realize who it's coming from.

"Ava, oh my God. Is that your mom?"

Ava and Kellan both turn to look across the yard at Avery as she leans down to grab her knees, out of breath as she laughs with the woman next to her. Ava's dad looks uncomfortable and stiff as he stares into the distance, trying his best to ignore the women standing near him.

"Yeah, we found out last year that our parents have history," Ava explains.

"Hope you like pie," Kellan says before walking away.

A young girl comes up to us, looking just as out of her element as I feel; Ava hugs her, asking her how she's been before introducing us. The girl brightens when Ava asks her if she watched the last episode of the vampire show I have been secretly addicted to for the last several years.

I feel my eyes widen as they gush about it to one another before blurting out what I think will happen. They both look at me in shock before squealing with excitement. I never told anyone that I was into Vampires. Everyone always gave Ava so much shit for liking horror movies, myself included, but it completely clashes with who she is.

"Tracy!" Ava screams over her shoulder.

Internally, I pull away as a girl with bright green hair stomps over to us. Her face says she will kill us all here without breaking a sweat if she wishes. The piercing above the bridge of her nose shines in the fireworks going off above us, and once she's closer, I count five more pieces of jewelry sticking out of her skin in various places. I take in the sight of her, staring at all the ink on her body and shiver. A small vine of thorns and leaves travels up her neck to her forehead while her hands are covered in tiny symbols that I can't make out.

Her presence is more terrifying than any man here as she comes up to us, a hate-filled scowl on her face until Ava speaks to her. She breaks into a smile when she hears what we were discussing and joins in, gushing about the storyline with us.

As the mask falls from her face, she's actually quite beautiful; I catch myself staring at her as she becomes more animated the longer she talks. I find it hard to believe this is the same person who just walked up to us mere seconds ago. These people are fucking weird.

Before I realize it, Ava has disappeared, and I'm left standing with the two women talking about characters from the show I had no idea was so popular with other people. Eventually, Ava interrupts everyone to make an announcement, and I'm forced to pick my jaw up from the lawn I stand on.

Engaged, yes. We all saw it coming. But, pregnant? Holy shit.

"That's crazy," a deep voice beside me says.

I turn my head to look at him, surprised that he approached me without making a sound. I look the man up and down, raising an eyebrow as I take in the view. He stands a head taller than me, wearing a green and black plaid long-sleeved shirt that's rolled up his forearms to show off naturally tanned skin that pairs perfectly with his beautiful smile.

My head snaps back in surprise as I stare at him. Where did he come from? I look around, as if I'm the only person that can see him, then find his gaze again. His broad shoulders block out the light shining from inside the garage as he turns to face me to stretch his hand out, offering it to introduce himself.

I stand still, taking in the size of his massive build. I swear the guy could fit two of me on one shoulder if he wanted. Good God, the biceps. I blink several times, trying to remember my name. His smile grows as he patiently waits for me to accept his extended hand, which I eventually take in mine, feeling his body heat as we hold on for a little too long.

"Cam," he says before releasing my hand.

"Amber," I finally find my voice.

"Would you like a drink?" He asks.

A New Year's Ride

I consider my options. I know I get a little out of control when I drink, and I know this night is more of a celebration for Ava and Kellan, but I think I need something to take the edge off.

A New Year's Ride

A New Year's Ride

www.ingramcontent.com/pod-product-compliance
Lightning Source LLC
Chambersburg PA
CBHW071546110726
47908CB00007B/2013